# FAME CAME EASY
# AND SO DID WOMEN!

"*Nicole*"—his thrilling first conquest in Central Park

"*Julia*"—the love-starved wife of his college professor

"*Eileen*" and "*Maggie*"—playmates of Greenwich Village sex parties

"*Helen*"—the voluptuous Parisian whose husband was never jealous

"*Tania*"—who surrendered in Fontainebleau forest

"*Claudine*"—the delectable temptress who left him lost to desire

"*Daphne*"—the elegant London beauty who offered him the most secret recesses of a woman's body

**MIRROR MAN** is an "exciting, sensuous, even naughty, tale which brings back quite a few memories and, I almost suspect, shared experiences . . . And just as soon as 'Paul Virdell' comes out from behind his pseudonym, I may come out from behind mine."

—John Smith
(pseudonym of a nationally known newsman)

## ABOUT THE AUTHOR

"PAUL VIRDELL" is a former radio and television newscaster and journalist. He was a correspondent for various news services during World War II in London, Paris and Rome. Under his real name he is also known as a best-selling novelist. He divides his time between the south of France and the New York area.

# PAUL VIRDELL

# Mirror Man

Futura

A Futura Book

This edition published in 1985 by
Futura Publications, a Division of
Macdonald & Co (Publishers) Ltd
London & Sydney

ISBN 0 7088 2799 3

Printed and bound in Great Britain by
Hazell Watson & Viney Limited,
Member of the BPCC Group,
Aylesbury, Bucks

Futura Publications
A Division of
Macdonald & Co (Publishers) Ltd
Maxwell House
74 Worship Street
London EC2A 2EN
A BPCC plc Company

# To the Reader

The protagonist of *MIRROR MAN* is called David Brent because that is not his real name.

His real name is known to you as popular author, Hollywood scenarist, and TV personality. But for reasons that will be obvious he has chosen anonymity.

In this novel, as told to Paul Virdell, he relives his rise to fame over a significant span of contemporary history. Wartime London, Paris and Rome, the world of broadcasting in New York and Washington and the Hollywood film community provide the setting for his professional activities.

But that is only the surface of the story.

For contrasted with David Brent's public image is his untold private obsession: the secret, compulsive sexual passions revealed in this book. It is a step-by-step, totally explicit odyssey of emotional discovery from obscure childhood to the summit of successful maturity, and the ultimate truths of its resolution.

# MIRROR MAN

*To starstruck tourists cruising along the coastal highway, it's "famed Malibu Beach," a strip of golden sand north of Los Angeles studded with million-dollar beachfront homes. To the Hollywood crowd it's simply the Colony, a special paradise separated from the less fortunate in life by electrified fences, a private road and entrance gates manned by armed guards around the clock. That is why, this night of murmuring surf and mist-hidden moon, the man who stood motionless on the sun deck had the world to himself. The beach was empty and silent, but the man was listening—listening to voices only he could hear, staring into the mirror of the past . . .*

ONE

# 1

In isolate brief flashes, sharp and searing yet discontinuous, with no before or after, he saw the countless fumble-failures of his growing up to sex—moments when awakening desire for the flesh swelled like hunger through his days and nights but still was mystery. Sight and sound from the earliest years: his sister's violet eyes and infant voice yearning, cajoling: *Mama, why can't David take his nap with me? . . .* Hidden rituals under the summer branches: *Turn around and let me see the front, too . . . But Davie, it's just like Cathy's . . .* Suddenly his mother's convulsive half-laugh, a thrilling whisper under it beyond the bedroom door: *Ben—wait—shh! The kids will hear . . .* as he peeped astonished through the keyhole, saw her supine with silk-stockinged legs inexplicably flung high, his father standing naked between them at the foot of the bed . . .

When Uncle George visited, kissing you arriving and leaving, why did he always stick his tongue in? . . . Freddie, nine, big, leading him into the tall grass and opening his pants for him, fondling where it tickled and jumped . . . And the milkman that time down by the cellar door, turning and seeing the child on the stairs, taking his huge thing out and showing it: *How'd you like to have one like this, little feller? . . .* A hillside in spring, sitting with Ann, groping at tight-held knees, murmuring, muttering, all at once consumed by agonizing need for her nearness, her openness . . . And boys, too—Tommy standing under the shower by the swimming pool, eyeing him oddly through the veil of water, somehow beautiful and desirable as a girl . . . Staying overnight at Phil's, looking at Phil stepping out of the tub before the pillow fight—why had the bronze-smooth skin, the velvet thighs, made him suddenly want to kneel, touch, worship? . . .

The summer Betsy came from Hartford, the intoxicat-

ing smell of her hair when she rode the handlebars; later,
beneath her, watching her climb the tree, both caught in
the spell of the singing woods, standing wonderstruck at the
glimpse of her pouting cleft quite clearly seen through
flimsy underdrawers . . . Old enough now to go alone to
afternoon movies, feeling his body freeze in fear the first
time a man slipped out of shadow to sit beside him and
take his hand, place it on hot, damp, straining flesh before
he realized what was happening and ran from him through
dark aisles . . . And, even more intensely, the dawn he
woke at climax of his first wet dream, frightened and ignorant, in guilty panic seizing the sheet and throwing it wildly
into the apartment courtyard five floors below . . .

No one spoke of it, or of anything else about sex. No
one explained, and you didn't ask. It was Joe Gavin, as
with so many other things, who told him the why and how
and took away his fear, put it safely in the past and understood. And it was Joe, his classmate and already at fifteen the sly sophisticate, cynic and sexmaster, collector of
dirty cartoons and organizer of group masturbation, who
led the way finally to true initiation. Of all his memories
this was the most dreamlike, even the girl's name forgotten, the place a darkened game room in a basement—Joe's
house? Briggsy's? He moved as fated, controlled by instinct
only, everything else blotted out now; automatically he
loosened his belt and approached her.

He stared at the face gone soft in shadow, separate,
detached from the disheveled mass lying on the Ping-Pong
table, the blurred body splayed and helpless, this flesh no
longer a person. Were the eyes open or closed, wanting or
dismayed, would the mouth speak again? It didn't matter;
he had come too far to turn away. *It was really happening
at last,* all dreams resolved in the feel and smell of reality
—the glistening sweat he touched with clumsy fingers, the
musky perfume in her upswept clothes, the odors of smoke
and raw wine, of Joe and Briggsy and his own, all com-
mingled. And the flesh received him, warm, slippery, not
welcoming, not resisting, but *there* for his dozen seconds
of wild and twisting motion to the great burst like a silent
cry and the stabbing pull deep in his back. Then it was
over, everything was achieved, and he had discovered it
was not as good as the dream, but it was done.

# 2

In the summer night he walked north through the park toward the Mall, past benches crowded with refugees from the heat. They sat there indolently fanning themselves, too spent to talk, and watched the cars flash past on the park roadway with a soft rush of engines, trailing snatches of voices and laughter. The sounds seemed to hang suspended until the next car went by, running over the sounds and leaving its own sounds behind to quiver momentarily in the air.

Farther along on the lamplit walk, where it was cooler by the lake, he listened to the murmur of desultory chitchat that mingled with the park's own sibilant voice, made of near and distant noises of cars and splashing ducks and carriage horses clopping on the asphalt drives. There were only faint reminders of the streets outside, like the dim boom of traffic behind the skyline to the south or a bus groaning its way up the avenue. Up here the air was different, part haunting sweetness of grass and the unfamiliar trees, part dust and the sickish odor of exhaust. And already he could picture the scene up on the Mall, the crowds gathering under the red sky in one big strolling throng all headed in the same direction, converging on the rows of seats around the dance area, the younger women mostly with men and walking with arms entwined, the older couples placidly finding benches along the Mall and waiting without impatience for the music to begin.

The kids were out too, until family curfew would banish them soon. They darted shouting and jeering among the strollers, intent on the games without names played at night in the park, full of the excitement of darkness. Was it only a half-dozen years since he'd been one of these, racing and chasing, knowing the deserted places like the back of his hand, the meadow lawns for running, the moss-covered piles of rocks and the caverns beyond the lake? It was almost too long ago to remember. He stared at the faces dodging past him under the lamps, looking for his own face among them. But he knew they wouldn't recognize each other, two lives that linked no longer. Tonight he was playing his own night game, the best game, the only game.

He didn't hunt with the bunch any more. He'd tried that and it didn't work. It was no good that way because the pickups stuck together in pairs and wouldn't be separated. Neither wanted to let the other know that she might put out, so at the end of the evening they just drifted off to wherever they came from, still together, and you had nothing. The only way to hunt was to hunt alone. It took time and luck to snare a single, but a single always put out, he had Joe Gavin's assurance of that. So far, patience hadn't paid off, but Joe had to be right. He missed Joe since the Gavins moved away, and with Joe gone the bunch began breaking up; anyhow it was only another year to high school graduation before they'd all be scattering to jobs or college. But he didn't need Joe Gavin anymore. He didn't need anybody.

Head high and eyes alert, he quickened his step in tense expectancy. In a moment he would be turning into the Mall and the hunt would begin. Before him stretched the long black promenade with its brilliantly lighted bandstand at the farther end—down there beyond the mass of swaying heads now pouring onto the central walk he could see the musicians in bright blue coats assembling with their instruments. And suddenly the arc lights blazed on; the crowd surged forward with a babble of anticipation. Just as suddenly the girls were all around him like chattering birds, carrying him along on a river of white and pink and green dresses, all hurrying with lilting steps toward the appointed place in shifting patterns of color and movement. The sight filled him with a deep, unreasoning hunger; he wanted them all as if they were one girl; they merged in a single image. But the image was shattered by the hoarse cries of the pack closing in behind him on the trail of potential pickups. In groups of three or four they were trying to turn their targets out of the mainstream and onto the grass on either side of the walk, pleading, clowning, calling back and forth in the jostling multitude. The chorus of entreaties smothered all separate speech. There was only the voice of the crowd.

Then the music began. Over the swirling crush this new voice burst through the loudspeakers high above the dance area and beat down upon them all like the glare of the arc lights, the boisterous, gay tune roaring out of the amplifiers, sounding over the whole park. With a happy shout the dancers surged forward, and he let himself be buffeted aside in the race to be first on the floor. So far he'd seen nothing of promise. In disappointment he worked his way to the edge of the crowd and beyond to the quiet of a deserted walk leading toward the zoo. He'd stopped to wipe his face with his handkerchief when he saw the girl facing him in the lamplight a couple of yards away. She was staring hesitantly past him as if trying to decide whether to join the crowd on the Mall, dark-haired and slim in a flowered dress, standing a little awkwardly on spike heels. At first she didn't seem aware of him at all but he stayed there, not moving, until she glanced his way.

He smiled. "Want to dance?" he said.

Her glance held but she didn't return the smile. She shook her head doubtfully. "It's too crowded."

"I'm game if you are. How about it?"

She grimaced prettily and shook her head again.

"You alone?" He moved nearer.

"Now I am. My friends are out there somewhere." She pointed vaguely at the Mall.

"You'll never find them in that mob."

A man walked into the lamplight and slowed his step as he passed them. He looked at the girl as if itching to put his hands on her, a long, cool stare starting at her ankles and sweeping up her body to her breasts and then her eyes, deliberately ignoring the boy who stood near her. She turned her head in scorn and waited until the man disappeared in the crowd on the Mall. "The way they look at you," she muttered half to herself.

"Let's get away from here," he said. "Want to walk over to the zoo?"

She gave a small shrug of assent and moved off with him down the walk. A single! And as easy as that. He felt a swelling sense of success and covertly observed her at his side as they passed under the next lamp: olive skin, hair glistening black and tied back tightly at her neck, thin lips and aquiline nose: she had to be Italian or Spanish. "What's your name?" he said. "I'm Dave."

"Nicky."

"Nicky?"

"For Nicola. Nobody calls me Nicola."

"You Italian?"

"How'd you guess?"

"I'm smart, that's all." Boldly he reached for her swinging hand and she let him hold it a moment before pulling it lightly away. "You work fast," she said, and for the first time she smiled.

"You like to dance, Nicky?"

"Not much."

"What d'you like to do most?"

She giggled. "Don't you wish you knew!"

"Is it what I think it is?"

"I don't know what you think it is."

"Aw, come on, Nicky!" He caught her fingers and this time he kept them.

"I'd never tell you that," she taunted.

"Why not?"

"Because you're too fresh."

They were laughing together. "Come on, Nicky—"

"Find out for yourself," she said.

"Okay, how's this for a start?" In the dark stretch between lamps he pulled her to the edge of the grass and kissed her, feeling her resist at first and then suddenly open her mouth to him. But it only lasted a moment. She jerked herself free and protested breathlessly, "Say—who d'you think you are, anyway!"

But he knew she accepted him. They were swinging hands as they sauntered on. There was a brick tunnel under the next crosswalk where he could grab her again; his body tingled at the thought. Still nobody passing them in either direction, luckily—dance nights everybody was up on the Mall. And this time in the denser dark she didn't pull away. He was holding her close and she put her arms around him. He dropped his hands below her waist and pulled her solid young flesh against him hard. *"Nicky . . ."* She could feel his erection and she didn't recoil.

*"Nicky,"* he said into her mouth. His body sang with excitement. *"Follow me."* He took her submissive hand

and led her out of the tunnel and up a grassy slope to a spot just under the crosswalk. He knew where he was going. He'd noticed the place before and marked it in his mind. Here they could sit in complete darkness, their backs resting against the tunnel wall, sheltered from all eyes. And still holding her hand he drew her down beside him on the cool grass.

"Okay, Nicky?"

She made no answer to his whispered words but her head dropped to his chest when his arm encircled her shoulders and he felt her full weight sway against him. No doubt left, she wanted this as much as he did! There were no more words between them, only her quickened breathing and the language of his fingers moving carefully downward under the low-necked dress, inch by inch, her skin hot and moist to their touch until they found their way inside the smooth, soft band that held her breasts, while his right hand pressed her bare knee and crept upward between her thighs. *"Nicky,"* he whispered again, inhaling the scent of her hair, and in unspoken answer she spread her legs so his hand could reach her all the way. He was kneeling beside her now, lowering her body full-length on the grass. He felt the wetness on his fingers as he pulled the panty down and threw it aside. Feverishly, triumphantly, he bared himself and straddled her, hardly hearing the husky whisper beneath him: *"Just . . . be careful . . ."* For more than the thrill of her pliant nakedness, more even than his desire, he knew the mastery of conquest. She had yielded to him, he had won the victory, and all of her lay ready to receive the gift of his power.

# 3

The low red-brick buildings made a square about the campus; there was an inner square of white colonnade. Summer was dying but the upperclassmen still moved carelessly and slow in their linen suits all cut to a fashion, walking by twos and threes and carrying books as if forgetful of them, as though it wasn't possible yet to feel in the college swing again. But for the freshmen this was an exciting day: in Main Hall the atmosphere was festive and tense for Incoming Reception, where they would meet the faculty for the first time.

Even now the line of professors and their wives had formed across the auditorium and the freshmen shuffled past, awkwardly shaking hands and putting on their best smiles. There was no time for more than a word or two with each teacher and his lady; to David Brent it was all a blur of faces, a little frightening in their poise and assurance. He wished he could reciprocate because he wanted to like them and he wanted them to like him.

Little by little, in the first weeks, some of those faces were remembered as he got to know his course instructors in class. And sometimes after class their wives would come to pick them up and nod pleasantly to the students as they came out of the building. But he knew it was all a meaningless formality; he still felt humble and anonymous in this new and strange environment. But he was coming to love the physical beauty of his surroundings: the blue range of hills circling half around the valley cradled the university town with its church spires and old clapboard houses. After his morning classes he liked to linger a while on the grassy lawns, looking out toward the beckoning countryside, just gazing, reluctant to return to the freshman dorm.

A car was coming along the road this afternoon as he started to cross the campus footpath. He waited for it to pass and was surprised when it slowed and halted beside him. The smiling woman at the wheel leaned across the seat and said, "Well, *hello!* It's David Brent, isn't it?"

"Oh. Hi." He stared back, puzzled.

She was looking at him quizzically. "Are you sure you know who I am?"

Now he remembered. "You're Mrs. Keith." But he wondered that a professor's wife he'd met only once would stop to greet him.

"Finished your classes for the day?"

"Yes, ma'am."

Her laugh was husky and warm. "Not *'ma'am,'* for heaven's sake! How you doing in my husband's course?"

He grinned, pleased now at her breezy informality. "I'm not sure yet. We've only—"

"Don't count on *him* to help you. He's a lousy English teacher, or don't you agree?"

"Well . . ."

She laughed again. "You're very diplomatic, David. Can I drop you off somewhere?"

"Oh, thanks, but I was just going back to the dorm."

"Rooming alone?"

He nodded. Her eyes were kind. "Isn't it sort of lonely, being new here and all?"

"I guess I'll be making some friends pretty soon. Right now maybe it's better to have some time to settle down."

"Right now you look lonesome, to me."

He knew he was blushing. "Not really."

She reached a tanned arm and swung open the car door. "Hop in and come for a drive, it'll do you good."

"Well, thanks!" Again he felt a surge of pleasurable surprise.

Now that they'd left the college grounds and taken a secondary road into the countryside he sneaked a closer look at the driver. She was wearing a short tennis dress furled carelessly, well above knees that were as brown and smooth as her arms framing the wheel. How old was she— forty? Thirty? It was hard to tell. Anyway much younger than the professor, a real geezer. She gave him a sly sidewise look. "Trying to figure my age?"

"Your age?"

"Of course you were. And wondering how I could be married to an old fogey like Henry Keith."

"Why, no, I—"

"You're not the only one who's wondered about that, including myself. It's a long story—or maybe only a short story." She dropped one hand to his thigh for a moment in friendly reassurance. "Don't feel embarrassed, David. It was a perfectly natural thought for a seventeen-year-old in this situation."

"I'm eighteen," he said. He could still feel the disturbing touch of her hand.

Again her amused glance. "But not very long since, I'll bet."

"That's right. Last month."

They drove on in silence. The road was practically empty. How quickly you came out into farmland from the college town that was really not more than a village. Already they were in the hills, everything brightly green under the sunshine. Houses were few and far between now. He felt relaxed and almost happy for the first time since he arrived, contented just to lean back and look at the lush rural beauty around them.

Mrs. Keith said, her eyes on the winding road, "Not so lonesome now?"

"That's right!" He felt clumsily ashamed for being so inarticulate but she didn't seem to mind.

"It's nice around here. I often drive out in the good weather, just leave my tiresome daily life behind."

"Getting away from it all," he said.

He liked her warm, swift smile. "Exactly. And you're invited to join me whenever you feel like it, how's that?"

"Well, thanks . . ." was all he could find to say in the flush of his gratitude. But in the new silence between them he was thinking there must be other students as well who benefited by her friendliness.

"You're wondering about who else gets to share in these little occasions," she teased, reading his mind again. "And, perhaps, how I recognized you out of all those faces."

"Why, no," he protested, but knew she wasn't fooled.

"I don't mind telling you," she went on, "because you just might be interested to hear. I've seen you several times since classes began, David. It so happens I've been attending Economics One for my own edification, and there you are, sitting a few rows in front of me. You wouldn't have noticed me in that hall full of a couple of hundred students but the back of your neck is quite familiar to me now." She paused. "Does that please you?"

For a moment he didn't know how to reply. Mrs. Keith smiled and touched his thigh again. "Don't try to answer. It was just my little joke."

"It does please me," he said. Once more he was blushing.

They were passing a patch of forested slope. "I want to show you a favorite spot of mine." With the casual suddenness that seemed characteristic, Mrs. Keith swung the car into a narrow side road which was little more than a track through the woods. Trees rose thickly on either side. So dense was the foliage overhead that the sun was almost shut out. All at once they were in a world of shade and seclusion; the wheels crunched softly against soil. "Here," she said, and cut the engine. They rolled to a slow stop. A small clearing opened at the track's end. There was birdsong somewhere above them. Mrs. Keith sighed with relief, sank against the seat and turned her head toward him. "Now, isn't this nice?"

"It sure is." His voice sounded remote to him.

For several minutes they both were completely still. She didn't speak and didn't seem to want him to say anything more. Despite the lack of sunlight he was conscious of an enveloping warmth that intensified the isolation of this place and the drowsy spell it was casting over him.

"Hot?" she said.

He shook his head.

"I am. You'll forgive me if I get more comfortable."

Facing him, she leaned forward, dropping her hands behind her back and pulling the short skirt out from between the leather seat and her body. It was a quick, lithe movement but not too quick for him to see that she was nude under the skirt. "That feels much better," she said in a half-whisper, and dropped back against the seat beside him, apparently unaware the front of her skirt was now almost up to her hips, or ignoring it. Again she let her hand fall onto his thigh, and this time left it there, her head turned toward him. He felt the blood mounting to his head knowing she was watching him and at last was able to face her, saw her smile lingering on him like a caress.

"Do you mind if I tell you something?" she said slowly

and softly. "Sitting behind you in class, I was fascinated by
the back of your head, the way your hair grows to a little
V on your neck, thick and dark. And I wanted to see all of
you, without any clothes on. Because I knew you would
look just like the portrait of the Greek lad that hangs
over my bed. The naked boy sitting with his chin on his
knees and his arms clasped around his ankles so you can't
see all of him." She paused. "Do you mind if I talk to you
so frankly?"

"No. No, of course not."

She was looking down at her hand on his thigh as if
noticing it for the first time. "Oh. Do you want me to take
my hand away? I will if you want me to."

"No. Please . . ." Something like terror seized him;
this woman was a wife! And his professor's wife!

Her little laugh was low and tender. "I know you
don't, David. I just said that. Because I know you can't
help yourself, now, and neither can I. And that's as it
should be. That's right. That's good." Her fingers twitched
and her hand moved inside his thigh. "Don't you think I
can see you can't help yourself? Is it because you saw
something you shouldn't have seen when I was pulling up
my skirt, David? But I wanted you to see it. Ah, you're a
big boy," she was murmuring, "and you want me to hold
you. Don't you want me to hold you?"

"Yes . . ." He heard his own voice trembling, tried to
control it.

"And you want to fuck me. Don't you? Don't you?
Say it. I want to hear you say it."

"I want to fuck you . . ." Was he really saying it, to
*her?*

Through his clothing he could feel the heat of her
hand closing on his penis, she was kissing his mouth with
rich wet lips while he sat transfixed, a drunken dizziness
rising through his body. "Is there a girl you want more
than me?" she whispered. "Tell me. Is there?"

"No. Nobody."

"But you've been with a girl before me. Of course
you have."

"Yes."

"Many girls?"

"No."

He felt her smile against his throat and her fingers

tightening. "Behind us in the back seat there's a mat rolled up on the floor. Take it out and spread it on the grass by the car. And don't be worried, darling, no one will see us, no one will hear us. But we will see each other. The first time you will come to me quickly and I will want it that way. The second time I will show you how to be a man. Would you like that?"

"Oh, yes. Yes," he whispered, "I want you to show me."

"You're eighteen." She laughed the low, intoxicating laugh and gripped him hard. "It's time."

# 4

Looking back, his freshman year seemed to open a new world to him—of books, of friendships, of freedom from family restraints, most of all of Julia Keith. Now, back in New York and working at a summer copy boy's job at the *News*—thanks to a recommendation from Henry Keith as a promising writer—he still couldn't believe the exciting things that had happened with the professor's wife. Did Henry Keith know? Sometimes he wondered whether this quiet, courteous little man, this bookworm who was laughed at by some students behind his back, was aware of what his wife was doing with David Brent, his best composition student; two or three times he thought he saw a glint of special understanding behind those glasses in their after-class conversations. But he couldn't be sure. He only knew another year of sexual adventure was in store for him with Julia; she'd promised that their little drives in the country would continue.

Meanwhile there was the *News*, a new world of its own. And New York, seen with adult eyes as if for the first time, a city he'd never recognized, was there. It was Jake Wethers who introduced him to the Village. They worked the same shift and usually—unless a big story was breaking—finished up at eight-thirty and came out just as the bulldog edition was being loaded on the Forty-first Street side. The job was exciting and he loved it.

Jake was twenty-three and a *News* veteran, a sort of chief copy boy with the assignment of breaking in the new guys and keeping an eye on them, but already they were letting Jake go out on minor fires and try his hand at squibs on the rewrite desk; he'd move up to cub reporter soon. He liked Jake Wethers, had a feeling there was more to their relationship than just getting along well together on the job. And he was sure of it when one night

18

after he'd been at the *News* less than a month Jake caught up with him as they were leaving and said, "Are you free? Come on downtown."

He'd been there, but he'd never really seen the Village until he saw it with Jake, who had a little apartment on Patchin Place and knew all the bars and eating places. That first night they rode down on the Fifth Avenue bus and went to Julius' for a sandwich and beer. There was something magical about the Village—the glow from the old-fashioned street lights in the soft summer air, the elegant old town houses, the smells and noise along Eighth Street, the kissing couples in Washington Square, an ambiance of variety and freedom all around him, refuge from the gray monotony of uptown. Walking over to Jake's apartment he felt the enchantment of it take hold and said he wished he lived there.

"Where you living now?"

"With my family on Seventeenth."

"I could maybe find you something cheap around here."

"I can't, Jake. I'm supposed to be saving to go back for sophomore year."

Jake spat into the gutter. "You want to be a newspaperman?"

"I think so, yes."

"You want to be a newspaperman you can't learn it in college. Look at me—I never finished high school."

In the apartment they drank coffee brewed by Jake in his kitchenette and afterward, over the applejack, Jake said, "Another thing about having your own place, you've got somewhere to take girls to."

"I'd sure love to have a place like yours."

Jake squinted at him. "You got a girl?"

"Not in New York." And he thought of Julia Keith.

"You want to come down here Saturday night? A couple of dollies coming who like a good hosing." He grinned and nodded toward the king-size bed that filled half the room. "Better plan to stay all night."

"I'd like that."

"They'd like you, too. You're a good-looking guy, Dave."

It turned out the two dollies were sisters from Brooklyn who worked for the racing paper, the *Morning Tele-*

*graph,* and Jake knew them well—both blue-eyed, black-haired Irish, about Jake's age. They were already in the apartment with Jake, well into the whiskey, by the time he arrived. Jake said, his arms around the two girls, "Whadd'ya think of my new assistant?"

"He's cute," one of them said. "What happened to Harry?"

"I demobilized Harry."

The other girl said, "It's about time. I'm tired of Harry."

"Harry's tired, too. You wore him out, baby." Jake laughed and pointed to the bottle. "Drink up, assistant. No, they're not twins, if that's what you're thinking. Eileen's got the legs and Maggie's got the tits, in case you have to tell them apart in the dark."

Maggie was smiling. "You all ready to go, assistant?"

"He's always ready to go," Jake said. "Take off your jacket, Davey—it's warm in here and gonna get warmer."

The courtyard lamp, a relic of horse-and-buggy days, threw mellow light on the facing rows of houses, and from beyond the street the distant clamor of a Village Saturday night rose into the lowering sky. Jake was opening a card table and dragging up chairs. "How about we start things off with a little poker? Okay with you, assistant?"

"Fine with me." He was relieved he knew the game and had some money in his pocket.

"I get to sit across from Maggie."

"That's a break for me," Eileen said. "I can play footsie with the assistant."

"Not till she loses one shoe—it's the rule," Jake warned him, and with a little twinge of excitement he realized what the stakes would be.

But Maggie lost both her shoes on the first two pots and Jake had to shuck his shirt on the third before Eileen lost a shoe. "When's the assistant going to lose a pot?" Maggie was complaining. "You cheating on us?"

"Maybe he's just shy," Eileen said. He felt a bare toe rub against his ankle. "You shy, assistant?"

"I play to win," he said.

"I play to lose," Eileen said.

"So that's why I'm always last man out," Maggie said, and everybody laughed.

Male luck began to fade after that. The assistant lost

both shoes and his shirt before Eileen lost her other shoe. Bare-chested, Jake barked at him, "Unfair! No wearing undershirts."

"If you say so." He stood up and pulled off the undershirt. He'd had his second whiskey by now and felt steady and good, no longer strange with the two girls. Eileen was watching him. "Now we're getting somewhere," she said, and lost the next two pots. This cost her, first, her blouse, then her skirt, leaving her in panty and bra. She stood up to step out of her skirt and he saw what Jake meant about her legs. He couldn't see through the bra but she looked pretty good up there, too.

Jake lost the next pot and his trousers. When he got up to shed them and pour another round Dave glanced at Jake's shorts and saw the hard swelling pushing up underneath. Maggie leaned over and tweaked it.

"Take it easy, girlie, I'm still in the game."

Eileen laughed. "It sure looks that way."

Maggie, wearing a short black dress, had only one outer garment to lose. That went with the next pot. She was stockier, with paler skin than Eileen. Heavy breasts stretched the restraining sheath and, below, the panty fabric wasn't enough to hide the dark massed hair curling around its edges. Across the way in the house just opposite, radio music blared suddenly into the court, punctuated by shouted laughter and a slammed door. "They're at it again," Jake groaned. "Last week the cops broke it up at six A.M."

"Shut up and deal," Maggie said.

"I'm going after your bra on this one, kid."

Eileen said, holding his ankle under the table with both feet, "She won last time. I think I'm going to like you better than Harry, Dave."

"Do socks count?"

"Not in summer when we don't wear stockings."

Maggie lost the next pot. Jake and Eileen jeered and the assistant watched the big, lovely breasts spill out of their covering, white and pink against the flushed skin. He was more excited now than Jake, suddenly aware the room was full of the heat and scent of their bodies. "I'm pulling the shades," Maggie said, and held one arm over her breasts while she covered the two windows. But she'd been seen; a yelp of laughter came from across the courtyard and a man's voice chortled, "Put it right here, sister!"

Jake, dealing the next hand, had hung the bra around his neck. Things seemed to be happening faster now—the game was reaching climax. The assistant lost his trousers and Eileen her bra. He found he could devour her nakedness with his eyes as unaffectedly as looking at a ring on her finger, and made her laugh when he said in his turn, "Now we're getting somewhere!" She was more daintily built than Maggie but he liked them both and wanted them both. He didn't care now whether any of them saw his erection. Shifting his shorts more comfortably he realized he was drunk and it made everything easier to control. When Eileen lost the next pot he joined the chorus of laughter and applauded as she stood up in pretended shyness to slip off her panty.

Jake cackled, "One down! I'm gonna win this yet."

"I hope your assistant's next," Eileen said.

"Thanks for the support," the assistant said, and lost the next pot. Standing up, swaying just a little as the blood mounted to his head, he loosened his shorts and let them fall to the floor.

Jake and Maggie were clapping their hands. "Didn't I tell you he's ready to go?" Jake demanded.

Eileen, her color high, her eyes glistening, stared at his face before deliberately dropping her gaze downward. "I knew I was going to like you better than Harry," she said, almost solemn. She put out her hand and took his hand, the first time she'd touched him. "We're spectators now, assistant—come on over to the grandstand." They sat down side by side on the bed while the other two battled through the final round.

"How many, friend?" Jake was saying.

"Three. And don't palm anything."

"I'm pat."

"Go ahead, bluff," she said. "It won't help you."

"Whatcha got?"

"You first."

He laughed. "Show me."

"Show *me*."

They put down their hands together. She had three deuces to his two kings. "You're out," she jeered. "Stand up and pay off."

The other three watched while he went through a peekaboo striptease, Eileen chanting, "Take it off, take it *all* off!" until he tossed his shorts away. Maggie stood up and grinned at him. "Okay, you showed it. Now let's see what you can do with it."

"You know what I can do with it."

"I think I forgot."

"You'll remember this time." He leaned and pulled her panty down to her ankles, holding her steady while she kicked it away. "Gangway!" he shouted to the couple on the bed. Eileen moved to the big chair opposite and Dave perched on the arm beside her. A special silence descended on the room. Maggie wasn't jeering any more. She reached for Jake's hand and looked up at him. Their eyes held. "You're something," he muttered. "Aren't you something?" Then she lay down on the bed and closed her eyes and drew back her knees and using one hand eased him into her body with a beautiful, natural movement. The two watchers stirred as his rhythm began. Dave leaned forward, intent on what he was seeing. Eileen was touching his penis without seeming to know what she was doing. And he knew how to wait now; Julia Keith had taught him that. In time, in good time, it would be their turn. In the house across the court a radio or something began to play.

# 5

He hadn't known exactly what to expect but he was somehow disappointed all the same. It was an ordinary apartment house in the west sixties and the elevator man didn't even give him a look taking him up to the fourth floor. Turning into the street where it was, he had a funny feeling that people knew where he was going. Was he mistaken or did several of them give him a sharp, mocking glance, almost a grin, as they passed? The thought of his sister Cathy finding out, for instance! He hadn't done anything like this before. He felt oddly guilty and alone.

There was a peephole in the apartment door, a bell button on the wall beside it, but the other doors in the quiet corridor had peepholes too, so there was nothing unusual about 407. Or were the apartments all in the same setup? He doubted it: while he was waiting self-consciously for somebody to answer his ring the elevator door opened again and a tired-looking man with a large grocery bag in his arms walked to an apartment at the other end of the corridor without even glancing at him.

Jake Wethers had given the address to one of the copy-readers a few days ago over beers at Costello's, and he'd made a mental note of it at the time. He wasn't seeing so much of Jake right now: Maggie was staying at the apartment in the Village where, Jake told him with a laugh, she didn't go for the idea of two men on one girl; they'd have to wait for Eileen to come back from vacation before they could arrange another poker game.

But there was always that address. He hadn't really intended to do anything about it—or had he? Anyway he didn't discuss it with Jake. But tonight as he was finishing work he thought of it again, and instead of going home he took the bus across town and walked the rest of the way. Twice he'd considered dropping the whole idea—for some reason he felt tense about it—but he kept walking, telling himself that if he didn't go through with it he'd regret it afterward.

They seemed to be quite a while answering the door. He was still nervous, and almost with relief he decided he must have the wrong address; he knew he wouldn't have the courage to ask the elevator man whether it was the wrong apartment. He was just turning away when the peephole clicked open, an eye looked out at him and after a sound of lock and chain rattling the door swung inward. Immediately he felt a pang of disappointment; the girl wasn't at all what he'd expected. He'd thought all of them were pretty and sexy, but this was a woman well into her thirties, angular instead of voluptuous under her faded kimono, with dyed blonde hair and a suspicious, hard smile. She looked over his shoulder into the corridor before she shut the door behind him, and still without saying a word led the way down the narrow hall past closed doors to a parlor at the end.

The room was poorly lighted and smelt of stale tobacco smoke. Two men in shirtsleeves sitting on a couch against the wall looked up briefly with identical opaque stares as the woman motioned him to a threadbare upholstered chair, then turned her smile on one of the men and said, "C'mon, honey." Carrying his jacket over his arm, the man followed her into a room off the hall and the door closed behind them.

He watched them disappear and listened but heard no sound. Apart from his first glance, the other man on the couch had ignored him. Was this one on line or was he finished and just waiting for his friend? It wasn't long before the question was answered: another door opened farther down the hall and a third man came out, followed by a woman with a towel in her hand who was completely naked except for house slippers. She was heavier than the other woman but it didn't make her any more inviting to look at. She had the same mechanical smile and dyed red hair that belied the rest of the hair on her body.

"See you soon," she said to the man who was with her, not even looking at him.

"So long, Daisy." He spoke without enthusiasm.

She let him out the front door and walked listlessly back to the parlor. "Who's next?" she said.

The man on the couch got up without a word and followed her back into the room she'd just left. Watching them go, Dave felt the silence close around him again, not a sound from either room where the women were. The feeling of dismay grew stronger; he didn't like this place or the people in it. Were all these joints like this? If something better existed he'd have to try again some other day; right now he wanted out, and fast, before the women came back.

Too late—he was trapped. Just as he stood up the one who'd let him in came out of her room, followed by the man. This time she was naked, like the one named Daisy, and even uglier without her kimono. The man had his jacket on again and preceded her down the hall to the front door. "G'bye now," she said dully, and he nodded unsmiling as she let him out. Coming back into the parlor she spoke tonelessly, absently. "Okay, young feller, it's all yours," and led the way to her room.

In the doorway he stopped, his last chance to tell her he'd changed his mind. But he couldn't find the words. She hadn't even noticed his hesitation; she was busy smoothing down the ratty bedcover. Her arching body as she bent over the bed was grotesque, disgusting, but she seemed oblivious. Straightening up again, she turned as if aware of him for the first time.

"How about you shut the door?" she said.

Still speechless, he closed it behind him and took a step into the room.

The frozen smile. "You forget something?"

"Did I?"

"The money, buster!"

He felt his face flame and fumbled in his watch pocket for the bill that was ready there.

"Who sent you, anyway?"

"Jake Wethers."

"You with the *News?*"

He nodded. She dropped the bill into a bureau drawer, saying, "Well, go on—strip down!" as if annoyed at him. Quickly and clumsily he put his clothes piece by piece on the wooden chair by the door—jacket, shirt, shoes, socks and pants, feeling her cold stare at every movement. As he took off his shorts she shook her head glumly and

spoke. "We're gonna have to do something about that—
c'mon over here and lie down."

He fought the impulse to hide his impotence with his
hands and obediently lay down on his back while she knelt
on the floor beside the bed. He had thought it would be
like Eileen and Maggie but everything—the woman, the
room, the smell of the bedcover—was repulsive and shame-
ful. Had he felt a real desire or only curiosity before he
rang that doorbell? All he knew now was a desperation to
get it over with, and how could he do that the way he
was? But the woman was showing him how. One hand
cupping and squeezing, she bent her head to him and
sucked with patient, supple jerks that drew irresistible sensation up along his legs and into his belly and chest until
he closed his eyes in surrender. Blindly he gripped her la-
boring shoulders and lifted toward her. Beyond his eyelids the room seemed to revolve, time suspended, all mind
lost. And "Yeah!" he heard her say. Her mouth had left
him. Like waking, he opened his eyes and saw her lying
beside him.

She spoke to the ceiling. "Climb aboard, sonny."

It was not himself but he was there, placed neatly, the
expert, undesired body drawing, driving, coiled beneath
him. Physically he had never reached so far, but it was like
someone else was doing it, outside him, removed—somebody staring down at the empty eyes that never wavered,
somebody who knew he was softening again, failing, and
knew that she knew it. And somehow, tightening, yielding,
tightening, somehow closer, hotter, deeper, irresistibly she
gave him back the strength to go on with it, taught him
this was happening and could happen to him without need
or will or longing, made him partner at last in her dis-
honored world.

For only a minute or two she let him rest there,
drained, humiliated, before she shifted his weight from
her, rose abruptly and went to the towel rack across the
room. Who was this stranger he'd wanted to call friend?
He didn't even know her name. He turned his head away
because he didn't want to look at her anymore. He closed
his eyes because he didn't want to look at himself.

The doorbell buzzed in the hall, repeated, insistent.

"C'mon, bud," she said to him. "Up and out."

# 6

He was late getting downtown to the bus station and made the ten P.M. departure by seconds. The last fight with Eileen had left him angry and troubled; tonight she'd told him she wouldn't be seeing him at Christmas vacation; she'd decided to go steady with the guy she'd met in Nantucket and there'd be no more poker games with Jake or anybody else, including Dave Brent.

That was what you learned about females. You couldn't count on them; you never knew what they'd do next.

And Julia Keith—would he find she, too, had changed her mind when he got back to school?

Frowning, uneasy, he made his way through the narrow, cluttered aisle, clutching his ticket in one hand and his suitcase in the other. He stumbled into the last vacant seat just as the bus groaned forward, its interior lights dimming to darkness. There had been only a moment to glimpse the passenger in the window seat next to his—a quietly dressed girl who glanced at him with open curiosity. Staring straight ahead, he sat steadying the suitcase in the aisle with one hand while the bus lurched and wheeled through deserted nighttime streets until it lumbered onto the smoother pavement of the brightly lighted river tunnel. Here it was possible for him to stand up and hoist the suitcase laboriously onto the rack above the seat. One more chance to size up his neighbor before they sped out of the tunnel and into blackness again. She was about his own age, nondescriptly blonde, and her mouth widened to a friendly smile as he looked down at her. Now as the bus gained the skyway, heading south, he settled into his seat again and dropped his head back against the rest.

"Heavy valise," she said in a small voice. "I wouldn't like to lug *that* around."

28

"It's not so bad."

"You goin' far?"—the musical Virginia accent unmistakable on her lips.

"Carolina."

"Carolina! You won't get there till *mornin'!*"

She seemed dismayed for him. "I don't mind."

The bus interior was taking shape—heads just visible in the pale gloom above the seats in front, long rows of baggage in the overhead racks, a dim light glowing above the driver's uniform cap, one of his elbows leaning negligently on the wheel. The girl spoke again in that soft little voice.

"Carolina. That where you live?"

"Where I go to school." He turned to look at her but could only vaguely make out her features. "You been visiting in New York?"

"How'd you *know?* I've been stayin' with my aunt." She said "awnt."

"Like it?"

She didn't answer right away, then said, "I guess not much. Y'all just go too fast for me." Her little laugh mingled innocence and ignorance. "I'm glad I came, though. Now I won't feel so sorry for myself I've never been there."

The bus was up to cruising speed. The motion beneath them settled into a steady rhythm and he could see people squirming around and getting comfortable along the aisle. He turned to his neighbor again. "How far are you going?"

"Washington." She said "Wahshinton."

"That's your home?"

"Now it is."

They rode on in silence and he closed his eyes. But after a moment she spoke again. "You're feelin' bad, aren't you?" she said softly.

It startled him. "Sick? No, I'm fine."

"I don't mean throwin'-up sick. I mean *about* somethin' . . ."

"No. Not at all."

Perhaps it was the sharpness of his tone; she turned away from him and rested her head against the window and he was sorry he'd snapped at her. But he didn't want any more questions. Instead he let his mind drift again to the days ahead, sophomore year beginning, and above all

to Julia Keith. Nothing he'd experienced this summer with
Eileen was quite the same as being with Julia. Intercourse
One, she called it, and gave him an A-plus for his first year
in the subject. He still suspected the professor knew
about him and Julia but still he wasn't sure. Such uncer-
tainties, and the fear always that they would be caught together, added suspense that only heightened the sexual excitement, especially the two times that Henry had been
away lecturing and she'd had him come secretly to the
house late at night. There for the first time they'd bathed
together, Julia massaging him with soap and so intensifying the sensation that he came in her hands. For that quiz
she gave him a C-minus, as she called it, for lack of control. They made up for it next time when he fucked her
standing up under a warm shower and felt her whole body
trembling with orgasm.

He stirred, realizing his thoughts were exciting him
physically. With a self-conscious movement he dropped
both hands over his stiffening erection. Had the girl observed it? He turned his head to look at her in the dimness: her head was back, her young bosom rising and falling as if in sleep, her eyes were closed, and for the first
time he noticed the almost voluptuous fullness of her
slightly parted lips. What would she do if suddenly he
leaned over and kissed her mouth?

At the same instant she opened her eyes, answered
his smile with her own, and shifted her body nearer to
him, letting her head sink sleepily against his shoulder
while her left hand closed around his arm like a child
nestling up to her father, comforted and secure.

It gave him a strange reaction. For a moment he sat
perfectly still, not responding to her in any way. Then he
put his arm around her shoulders and drew her yielding
body closer to him. As naturally as a lover, she dropped
her hand to his lap and reached for the hand still lying
there, gently pushing it aside and letting her hand rest
lightly on his erection. He felt it throb under her fingers
and in his astonishment he looked down at her face. It
was serene and composed as though she was living a peaceful dream. She hadn't opened her eyes again.

Still feeling wonder at what was happening, he glanced
uneasily across the aisle at the only two passengers who
could have noticed. He couldn't make the two women out

very well in the faint light but they both seemed safely asleep. He was alone with the southern girl in a small compartment of isolation. He looked down again at her hand on his lap. The fingers lay there light as lace, motionless yet somehow aware of what they covered, only a layer of clothing beneath. But were they aware? Was she truly asleep? Again in spite of himself he throbbed under her hand, and now she spoke, a whisper: "Aren't you warm in your jacket? You'll feel cooler if you take it off." And he was obeying as she withdrew, reached up to help him off with the jacket, spread it over his lap. "Don't that feel better?" she was whispering, and once more snuggled under his arm. He felt her hand stealing back across his thigh, concealed now, and softly, deliberately, unbuttoning his fly while he sat hardly believing what she was doing. She had all the buttons undone and was loosening his belt buckle, tugging his trousers apart. Already he could feel the heat of her fingers. Then they found the opening in his shorts and with a single swift motion closed around his penis with the tenderness of embrace.

Once more he tried to see her face, but it was buried in his shoulder now and only her fingers told him she was aware. He shifted slightly in his seat and dropped his head back, opened his legs in delicious surrender to her touch. The hand was quiescent, tentative at first, the fragile fingers fluttering with brief involuntary movements along the smooth, hard shaft. Each time, he quivered, and each time she gave him back a slight responding pressure, before the fingers darted upward to the tip or down with exquisite lightness to brush the base. He could feel her breath rise and fall more quickly against his chest. No need for words; they were saying it all in another language. His hand slipped from her slender shoulder to cup her breast; its heaviness surprised him. Again she responded by tightening her grasp a little more, and now the fluttering motion became a steady, slow jacking, bringing sensation that came from far back, deep in his loins. He knew he couldn't take this for long, and she too knew it—the hand paused at its lovely work and she whispered, her voice muffled in his shirt: "*Handkerchief? . . .*" With his free hand he fumbled in his back pocket, brought it out, pushed it under the jacket so she could take it and cover his penis. There was barely time; the orgasm had begun. Straining to hold himself motionless, he could feel the sweat break out on his skin. With fierce effort he stifled the gasp half ecstacy, half pain that shook his whole body, and felt her hand closing on him like a vise, her torso half across his lap now bearing down on him, staying with him to the end.

She was still there, patient and tender, when at last his breathing quieted. He was aware his eyes were closed and he opened them with disbelief that this had really happened. His body's paroxysm ebbed toward sober reality again but a new emotion remained—a warm feeling of gratitude toward this girl he'd never seen before, who knew no more of him than he did of her, and whose hand under the jacket was now withdrawing the handkerchief between expert fingers, leaving him dry and clean. Gently he drew her back into the seat beside him, and for several minutes neither spoke. But when he leaned toward her and tried to put his hand between her knees she stiffened and resisted.

"Why?" he whispered.

Her only answer was a swift, small kiss at his cheek.

"But don't you want me to touch you now?"

Very slightly she shook her head. He could see her faint smile in the dimness. The handkerchief lay in her lap, "Rest now . . ." she said, and took his hand between her hands. All at once he realized how tired he was, and dropped his head back against the seat, deliciously sleepy. The bus rolled steadily through the night and he wondered for a moment how far they had come.

It was all he knew before he ceased to know. Once, as in a dream, he blinked at passing lights, and was aware the girl next to him still held his hand. Another time he felt himself come slowly awake, the bus lights were on, they were stopped at some kind of indoor platform and people were struggling up slowly and shambling with their luggage toward the front door. He turned his head and saw the girl standing in the aisle beside him with a shabby suitcase in her hand.

"Where's this?" he mumbled, staring with bleared eyes.

"We're in Wahshinton, darlin'."

He started to get up but felt her restraining hand on his shoulder. "You're stayin' on, remember?"

"But wait a minute . . ."

It was like seeing her for the first time, and suddenly

she was a stranger again. Not pretty, not desirable, not the girl who touched him in the darkness. She stood looking down at him with a wistful smile that somehow reminded him of his sister.

"You feelin' happier this mornin'?" she said.

"Thanks to you . . ."

"I'm glad."

"Can't I see you again?"

She was shaking her head. "Can I keep your handkerchief?" she said.

# 7

He stood within the protective shadow of the big trees and for several minutes fought to control his drunkenness. Once he shivered with nausea and leaned forward a little, feeling the strong, raw taste of the moonshine come back to his throat; he'd never been as drunk as this, not even freshman year when the upperclassmen stood around you in a circle and made you drink a full tumbler without taking a breath. But inside him a single lucid spot of thought watched the struggle with confidence—he had to control it, he must. That's why he'd stopped, halfway back to the dorm from the tavern, to give himself time to recover. He wasn't about to face his roommates in this condition, hear their laughter and jeers.

There was sweat on his face and hands but already he was feeling cooler, stronger. The worst was passed. In a little while, working at it, the stagger and drowsy weight would go, he would have again that feeling of new strength forever, as though waking refreshed from sleep. But he knew, even as he straightened and was able to look around him, there was more to recover from than the whiskey he'd swilled down like a lunatic at that table in the back room: Julia's words ringing in his head like the voice of doom. A part of him was still dazed, bewildered. Something had happened that had never even come to his mind.

He shook his head as if to shake off a blow, turned and resumed his walk on the other side of the street. They called it Fraternity Row, the stately Colonial houses bathed in the moonlight of late evening, the scent of summer redolent in the hedges fronting the lawns. Sounds of talk and laughter floated from the downstairs rooms, upstairs the lights in the bedrooms were already winking out. In one of the houses as he passed, walking carefully, still a little dizzy, a victrola sounded the plaintive strains of "Ramona."

34

"Hey, Brent!" The greeting came from a solitary figure standing at the gate of the last house on the Row. He looked up to see Galloway grinning at him. They had a history class together and were nodding acquaintances. Galloway was one of those easygoing southerners, graceful and well-dressed, who always looked slightly amused and skeptical no matter what was going on. He stopped and Galloway took a step toward him.

"You all right, Brent?" The voice casual and genial. "Look kind of woozy."

"I'm all right." But he swayed a little as he said it and Galloway took his arm to steady him.

"I'd offer you another drink but that's the last thing you need." The low, pleasant laugh. "Better come inside and sit a while, Brent."

"I'm all right." The touch on his arm was somehow reassuring but he drew away; he had to show he could hold his liquor as well as anybody on the Row.

But the hand was on his arm again, gently propelling him through the gate and up the flagstone walk to the house. This time he allowed himself to be guided. His head was fully clear but the rest of him still wobbled a little. "Where you been?" Galloway was saying. "Nothing over that way but the tavern." He chuckled. "Don't tell me."

"Right the first time." They went into a kind of parlor to the right of the front door and Galloway eased him into a big chair. The guy was being friendly and helpful; he liked him for it and was glad now they'd come in. The Delta house was quiet tonight, though other times, especially weekends, it was one of the noisiest on the Row. The members were mostly reputed to be rich and wild but Galloway had something about him, something mature or controlled, that didn't quite fit the image.

"How you feeling now?" Galloway sat down opposite him and looked sympathetic.

"Fine. Don't I look okay?"

"A little worried, that's all. A little wounded."

"Wounded?" He stared back, startled at the word.

Galloway only smiled. "Something eating you, Brent? I mean besides that corn likker?"

He shook his head. "I'll be all right in a little while."

"Drinking alone?"

"Well, yes. I got some bad news tonight."

Galloway looked grave. "Not from home, I hope."

"No, not from home. From somebody I know right here."

"A female, right?"

It startled him. "Why d'you think that?"

"I read you like a book, Brent."

"I didn't say it was a female." But something in the way Galloway was talking soothed the hurt he felt; he had a sudden warm desire to confess in comradeship. "I'll get over it," he mumbled.

"Of course you will. They're all the same—no good, especially this one."

"This one?" He stammered it.

"Oh, come on, Dave." The low, easy laugh. "You know who I'm talking about. Listen, two years ago when I first came to school here she tried it on me, too."

A silence. He was trying to look Galloway in the eye without turning away. Galloway spoke evenly. "Did she tell you she has a new boy, is that it? That's no surprise. I saw her with him yesterday, in her car. Last year I saw her with you, too. Two or three times." More gently he said, "Believe me, it's not worth getting piss-drunk over."

Another pause. He felt the blood flame to his face. "How do you know all this?"

"I just told you, I saw you. Everybody around here knows Julia Keith. You think she could get away with it without being found out?"

"You mean the professor knows?"

Galloway shrugged. "If he doesn't, he's stupider than he acts. I'd guess he wants it this way, if he can't take care of her himself."

No use pretending further. He'd already admitted it. Instead there was a feeling like relief, something comforting in the way Galloway sat there like a wise older brother taking it all as a matter of course, making a routine thing of it. "The bitch," Galloway was saying, "that's all she is, a bitch in heat every day in the year. Only reason they both haven't been kicked out of here is the college is afraid of the scandal. She's the type who'd make him start a lawsuit." He chuckled. "Poor Henry, what else could he do—challenge a couple of dozen students to a duel? Either way, his old mother down in Charleston would just about die of shame."

The voice trailed off, and everything seemed to break in him at once. Suddenly he was exhausted, unable to care about it anymore, to care about anything. Galloway seemed to understand. He got up and put a hand on his shoulder. "I know how you feel," he said quietly. "You'll get over it after a good sleep. And you're going to do that right here—there's an extra bed in my room and you're more than welcome."

He nodded unprotesting, got slowly to his feet and side by side with Galloway climbed the stairs. On the second floor the house was hot, dark and close. A sound of snoring came from one of the rooms. Galloway guided him to the end of the hall and into his room to a bed under the window, patted his shoulder again and said, "Night-night, Dave boy." He could hear the little smile in the voice and thought: I've made a friend. He had just enough will left to strip and fall flat out on his face before he slept.

It must have been near dawn when he woke, like coming to himself from far away. He was thinking nothing. He was very gradually aware only of the touch of bare flesh against bare flesh, *his* flesh, warm fingers tracing as with infinite care a faint design in the small of his back, lightly probing between his buttocks, and above him he could hear unseen a presence, an intensity of suppressed breathing. His eyes were still closed. He did not all at once believe what he knew was happening, then with a guttural cry arched his body violently, rolled and sprawled to the floor before springing up again, shivering with shock and anger, fists clenched, to face the naked male who faced him. "What do you think you're doing, are you *crazy?*" he gasped.

"Come on, Dave," Galloway whispered, and moved a step closer, "you know you want it."

"No," he said, *"don't touch me."* And again he said, "No!" and reached for his clothes.

# 8

His father died suddenly late in his second college spring, in the midst of final exams. It was the culmination of a long, ill-fated year. Since his break with Julia Keith the night of the incident at the Delta house he'd not been able to find a girl who could substitute for the excitement and satisfaction of their relationship, though he admitted to himself that in his bitterness toward Julia he'd not tried very hard. Was it a hurt pride that had seemed to cut off his sexual feelings? Had he really loved this woman so much older than himself, discovered the wretchedness that love could bring? Even her husband had changed toward him, no mistaking that. She must have said something to him. There was no more talk from Henry Keith about a junior-year scholarship that would have relieved the financial pressure resulting from his father's death.

On a wet, sullen night in New York he sat in a booth at Costello's with Jake Wethers, the first time they'd talked since the funeral. The wind drove bursts of dirty rain along Third Avenue, snapping umbrellas inside out and chasing a few early evening pedestrians into the precarious shelter of doorways. He could see Jake was being particularly cautious and watchful with him, careful to avoid saying anything that might touch too directly on his bereavement, and he wanted to tell him he was all right, it wasn't painful any more. He'd been stunned for a while; his father was only forty-seven. But you had to put it behind you. It was only the future that mattered now.

Jake said with his cautious grin: "I guess you'll be glad to get back to college."

He shook his head. "I'm not going back. No money to pay for next year. Got to get a job, Jake."

"Sure. You're the head of the family now, right?"

"It's not like that. My mother has the insurance and

Cathy's in nurse's training, they'll be okay. I just have to take care of myself."

Still cautiously: "You weren't so dead set on school anyhow, as I remember."

He shrugged. "I guess not. My father was."

"Dads are like that, Dave."

Once more he felt the shock of sadness return, but it was briefer each time now. He wondered again if he and his father had ever been friends—was he a son or just a responsibility? He had thought he might cry at the graveside but when they lowered him in only Cathy cried, her hand holding tight to his own. In the sorrow of the moment he felt his sister had grown closer to him than ever before, somehow closer even than his mother.

Jake was saying, "What the hell. Sometimes the worst things turn out for the best. Remember when I used to tell you a newspaperman didn't need college? You start early and stay with it, that's all."

"I was going to ask you about it, Jake. I figured if I could get my old job back at the *News . . .*"

"They're not hiring. Seems like nobody's hiring right now. In fact they're laying off all over town. I'm lucky to have my own job, you want the truth."

"I was afraid of that."

Jake looked at his watch. "But I'll talk to Mahoney tonight. No harm in trying. I'll tell him about your—" He broke off and stared at the door, then laughed. "Well, I'll be damned!"

Turning, Dave saw the couple coming in from the street, a heavyset man in raincoat and beret with a slim, attractive woman somewhat younger. They'd recognized Jake Wethers and came up to the booth shaking the rain off their clothes.

"Thought you were in Paris, Hap!"

"I was and I will be. Here for a couple of weeks."

"It better not be any longer or I'll go back by myself," the woman said. She smiled with cool gray eyes. "Meanwhile, I want a drink."

Jake scrambled up and ushered her into the seat next to him. "Got to leave in a minute. Dave, meet Hap and Helen Osgood, Dave Brent. Hap used to be on the *News.* So did Dave."

He thought the man looked at him without any interest, but Helen Osgood turned that easy, friendly smile in his direction in a way that seemed to appraise all of him at a glance. "You're too young to retire," she said.

"Far from it. I'm looking for a job."

"I hope you aren't saddled with a wife and kids, in these times."

He shook his head. "No plans for that, so far."

"Luckily, Hap and I got out just in time. In Paris they don't even know the meaning of the word 'depression.' Yet."

Beside them Jake and her husband were deep in talk about the *News*, interrupted only by arrival of the drinks and a welcome-home toast. Dave found himself talking to Helen like an old friend, telling her about his father and college, asking her about Paris. And she listened, giving him a feeling she was warmly sympathetic to what he'd come through these past few days, understood his anxious uncertainty.

"Why don't you give Paris a try?" she said. "Maybe Hap could fix you up with a job on the *Trib*."

Paris! Just hearing her say it excited him. "You think there's a chance?"

"I'll talk to him about it."

"Say, that's nice of you, Mrs.—Helen."

"Why not? I like you, Mr.—Dave."

They laughed and he felt himself blushing for no reason. Was it because she was maybe ten or twelve years older than he was? For a moment the image of Julia Keith flashed across his mind, but there was no comparison; Helen Osgood was different in every way, including age. Then Jake was leaving to go back to the *News* and all at once Hap Osgood's manner changed, he was cordial and interested and wanted to know all about college, particularly student activities.

"What about the sex life, Dave?" he laughed.

"Pretty good," he lied, not saying that since the night at the Delta house he'd not laid a finger on a girl.

Hap ordered steaks for three and a third round of drinks, then launched into a vivid account of life in Paris, the easy working hours, the favorable currency exchange, the food and wine.

Helen said, "Dave has a problem. He has to go to

work and he can't find a job. I thought maybe you could help him connect in Paris, Hap."

Osgood looked at him. "Well, first he'd have to come over. Think you could scrape up the ship fare?"

He hesitated. "There's something maybe Jake didn't tell you, Mr. Osgood—"

"Hap to you."

"You see, I was only a copy boy at the *News,* so if it was for a reporting job, or rewrite—"

Osgood laughed. "Any intelligent kid can learn the basics of newspaper writing in half an hour. The rest is experience. Don't worry about that. Just get yourself to Paris and be prepared to wait around. Eventually you'd get aboard. They all do, sooner or later, if meanwhile they can feed themselves and have a place to stay."

"He could stay with us," Helen said.

"Sure he could." He spoke without hesitation. "But he's still got to find the fare and enough money to keep from starving. Think you could manage it, Dave?"

He could feel his heart beating fast. "It's a great idea. And it's great of you both to offer to help me."

"Your steak's getting cold," Helen said.

Was it just the liquor or did he feel a sense of living again, of being alive and hopeful, for the first time in months. He listened fascinated to the Osgoods' gay banter about Paris and recalled now that Jake had talked in the past about a couple who'd helped him when he was just starting at the *News.* Grateful and happy, he accepted their offer to share their taxi on the way uptown. It seemed perfectly natural, sitting between them, that Helen would slide her hands through both their arms and hug them all closer together in the chilly night.

"I'm squiffed," she announced with a little laugh.

"Course for the par," Hap said. "How about you, Dave?"

"I feel good."

But it was better than that. He was conscious of the nearness of Helen Osgood's body and the pressure of her arm, a tantalizing perfume lingering in her hair. By the time they reached his street it had been decided he would go on with them for a nightcap to the apartment lent them by a friend who was in Italy. She took his arm again as they hurried into the lobby, shivering and huddling close to him while Hap paid the cab.

"This rotten, filthy weather," she said.

"I guess it's better in Paris."

"Worse!" And she laughed, squeezing his hand.

Upstairs Hap opened a bottle of Martell cognac and after they'd sampled it Helen went into the bedroom to change her damp clothes. He sat with Hap in front of a fresh fire, both of them silent and comfortable. Hap was lucky with such a wife. Someday, somewhere, he'd have a wife of his own, and he realized suddenly that he'd hardly thought about that so far. Anyway he couldn't imagine being married, or even the kind of wife he'd like to have. He smiled to himself. He was no gentleman; he preferred brunettes, like Helen Osgood.

She came back into the room just then with a swift gliding step and he caught his breath in astonishment: she was wearing a filmy white nightrobe and apparently nothing else. As she reached for the drink she'd left on the fireplace mantel the outlines of her naked body were suddenly revealed.

Hap grunted. "What's this—ready for bed already?"

She turned and faced them, her smile gleaming with challenge, her drink in her hand, her legs wide apart. "Ready for bed? You could say that. But not to sleep."

Her husband laughed and wagged his head. He didn't seem surprised at all. "What are we going to do about this gal, Dave?" And to Helen: "I suppose you realize that with the firelight behind you our guest can see right through that robe. You're showing him everything you've got."

She laughed. "Sorry. It was intentional. Will you forgive me, David?"

Speechless, he felt his face flame hot and his erection straining against his stomach. Her slimness, dressed, had been deceptive; her body was voluptuous, heavy-breasted, the slender legs tapering from rich, full thighs. She made no effort to change her stance but only raised the brandy glass to her lips in a mocking gesture. Slowly, deliberately, she drank, and said again in a low voice that thrilled him: "Are you going to forgive me, David?"

He waited for her husband to speak, but Hap Osgood just shrugged and chuckled. "What are we going to do with her?" he repeated to Dave, and then sardonically to his wife: "Shall we try a profile view, my dear?"

Immediately she pivoted like a dancer and stood with her back curving, her breasts thrust provocatively forward, the nipples tensed and tight. "Well, go on, go on," Osgood was saying, "you might as well complete the routine." And smiling the taunting smile she turned her back with a supple, graceful movement and raised the robe above her hips, baring a bottom that shone lustrous satin-white. For a long moment she stood motionless, then lifting the gathered gown still higher, almost to her shoulders, she turned to face them again. The breasts swung insolently free; the mass of soft dark hair curled deep between her thighs and halfway up her belly.

Osgood's grunted laughter broke the silence. He was applauding, clapping his hands heavily together. Dave sat electrified, unable to move a muscle. And just as swiftly as she had come in Helen glided back into the bedroom and out of sight. Osgood turned to his guest. "I don't know whether to apologize or boast," he said. "Just don't tell anybody what that naughty lady of mine just did."

"David!" They both looked up at the voice from the bedroom.

Osgood groaned. "What is it now, Helen?"

"I didn't call you! David, will you come here a minute?"

He glanced at Osgood who muttered, nodding, "Better see what she wants. I can't do anything with her."

He stood up unsteadily, realizing that he was drunk, and walked into the bedroom. Helen Osgood lay nude and smiling under the lamplight in the middle of the wide bed, her hands clasped behind her head, her legs spread indolently apart on the black counterpane. As he came to the foot of the bed she lifted her knees very slightly and he could see the glitter of moisture inside her thighs. She spoke with soft impatience: "Take off your clothes . . . quickly . . ."

"But—him . . ." He stammered the word.

"Don't you understand?" she whispered. "He wants it to happen."

He stared in disbelief and for a moment, torn, he hesitated. A sudden wave of denial was rising in him, as if in succumbing to this wild temptation he would not only

be betraying Hap Osgood but would be renouncing Julia
Keith and all she had meant to him. Just once he glanced
backward, saw Osgood smiling in the doorway. But already
he was powerless to question or fear, knew he must seize
and possess what lay offered under his eyes. As though
hypnotized by his body she watched him strip swiftly, leaving his clothes in a heap at his feet. She gave a little murmur of gladness as he moved toward the bed, toward
opened arms that reached and drew him close to her. With
a sudden motion she raised her head and ran her tongue
over his stiffening penis, then pulled him down upon her,
one hand coming delicately to rest below his buttocks. He
felt her body suck him into her like a hungry mouth. In a
dizzying ecstacy he closed his eyes, conscious only of the
pounding drive and ebb of the rhythm they made together,
as perfectly synchronized as music. It was she who was
making it happen, matching his every movement with the
magic of her own, as if her hand lying lightly on his thigh
could by faintest pressure control the tempo, the counter-
point of flesh against flesh. Somewhere deep in the back of
his mind he was hearing a sensual metronome, increasing
his delirium of pleasure as the beat quickened, gradually,
steadily, out of control, until at last it burst in orgasm like
a mighty orchestral chord.

# 9

The night with Helen and Hap Osgood had been the most complete sexual thrill and satisfaction of his life so far, and in a strange way Hap's presence in the room only intensified it. After his first orgasm, Hap was ready to take over immediately, and from then on, until dawn, she had taken them by turns, three times each.

It was not to happen any more, at least in New York, because two days later the Osgoods left for San Francisco to visit Helen's parents. Meanwhile, thanks to Jake Wethers' intercession at the *News,* he got his old job back. Luckily it was the vacation period and he could fill in. And maybe, Mahoney said, somebody would drop out by September and he could stay on, but with jobs so scarce these days that wasn't likely.

He didn't want it to be likely. By September he should have enough for ship fare to France, with some left over to keep him going awhile, and that was all he cared about now; he was working for it and dreaming of it every hour of the day. Once he got over there he could trust in Hap Osgood to get him onto the *Trib,* where both Hap and Helen had jobs. Meanwhile, he was getting a paid training course at the *News.* The word came down that Mahoney thought he was a comer. In between copy-boy chores they were letting him write filler squibs and minor obits. By now he knew at least one thing about himself: he loved to write—anything, any kind of writing. He looked around him at the city-room types and saw a fictional story in every one of them.

It was his summer for good luck. When Jake Wethers moved to Brooklyn Heights he sublet the Patchin Place apartment to him until October, when the lease expired. It was also the summer he met the girl from Newark.

He noticed her through the window of Rikers on

Eighth Street as he passed one hot night in late June on his way home from work. His habit these nights was to go directly home and work on his fictional writing experiments—nothing good enough yet, he was sure, to make a publishable story, but he felt he was getting there, slowly. He learned through imitation—Stephen Crane, Sherwood Anderson, Scott Fitzgerald, reading their short stories carefully and copying their styles. Odd how fiction writing gripped you with a kind of passion! Was he doing it because it was the hardest thing? Compared with journalistic style it was infinitely more a challenge.

But tonight, passing the lunchroom on Eighth and seeing the girl sitting at the counter, he dropped his usual routine. Probably he'd be too tired to work well tonight, anyway. Something about her body, seen from the back, had changed his mind for him. He hadn't even seen her face, but the tiny waist and broad hips as she sat on the counter stool, the sleek black hair that clung to her head, aroused him. He went in and slipped onto the vacant stool beside her.

She was finishing a dish of scrambled eggs and taking little sips of coffee and she didn't seem aware that he was covertly watching her—the round, snub-nosed face, the stubby fingers holding the cup, bare knees visible below the short skirt. She must be about his own age, and he wondered what this cute kid was doing here, alone, at such a late hour, whether she had an evening job like his or what. It could be interesting. You never knew what you might meet up with in the Village; he was learning that. The first night after he moved into Patchin Place he'd picked up a tall, unhappy-looking girl named Bella sitting at the bar in Luigi's. He bought her four Applejacks and got a little drunk himself doing it. They didn't talk much, but when he suggested taking her back to the apartment she readily agreed. As they were crossing Sixth Avenue she said abruptly: "You think you're gonna get it from me, right?"

He laughed. "Well . . ."

"I'll only take it one way."

He was puzzled. "How d'you mean?"

"Like I was a boy," she said harshly. "Otherwise, we're wasting our time. So don't figure I'll change my mind. I won't."

He thought it over while they walked in silence the rest of the way. At the corner of Patchin Place she said, "How about it, yes or no?"

"Some other time," he said, and turned unsteadily and left her there.

He sat beside the girl at the Rikers counter and remembered Bella unpleasantly. When the counterman brought his coffee she pushed her plate away, lit a cigarette and glanced at him just as their eyes met. It was a frank, open look and he smiled, saw her smile in return.

"Kind of warm," he said.

"It'll get worse before the summer's over . . ." a calm young voice, attractively husky.

"You live in the Village?"

She shook her head. "I wish I did."

He sipped his coffee and waited for her to say something more but she didn't. He was about to reopen the conversation when she took a small, worn change purse out of her handbag, paid her check and stood up. "Goodnight," she smiled, and went out. He put down the money for his coffee and caught up with her at the door as she hesitated a moment, looking uncertainly up and down the street.

"Lost?" he said.

The swift smile again. "I'm trying to decide whether to go home yet."

"How about a drink while you're making up your mind?" He motioned to the bar across the street.

"Okay."

Suddenly he felt refreshed, gay. He took her arm. It was nearly midnight but Eighth Street was zinging along pretty good; even weeknights it was the liveliest street in the Village. The piano player nodded to them as they came in. He found a table in the back where they could hear each other talk and they sat in a booth exchanging identities over gin fizzes. Her name was Jean Lobowski and she lived in Newark, but she came to New York whenever there was work because her husband was out of a job.

"What kind of work, Jean?"

"Sometimes a little modeling, or if not I give blood. Like today."

"You gave blood today?"

"Two pints. That's fifteen dollars." She looked at her empty glass. "So I can pay for another drink."

"It's on me." He ordered it. "Don't you feel weak after losing all that blood?"

"I've got plenty where that came from, don't worry."

"If I was your husband I'd worry."

"Stan?" She seemed surprised. "Stan doesn't worry about nothing except where his next beer is coming from."

"What kind of modeling do you do?"

"You want to see?" She fished in her purse and brought out three snapshots in profile of herself, innocently naked in all three. It was a handsome body, compact and shapely.

"I thought you meant clothes modeling."

"Naw. There's this camera studio—five bucks an hour for naked posing." She sipped her second drink and giggled. "They pay double if you pose with a guy, but Stan'd kill me if he ever saw me in one of those."

"But he lets you come into New York alone and stay out at night like this."

"He should care what I do! Anyway I tell him I'm with my girlfriend."

They had a third drink. She was a little flushed now and her eyes were wistful listening to the piano. "I like this place," she said.

"You've been in here before?"

She shook her head. "I'm glad we came in here."

"I'm glad I spoke to you. I went into Rikers because I saw you sitting there."

"No kidding!"

The way she said it made him laugh. "You think I was just out looking for a pickup," he said.

"No I don't. But even if you were, I'm glad you did."

"I guess you've been picked up before."

"They tried. But I didn't like their looks."

"But you liked my looks."

"Yeah. I guess *you* tried a lot yourself."

"Not a lot. The last one I picked up turned out to be a lesbian." He smiled. "You know what a lesbian is?"

"I found out. They tried, too." She paused, then said, "You really went into Rikers because you saw me at the counter?"

"That's right, Jean."

"But all you could see was the back of me."

"I've seen all of you, now."

She giggled. "Did you like what you saw?"

"I sure did."

"Then you can have the pictures." Impulsively she reached into her bag again and handed them across the table. "It's okay, I've got copies."

When he took them from her he held her fingers and she didn't try to withdraw. "I like *you*, Jean. Never mind the pictures."

She was looking over his shoulder at the clock above the bar. "Oh-oh, look at the time. I can't go home now."

"You said you could stay at your girlfriend's."

"Her mother'd kill me if I phoned this late."

"You better come with me, Jean."

"Maybe I better."

They finished their drinks and walked up Sixth Avenue together, swinging hands like high school sweethearts. He still couldn't figure her out. If she knew total sex was implicit in the situation she gave no sign, yet he felt a happy acceptance between them that was closer to lovers than friends. It was the same when they climbed the stairs in Patchin Place; in the dark, suddenly, he stopped and put his arms around her, and she returned his first kiss with the naturalness of long intimacy.

She stood watching him across the room while he switched on the floor lamp and drew the shades down. "It's nice," she said softly.

"I didn't make the bed this morning."

"I know."

There was no more talking. As he began to undress she turned her back to him, slipped out of her shoes, and still standing straight pulled her brief dress over her head and tossed it on the bed-table. The bra went next and then, with a sinuous twisting movement, she dropped her blue panty to the floor and kicked it aside. She turned back to him, warm flesh glowing in the lamplight, and watched him finish taking off his clothes.

"I hate to turn out the light," he murmured, looking at her.

"Leave it on then."

But he switched it off and went to her in the soft sum-

mer darkness and wrapped his arms around her again as
he had on the stairs. She was breathing quickly and heavily,
locked in the kiss, but when he started to bear her body
back toward the bed she resisted and he didn't try to force
it.

"What's the matter?" he whispered. "Don't you want
to?"

"This is what I want. Will you let me? Please let
me . . ." Without waiting for answer she went down on her
knees, clasping his thighs with both hands, and almost before he knew what she was doing took him in her mouth.

The sensation of it went through him like electricity.
He felt her lips close on him, softly, lovingly, her tongue
darting with swift little stabs, one hand reaching between
his legs now to tug at his scrotum while the other fingered
him between the buttocks, arousing a new, hot reaction all
through his body. For a moment she withdrew her mouth
to murmur something he couldn't catch, she found his
hand and put it on her head. *"Pull my hair!"* she was murmuring, he heard the words now, muffled, impassioned, as
her lips returned to him and he obeyed. "Yes, yes, yes!"
she whispered even as she held him in her mouth, *"Harder, harder . . ."* the words gulped, choked in her frenzy.
And suddenly he felt her body sag and collapse against
him with a long sigh, her hands gripping his thighs
again, her mouth releasing him, the words coming again
in an anguish of gratitude, "So good, so good, you're so
good to me . . ."

But now it was his turn. He picked her up, almost
carried her to the bed where they fell together, his body
sprawling on top of her in a tangle of legs and arms. As
if by accident he felt himself slip into her, caught, clutched
in the soft black dripping gorge, and heard his own groan
of pure delight. He'd never felt as hard or as big, not
even with Helen. And her thighs widened under his weight
and drew back, yielding; he went deep, deeper, deeper
still, until she shook under the steady, shocking blows.
*"Don't—want—to—hurt . . ."* he whispered, gasping, her
hair wet in his mouth.

"You can knock me through the wall if you want,"
she said.

# TWO

TWO

# 10

What was it about this girl, this Jean Lobowski who had wandered into his life as he had wandered into hers, that made the rest of the summer pass so quickly, so easily? From that first moment, meeting her clear, frank glance at the lunch counter, he'd felt totally at ease with her, totally himself, as she was herself with him. It was a relationship based simply on their individual sexual needs; neither asked the other for more than that. They saw each other regularly but not too often; he was learning to pace himself, and adjust as well to her own desires. And always she satisfied herself on his body first, touching him, kissing him, sucking him, while he hurt her physically—not too severely, no bruises, no scars, only to the limits she sought. Then as on the first night it was his turn to take her as he would, the glowing welcome of her young and freshly aroused body, relaxing, satisfying, renewing him for his work.

She was always ready, never made demands on him of any kind, never asked him—even on the night before he sailed for Europe—whether they would see each other again. For the last time he listened to her simple, artless talk and knew that no matter what lay beyond the horizon he would miss this precious summer in New York that had flowed so swiftly through their fingers.

Neither raised the question as to whether she would come to see him off on the boat. His mother and Cathy came aboard to say goodbye, then joined the crowd on the pier to wave a last bon voyage: his mother buoyant and strong, even more so than she had been before her husband's death; Cathy wistful and straight and boyish, reminding him still of her vanished childhood.

And suddenly, standing in the crowd only a few feet away from them, he saw Jean, looking up at the deck rail

53

where he stood and smiling at him as the *De Grasse* slowly moved away from the pier and out into midstream Hudson and down toward the bay and the ocean and the new Old World. It was Jean's face that lingered longest in his mind, but even Jean had faded by the second day out, lost in his excited anticipation of the life that lay ahead. Paris! And the *Trib*. And Helen Osgood ...

# 11

The Osgoods met him at the boat train, lodged him temporarily in their extra bedroom on the Rue Boissonade, took him to dinner at the Coupole and climaxed his introduction to Paris with a brandy at Le Sphinx. It was like a big, colorful indoor cafe, couples and groups sitting around tables talking and drinking, but he realized almost at once he was in a brothel.

Hap and Helen had been waiting for his reaction. "We had a bet on how long it would take you," Hap laughed, and Helen said, "You catch on quick, Davie. Been hanging out at Polly Adler's in New York?"

He grinned and shook his head, and didn't mention that moth-eaten apartment in the west sixties which was his first whorehouse. But this was what a whorehouse should look like! He glanced around him, giddy with the excitement of his first day in France, rapturous over the wine and food, the September beauty of the city. Three women were approaching the table, smiling, murmuring French greetings. These were whores? They looked more like models or actresses in their fancy hairdos, pattering along on high-heeled shoes, their breasts spilling half out of their filmy bodices, their loins barely covered with brief, beaded scarves. He smiled. Enticing, seductive bodies every one, each different from the others—and as if chosen for an ad, a redhead, a blonde and a brunette.

He decided instantly that the dark-haired one was the best, but as Hap invited all three to join the party, she'd already fixed her attention on Helen who launched a conversation with her in French. The redhead was smiling at Hap, so that left the blonde, who reached across the table and touched his wrist with long lavender fingernails.

"You speak French?"

"Not yet. But your English sounds okay."

55

"My English very good. You American?"

"That's right." He smiled and looked down at her half-exposed breast. It was a quite beautiful breast.

"You like this?" she said, and flipped it out the rest of the way.

The redhead laughed and said something reproving to her friend, who tucked it back in again. "What's your preference, Dave?" Hap said. "I'm treating you."

"He likes the brunette," Helen said. "I could tell by the way he looked at her."

The brunette wanted some translation and the blonde gave it to her, but she didn't like what she heard and she looked across the table at him without smiling. "Just tell her I like them all," he said, and when Helen translated the blonde and the redhead tittered but the dark one still wouldn't smile. She tried to resume in French to Helen but Helen ignored her. The blonde leaned forward, cajoling. "Josette likes you, Madame."

"So I noticed. But my friend from New York likes Josette, and that's what she's here for, *ne'st-ce pas?*"

The brunette demanded more translation, then frowned and shook her head. "She don't want to go with him," the blonde said, "she want to go with you, Madame."

Hap Osgood was vastly entertained. He looked at his wife. "How about it, Helen?"

"I'm flattered. Maybe some other time." She turned away from the brunette. "What are you waiting for, Davie? Aren't you going to take her upstairs?"

He started to get up but stopped when Josette spoke rapidly, almost angrily to the blonde. Hap chuckled. "Let me handle this, Helen." He looked across the room and beckoned to the woman in the black dress standing by the stairway. Immediately she waddled over to the table.

"Something wrong, Monsieur Osgood?"

"This girl, Josette, is annoying my wife. Our friend from New York has selected her but Josette doesn't seem to like the idea." He grinned. "Perhaps you reserve Josette for lesbians?"

"*Ah, non,* Monsieur! No one is reserved at Le Sphinx." She turned and glared at Josette while the two other girls waited uneasily.

Helen said, "Never mind, Madame. We'll come some other time," and she made as if to rise.

"*Non*, please, Madame! This girl is new, she don't know." She smiled apology and unleashed a torrent of exasperated French at Josette. People at nearby tables looked on, mildly amused. Finally the brunette stood up and walked unwillingly toward the stairs.

"Okay, Dave," Hap said, "you're all set. Enjoy yourself." The manageress smiled benignly at him as he left the table. At the foot of the stairway Josette snatched at a towel on the rack against the wall and flung it over her shoulder, not looking back. He felt awkward and embarrassed following her up the stairs and was glad when they were out of sight of the room below.

She led the way down a long corridor lined with doors on either side. At the next to last on the right she stopped, listened a moment, twisted the knob and went in, still silent, still ignoring him. He shut the door behind them; maybe now she would be pleasant. But she didn't turn around, and he stood there watching her as she sullenly dropped the two scarves from her body, revealing delicately curved shoulders, a slender back and soft, perfectly placed buttocks.

A wave of warm desire went over him despite her attitude of rejection. He wanted to say something in French, to go to her, touch her, but the few phrases he knew wouldn't come. He heard himself say softly, "I'm sorry I can't talk your language, Josette . . ." but there was no response; it was as if he wasn't even in the room with her. She was turning now, balancing that exquisite body on absurd high heels, and he saw her breasts fully exposed, delicately lovely like the rest of her, the pretty face clouded, sulky. With a resentful little twist of her shoulders she lay back on the bed and crossed her arms under her head, staring unseeing at the ceiling, awaiting him with unconcealed resignation. Helen Osgood had lain like that, the wonderful night in New York, but it was this woman, this Josette, that he wanted now in this moment; and Helen wanted him to have her, like the gift of Paris.

Maybe she would change when he took her in his arms. He told himself that as he slipped quickly out of his clothes, freed his erection, moved to the side of the bed. Josette stared stubbornly away, and when he knelt over her, straddling her body, he had to separate her legs with his hands because she wouldn't yield. Too late now to care about that, though she still resisted, subtly, cunningly, as

he forced his penis into her, pushing her legs wider and
back to sink it all the way. Only then, breathless after his
effort, panting, did he look down at her face again, and
saw the contemptuous smile begin at her lips, the bitchy
look in her eyes. Instead of taking him she countered his
steady rhythm with little sinuous jerks and parries aimed
at spoiling his pleasure as much as she was able—her protest, her revenge, her rebellion. And when in his paroxysm
he gripped her shoulders hard and bent to kiss her mouth
she ripped it away from him with a tiny guttural snarl,
bruising his lips, in the same motion twisting her pelvis
in a final violent spasm designed only for his pain.

She had succeeded. Spent and yet unsatisfied, de-
feated, he lay heavy on her for a long moment before releasing her and slowly getting to his feet.

Her burst of spiteful laughter followed him down the
hall.

Hap and Helen Osgood awaited him at the table, but
the blonde and the redhead had moved on to other customers. The blonde was at a nearby table and for an instant
he caught her glance, mocking, malicious. She was laughing
at him because she knew what had happened upstairs.
Helen knew, too; women always guessed these things. But
how different was her smile, her eyes merry, searching,
soft. "Well?" she said, taking his hand between her hands.
"Was it a proper introduction to La Ville Lumière?"

"Yes and no."

"Dear me, didn't it go well?" as if she didn't know.

"Josette wasn't very—cooperative."

"Poor boy," Helen said, "we'll have to make it up to
you," and Hap chuckled. "Better luck next time, kid." He
motioned to the fresh brandy on the table. "Drink up!"

# 12

As Hap had warned, there was no immediate opportunity to join the *Trib* staff. But the managing editor, an easy-going guy, held out some hope for him. The turnover was high, especially when the weather got colder, and if they took him on they'd give him a job on the hotel beat at the lowest level of pay; but it was enough to keep him afloat. It was also the lowest level of competence, practically a training job for a cub reporter. Each day you went around to the central hotels, picked up the list of new guests for the society editor and interviewed anybody noteworthy who might be passing through Paris. Hap promised to help him learn to write a simple interview story so it would satisfy the copy desk.

He was thrilled at his first visit to the *Trib*'s little city room and imagined himself as one of the vagabonds, as Helen called them, lounging at their typewriters and exchanging cynical wisecracks about the day's news. More than anything, he wanted to live their way of life—bohemian, eccentric, challenging the conventional, conformist, comfortable American tradition in everything they did. But it would be a while before he could become a member of that glamorous company, and meantime he would spend his days getting acquainted with Paris and his evenings with the Osgoods. As soon as he was signed on by the *Trib* he could afford to move into his own quarters. For now, Hap and Helen seemed happy to have him.

And the city was a delight. Provided with suggestions from Hap, he explored it methodically, starting from the Ile de la Cité, where Paris was born, proceeding through the Tuileries gardens to the Place de la Concorde, from there up the Champs-Elysées, past the Arch of Triumph and on into the Bois de Boulogne. On another day he covered central Paris—the Opera district, the Palais Royal

and Comedie Francaise neighborhood, the stately Place
Vendome and the maze of shopping streets—tourist
haunts—encircling the area. Two days he reserved for the
mighty Louvre, and another was devoted to the length of
the Grands Boulevards from the Madeleine to the Fau-
bourg Montmartre. A surreptitious observer, he acquainted
himself with the lobbies of the leading hotels where soon,
he hoped, he would be returning in the role of reporter
from the *Trib*. And everywhere he went he tried his fum-
bling college French on anyone who would answer his
questions, spent his lunchtimes in obscure cafes reading the
French newspapers with the aid of a pocket dictionary, listened to the conversations on the street, in the little out-of-
the-way bistros standing at the zinc counter and dallying
with a tumbler of white wine.

The Left Bank he loved most of all, from St. Ger-
main-des-Prés to Montparnasse, from the Eiffel Tower to
Notre Dame and the Ile St. Louis. And to cap it all, he
climbed the Butte Montmartre and from the steps of
Sacré Coeur surveyed the scenes of his exploration, returning that evening to report to Hap and Helen that his
travels were completed.

Except for the first day at Le Sphinx, there had been
no further sex since his arrival. This disappointed and puzzled him; he had looked forward to living with the Osgoods
as a kind of continuous sensual experience like the night in
their New York apartment. But the Osgoods at work
were different from the Osgoods on vacation—frequently
they worked overtime and came home visibly tired, content
to cafe-sit in nearby Montparnasse, enjoy a late dinner at
their favorite restaurant, the Nègre de Toulouse, and listen
to their house guest's report on his wanderings through
the city before saying goodnight and retiring to their own
room.

Then, quite suddenly, the mood changed.

It appeared to develop without prior arrangement,
quite casually, on one of the last balmy days of the year
in early October. The three of them had dined at the
Nègre as usual and Helen had decided she wanted a cognac at the Dôme before returning to the apartment. The
terrace was crowded, but two American women whom the
Osgoods knew made room for them at their table and all
five squeezed in around it. The women were not bad-look-

ing and about Helen's age; he realized after a few minutes
that the dark one, Irma, was British. By contrast to her
cool, clipped manner the fair-haired one, Margo, was distinctly less reserved and more open, talking and laughing
a lot and referring several times to San Francisco, evidently her home town. Both of them were flatteringly attentive
to Helen rather than Hap, but it wasn't until Helen told
the story of Josette at Le Sphinx that it became obvious
to him Irma and Margo were lesbians.

"But, my dear," Irma was saying, "why did you reject
the offer? Josette sounds attractive."

Helen laughed. "She's just not my type, I guess."

"We'll have to drop in on Josette some evening, Irma."
Margo looked at Helen. "We're always ready to encourage new talent."

Hap Osgood leaned forward. "Helen's never had a
lesbian experience, by the way. I suspect she'd like to."

Irma's eyes were bright. "Is that true, Helen?"

"I've thought about it, yes. And, Hap, if you don't
mind, I'm quite capable of speaking for myself."

He laughed. "Sorry. Just wanted to reassure our
friends here I have no objection, as your husband, to your
amusing yourself with anyone you like."

"That's generous of you, Hap. You know I would
anyway. Davie's proof of that."

All three women's eyes were on him, Irma's and Margo's as though they'd just discovered he was there. He
felt himself blushing. "Lucky Davie," Margo smiled. "I
envy you."

"So do I," Irma said.

"How about another round?" Hap said, and ordered
drinks for them all.

"I'll be squiffy!" Helen warned.

"That's okay. We like you squiffy, don't we, Dave?"

All he could do was nod and grin in response; he felt
clumsy and ignorant, out of his depth with the lesbians;
they were too worldly and sophisticated for him. He gave
up trying to join the catty conversation that followed about
the writers and artists who lived in Montparnasse and their
quirks and escapades. Yet he sensed that underneath the
bright patter of gossip another, subtler dialogue was going
on between Helen and the other two women—an unspoken dialogue, communication with their eyes alone. With

the liqueurs Helen's color was heightening, her speech became more animated, and the other two never took their eyes off hers. There was no further talk about Josette, yet he felt that somehow they'd never left the subject and its implications; a feeling of challenge lay just beneath the surface.

So he was not surprised when Helen suddenly drained the rest of her cognac, stood up a little unsteadily and said: "You're invited to continue the discussion at our place." And Hap, amused, said, "Good idea. Come along, children."

It was like a summer night. The boulevard was crowded with strollers as they left the Dôme and turned toward the Rue Boissonade, the three women in the lead, Helen between the other two arm in arm, the two men following. For the first time he felt himself a part of the hidden excitement that ran like a deep undercurrent among the women; or was it just the alcohol taking over, a warm fuzzy glow in his head, a quickening deep in his stomach? This was a night that anything could happen, this was Paris! And he wondered if Hap Osgood was feeling the same sense of imminence.

Again he was not surprised when just inside the apartment-house vestibule Helen turned suddenly to Margo, threw her arms around her and clung to her in a long, breathless kiss, while Irma, tall and calm, smiled at them in the dim light. Slowly the little group climbed the stairs to the second floor. At the top landing, while Hap Osgood fumbled for his keys, Irma moved close to Helen and whispered in her ear. Helen listened, then nodded with an enigmatic half-smile and disappeared ahead of them into the apartment.

"More of the same?" Hap asked affably, a fresh bottle of Courvoisier in his hand, as he ushered his guests to seats on the big couch that filled the window side of the salon. The two men took seats on easy chairs along the opposite wall. Margo was flushed and silent, but Irma carried on the conversation as coolly as before, as though totally unaware of the electric atmosphere. Outside, ragged wisps of cloud crossed the face of the moon. Hap stood up and drew the window curtains, dimmed the light of the two floor lamps that flanked the long couch. He had just settled himself in his chair again when Helen came into the room.

At first glance she was unchanged, except that she was barefooted and was wearing another dress, a dark, loose-fitting garment that came just above the knees, accentuating the whiteness of her bare arms and legs. But she had done something to her hair—loosened it, fluffed it so that it had a windblown look of abandonment matching the high natural color in her face.

"Pour you a drink, darling?" Hap said, half rising.

She shook her head, almost as if she hadn't heard him but was absorbed in some private thought of her own. She was facing the two women on the couch and seemed hypnotized by their presence. For a long moment all three were motionless, trancelike, caught in a spell of their own making. Then with a sudden, swift movement Helen moved toward them, dropping facedown full-length on the couch, her head buried in Irma's lap, her knees across Margo's thighs. She gave a long, sibilant sigh and relaxed utterly. Irma's hand dropped caressingly on her hair; Margo stirred and threw her arm across the shapely, smooth calves, drew them closer to her.

A faint sound of singing came from the boulevard at the end of the street below, otherwise the room was completely still. An air of expectancy hung over the salon; the two men, ignored now as if they weren't present, watched and waited. They saw Irma bend and touch her lips to the soft hair at the nape of Helen's neck while her hand tightened on the slender prostrate shoulder. And they saw Margo, using both her hands, begin to squeeze and knead the supple flesh that lay willing before her, beginning at the ankles and moving up and down to the knees and back, the strong, soft fingers working like those of an expert masseuse. But it was more than that—each movement of the hands was sensual, cunning, as tender as the kisses that Irma left on Helen's hair, and softer, more tender still as the hands moved now under the skirt and upward along the inner thighs, inch by inch, moving and returning, higher and softly higher until they found the buttocks, surrendered in their hidden beauty to the hands that took them at will, worshipping the pliant flesh.

The sound was Helen's groan, a faint gasp of gratitude

for what was happening to her, and with a sudden twisting movement she turned on her back, reached up with
both arms and drew Irma's head down, kissing her lips.
At the same time her knees swung apart in a wanton motion that drew her skirt halfway to her waist and give
Margo's hands free play between her thighs. And now
Irma's hands were moving, caressing the cheeks, the ears,
the mouth that lay offered to her, slipping little by little
under the loose top of the dress until they found the
breasts, naked and free. Helen's eyes were open very wide
but as if unseeing, but she closed them as Margo's fingers
deftly lifted the skirt back over the softly heaving belly,
exposing at last the moist dark curling mound that they
had sought so surely.

The sight brought a little sobbing cry from Margo.
Her mouth twitched in avid desire and abruptly she slid
from under the supine body and went to her knees on the
floor beside the couch. Tenderly she drew Helen's knees
toward her, opened them again, bent forward and sank
her face into the wet depths that eagerly awaited her. The
men watched the lunging, weaving head, heard the famished sucking sounds, saw the glistening belly contract in
ecstasy. Above it, Irma's hands had lowered the top of
Helen's dress to expose the breasts and now devoured them
with her mouth, shifting back and forth between them, fingers twitching at one nipple while she tongued the other.
And by some wild chance all movements fell into the same
swinging rhythm—Irma's darting, swooping head, Margo's
diving, plunging assault; most intense of all the writhing,
moaning body they possessed together, that came to them
in orgasm with a final shuddering cry of ecstasy that was
almost a scream.

Then silence again, and profound stillness of all three,
Irma's head finding rest between softening breasts, Margo's
tongue still licking up the last drops of its feast, Helen's
ravished contours sagging in sweet exhaustion. For uncounted minutes they lay thus, eyes closed, unconscious of
their surroundings, lost in slowly subsiding passion. For the
first time Hap Osgood stirred in his chair, like a man waking from a dream; but it was no dream; the other man,
turning to glance at him, saw the huge erection still standing under his trousers and was aware his own penis was
still hot and hard.

Hap smiled and spoke in a low tone. "We'd better go to bed and leave the field to the ladies, Dave. We're not needed tonight."

If any of the women heard they gave no slightest sign. At the salon door they looked back one last time; the women hadn't moved.

But Hap was wrong. Toward dawn his laugh woke the house guest from fitful sleep. Judging from ensuing sounds from the Osgoods' bedroom Hap was needed, all right; he could hear Helen's muffled, urgent tones and the creaking of their bed in steady recurrence, then the final quickened thrusts and her grateful cry.

It was like the night in New York—she was insatiable. The listener gripped his erection and tried to put her out of his mind. Surely she must know he too was waiting for her. But she didn't come to him. Finally he dozed again, slept, dreamed he awoke to the touch of her fingers and saw her crouched at the edge of his bed in the morning light. The dream voice whispered: "Can I come in with you? Just for a very little while?" the words wistful, wheedling. A wave of relief swept over him; he put his arms around her and drew her into the bed beside him. "I wanted you all night . . . but I thought the women gave you all you could take," he said.

"Sweetheart, when a woman's really aroused she could take a regiment, didn't you know that, didn't you know that, didn't you know that . . . ?"

He started up. He was awake. There was no voice, she wasn't with him, the house was silent. Fresh sweat broke out on his body. The dream had excited him unbearably. His hand went to his belly, grasped the rigid column of flesh, ground his fingers in a kind of desperation. He was doing something to himself he had sworn after Jean Lobowski he would never need to do again. He closed his eyes and saw the three women on the couch, devoured Helen's pillaged body in his imagination as Margo and Irma had done with their hands and lips, a helpless fantasy in which she came to his bed as in his dream and gave herself more fully even than the New York night, her knees drawn back to her shoulders, open and ready for the plunging drive, then the fluttering membrane closing sticky and delicious around him, her hands slipping downward along his back to his buttocks to pull him closer with every stroke, with every pulse beat, her whole body rising against him for their climax, thrust for thrust, begging him breathless, half-strangled, to come, to come, to *come* . . .

He gave way to orgasm and turned, cheated, angry, on his face in the bed, joy gone from him as quickly as it began, instead the guilt from childhood, the humiliation of this make-believe. He pounded his fist in the pillow: she had forgotten New York; she would never come to him again.

# 13

It was nearly the end of October now and the *Trib* job hadn't yet materialized. His money was gone but Hap Osgood was carrying him from day to day, confident that he'd finally get aboard when Jud Purcell made good his threat to quit and hike the wine country with some friends recently arrived in Paris. He didn't like living off anybody, especially the Osgoods, but a lot of people around here were doing just that, and if you had to be broke and dependent, this was the place for it. Something in the carefree beauty of the city and its life made it exciting just to be here. He had never felt as alive, as sensuous, as easily affected by the vibrant, colorful activity around him.

It would have been difficult to say whether he'd picked up Tanya or she'd picked him up. More likely it was just bumping into each other by accident between rows of bookshelves, smiling apologies on both sides, and a walk through the *allées* of the Champs-Elysées when they left the American Library at the same time, again apparently by chance. Tanya was White Russian, about his age, the daughter of well-bred emigrés who were somehow scraping up an existence in Paris giving English and Russian lessons. Which was why Tanya herself spoke such good English.

She wasn't a conventionally pretty girl but her lively expression, huge dark eyes and lovely smile made her attractive in her own very individual way. Especially he liked her soft, husky voice and the somehow surprising lustiness of her laugh. When they said goodbye that first afternoon it included a date for the next day, same place, same time, and he knew they had liked each other right away. But he didn't tell the Osgoods about her at dinner—something about Helen's probing look warned him off, although he had no reason to believe she wouldn't approve; still, he was cautious.

"You're happy, Davie," she smiled across the table.

"I'm always happy."

"I mean tonight, especially tonight."

"No more than usual."

"You got laid," Hap observed with his grunted laugh.

"No. Absolutely no."

"You were up to *something*," Helen persisted, teasing.

"Look, I don't know why you think so! I spent the afternoon at the library as usual. Believe me, if anything special happens to me I'll always tell you."

The talk went on to other things after that, but he wondered if they'd believed him, particularly if Helen guessed a girl was involved. She was uncanny in her perceptions. Maybe Tanya wouldn't amount to anything, but for the moment he felt something precious about this new friend that he wanted to keep to himself.

Maybe it was because, except for his relationship with the Osgoods, he was lonely. Having no money of his own was part of it; everything he did was circumscribed by this. These days he couldn't even sit in a cafe, let alone treat an acquaintance to a *café crème*, and everywhere he went he had to walk. He didn't mind; he enjoyed every minute, and he treasured the Osgoods' friendship. But Tanya was something new of its kind, the first relationship he was establishing on his own. And she was as warm, as eager as he was, at least it seemed that way. In only their second walk, this time in the Tuileries, he found himself confessing to her freely about his situation and explaining why he wanted to take her for a drink or dinner and couldn't.

"But I will take *you*," she laughed, and they sauntered over to a little bistro on the Rue St. Roch where she treated him to coffee and listened raptly to his impressions of Paris. When it was her turn she responded just as willingly to his questions: she was preparing to take her *bachot* degree and studying hard; she lived with her parents in the Grenelle *quartier* and earned pocket money tutoring other Sorbonne students in English and Russian. But what she seemed most interested in was America; she kept returning to his life there, his family background, his experiences in college. It was growing dark when they realized they'd been talking for two hours, and they rode together on the back platform of a bus until he dropped her off a block from her home.

She gave him the firm, frank students' handshake as she said goodbye.

"Tomorrow?" he said.

The warm smile flashed affectionately. "Until then, David!"

This time they wandered through the Jeu de Paume museum looking at the Impressionists. Tanya was surprised that he'd been in France this long without seeing any of the countryside except glimpses from the boat train, and proposed they make an excursion to Barbizon together next morning, when she had no classes.

"Barbizon? What's that?"

"A village. You'll see. You'll love it as much as I do."

"But I haven't any money, Tanya—I told you that."

"It is small cost. You will repay me when you have your job." And like a fellow-student she squeezed his arm and smiled her generous smile.

"You're a pal, Tanya."

"And you are a true camarade!"

They met at the Gare de Lyon on a bright, crisp morning and ran along beside the track just in time to catch the Melun train. Her lithe young body was clad in a swinging skirt and shirtwaist, a sweater around her shoulders, her bronze hair tied tightly behind her neck. She looked so glowing, so vital he wanted to throw his arms around her and kiss her, and saw in her eyes that she knew it, but somehow he felt shy with her in a public place and held back. He wasn't quite up to Paris street habits, yet, though the kissing was all around you wherever you went and nobody was in the least self-conscious about it. And he wondered about Tanya's friends at the reputed free-living and free-loving Sorbonne.

The train rattled through the *petite banlieue* and into a world of broad green fields and colored houses. "I guess you have a lot of true camarades, Tanya," he was saying.

"A very few."

"No special boyfriend?"

She smiled and shook her head. "He would want me for a *maîtresse*, David."

"Well, what's the matter with that?"

She colored faintly and looked serious. "I suppose I am old-fashioned. I still believe in old-fashioned virtues."

"In *Paris?*"

The way he said it made her laugh. "If my father and mother even knew I was running off to the country with you this morning, David, they would be terribly shocked, you know. So I didn't tell them. I'm not *that* old-fashioned."

At Melun they changed trains for Barbizon, and there awaiting them was a quaint little two-car vehicle hauled by the kind of steam engine you see in amusement parks taking kids around. Hissing and puffing, it started off with half a dozen passengers through sunlit wheat fields and tiny hamlets that looked like paintings they'd seen at the museum.

Tanya was smiling at him. "Does it look familiar to you, David?"

"It's beautiful, I'll say that."

"Millet painted it, you know. The *Angelus* was painted in one of these fields. And many of his paintings."

And Barbizon was where he lived, along with other painters and sculptors whose studios lined the little main street that couldn't have been a quarter-mile in length. Beyond it, green and lovely, stretched the forest of Fontainebleau, and it was there they picnicked together in a remote corner of the woods on pâté sandwiches and strong white wine Tanya bought at the *charcuterie* in Barbizon.

"I want you to know something," he said to her. "This is the happiest day I've had in France."

A curtain of quiet seemed to conceal them from the world. Midday sunshine made the little glade as warm as summer. For a moment he remembered his first meeting with Julia Keith—how long ago it was, another lifetime!—but only for a moment. He was looking at the girl who sat near him, her back against an ancient tree trunk, who in these past few days had come to symbolize his new life in France. She'd taken off the heavy walking shoes she wore and tucked her slender feet beneath her, and she returned his look with a tenderness he saw in her eyes for the first time.

"What are you thinking, Tanya?"

"For me too it is a happy day."

Involuntarily he moved close to her and dropped his

arm around her shoulders, and with a small sigh of contentment she let her head fall to his shoulder. Her skirt had risen carelessly above one knee and he could see the warmly tinted flesh of her young thigh. At the same moment she seemed aware of this and lowered the truant skirt. They both were smiling at her gesture.

"What's wrong, Tanya? Afraid of me?"

"Of course not!"

Emboldened, he kissed her. Quickly, before she could turn her head away. And seemingly despite herself she returned his kiss in a sudden burst of very real passion. Then, just as swiftly, she pulled away, breathing quickly, her eyes warning him.

"No, David, please!"

"You don't mean that." All at once, for the first time, he wanted her body with a fierce desire.

"Yes, I mean it."

"But you want it!"

"David, please . . ."

He was pulling her close to him, holding her hard, and she was resisting with a stubborn strength as great as his. Twice he tried to find her mouth with his lips and each time she eluded him. His hands sought the heaving young breasts against alert resistance. Finally he dropped his arms, panting with his fruitless exertion—they were like a couple of clumsily necking school kids and he was beyond that now.

There was a long silence between them. The forest sang its subtle noonday melody of chirping birds and breezes sifting through the high branches. And as abruptly as she had pulled away from him she turned back now, wide eyes brimming with unexpected tears, both hands reaching for his arm and clinging.

"Poor David, I am so difficult to you."

He drew back in his turn. "It's all right, Tanya."

"No, it is not all right. *You* are right to expect more from a girl who leads you to the woodland. It is not because I don't care for you. Please try to understand, David . . ."

"Can you understand this?"

On savage impulse he ripped open the front of his trousers and freed his bulging penis to her stunned look.

"I can't help it, Tanya. It's out of my control."

He had acted without thought, impelled by pure emotion. Was she going to recoil in disgust, get up and leave him? They both were looking down at his naked sex, seeing it grow and stiffen before their eyes, but when he lifted his gaze to honestly meet her own he saw her still staring down at it.

It was as if she was watching a strange, separate organism no longer part of a man's body, complete in itself. And slowly, riveted, she bent her head toward the straining penis, closer and closer, one hand creeping up his chest as though unaware of what it was doing to gently push him backward to the forest floor, while the other loosened his belt and opened the trousers further, pulling his shorts halfway down his thighs.

He was fully exposed now, could feel his scrotum tightening with excitement, could feel the involuntary movement of his knees drawing apart, his body yielding, settling on his mossy bed. Holding his breath, he waited, watching through half-closed eyelids the flushed young face, her hair in lovely disarray, poised hovering, almost as if in fear over her discovery. But only for a moment longer, then her mouth descended with a tiny gasping exhalation to take him deep into its warm, wet recesses, closing on the shaft, sucking awkwardly, her slender fingers caressing, clasping the balls and drawing them downward in a softly jerking motion.

Was it pure instinct? Was this her first time? He was sure it was. For an instant, as he lay quiescent, throbbing under her ministering lips, his mind flashed back in revulsion to the first time this was done to him—the whore's brutal ugliness, the tawdry room, orgasm without joy. Even with Jean in New York it was more for her need than his. But he knew, now, was learning with each second, what this could be, a sensation like no other, that embraced, enveloped, lifted toward the ultimate overwhelming, when truly it was an act of love.

Tanya had made it that. Already, powerless to lie still a moment longer, his loins began to stir with her movements' rhythm, feeling the far-back, deep contraction start, and swell, and draw again, mounting as his body surged to meet her, knowing she knew by instinct the supreme moment was coming, was here upon them both, and again by instinct that she must stay with it, crushed to him, and swallow all he gave as he burst and spurted and pulled her head down on him with both hands.

Afterward she lay for endless sweet minutes utterly motionless, her full weight relaxed against him, while he felt himself slowly dwindle in her mouth and at last slip out. She let it go with a tremor through her body and slowly sat up, pale and composed. Somehow it seemed to him the child had become woman. She smiled, straightening her straggling hair.

"Did I do what you needed, David?"

"Everything," he said.

"Did I do it right?"

"You were unbelievably wonderful."

"You were quite wonderful, too." Again the tremor through her body. "I never imagined I—" She stopped and color flooded into her face.

"There's only one thing I want to say, Tanya. Next time, let me make you as happy as you made me."

Slowly and a little sadly she shook her head. "No, David. Not until marriage. It is a risk I cannot take. It would kill my father."

It was not the moment to question her conviction. His arm around her waist, they walked slowly back to the village in a soft daze of contentment he hoped she shared. Rattling through Millet's wheat fields in the little train, they held hands in silence and she curled up against his shoulder.

But she didn't meet him the next day as usual. Instead, the librarian handed him a note from her apologizing for breaking their date. It began, *Très Cher David,* and said simply that their relationship, for reasons she could not help, had to come to an end. He must not think that she regretted a single moment; they'd had fun together and learned from each other. But the inevitable turn their friendship had taken was not what she wanted. She wished him a great success in his life. She knew he would become a brilliant and famous journalist. She hoped he would remember, as she always would, their times together, their visit to the Jeu de Paume, and especially, she said, their walk in the woods that day at Barbizon. The note closed with a politely informal *Bien à Vous* . . .

He could hear her sorrowfully speaking the last words aloud.

# 14

He told Helen Osgood about it a few days later, after he'd haunted the library each afternoon and even walked up and down the street in front of Tanya's house in hope of catching a glimpse of her, but without luck. They were sitting on the terrace of the Sélect over a Mandarin-Curaçao, Helen's current favorite apéritif, waiting for Hap to join them from the office.

Helen was not surprised.

"But what I don't understand," she said with that teasing smile, "is why you seem to care so much after such brief acquaintance."

Indirectly at first, then more explicitly, he told her what had happened in Fontainebleau forest.

She laughed. "Paris is full of women who go down on it, Davie. I don't happen to be one of them, although I've been known to obey the command if I'm drunk enough. Did she drink it?"

He nodded. "But it's not only that, Helen. We were *friends*. I can't believe I'm not going to see her any more."

"Don't count on it. These White Russian families are fanatically stuffy. The better the class, the more likely she'll obey. Even the taxi drivers tote little icons and hold candles outside their church at Easter."

"It was more than sex, Helen. We *liked* each other." And in a warm gush of memory he thought of Jean Lobowski in New York and how she'd made his life bearable during the long summer while he was saving up to come to Paris. Was she wandering around the Village right now, looking for a new companion? And what right had he to resent it if she was; still, he was jealous of the guy. What was so precious about the thing Jean had given him—unquestioning loyalty, devotion, always there when he wanted her, asking nothing in return? . . .

"You're reminiscing," Helen teased.

"I'm sorry. I just wish I knew how to get Tanya back."

"Better you put it aside and look elsewhere, David. As I told you, Paris is full of easy girls—you're going to learn just how easy women are, baby boy, before you're much older. Meanwhile"—she was smiling—"meanwhile there's always Mrs. Osgood."

He wanted to say what he was thinking but didn't— that Helen had Hap. Hap was first. And that was what made the difference. He wanted his own girl and he didn't want to share her. All the way back to Karen and the gang-bang he'd shared them—Nicky, the girl in the park; Julia in college; Jake's friends Eileen and Maggie; the whores along the way. He wanted someone to live with, to sleep with every night, naked in each other's arms under the warm covers, like Hap and Helen that night of the lesbians when he'd waited for her, needing her, in vain. He knew he still resented her for that.

She was speaking again, her eyes holding him, something insistent in the low, caressing tone. "Did you hear me, dreamy? I said there's always Mrs. Osgood. She can make you forget all about Tanya. What do you say to that?"

"You know how I feel about you, Helen."

"Prove it!"

"Prove it?"

"Prove it right now!"

He stared at her, startled, while she put some money on the table, told the waiter they would meet Monsieur at the restaurant, and stood up, smiling down at him.

"That's the nicest thing about Paris, Davie—there's always a little hotel just around the corner."

Still surprised, he let her take his arm and guide them down the Rue Vavin to the dingy little hotel he'd often passed on his walks through Montparnasse. Outside the entrance she slipped a hundred-franc note into his hand and whispered her instructions.

"*Une chambre pour une heure,*" he said to the man behind the counter.

"*Certainement, Monsieur . . .*" He hardly looked up at them.

Suddenly he was excited in a new way, and knew Helen was, too. They were strangers to each other. She was

the whore he'd just picked up in the street, had never seen
before. On the dim stairway he glanced at her face and saw
it subtly changed, the eyes with a sudden feverish glitter
far back, her body's movement loose and coarse. She muttered something to him in French—words he didn't know
—in a lewd undertone, in a voice he'd never heard from
her, abruptly gripped his hand and put it to her breast,
rubbing the hardening nipple.

He turned to ask her what she was saying but she
only went on murmuring to him in the same obscene
sounds. He realized then that it was more than playing a
part, she'd transformed herself, slouching a few steps ahead
of him as they went down the narrow hallway, her hips
swaying, stopping in front of number seven and leering at
him with a dirty smile. Opening the door he felt her hand
on his crotch, and closing the door behind them she
reached the naked balls and clutched them lasciviously;
he looked into her eyes and no longer recognized the
woman who now with a lecherous low laugh squeezed the
stiffening column and, still clasping it with her fingers,
physically pulled him toward the old-fashioned bed with its
heavy brocaded cover.

The room was in pale darkness, its curtains drawn, but
when he reached out to turn on the lamp she shook her
head. Still speaking the muttered, undecipherable French
she jerked open his belt, dragged his trousers and undershorts down so they fell at his feet, then turned her back
to him, leaned over the bed and in a savage twisting motion yanked her dress high above her hips. The flesh was
bare beneath it, the white thighs and buttocks lying helpless and totally offered to his eyes; she was all animal,
the upthrust red lips gaping and quivering, already a trace
of foam gleaming in the depths of soft dark hair. He had
never seen a woman so open, so exposed, so ready to
take cock, and the sight filled him with a savage desire
that sent the blood pounding through his body. He staggered a step nearer, not even kicking away the trousers
around his ankles, seized her body in both hands, fingers
pressing the soft round belly, and in a single lunge sank
the staff to its root in the cavern awaiting him. Her breath
was expelled in a moan with the violence of his thrust,
but facedown she was returning each stroke now with the
full strength of her thighs, smacking hard against him as

he plunged it again and again, reaching further to grasp her breasts from behind, riding the arching, bucking animal that surged beneath him. A film seemed to descend over his eyes; he was no longer himself; his identity was unknown; he was fucking a whore in a Paris hotel room and only this mattered all the way to the final furious assault, faster and faster, her groans rising to wails half-muffled in the bedcover, her pleading, begging cries for more until at last, his own voice joining hers, they exploded together and she collapsed under him with a grateful sob of exhaustion.

Slowly, very slowly, he came back to himself. They were lying side by side on the big bed. Had he slept? He couldn't remember. The room was black dark now; outside, the Montparnasse evening echoed through the street.

"Are you sleeping?" he whispered.

"No. You were, for a few minutes." He thought he could see her smile in the darkness. "You're so good for me, Davie—so good I'm a little afraid."

"Afraid?"

"If we get in too deep I'll want you all the time. And nobody else. But there's Hap . . ."

"I know, Helen. I shouldn't be living in the same house with you. It's a lousy arrangement, but I'd hoped by now I'd have my own room somewhere, maybe in a hotel, like this. It's not fair to either of you, and I wish—"

Her warm smooth hand was over his mouth. "You know Hap wants you to stay as long as you need to. So, no more talk about that . . ."

A long silence. Her hand was softly, as if absentmindedly, playing over his chest, tracing little circles over his belly. He felt it move with each new brushing stroke a little farther down.

"What were you saying in French, Helen?"

"Nothing. Gibberish. I don't remember."

"Yes, you do. I know it was something—dirty. Dirty things."

Her smile in the dark again. "Too dirty, Davie. Too dirty for your young ears."

"Not any more. I'm not a kid any more. Tell me what you were saying in French to me, Helen."

In answer she sat up, bent to leave a light kiss and rose gracefully to her feet. "Poor Hap," she said. "He's probably wondering what in hell happened to us. Hurry, Davie."

He dressed quickly while she used the bidet. Turning on the lamp for the first time, she took a tiny comb from her handbag and straightened her hair before applying fresh lipstick.

It was barely a five-minute walk to Le Négre, where Hap Osgood sat composedly at their usual table on the terrace nursing a long drink. "Hi, kids!" he said, not asking why they were late. He included them both in his grin. "I've got some news for you, my boy—Jud Purcell quits Saturday and I'm authorized to inform you that you're hired for the hotel beat beginning Monday."

He had the job! Life was on the upswing again, Joyous, he reached across the table and wrung Hap Osgood's hand. "I won't soon forget what you've done for me, Hap. And I'm going to pay you back for every sou you put out for me."

Osgood shook his head and laughed. "Not a chance, son. Try anything like that and I'll be very, very vexed."

"So will I," Helen said.

She was smiling but her voice caught a little. With a sense of relief that surprised him, he saw in her eyes and heard in her voice that she knew he knew it could never again be quite the same between them. He was on his own at last. He was a free man.

# 15

His first week's salary was like inheriting a million dollars. With it, he moved out of the Rue Boissonade and into a tiny hotel on the Impasse des Deux Anges, into a room vacated by Jud Purcell, who said in the doorway, departing: "The bed was made for heavy duty, Brent. Good cunting!"

The room was like the seven others in the hotel, large and box-shaped, with a French window giving on the court, a shabby coverlet on the bed, an old fringed lamp standing by a tattered armchair, a cracked bowl and pitcher on the washstand under a smoky mirror, a frayed towel covering a rickety bidet, and a warped bed-table with chamber pot beneath. Jud had bequeathed his pipe rack and a half-filled bookcase, mostly French paperback novels.

Before he left on his wine tour and an indolent future Jud filled him in on the occupants of the other rooms: an Irish drunk, a Eurasian mystic, two Danish lesbians, a Parisienne who danced at the Bal Tabarin, a Spanish guitarist, two Croat political exiles and three French students at the Ecole des Beaux Arts, one of them a girl, all three living in the same room. There was only one tub bathroom in the hotel, extra tariff, not counting the tiny sit-down toilets located one to each of the four floors. The *valet de chambre,* Auguste, who painted in oils in his spare time, lived in an attic aperture cut into the roof and reached by a ladder to a skylight. Mme Alric, the proprietress, resided in a lightless, airless cubicle off the entrance hall and was rarely seen except on rent-collection day, when she made the rounds of the rooms and could often be heard expostulating at overdue tenants.

The *Trib* staff were another mixed lot, though most were Americans. He quickly fell into their eating and drinking habits, a routine which began in late evening when the paper was put to bed, first with several rounds of Pernod at the Bar des Sports across the street, then dinner at the Balzar or one or two other brasseries favored by the staff at which wine was copiously drunk, finally what Hap Osgood called the serious drinking at St. Germain des Près. But Hap and Helen were seldom seen at these midnight-to-dawn sessions because Hap's work was finished early in the evening and the Osgoods preferred the quiet atmosphere of the Nègre in Montparnasse for dinner. The rest of the staff could sleep a lot later in the morning but both Hap and Helen had to be in the office by ten.

He wrote about them all—the hotel guests, the *Trib* staff, incidents of his daily life in Paris—in a series of letters to Cathy in New York. Curious that now they were separated by such distance, they were renewing in their correspondence the ties that had bound them in childhood. Cathy's letters were funny and sharply observant, although a troubling note was her report that their mother's eyesight was beginning to fail somewhat. He wondered if it was more serious than that, and whether Cathy always told him everything he wanted to know. For his part, Brent had held back on some things, too, particularly his relationship with Helen and Hap Osgood, referring to them only casually. And of course he made no reference to whorehouse adventures or the sleazier side of Paris life, feeling that Cathy and especially his mother would be shocked and repelled.

Did Hap and Helen resent the fact that their protégé was seeing very little of them now? He was sure they understood that being with his new colleagues was necessary to his learning the newspaper trade. And with helpful advice from the men on the night shift he was learning rapidly. His first efforts at interviews on the hotel beat had to be largely rewritten, but he soon acquired the knack and, within a couple of weeks, thanks to diligent reading of the French press and use of the dictionary, he was even translating simple news stories out of *Le Matin* and *Paris Soir* and rewriting them for the *Trib*. The more proficient he became the more they gave him to do. As a result he was kept so busy the first month he hardly had time to think about Helen or Tanya and his sex experiences since arriving in France.

But gradually the novelty of evenings with the "vagabonds" wore off and the old, gnawing sense of loneliness for a girl began to well up in him. The staff bunch seemed more interested in drinking than in women, although several of them were living comfortably with attractive wives and had no apparent reason to look beyond. For those without regular mates the favored sex outlet appeared to be a drunken visit en masse to the cathouse at 32 Rue Blondel, but the first time he was invited to join this expedition he begged off, lying that he had a date at his hotel; his memory of the girl at Le Sphinx was still too fresh. Anyway, he thought he'd had it with brothels.

Later, alone in his bed in the hotel, he half regretted his decision. A persistent, recurrent erection had been bothering him for several days. Even in the midst of his daily work he had haunting flashes of memory, images of Julia soaping him in the shower, of those nights in Patchin Place when he and Jake changed off with Eileen and Maggie, of the night bus to Washington with the southern girl, the unforgettable first time with Helen Osgood. He guessed Helen would welcome him again, any time, but he didn't know how to make the approach without telling Hap as well, and he concluded that all he could do there was wait for a sign from either of them.

Those sounds from the next room didn't make it any easier for him. Moving closer to the wall he listened intently—the girl who danced at the Bal Tabarin was entertaining a late visitor, as she had several times before. He could hear the man's gruff undertone and the girl's fresh young laughter, sudden little yelps of pleasure, then smacking kisses and slaps—whatever they were doing to each other it was exciting fun. He'd seen her a few times and responded to her bright, impersonal smile—a trim, long-legged kid with goo-goo eyes, black bangs over her forehead, full breasts and a big ass belted into a short trenchcoat. Altogether delectable and desirable, but obviously very, very busy, like now.

He turned away and buried his face in his pillow, pressed his erection hard against the rough sheet and tried to forget what was going on beyond the wall. The wine and drinks he'd had during the evening were pounding in his head and he made his usual resolve to ease up on the alcohol. Hap Osgood had warned him about it during his first days in Paris: observe the French; they handle the

drinking problem very well. Just enough wine and no hard
stuff except maybe an after-dinner liqueur, all of it directed toward the same purpose—as a part of lovemaking.
It excited the imagination by removing inhibitions while it
slowed down your eager physical reactions to just the right
degree, giving the woman more time to develop her own
pleasure process. But if you overdid the drinking, or didn't
drink enough, it spoiled it for both of you; you were
either too quick for her or you couldn't get it up and
passed out.

He went to sleep missing Hap Osgood's wisdom and
hoping Helen would arrange something soon. Maybe they
were deliberately letting him have his head for a while, get
the Paris excitement and working on the *Trib* out of his
system. One thing he knew: they were two of the best
friends he would ever have.

The room beyond the wall was quiet now. He didn't
have to imagine any more.

A pale autumn sun was streaming through his window when he woke. It took him a while to realize it was
Sunday, the *Trib* day off—a day for lazing, strolling, luxuriating, sitting on the terrace of the Deux Magôts and
watching the world go by as you sipped your *café noir*.
He sat up and listened: no voices or movement in the
room beyond the wall, but the gurgle of bath water
sounded from down the hall; one of the tenants would be
having their weekly tub. He had washed his hands and face
and was combing his hair when he was surprised by a
knock at his door.

*"Qui est là?"* he called.

A young voice with a trill in it. *"Votre voisine, Monsieur. Je peux vous déranger un instant?"*

*Voisine* was neighbor. He recognized the trill. She
certainly could disturb him for a moment! He reached the
door in two strides and opened it.

She was wearing a worn wrapper and was obviously
naked underneath it. She was also wearing an enchanting
grin. *"Vous n'auriez pas un morceau de savon à me
prêter?"*

Lend her a piece of soap? He certainly could. He got
it from his wash basin and was greeted by another be-
witching smile. She added, *"Sank you!"* and he watched

her walk down the hall to the bathroom before he closed his door.

Where was her friend of last night—still asleep in her room? Or had he gone early? Or was he waiting for her in the bathtub? He wondered about this while he shaved and dressed but could hear no voices, only the bath water, running out now. Surely they would be joking and splashing if they were in there together. Instead he pictured her climbing out of the big tub and rubbing down those beautiful legs, drying her breasts more gently, shaking out her tousled hair and standing a moment looking at herself in the misted mirror. When he heard the bathroom door open it took a physical effort to keep from opening his own door and looking at her as she came down the hall.

He needn't have worried. And this time at the knock on his door he didn't wait to ask who it was.

She held her wrapper carelessly close to her with one hand while proffering the soap to him with the other. "Sank you!" she said again.

*"Pas de quoi, Mademoiselle!"*

She was peering past his shoulder into the room, looking around curiously. Would she come in? He stood aside and made a gesture of welcome.

She would. Suddenly he realized he hadn't yet made his bed. *"Oh, pardon, Mademoiselle . . ."* He closed the door behind them and hastened across the room to the bed but, laughing, she came up behind him, took the sheets and blankets from the other end and shared the chore. Her wrapper fell open in the moment's exertion, her breasts poured out like a little golden cascade and her body was revealed at full length, the skin pink and glowing after the bath, the massed dark hair at her crotch soft and shining like kitten fur.

She didn't cover herself immediately, noting the incident only by giggling and rolling her eyes like a child. Her breasts swung free as she finished making the bed, waving him aside with housewifely impatience. Then, the job done, she gathered the robe around her again, perched on the edge of the chair and asked for a cigarette.

He couldn't have described how they communicated from then on. Claudine—their "conversation" elicited her

name—spoke virtually no English, and his French was still
scanty. Yet somehow, together, they managed to convey
everything they needed, including his invitation to join him
for breakfast at the Flore, where they sat together in perfect contentment without exchanging a word. Walking
back to the hotel together he took her hand and felt the
answering squeeze of her fingers, and it was no less natural
for them both to go to his room. The hotel was quiet—no
sign of Mme. Alric or any of her tenants. Beyond the
window Paris strolled in its Sunday mood, familial and relaxed. Without asking him, Claudine went to the window
and closed the shutters against the afternoon sun, which
filtered more gently now through slatted apertures and cast
a yellow pattern on the floor.

For a long moment she faced him again. Neither
spoke; no words seemed necessary. Then, loosening her
dress behind the neck with a swift, graceful movement, she
let it drop to her feet. She stood there clad in nothing but
her shoes—no bra, no panty, only the full, fresh, vibrant
smile that seemed to envelop the whole room. He felt her
presence like a man in a spell, and followed her with his
eyes as she kicked off her shoes, moved to the bed and lay
down. She didn't move again except to raise her arms and
open them wide, awaiting him with her smile, her eyes
shining with serene content. And as he shed his own
clothes, still watching her, her eyes never left his. He was
lying beside her, and her smile faded obedient to his kiss.
Their bodies touched from head to foot. He felt her shoulders cool and firm under his arm, felt her fingers tightening
a little on his back as she stirred to move closer against
him. So they lay in utter silence for uncounted minutes,
knowing that at the end of it she would open to him and
take all of him, knowing that he would enter her warm
depths and the other man, the other men, would be forgotten. This was being alive. This was all there was. The
sounds of Paris entered the room intimately in the cool,
happy afternoon, and this girl became Paris, and Paris
was his mistress, and he would take her now.

# 16

Days when the happiness of being in Paris with Claudine was like seeing Paris for the first time. From that first morning she came to his room, their relationship was settled—each free, of both necessity and choice, to pursue his/her own life, with no questions asked. She declined his invitation to move in with him and save money on rent, and sometimes he wondered if she had daytime lovers, more or less accidental, when he was working. But jealousy was not a part of the relationship. It was not the Paris way. There were no obligations each to the other, and no recriminations: no time for that in the joy they knew together.

A glorious fall slipped imperceptibly into winter, but it was a mild winter; no extreme weather he was used to back home. Now even the phrase "back home" was meaningless: Paris had adopted him. The day began with Claudine coming to his room to wake him, or vice versa, and lovemaking like the first time of making love, then a long nap before he had to leave for work. He didn't see her again until midnight, when he waited in their habitual *café* down the street from the Bal Tabarin until she emerged, flushed and exhilarated, as happily excited to see him as if they'd been separated a month. Usually she was hungry after the show though it was too soon for him to eat again after his late dinner, so he watched her fondly while she wolfed down a large *croque madame* and joined her in a couple of glasses of mellow Alsace beer. On a fine night they would walk home by way of Les Halles (more beer while watching the market trucks arrive) and cross the moonlit river on the Pont des Arts, stopping halfway over to kiss—backing her suddenly hard against the railing to find her laughing mouth with his lips, his hands

up under her skirt to pull her closer to him. Often, because by now he was hungry again and so was Claudine,
they would saunter on and join the *Trib* crowd at Lipp's
before going to bed, for yet another round of beers, maybe a *cervelas remoulade* for him, a *choucroute garnie* for
Claudine, under the approving not to say lustful eye of the
other men present. And at the end, slow and delicious in
the dark room, the tenderness of sex. Sometimes in her
paroxysm her teeth brought blood from his shoulder, from
his chin. And always he heard her little cry of gladness at
the end: *J'arrive!* . . . Eating, drinking and fucking—was
there anything else? That was the view expounded at
Lipp's. Who cared about the news? Reporting, copy-edit-
ing, proofreading was a livelihood. Politicians were fools,
economics a bore, crime a commonplace. A boss was
meant to be laughed at or ignored. As for the world depression—*sauve qui peut*. France had everything and Paris
was its capital.

Sundays off were best of all. If they were lucky, a
splendor of winter sunshine made it seem as if the whole
city was on vacation. Late morning sang in the Impasse
des Deux Anges, and Auguste brought in the special Sunday treat—rich, crisp *croissants* with steaming *café au lait,*
pretending not to notice that Claudine sitting up in bed
made a lovelier nude torso than any he'd ever painted in
his attic. It might be two hours before they rose and
dressed, so hungry again that they wanted to run, and did,
down the Rue Bonaparte to the restaurant in the tiny, narrow Rue Visconti where they liked to have their Sunday
lunch.

Maybe they started with a white Côtes du Rhone for
their apéritif, drank the rest of the bottle with the baked
filets of sole in cream, changed to the garnet-red Macon
that came from the cellar barrels with their cassoulet, and
finished up with a chèvre or a port du salut they swore
they would never forget. At least an hour was needed on a
terrace by the river to reflect on what had been eaten and
bless it with *marc* (Claudine meanwhile disposing of a
tangerine), then they could jump aboard a *bateau mouche*
and ride out to St. Germain en Laye for a wandering
walk under the trees, conversing together quite well with
his improving French, and have early dinner at a *guingette*

by the water, watching the Seine shimmer like a Monet at sunset.

For a moment Monet had made him remember Tanya and their visit to the Orangerie. It was the first time he'd thought of Tanya since he met Claudine, and he felt a passing pang of astonishment that now she meant nothing more than a vaguely pleasant afterthought.

Evening would lie blue along the quais when they came back, perhaps with showers, fine as a woman's veil. It did not deter them from strolling, laughing, through the Latin Quarter where a carousel turned raucously in the midst of a street carnival and they stopped to watch while a pig labeled *Ma Concierge* made its eternal round. There was a shooting gallery where the grand prize was awarded for hitting the bullseye over a bed in which a real live girl lay under the covers. If you won, she tumbled out in a scanty nightgown, shrieking with fake modesty, and the crowd applauded you.

It was on a night like this, back at the hotel again and holding Claudine close in bed, that he realized how much she had come to mean to him—so much, he knew now, that he could ask her if she'd had any other men since their first time together.

"*Non, chéri.*" She kissed him with the words.

"Who was the man I used to hear in bed with you?"

"A *caissier* from the Tabarin. It is without importance. I don't see him any more."

"Does he try?"

She laughed. "You are being foolish, *chéri*. Yes, he tries, but it is no use."

"Why did you like him?"

"*Like* him! He helped me to get my job—*voilà tout!* And so, I owed him payment."

"There's nobody else, Claudine?"

"*Mais non!* You are having foolish thoughts. Please, no more of this . . ." And she kissed him again, clung to him a moment, then turned as she always did when it was time to sleep, arched her body and thrust her shapely haunches against the nest of his thighs.

Suddenly he felt warm with a new and special pride of possession. It hadn't mattered to him before what Claudine did when she was away from him, but now somehow

it mattered very much. And for the first time he wanted
Hap and Helen Osgood to know her. Once or twice Hap
had seen Claudine with him, at a distance, and leered benignly in their direction, but Helen had never met her.

Next day at the office, a little nervously, he fixed the
rendezvous with Helen. They would join the Osgoods for a
drink at the Sélect tomorrow evening before Claudine left
for the Tabarin. Why did he have to feel on edge about
this; it wasn't possible that odd glint in Helen's eyes could
signify jealousy because of their past intimacy! She must
have been just laughing at him in her way—a kid wanting to show off his best girl.

He told Claudine about it after the show and was surprised to see a troubled look flit across her face.

"What's wrong, *chérie?* There's nothing to be nervous
about, you'll like each other."

She hesitated. "It is not that. I don't have a good dress
to meet your friends."

He was laughing. "Everything you wear is good! Anyway, they never think about such things."

But the double date didn't go well. Somehow, despite
his efforts at conversation, constraint was in the air, and he
wondered how much the others were feeling it as he did.
Claudine had never looked prettier, but she was tongue-
tied, as if awed by these two older Americans, which was
not like her breezy, insouciant self. Helen smiled a lot but
was nothing like as cordial as he knew she could be. He
could understand some resentment in Helen perhaps, but
Hap—good old Hap!—treated them both with indifference
just short of outright rudeness, wouldn't help with the small
talk and just sat watching the street. It wasn't surprising
that Claudine said *bonsoir* even sooner than she had to,
giving a rehearsal call as excuse.

There had to be a reason for the Osgoods' attitude.
Wounded in his pride, he tried to find out after Claudine
left. But all Hap would say was, "Nice girl, Dave." And
Helen, still smiling, teased, "I must say she's cuter than
anything the *Trib* boys have collected."

In his hurt and embarrassment he felt he couldn't go
through dinner with them, gave a lame excuse and left the
cafe abruptly without being urged to stay longer. Walking
slowly down the Boulevard Raspail he began to reproach
himself for the whole fiasco. Probably it was his fault for

setting up a meeting instead of letting it happen casually, as it would have in time. It wasn't the *Trib* style; he should have known that. The best thing to do now was act as if it had never happened. It would work itself out in the end.

By the time Claudine joined him after the show he'd decided not to mention it. Neither did she. If she felt his disappointment at the meeting she didn't say so; was it simply not in her nature to brood? They walked across the city together as usual, talking of everything but the Osgoods, eating and drinking on the way but avoiding the Lipp's crowd as if by unspoken agreement. At last in bed together, the doubts of the day were finally dispelled: the world was shut away; Claudine made this the only world. And tonight he took her with a tenderness of emotion that almost overwhelmed him, felt her respond to it with a reassurance that touched him deeply. He noticed as they finished and lay exhausted, side by side, a small tear trickling down her cheek.

He kissed it off without words. She too had felt the humiliation of the encounter in the Sélect.

By morning life was back to lighthearted normal. Bright winter sunshine lay over Paris and there seemed even a hint of spring in the air, though spring was still far off. His mood was so relieved, so carefree, that he'd almost reached the office before he realized he'd left both his watch and his wallet at the hotel. He laughed and shrugged: nothing to do but go back and get them. In the Metro he scanned the day's news in *Le Figaro* and found nothing of interest, discarding the paper as he left the St. Germain des Prés station. It was a brisk five minutes' walk to the hotel. He bounded up the carpeted stairs and along the hall, gaily calling out *"C'est moi!"* as he turned the key in the lock and stood for a moment in the open doorway as if his heart had stopped. Hap Osgood, naked on top of Claudine's naked body, raised his head and saw him.

# 17

The rest of the day was something like a trance. At some time after two, after walking dazedly around the Latin Quarter, he found himself sitting on a bench in the Jardin des Plantes, staring at nothing. He remembered then that he hadn't checked in at the office, went to a phone booth in the Halle aux Vins and said he was on his beat and would be back at the end of his normal routine calls. But he had no heart for the job and spent the rest of the afternoon numbly picking up the hotel lists of new arrivals without even looking at them for a possible interview.

He was still staggered by that moment in the doorway of his room. Had he spoken? How long had he stood there, as if struck by physical concussion? Had Hap Osgood spoken, or Claudine? He couldn't remember, didn't want to remember. He couldn't even recall leaving the hotel or where he went first, but he was vaguely aware of having had some drinks at the bar of the Bonaparte that made him feel like vomiting a little while later. It wasn't the drinks, though; he knew it was the sickness of shock, of emotional hurt, of disillusion, so severe that he still couldn't quite believe it had happened. Certain it was that if anyone had told him it was going to happen he would have been incredulous. Not Claudine. Not Hap!

By evening when he returned to the office he was more or less in control again. He purposely arrived late to avoid seeing either Hap or Helen and was relieved they had both left. Nervously he wondered whether Hap had told anyone, maybe joked about it in an effort to laugh it off in advance of a possible scene. If he had, nobody seemed any different toward him than usual. But of course Hap had told Helen by now—or had he? What did Helen know about Claudine and Hap that she'd never told? Because today couldn't have been the first time. Now,

his mind cooler and clear once more, he was sure of that.
And yet hadn't he himself gone to bed with Claudine the
first day they'd spoken to each other?

It was torture thinking about it. He resolved to put it
out of his mind, but he couldn't face the prospect of dinner
with the *Trib* crowd; instead he avoided the usual haunts
and ate by himself at the Petit Riche near the boulevards,
dawdling so late he was the last patron in the place. Coming at last out into the chilly, noisy streets he realized it
was almost time to meet Claudine after the Tabarin show,
and from sheer habit turned into the Rue Montmartre before he stopped, angrily, and headed back toward the Left
Bank. His inadvertence plunged him into the bitter mood of
the afternoon and he stopped at the nearest *café zinc* to
add two cognacs to the brandy and wine he'd drunk with
his dinner. To avoid walking off the effects, so he would
sleep better, he took a taxi back to the hotel.

To his astonishment Claudine, fully dressed, was sitting solemnly on the edge of the bed, waiting for him.

For a long moment neither spoke, then she said in a
small voice: *"Bonsoir,* David . . ."

Slowly he closed the door behind him, heard his own
harsh rejoinder in French, like another man speaking:
"What are you doing here?"

"Why should I not be here, David? I live here, with
you."

"Not any more."

In answer she went to the washstand and poured some
water into a glass, then walked deliberately to the closet,
took the bottle of cognac from the shelf and mixed a
drink. *"Voici,"* she said softly, and handed it to him.

"No."

"Please, David. You need it. You are upset."

His hard laugh rang in the room. "And you're feeling
fine, right?"

She tried to take his hand but he jerked it away from
her. "No, David. I am not feeling fine. I have had a very
difficult day. Monsieur Osgood, your friend, came here. I
think he was drunk, very drunk, but not showing it. I could
not get rid of him."

"So you stripped down and opened your legs, right?"

She went on as if she had not heard him. "I did not
go to the theater tonight. I phoned to say I was ill. Per-

haps I will lose my job there, now. But I had to wait here
for you." She paused.

"Is that all you have to say?"

She shrugged faintly. "He is a big man, David. He
made me afraid of him."

"He's big, all right. You discovered that. And you like
them big, right? As big as they come."

"I knew I must not make your great friend angry.
After all, you told me he has done so much to help
you . . ."

He was staring at her, incredulous. "And that's why
you let him fuck you? Is that what you're trying to make
me believe?"

"It was nothing," she said. "You can believe me. I
have already forgotten it all."

In the silence he shook his head. "Try to tell the
truth, Claudine, for the last time. How long have you
known Hap Osgood? How long has he been fucking you?"

He saw her eyes widen. "I never saw him before last
night, with you, David."

"You're still lying. I've pointed him out to you at
Lipp's."

"That, yes . . ."

"You knew him before I ever came to Paris."

She hesitated. "I think, perhaps . . . once, with Jud."

He was trying to keep his voice down. "Of course.
Purcell, your next-door neighbor. You were fucking him,
too. You were probably fucking the whole *Trib* staff. And
I thought—"

"David, please. You are talking about such a small
thing. Those times are forgotten, I told you." She went
back to the bed and sat down, facing him, her knees
wide apart. In the lamplight he could see the soft dark
patch at her naked crotch. "Come here, David," she was
saying, her voice a soothing murmur now. "Come and sit
beside me . . ."

He was thinking: No wonder Jud didn't tell me
about her. She was Hap Osgood's property. *And Helen
knew, too, she must have known, and never told me.*

And I'm supposed to do the Paris thing and take the
whole situation as normal, pass it off with a shrug!

"Do you know how I felt about you?" he heard himself saying to her in a broken voice. "Do you know how

much you meant to me? I thought we had something
—something that we both . . ." He shook his head again.
"What am I trying to say to you, Claudine? It's useless.
It's hopeless. Are you going to make me believe you didn't
know he was coming here this morning or he didn't know
you were waiting for him? You think I don't see now you
both probably worked this little game on his way to
work after I left here many times before—washing me out
of your ass and all ready to take him on the minute he
walked through this door? And do you think after this I
could ever believe a word you said about anything or
want to be with you ever again?"

She stood up and moved to him. "You don't mean to
say this, David." She put her arms on his shoulders and he
pushed them away from him. "You say I have done a terrible thing, but you cannot say you don't want to be with
me ever—what you just said, David—listen, listen to
me . . ." He held his head away from her seeking mouth
and she clasped his waist, her body sagging, going to her
knees, weeping tears that dripped on his resisting hands.

"It's over," he said.

"David . . . David . . ." Her arm tightened around his
knees and as he felt her mouth pressed between his thighs
he recoiled from her, leaving her kneeling, crying, her
head down.

"I'm going out now," he said to her. "I'll find a place
for the night and when I come back in the morning I
don't want you to be here, Claudine, not any more! Get
your things out of here when you go—I don't want anything of yours in this room when I come back to it."

He went out without looking back at her. The door
slammed behind him and her sobbing followed him down
the hall.

# 18

The next few days were easier on him than he'd expected: once he had firmly put Claudine out of his life he could face himself and his job again. He could also face the idea of the others involved; he avoided speaking to Hap and Helen in the office and they made no overtures in his direction. As for Claudine, she had moved back into her own room. She made no further effort to seek him out and, luckily, they didn't meet in the hotel hallway or elsewhere. There was no sound from her room at night; if she was seeing Hap Osgood or other men it was happening somewhere else.

To keep the whole episode out of his mind Brent applied himself to his work with a new intensity, starting earlier in the day and remaining in the office later at night pounding out extra rewrite and turning in more interviews than there was space to handle them. But he knew he was pleasing Dick Robertson, the managing editor, with his rapid progress. Most of all he was pleasing himself; he had a knack for news work and he set his sights on the future. So he wasn't altogether surprised in February when Robertson gave him a small raise in pay, enough so he could consider moving to a slightly better hotel handier to the office.

He'd been happy in the Hotel des Deux Anges until the break with Claudine, but those memories were overshadowed now by her presence in the next room. A deep-buried sense of guilt began to nag at him: wasn't her way the civilized way, after all? Weren't Hap and Helen, to whom he owed so much, right in their view of life? And had he left his adolescence behind him, as he'd thought, or was he still behaving like a kid about the whole thing? As long as he stayed where he was these doubts would assail him; he knew he was developing a neurotic dread of the first night he would hear Claudine with a visitor beyond the wall. He found a quiet Right Bank hotel that was within his means and gave Mme. Alric a week's notice. Even with that decision made, he felt uneasy about leaving. It would mean cutting off Claudine entirely, and was he sure, really sure, they might not somehow be together again?

Dick Robertson unexpectedly resolved whatever problem remained: the *Trib*'s resort correspondent on the Riviera had abruptly resigned to return to America, and David Brent was hereby instructed to proceed to Nice without delay to take over the job for the rest of the season. He greeted the assignment with unconcealed excitement; his new beat was the whole coast between Cannes and Monte Carlo! It was a real plum for a cub and the managing editor moved fast to avert jealousy among the older hands: within twenty-four hours, bag and baggage, Brent was aboard the Train Bleu and on his way.

He knew he would always remember the enchanted morning he woke in his berth as the train pulled out of Marseilles and started its winding trek along the *littoral*. After the fog and chill of Paris this was instant springtime. Warm sunshine poured through the window above his head, bearing with it the scent of mimosa; vineyards and olive groves spotted the countryside, and beyond lay the Mediterranean, the azure sea, an endless sheet of crystal under the cloudless sky, splintered along the edges by a gentle surf that broke across the sands of sheltered beaches, swirled in rocky coves. He dressed and sat fascinated at the window as the train rattled through stations with magic names . . . Bandol, Hyères, Ste. Maxine, Cannes and finally Nice, to be his headquarters during his stay on the Riviera. Basically the job would be similar to his work in Paris: to rove the smart hotels, collect celebrity interviews and write features about resort life.

Beyond that, it was an escape from the life he'd lived these past months and the souring of the relationships he'd formed and seen destroyed. Suddenly it was a new phase, a lucky change at the moment he needed it most.

He flung himself into the work with the confidence of a veteran, reconnoitering his territory quickly and thoroughly. The hotels were full of Americans, some of them rich, permanent expatriates, others prominent refugees from the depression at home who vowed to outlast it in the surroundings of luxury Europe. Most conspicuous were the movie and theater people—stars like Chaplin, who was staying at Juan-les-Pins, and Noel Coward, near Cannes. Other celebrities abounded, and scattered along the coast in vast secluded villas lived a clutch of multimillionaires who for one reason or another, usually embezzlement, had absconded from their native countries before the law caught up with them. They were fair game for gossip and interviews and color stories, and Brent lost no time starting a steady stream of material by mail and telegraph and telephone to Paris.

Most of all there was the sunshine, illuminating this glamorous pageant by day as the casinos lighted it at night. Winter was forgotten; there was no such thing as winter. The sun gave its blessing to all who moved beneath it, and for Brent it meant the reawakening of sexual urges dead since the bitter parting with Claudine. Desire grew as he settled into the new job and began to find breathing time, especially at night. But as yet he'd found no one he wanted to share his yearnings.

March came in and with it the Riviera spring like summer. The days were hot now, nights under the canopy of stars heavy with the odors of bloom. The Battle of Flowers was celebrated at Cannes. Beaches all along the coast were crowded with bathers. And the parties went on and on, around the clock, beginning with drinks by the pool when the sun went over the yardarm, long, winey luncheons under the awnings of the smart restaurants, back to the hotel or villa for siesta, then the round of cocktail parties on terraces overlooking the sea, dinners even longer and more elaborate than lunch, dancing perhaps, under the brilliant sky, champagne and more champagne, endlessly, and the gambling till dawn when at last, weary and reluctant, the revelers return to their beds, resigned to the inevitable hung-over awakening and fated to begin it all again.

David Brent, young reporter and spectator on the fringe, watched it happening and learned the ways of the rich and famous. Indefatigably he covered his beat, pursuing the wary, smiling at snubs, writing it all down. A phone call from Dick Robertson tipped him on the incognito presence of a celebrated American screen beauty who'd walked out on her fourth husband in Rome and driven alone up the coast to the Réserve at Beaulieu, where she was holed up in her suite and refusing all calls. For Robertson himself to have put him on the story meant he wanted it bad for the home edition in America. "Give it the all-out try," Dick urged. He sounded tense or tired, as if he'd been worrying about something. "It means a lot for us to deliver on this one," he said.

Dutifully, dressed in his new linen blazer and freshly pressed trousers, he bussed and taxied to the Réserve in bright midday sunshine. Politely he chatted with the concierge, then the manager, was told with polished courtesy there was no such person registered at the Réserve. He'd expected that, thanked them and instead of leaving immediately wandered out to the pool and the glorious view. It was a little too early still for the pool; only two children playing and splashing each other at one end, a lithe blonde teenager doing laps with powerful strokes. She was a beautiful sight, tanned arms flashing in the sunlight, wet yellow hair glistening. He stood beside the pool and watched her. As she returned to his end she glimpsed him suddenly, pulled up without making the turn and looked at him.

"C'mon in, the water's great!" She squinted with smoke-blue eyes and grinned a very wide grin.

"Wish I could. I'm not staying in the hotel."

"What if you're not? They'll have a pair of trunks for you. In there." She pointed.

He was looking straight down at the cleavage of high, full breasts. Maybe she was older than he'd thought. "Thanks," he said. "I'd settle for a drink, if they'd sell me one, which they won't."

"D'you like Tom Collinses? That's *my* drink."

He laughed. "Sure. Do you tend bar here?"

"Don't be silly." With a rippling of burnished shoulder muscles she surged up out of the water and ran, dripping, to the hallway beyond the pool, shouting her order in very clumsy French. And ten minutes later, wrapped carelessly in a beach robe, hair combed back like a boy's, long legs stretched out, she was sitting opposite him at a poolside table over their drinks. He already knew her name was Jamie Blake—Ojai, California—she knew he was a

*Trib* reporter, and he'd already told her the truth when
she asked him what he was doing at the Réserve.

"Naturally she won't see you," Jamie said.

"You know she's here?"

"I've heard the clerks talking. Nobody's seen her yet,
but for your information she's in number fourteen, up that
stairway in the back to the second floor, end of the hall."

"Want to make a bet, Jamie?"

"You sound like my father. What is it?"

"I'm going to get an interview with her. Right now."
She leaned forward. "Can I come with you?"

"I'm sorry, no. But I'll meet you here right afterward."

"You're on." She giggled and watched him walk swiftly to the back stairs and out of sight. "And good luck,"
she whispered.

It was quiet in this part of the hotel. No sounds, and
nobody, guest or servant, in sight. On the second floor
landing he looked around him, still no one, then tiptoed
down the softly carpeted hallway to the facing door at the
far end. He felt his temples pulsing; he'd never covered a
story quite this way before; well, he could always say he
was lost. He stood for a moment outside the door, breathing a little faster, and decided not to knock. Very quietly
he turned the knob; the door opened inward; no sound
came from within.

He was in a richly furnished foyer that opened into a
small sitting room, beyond that a half-open door led into a
larger room with tall French windows giving on the sea.
But the drapes were drawn in both rooms, shrouding them
in pale darkness. Feeling like a thief, half reluctant to keep
going, he walked noiselessly across the sitting room to the
inner doorway. A rose lamp burned beside the huge bed.
An open bottle of champagne stood in its bucket on the
same table. And *she* was sitting up against the pillows in
white negligée, a glass in her hand, staring at him.

She was as beautiful as he'd ever seen her on film;
more beautiful. She was also drunk, he was almost certain
of that in the oddly calm way she looked at him. She
even smiled slightly; his heart stirred at the famous smile.
And the husky voice, when she spoke.

"Are you sure you're at the right address?" she said.
"And who are you, anyway?"

He hoped his smile didn't show nerves. "The Paris *Tribune*," he said.

She began to laugh, throatily. "The word gets around, doesn't it? Come a little closer, I can't see you in this light. But don't open those curtains, I hate that damned sun." She drained her glass. "Six years of Hollywood and I'm still hating it. You know, whatever your name is—"

"Dave Brent."

"I miss Pittsburgh."

He was standing beside the bed. He noticed the empty champagne bottle shoved into the wastebasket under the table—had she already finished that this morning? She held out her glass imperiously. "Fill that, and find yourself a glass—think there's one in the bathroom."

The negligée slipped off one shoulder as she held out the glass, disclosing half a perfect breast. She was not the first actress he'd interviewed but she was the most undressed. And he saw now that she was older than he'd thought: very faint lines were visible in the pale skin, but the bone structure beneath was as young and fresh as a girl's.

"Aren't you going to join me, whatever your name is?"

"Dave Brent."

"Forgive me. You've already told me that." The smile again. "I promise not to forget. Now go get your glass."

He went hurriedly. Was it a diversion so she could call the desk and have him thrown out—worse, arrested? The bathroom was huge and smelled of perfume. It was also in a mess. Quickly he found a glass and returned to her. "That's better," she said, and they clinked glasses. "I suppose you're after all the dirt."

"I was hoping for an interview, yes."

"What makes you think I'm going to give you one?"

"Well . . ." He was trying to control his excitement at the prospect.

"Feather in your cap, wouldn't it?"

"It sure would."

"Better men than you've been turned away."

"I guess they have."

She laughed and held out her glass for more. "You're cute, whatever your name is. How old are you?"

"Twenty-five."

"That's a lie." She appraised him. "I doubt if you're much over twenty. Never apologize for being twenty. Best time of life, you'll learn that. Well, am I right?"

"I guess you are. Is it true that you've left your husband?"

"Ah-ah—no interview, yet. You're going to have to earn it."

He grinned, feeling the champagne gladden him and scenting success. "I'll do my best."

"Wait—be right back . . ." With a sinuous movement she slipped out of bed and walked on dainty feet to the bathroom. Was all this for real? It was a scene from one of her pictures. He watched her stand a moment before the mirror, raising her hands to her hair and scrutinizing her face, before she faced him again and as if totally unaware of his presence lifted the flowing negligée and sat down on the toilet. Even that casual movement she made graceful, with an exquisite flash of thigh. He fought his fascination and turned his head away, hearing her throaty laughter then.

"You're cute."

He was studiedly refilling his glass when she returned and got back into bed, but this time left the sheets off and lay against the pillows with only the satiny thin robe covering her body. She was smiling at him. "You know, Mr. Brent, with a little more grooming and the right clothes you wouldn't be a bad-looking man."

"Thank you."

"It will come in good time. Right now you're probably best with no clothes at all. Let's have a look at you."

He stared at her, heard her impatient command. "I mean it! Chuck that jacket and drop those pants. You want an interview, don't you?"

It was so unexpected he froze for a moment, trying to smile, trying to adjust.

"Will this help?" she said, and pulled aside the negligée. Her body lay lazily naked from the waist down, a blonde, more voluptuous than Olympe by Manet. He was living an instant that a million men had fantasized. And he realized in that instant that maybe never again in his life would he see nudity more beautiful as object, more desirable in and of itself—the softly rising and falling belly in the bowl of rose light, the pink lips parted slightly to bare the paler pink deep in the mound of silken hair, the creamy contours of the thighs, provocatively open, one golden, indolent knee drawn back as if expectantly. "Come on, then!" she was urging, her voice lower, intent. "Or will I have to undress you myself?"

Still as in a dream he responded, dropped the jacket and shirt and undershirt swiftly, slipped off his shoes, let his trousers and shorts fall forgotten to the carpet, stood naked and fully erect before her.

The low tones had a new note. "Now we're getting somewhere! Know the next move, David?"

"Yes!" He took a step toward her and knocked his glass off the bedtable, heard it splinter against the polished wood leg.

"Ah, not so quick, my sweet. The next move is here" —her legs opening wider—"with your kisses."

He hesitated, confused, and she spoke again. "You've never done that? Oh, David, such an ignorant boy . . . Come closer, put your head down, let me show you . . . like this . . ."

For a moment he lay there, his head between her legs, overcome by the scent of her nearness, overwhelmed by the knowledge of *whose* nearness, then felt himself blaze with sudden uncontrollable excitement, lifted his body till they were face to face, mouth to ravenous mouth, and plunged to her depths in the name of a million anonymous men.

# 19

It was several days before he really believed it had happened to him. But he had his interview, front-paged in the Paris edition, to persuade him it was true. She had, finally, talked a little about her break-up with the latest husband, and salted it with some racy observations about movies and moviemakers, especially some directors she hated. The sexual act had in some way sobered her, changed her. She was a bit imperious with him after that, but she made no complaint about his failure to obey her specific instructions at the moment before he entered her; she seemed to have forgotten what she'd asked him to do. And the other entry—like a thief coming into her suite—only amused her; she praised him for his nerve and predicted his success in a long newspaper career. He must have been with her an hour and a half when, abruptly, she dismissed him.

"Sneak out," she said with a very slight smile, "the way you sneaked in. Whatever you do, keep me out of it!"

It was only after he was in the taxi and on his way back to Monte Carlo to catch his bus that he remembered the girl, Jamie Blake, he'd left at the pool. As soon as he'd filed his story from the telegraph office in Nice he wrote her a note, addressed it to the Réserve, and contritely apologized, explaining that his departure had to be hurried and stealthy. He said he hoped he'd see her again before she went back to California, and enclosed his address and phone number.

Two days later, waked out of a sound sleep at eight A.M., he heard Jamie Blake's voice on the line. She sounded exuberant and amused. "What's all this about going back to California? I'm staying here till my father gets tired of the Casino, and that could be never."

"Wonderful, Jamie."

"Seen the paper yet? All about your girlfriend."

He sat up. "What about her?"

"She's back in Monte and with her husband. They're rosy-cosy again, what do you think of that?"

He laughed. "Nothing she does would surprise me. Anyway, I owe you a Tom Collins, Jamie. I have to go to Cannes today but how about tomorrow?"

"I can't wait to hear everything about her."

"Same time, same place?"

"Oh—we're not at La Réserve any longer—Daddy's rented a place in Beausoleil." She gave him the directions. "And don't stand me up again, David."

"Never again, Jamie."

"I know you reporters. I'll believe it when I see you."

"Count on me from now on."

Whoever Daddy was, he was in the money. The Beausoleil place was a villa on several flowery acres with a magnificent view of Monte Carlo and the sea. A little red Bugatti stood in the driveway and, beyond, Jamie was waving to him from beside the pool, her glistening wet suit clinging to the contours of that tall, athletic body.

"It's not as big as the Réserve," she grinned with a sweep of her arm, "and we have to make our own drinks, but you should see our place in Ojai."

"Maybe I will, one of these days."

The smoke-blue eyes squinted friendliness. "Right now you'll have to settle for this."

The makings for Tom Collinses stood on a table by the pool, and from the first sip the conversation flowed as between two old friends. She seemed curious, perhaps with feminine intuition, about how long he'd stayed in the suite at the Réserve and wanted all the details. He was curious, too.

"What's a girl like you doing out of school at this time of year—or is it your spring vacation?"

"Had two years of Stanford, David, before they told me college was not my style."

He laughed. "Another thing: I can't understand why you're not being chased around by half the boys on the Riviera."

"Oh, but I am! Trouble is, they all want the same

thing, and when they find out they can't have it, they run."

He feigned perplexity. "The same thing? What same thing?"

"Do I have to spell it out for you? S-E-X."

"What's wrong with sex, Jamie?"

She shrugged and grinned. "I dunno. Maybe I don't feel ready for it yet."

"You mean going all the way, or any sex at all?"

She was serious now. "Oh, I like the smooching kind. Even the touching stuff, up to a point. But I know where it's leading, and that's where I draw the line."

There was a silence. He said then, "I'm surprised, in a way. You seem so easygoing, so free and relaxed. If I'd had to guess, I'd have said you'd already had plenty of sexual experience."

She was mixing their second drink. She looked up at him and grinned the urchin grin again. "I've got a lot to look forward to, right? Well, there's plenty of time. I'm young."

"And beautiful, Jamie."

Something in the way he said it made her blush a little. She took a big slug of her Tom Collins and stood up. "Let's dip!" She ran to the edge of the pool and made a perfect racing dive, surfacing at once, whirling around and calling to him from the pool. "C'mon in!"

"Got a pair of trunks?"

She shook her head. "Didn't you bring your own?"

"Sorry. I should have."

She laughed, treading water. "C'mon in anyway! I don't care, if you don't."

He took another long drink and stood up, looking around him; nobody was in sight. "Okay," he called, and stripped down. He felt calm and good about it, standing there naked at the edge of the pool, not in the least self-conscious and aware that though he was excited inside, his penis was relaxed. From the center of the pool Jamie Blake was staring at him in unabashed curiosity.

"You're pretty," she decided, and he plunged awkwardly into the water, swimming toward her under the surface and seeing her legs, her floating, swaying body, come closer through the blue blur until he grasped them, then her waist, and surfaced laughing face to face with her, holding her shoulders.

"This is great, Jamie!" She made no effort to pull away from him.

"It's good to swim naked, isn't it? I do, when I'm alone."

"Pretend you're alone now."

She hesitated only a moment, then laughed and with a swift graceful movement dropped her shoulder straps and let the black sheer swimsuit fall away from her body. The beautiful breasts floated free, undulating with the water, and with a sudden splash she lurched away and started her slow, powerful crawl stroke toward the end of the pool. He was no big swimmer but he followed along, keeping up with her for three laps until she stopped near the poolside table where their drinks were. Coming up beside her, he drew her toward him, her body as light in his arms as a baby's. He gathered her up and looked down at her laughing face, felt her breasts against his chest, felt his cock rise suddenly to touch her between the legs. Just as abruptly, still laughing, she pulled away and announced, "All this water's making me thirsty!" and climbed out, giving him a brief, dazzling glimpse of crotch.

Lithe and lovely in the sun, throwing her wet blonde hair back over her glistening shoulders, she ran down to the poolhouse at the other end of the patio and brought out a couple of towels. And again they sat facing across the table, draining their second drink and starting their third. His towel lay across his lap and hers swathed her body carelessly, one breast almost fully exposed, the rosy nipple peeking. And he wondered whether this insouciance was deliberate provocation or just the innocence of un-awakened youth.

"You were telling me about your interview at the Ré-serve," she said, "and I have a feeling you didn't tell me everything."

He blinked. "Did I leave something out?"

"Don't lie, David."

It made him laugh. "Even if I told you, you wouldn't believe me."

She sat up and the towel fell away from one shoulder; the rosy breast shone in the sun. "You mean she—you—"

"I told you you wouldn't believe me."

"I'd believe anything about *her*," she said scornfully. He noticed she was slurring her words slightly over the third drink and he was feeling a little drunk himself with the combination of liquor, sun and most of all Jamie Blake. "Well?" she continued, challenging. "I helped you find her—now you tell me what happened."

He smiled. "I thought you were against sex."

"Come on, David! Out with it! You fucked her, right?"

He had a plan of action now. Still smiling, he shook his head. "That wasn't what she wanted, Jamie."

"What d'you mean?" She looked blank. "What else is there?"

"It's a little hard to explain." He was stiffening again under the towel. "I could show you, but I don't think I can put it in words."

Jamie was taking a long, gulping drink. She put the glass down and stared at him. "All right, show me!"

"Not out here, where everybody can see. Is there someplace we can be alone?"

By this time her curiosity was obviously tormenting her. She looked around them. "How about the pool-house?"

"Why not?"

She got up a trifle unsteadily, holding the towel around her, and he put his arm around her waist to steady them both as they walked down the patio, his towel knotted over his hips. "Will we be disturbed?" he murmured in her ear.

"Nobody in the villa—Gervaise doesn't come to clean till two."

"But where's your father?"

"Always has lunch in Monte. With one of his girls."

"He sounds interesting. I'd like to meet him some time."

"You will."

And then they were inside the cool, shadowy one-room cabin. A low, broad couch filled the corner, covered with a smooth black cover. He motioned her to it. "Lie down there, Jamie." And as she hesitated, he smiled and said: "Don't worry. No violence. You wanted me to show you and I will."

He stood at the foot of the couch as she lay down

obediently on her back and stared up at him with soft wide eyes. "Don't try to take advantage," she muttered with a trace of mutinous anxiety.

He smiled. "I promise. Now open that towel so I can see all of you."

Her turn to smile. "You too, David, if I do."

In answer he dropped the towel from his hips and stood naked again, the ramrod column standing out in front of him. And she, slowly, reluctantly, drew the towel away from her and lay nude under his eyes, every inch of smooth, tanned flesh bared, the golden mound at the crotch still damp from the pool water. Gently he leaned forward and parted her knees while she watched him in submissive silence. Afterward she spoke, almost in a whisper. "What did she want you to do, David? Tell me. Tell me . . ."

For a moment he was unable to speak in answer, his gaze enthralled by what he saw, tendrils of blonde hair clinging, curling around the parted pink lips, as fresh as young fruit with the dew still on it, virginal and unsullied as a spring flower. Because he knew now that for the first time he wanted to take this fruit in his mouth as women had taken him—to taste the full flavor of a beautiful girl in the early prime of her flowering, to savor her to the depths, to breathe the warm, delicate scent of this most intimate of all flesh. And he knelt almost reverently before the altar of her glowing youth, bent his head in tribute, bent his lips to the lips that lay open before him, his hands moving upward over the firm young belly to the rich young breasts above, over the perfect body that suffered his touch without resisting, only stirring a little as though in astonishment at what was happening to it.

And then he was lost in the intoxication he had never known. She too was lost; he could feel her anxiety ebb under his lips, under his hands. As naturally as an animal grazing in green fields, snuffing for the tenderest herbs, kissing and sucking at the source of earth's joy, he felt the hot softness grow softer, wetter still as he wallowed in her. And he heard her moan in a kind of wonder, a revelation, that drew her thighs helplessly farther apart and lifted her knees to take his flicking, plunging tongue deeper, as deep as it would go.

Her orgasm came so suddenly that he was totally unprepared: a sharp, yelping explosion of breath, her thighs coming violently together with all the strength of her powerful young muscles, seizing his head in a vise and keeping it clamped between them as though to crush him, swallow him. His head came up with her as her buttocks rose off the bed in a thrashing, twisting climax, before she fell back in overwhelming release, yielded him, and lay quivering with sweet exhaustion. In the same instant his own paroxysm overtook him, would not be denied, and he sprang up, groped for the towel beside him and clutched it to his belly just in time to arrest the spurting semen in its folds. Like her he was panting as from a fierce race won, a high peak scaled in triumph, and indeed it was a breakthrough for him, a breathless new sensation that gripped his whole body, as it was for Jamie Blake the crossing of a threshold toward new horizons of sensuality.

Like coming back into another world he became aware she was watching him, the smoke-blue eyes softer than he'd ever seen them, the warm mouth curving in a secret smile.

"Jesus Christ in the foothills!" she said in a small, awed voice.

"What was *that,* Jamie?" He laughed.

"Something my father says when he's really stunned by something. I mean he means it's too wonderful to believe. And how do *you* feel? I suppose it was just routine for you."

*"Routine!* I've never done this before, Jamie. And I'll tell you how I feel about it—I feel drunk with some marvelous new liquor. Or dope. Or perfume. Or all of them at once. And even that can't describe it."

"And I never even *heard* of it, David! I guess I've got a lot to learn."

He smiled. "When's the next lesson?"

"Tomorrow? Noon?"

"I'll be here."

"And what are you going to teach me next time, Professor?"

"Maybe you'll teach me."

Her impish grin. "Come here and sit beside me."

He sat at the foot of the bed and held one of her shapely ankles while she rubbed her toes into his thigh.

Her voice was soft and musing. "D'you think I'm ready to graduate?" she said.

"With honors, Jamie."

But school wasn't held. When he got back to Nice that afternoon he found a telegram from his managing editor ordering him to pack and return to Paris by the night train. No reason was given—could it have been an angry reaction to the Monaco newspaper's beat on the star's reunion with her latest husband? Knowing Dick Robertson, he doubted it. He remembered Robertson's worried voice on the phone the other day; something bigger was going on.

And when he walked into the city room next morning he didn't have to ask: the funereal faces around him showed just how serious it was. He already knew it in his bones by the time Dick Robertson called him into his office and told him. The *Trib* was about to die, killed by the Depression.

It was a quick passing. The final issue, two days later, was followed by an eighteen-hour drunk in which the whole staff participated excepting only Hap and Helen Osgood. Reassigned to safe jobs by the home edition, they'd caught the *Mauretania* back to New York the same morning he'd arrived from Nice. Robertson too would be returning to home headquarters after he settled the Paris edition's final affairs. The rest of the staff were high and dry on the beach.

"What are your plans, kid?" Dick asked him. It was their last meeting in his office, the door closed.

"Plans?" He shrugged hopelessly. All the light had suddenly gone out of his life. Was it possible that only four days ago, that wonderful moment with Jamie Blake on the Riviera, the future so full of promise . . .

"Don't take it so hard, Brent." Robertson smiled faintly. "It's all part of newspapering. You're young. And I like you. If you'll agree to say nothing to the rest of the boys, I can fix you up with a job in the London bureau, what say?"

His heart rebounded in relief, so happy he felt the tears come to his eyes. *"London?* Yes, sir!"

He tried to keep his joy secret as he walked through

the city room on his way out, but they were all weighed
down with their own troubles; nobody even looked up at
him.

Later, sitting alone on the terrace of the cafe across
the street, he faced a double sadness: he would lose
Jamie, and he would lose France. Wasn't he falling in
love with both, now it was too late?

Just what was love, anyway?

Gray clouds parted suddenly over the city, and the
vagrant sun broke through.

# THREE

# 20

He was to remember for a long time the Englishman he met on the Channel crossing from France. Brent had spent much of the time in the ship's bar nostalgically rhapsodizing about the Paris he was leaving behind. The Englishman had done very little talking, just quietly hearing him out while smoking his pipe. It was not until they were interrupted by the warning that they'd be docking soon, in the midst of Brent's wistful description of the beauties of the French capital, that the Englishman made his first and last observation.

"Odd you should feel this way about Paris," he said, rapping out his pipe. "Actually London's a better place."

Now, after nearly two years in the *Trib's* London bureau, Brent was beginning to appreciate his English friend's laconic comment, smugly superior as it was and without relinquishing his nostalgia for France. London was not Paris, by no means, but there was something about it, something unique. Somehow it grew on you, with all its shortcomings—dreadful climate, terrible food, and compared with Paris, drab architecture. After a while you began to see the virtues of restraint, of understatement, so much a part of the British psyche. London was a comfortable old shoe, and he had the feeling that later in his life he would look back on it with the affection he now felt, so different an affection, for irrepressible, outspoken, sensual Paris.

Not that he had much time to think about these things during the process of winning a steady job with the bureau: he was mastering a brand new kind of newspapering. Whereas in Paris he'd been a minor cog in a sizable reporting staff, with most of his work outside the office, here he was general utility man in an organism of four persons where, except for an occasional interview, much

113

of his time was spent poring over and rewriting the British press, boiling it down to capsule size and transmitting it by cable to New York in competition with Associated Press, United Press, Reuters agency and the correspondents of major American newspapers.

But the work was more important than it sounded, particularly as to his personal development. In Paris, even on the Riviera, he'd still been a fledgling, trying his wings, grasping the fundamentals of his trade. Now he was an established journalist with recognized responsibility, of whom a fixed standard of performance was expected. He was learning that a newsman's job could hardly be separated from his life; *was*, in fact, his life, twenty-four hours a day. Moreover the whole atmosphere of the news had changed: international tension was rising over the emergence of a threatening Nazi Germany, the daily news was predominantly political, and a sense of foreboding was beginning to grip all Europe.

David Brent had a lot to catch up with if he was to progress as a chronicler of world events. He was entering a new phase of maturity. Preoccupied with his work, digesting an almost overwhelming mass of material, he hardly noticed the passing of the months which, in a strange way, seemed both swift and slow at the same time, so intense was his study of political history as the background to the fast-moving contemporary situation. Realization came only gradually that his emotional outlook, the very chemistry of his body, was changing. He hadn't had a sexual experience since France; that hardly seemed possible to him but it was a fact. And he wondered about it. Although his professional colleagues offered casual friendship, he'd become necessarily something of a loner, which wasn't like him. Was it a matter of the British food he ate, the beer and ale instead of wine, that was altering his sensual perceptions? Was it the cool, stodgy ambiance of the great gray city of London itself?

Through Jack Hawley, the dignified middle-aged bureau chief, he'd luckily found and kept a tiny apartment off Montagu Square and had settled into a comfortable routine. But lately, almost in spite of himself, he'd begun to remember his Paris life again, and especially those days on the Riviera, with a poignant longing. Early in his London stay he'd exchanged letters with Jamie Blake, but he soon realized that Jamie was no letter writer, and to his disappointment the exchange dwindled and died.

His own sister was a better correspondent than anybody he knew. Faithfully, at intervals of a month or so, Cathy had written the family news, which wasn't much but she made it seem so with her unfailing cheerfulness and sly sense of humor. His mother was having more trouble with her eyes so Cathy wrote for two. She had graduated from her nursing course, at long last, and could have become an RN but decided she didn't like working with doctors. (Brent wondered if sexual considerations had entered into the decision, but couldn't picture Cathy—thin, slightly gawky Cathy—as a sex object.) She was much happier now, she said, working as a receptionist in a Madison Avenue advertising office. And, closing this latest letter as she always did, there was her half-teasing reference to his own sexual considerations—*What*, no steady girl yet!— and so on.

Why was there no female friend of his in England, at least so far, who seemed worth more than a casual glance? English girls had a charm of their own, of course—the famous complexion, for one thing, and a sturdy, fresh cheerfulness. But somehow they lacked the American flair of a girl like Jamie, the smoldering sex attraction of Claudine, the disarming appeal of Tanya. Tanya! How long ago it seemed, and how much had happened to him since then.

Tonight, over his usual bedtime drink in the pub near his apartment, he lingered and ruminated about the past —about Helen and Hap Osgood especially. He no longer felt anger toward Hap; he wished him well. He missed Helen; she had been a friend, and somehow he felt she always would be. Wherever she was, she had a part of him with her. And he grinned in his reflections—he knew which part of him *that* was; he could hear her saying it, see her smile.

Around him in the smoky pub the talk was all politics and imminent war. His journalist colleagues all regarded war as inevitable now. They were a serious, sober-minded lot, especially the British. The only one of the bunch who seemed to be having a gay time was an American, Hank Fisher, the number-two man in the UBC radio bureau, and right now Hank was sitting in this pub by the window with Beryl Downing, Jack Hawley's secretary at the

*Trib.* At least they had been there when Brent came in; he turned and glanced in their direction and they were still sitting there.

Hank saw him, grinned and waved a beckoning hand. Brent took his half-finished drink and joined them. Beryl was leaning on Hank's shoulder, flushed and full of food and drink. She was wearing a skirt that ended about two inches below the crotch. Brent grinned at her, then at the skirt.

"Would Jack Hawley approve?" he asked.

"Fuck Jack Hawley," said Beryl.

"Fuck him?" said Fisher. "You can't even approach him. Irish coffee, Dave?"

"I don't mind if I do." He swallowed the rest of his Scotch.

Beryl seemed to be sizing him up. It was the first time he'd seen her, outside the office. "You know, Brent, you're not half bad-looking."

"Thank you." He raised his glass and bowed. "I kind of like your looks, too."

"No shit?" she said, and giggled.

He was grinning. This was the correct and composed Miss Downing? She must have got her Americanese from Jack.

"If you like her looks," Fisher said, "you should see her girlfriend." He looked at his watch. "As a matter of fact we're supposed to be meeting her just about now."

Beryl said, "Oh-oh, mustn't be late, Hank. We promised."

Fisher was paying the check. "C'mon along, Dave, we'll make it a foursome. And don't look at me that way —I'll bet it's the first night you've been on the town since you hit London."

"Almost," he admitted. "But I've got a heavy day tomorrow."

"You'll like the place," Beryl drawled. "Just a quiet little pub called the Cock and Balls."

Hank guffawed. "She's pulling your leg, Dave. If there's one thing it's not, it's quiet."

"I'd *like* to pull his leg," Beryl said, "only tonight I'm pulling *your* leg, Hank."

"Maybe some other night," Brent said.

"Ah, no you don't!" Beryl was standing beside him

now and holding tight to his arm while Hank paid the bill. "When you see Audrey you'll be sooo glad you came."

He allowed himself to be coaxed. The combination of Scotch and Irish whiskey was beginning to do something to him, the old feeling of anything goes he hadn't had since the Riviera.

There was no sign outside when the taxi drew up to the door. It was a low-ceilinged place with a service bar at one side and candlelit tables; Hank paid some kind of club fee for him as they came in. Audrey was sitting at a table in the corner, very blonde, quite young and busty. She flashed them a brilliant smile. "Look what I found for you," Beryl told her as they came up.

"Ooh!" said Audrey, barely audible in the noisy room.

Fisher ordered Scotch all around. It tasted thinner than the drink at the pub. Brent said, "What do you do, Audrey?"

"I'm like her, ducks, I'm a secretary, what did you think I did?"

"Model, perhaps."

She crowed. "I have done, here and there. Beryl, luv, I like your friend." But Beryl was concentrating on Brent.

"I want to ask you a question, David, you don't mind if I call you David? Hawley doesn't like us to use first names in the office but I knew right away you weren't a stuffy bastard like him, okay?"

"Okay."

"Don't you think Hank and I should get married?"

"Of course you should get married." He grinned at Fisher.

"I told you so!" she cried, and hugged Hank.

"I have to get rid of a wife first," Hank said.

"You've been saying that for a year!"

"And any guy lucky enough to get rid of his wife is crazy if he gets married again, right, Dave?"

Brent laughed. "I'm staying out of this."

Audrey reached over and took his hand and put it in her lap and held it there. "I don't like this place," she pouted. "I want to go somewhere and dance."

"I'm in favor," Brent said. She felt warm and soft under the thin dress and the drinks buzzed happily in his head.

The others were agreeable, and all four crowded to-

gether in the taxi. He had thought the first place was noisy;
the next one was pandemonium, much bigger, jammed with
dancers on the small smoky floor, and with a live, long-
haired band that never stopped shouting. Audrey was
clinging to him as they lurched in the smoke haze. "Is
New York like this?" she was saying at his shoulder.

"Sort of."

"I think I'll give New York a whirl."

"Why not?"

"They want us, you know."

"I've heard that."

"Will you be there?"

"Who knows? Maybe off and on."

"That sounds nice," and she laughed.

"What sounds nice?"

"Off and on, with you." She was rubbing her thighs
against his legs as they moved and he held her closer.

"I'm sorry I'm not a good dancer."

"What, ducks?"

"I said I'm sorry I'm not a better dancer."

Laughing again, "How are you in bed?"

"A matter of opinion, I guess."

He hadn't had this much to drink since the *Trib*'s
farewell party in Paris, and maybe it was what he needed
now and then. Audrey was like a ripe peach in his arms;
he had a sudden desire to see the big breasts that were
pushing at his chest. Back at the table Audrey was restless
again, so they all resumed their swaying progress across the
city, stopping next at a gambling club in Mayfair where
Hank had done a story for his network and was welcome with friends, drinks on the house.

Next it was an amateur striptease dive in a little street
off Leicester Square. They had to push their way through a
motley mob of young people congregated outside to get
into it. "Filthy scum!" muttered Beryl in her best office
manner, but she watched with fascinated attention, and so
did Aubrey, once they were settled at a table. Once Audrey gripped his arm and whispered, "I can show you better than that," and he laughed and kissed her cheek. Hank
Fisher leaned over and leered at them, "You like this one,
Dave, she's yours!" and Audrey said, "Oh, shut up, Hank,
don't be disgusting!"

To Brent the parade of volunteer strippers, with its

quality of awkward innocence and anxiety, was more
touching than sexually exciting. It was Audrey's hand that
was arousing him, lying as if unaware on his lap but he
knew she could feel him hardening through his trousers.
Half an hour later, as they were leaving, he heard his own
voice blurred and halting, "Listen, Hank—I owe you half
on tonight, only got a couple of pounds left—"

"Forget it," Fisher said. "And the rest of the night is
free for both of us."

Hank's digs were the upper floor of a small Georgian
house on an obscure street that had seen better days. The
first light of dawn was visible in the misty sky as they went
in and stumbled laughing up the stairs. Fisher lost no time
once they were in his flat. He took Beryl by the hand,
"Come on, baby!" and they vanished into the bedroom,
closing the door behind them.

Still laughing, Brent and Audrey looked at each other.
"It's the usual drill," Audrey said, and he thought she
chose her words well; he took her in his arms.

"You'll do the right thing by me, sir? You'll leave 'arf
a quid on the mantel?" The tinge of cockney in her voice
broadened to the full twang.

"More, my good woman, if you make it worth my
while."

But already he was beginning to realize he didn't want
it that much—not this, not Audrey. He could tell in her
kiss she had been used a lot. The big breasts were soft,
too soft, in his hands. And it was all too calculated. Was
it Jamie Blake who had changed him, spoiled him for
the casual encounter? Oh, he'd take this English girl, now
they'd come this far, but would it mean anything? He
looked down at Audrey lying on the couch and looking up
at him, her dress pulled down to her waist, the skirt up,
her eyes saying, "Well? *Well?*"

"In a minute," he heard himself say to her. "First, is
there anything to drink around here?"

# 21

He didn't see Audrey again. And somewhat to his surprise, given the circumstances, she made no overtures. But that was like the English. He had sensed, in the very act of intercourse, that she knew his heart wasn't in it despite his vigorous efforts to fuck her well and soundly. And she reciprocated with a lusty zest of her own, whispering cockney obscenities in his ear to intensify the orgasm.

There was no change in Beryl's attitude. In the office she was as cool and polite as ever, giving the boss no opportunity to complain of her familiarity, though Brent suspected Hawley was aware of Beryl's free and easy life on the outside. By chance Brent was alone in the lift with her one evening a few days after the pub crawl with Hank Fisher. Their eyes met and she smiled like her other self.

"How's Audrey?" he said.

"Pulling along. Did you have fun the other night?"

"Very much."

"Audrey says you don't fancy her."

The bluntness of it startled him a little. "I liked her," he protested.

"But it's not the same thing," she smiled. "G'night, David!"

He let her flounce on ahead of him and into the London night, and wondered if she was trotting off to meet Fisher. For once, the city was experiencing the rare thrill of a prolonged dry spell, and he decided to walk home instead of queuing up for the bus, his usual routine. For over a week now there had been no real rain, and London basked happily in the sunny days and starry nights, enjoying every minute while it lasted. But Brent felt there was more to it than that, and was sure the English knew, too. It was as though they were becoming aware that Britain was drifting into a deepening political crisis that might soon

120

envelop the whole Western world in war, and were determined to enjoy these fleeting days of peace and stability to the full while they lasted; who knew how long it would be before Britain would see such tranquillity again.

Strolling along in the fading rays of twilight, he crossed the imaginary border of Mayfair and found himself on Whore Street, as Hawley bitterly termed it. A long-time resident of Mayfair himself, the bureau chief had recently moved with his wife and two young sons to St. John's Wood to escape the rapid decay of what was formerly London's most elegant residential neighborhood. Now as darkness fell it seemed there was a woman, sometimes two or three, standing in every doorway of once smart townhouses and even reaching out to grasp the arm of a likely prospect as he passed. Many of them were West Indians, calling in low musical voices from the gloom of areaways; then, farther along, the whites took over, a motley crowd of all sizes, ages, some astonishingly young—fifteen, fourteen—rakishly dressed with lewd painted faces like Rowlandson portraits. And a forgotten verse rang suddenly in his head, something by William Blake he'd memorized in college . . . *The harlot's cry from street to street/Shall weave old England's winding sheet* . . . Had London changed so much since Blake's day?

Near the end of the block a woman thrust herself suddenly in front of him, illuminated by the street lamp overhead in dramatic silhouette. Beside her stood a girl who couldn't have been over sixteen, and in the moment of encounter Brent saw their likeness to each other—the bold, fresh features, the jaunty smile. " 'Ere now, there's a sport!" the woman said. "Looking for a bit of fun, I shouldn't wonder."

He paused in his step and looked from one to the other, half responding to the contagious smiles. Instantly they moved closer, as though to surround him. He laughed in spite of himself, at the same time piqued by their boldness.

"Take it easy," he muttered.

"I'll take it any way I can get it if the price is right," the woman laughed. She was looking him up and down. "How much does the gentleman offer? You got a bargain, y'know. Two for the price o' one."

"You must be sisters," he said.

"Correct the first time!" She grinned cockily up at him. "And you must be American, am I right or am I right?"

He hesitated. He had been about to brush past them but the unexpectedness of it had caught him unawares, and he realized now he was curious about them; he wanted to know more. But he couldn't just stand here in the street with them, and he couldn't take them to his apartment or even to a bar, not in Mayfair. Now that he'd observed them, they weren't respectable-looking by any means but they weren't repulsive either; they both looked healthy and clean under all the makeup and there was something genuinely friendly in their approach.

The younger one hadn't spoken at all. The other watched him with knowing appraisal. "Tryin' to make up your mind, are you? Just take your time. And don't fret over a place to go—Becky and I've got a cosy little nest for you right around the corner. Discreet, you might say." She chuckled. "But remember—it's both of us together or nothing. I keep an eye on Becky."

That was what decided him. A strange little setup—sisters, and sticking together. He smiled and knew they knew they'd made a deal.

"I'm Mildred," she said. "We'll talk the money later."

And he found himself walking between them, each holding an arm, as they strolled on.

Their place, the second floor rear of a neat little house off Shepherd Market, was only one room with bath but surprisingly clean and well-furnished. He wasn't sure yet what would happen—maybe nothing, but the adventure of it gave him a pleasant sense of excitement. Mildred took a bottle off the mantel and poured them each a modest whiskey. She gave Brent her engaging grin. "What do we call you, ducks?"

"Call me Ducks." He looked at the younger girl. "Cat got your tongue, Becky?"

She had a lusty little laugh. "Mildred handles the business, Ducks."

Mildred was still smiling but her voice had an edge to it. "Shall we get the business over with? We shan't haggle. You're a gentleman, Ducks—I could see that soon's I laid eyes on you. Let's say you put two quid on the shelf there and whatever more it's worth to you when you leave, now isn't that fair?"

"Very fair, Mildred." They watched him as he laid the two bills on the mantel. He knew enough to be cautious— waited for them to sip their drink before he touched his own; he doubted they'd use knockout drops and rob him of the rest of his money but he couldn't be sure of them. He turned back to them, smiling. "Nice little flat you've got here."

"Maybe you'll like it well enough to come back some time. Over here, Ducks." Mildred patted the pillows on the big bed. "Now lie down there like a good lad and relax a little."

Obediently he followed instructions and let her loosen his collar and unbutton his vest and shirt. "Now, isn't that better?" Her fingers slipped inside his shirt and lightly, expertly roved over his bare chest, flicking the nipples with a sensitive touch. At the same time Becky joined her sister sitting on the bed and slipped off his shoes, softly rubbing his ankles with warm hands.

He closed his eyes and let them have their way. His body was responding, the nipples hardening like a woman's and his penis stiffening inside his trousers. "That good, Ducks?" Mildred was crooning as her fingers crept lower over his belly. With the other hand she loosened his belt, opened his fly and pulled very lightly at the hairs below, still not touching the cock that rose now toward full hard. Behind her, Becky was reaching up under his trouser legs along his calves, kneading the muscles, steadily moving higher until she reached the knees, then withdrawing with small squeezing motions to the ankles again, slipping off his socks one by one.

He spoke, barely above a whisper, his eyes still closed. "You two know your job."

"We enjoy it, don't we, Becky? Specially when we get a young gentleman like you."

"How old are you, Becky?"

Again the lusty little laugh, but no answer.

Mildred said, "Sit up now and let me peel off the jacket." Obeying, he felt for a moment like a man in a hospital bed being cared for by two nurses, but no hospital was like this. As he lay down on his back once more

Mildred expertly pulled off his trousers. Then it was Becky's turn. Leaning forward, she slipped down his undershorts and left him naked.

"Better, isn't it, Ducks?"

He smiled and nodded, looking past Mildred toward Becky who was looking at his distended column with a little smile. It stretched out flat against his belly, straining to full length and stirring with life of its own. He saw a pearl of mucous liquid slowly forming at the tip and his body shivered involuntarily with excitement. More than anything he wanted to be grasped and held, and Mildred knew; Mildred knew everything. With her crooning sigh she took the cock in both hands, caressing, squeezing, as he lifted his body to meet it. "He likes it, he likes this . . ." Mildred was saying like a mother to a baby. "Look at 'im, Becky . . ." But Becky was doing more than that. With a swift, easy motion she dropped forward between his open legs, her warm breath suddenly at his crotch, and he felt her tongue flicking at his balls, at the insides of his thighs, her lips tugging gently at hot flesh, licking, sucking, kissing, while Mildred's hand along the shaft tightened and began a soft jacking motion, urging the skin up and down.

He knew he couldn't stand this much longer, feeling the penis swell and the scrotum tighten helplessly while exquisite sensation spread through his belly and thighs and radiated over his whole body. Mildred knew. Mildred always knew. She bent close to his ear and whispered, "Want it this way, Ducks? Want to come off?" But he shook his head—that was too soon, too quick. He wanted to savor his delicious experience; he wanted . . .

Opening his eyes again he saw them both withdraw from him as if by subtle, silent intercommunication. They were smiling at him and Mildred, as always, spoke for his desire. "He wants cunt, Becky. A man needs cunt to satisfy 'im all the way. That right, Ducks? You know it is. A woman wants cock, too. And don't think I don't want that big lovely thing rearin' up at me right now, because I do. I really do."

He lay there watching her stand up and strip off her clothes, watched a strong, compact body emerge before his hungry eyes, with firm breasts, swelling hips, rich delta of blonde hair at the belly. She was better than he could have expected, but in this moment of overpowering lust he would take anything, whore or angel. Becky stood up and moved to the other side of the bed, never taking her eyes off her sister, watching her as she lay down beside the stranger whose body Becky had just tasted with her mouth and hands, watching the man rise and kneel between the opening thighs, the hand that guided the straining cock into its waiting furrow, watching like a student at an operation.

He pumped hard and joyously, grasping the pumping buttocks under him, striking deep, feeling new strength with each lunge, doing this better than he'd ever done it, he knew that now, and knowing it was because Becky was watching. Was Mildred feeling that too?—feeling her sister's eyes avid upon them, seeing her sister lean over behind him to watch the glistening instrument that plunged and withdrew from the dark recesses? She would see it all now because far back he felt the tightening ecstasy of orgasm begin, it would be soon now, very soon, a minute or less, the seconds intensifying, and as the final moments increased the pace to headlong frenzy he felt Becky's fingers close on the plunging balls, swinging with them, squeezing, tighter and tighter until with that last supreme plunge they seemed to squeeze the last drop of semen from his body.

For a long time he lay there in silence after he withdrew, feeling not exhausted but renewed and revivified. Mildred got up and went into the bathroom, and as he watched her go he wondered about whores. Was she really as moved, sensually, as she had seemed to be? Surely there was no difference between her enthusiasm for what was happening and the transports of a lover. Whatever she felt, he felt grateful to her for the deep pleasures she had aroused in him. And what of Becky? She was sitting quietly in the big chair across the room, smiling at him. What had been her feelings as participant in the scene, when she had reached and held him as intimately as a woman can hold a man?

"Come over and sit beside me again," he said, and obediently she rose and sat down on the bed. He took her hand. "I guess I'm taking up a lot of your time, Becky. I guess you and Mildred want to get rid of me now and go after your next customer."

She shook her head, still smiling. For the first time, looking at her voluptuous young body, the knees slightly apart, he saw that she wore nothing underneath. Immediately he felt reaction in his loins. "I noticed how closely you watched me with Mildred. Why did you watch so closely, Becky?"

The question amused her. "Learning," was all she said.

"You mean you haven't had a man yet, yourself?"

She chose not to reply, and her enigmatic little smile aroused him further. He felt his cock stiffening and put her hand on it. She didn't resist his gesture but her fingers lay passively, not moving, while she watched him with dark blue eyes alive and alert.

"Does it excite you to see Mildred with a man, or are you used to it?"

She gave the faintest of shrugs. "Sometimes I like to see it."

"Did you like to see it tonight?"

The little smile widened. "Couldn't you tell?"

"I'll tell you something, Becky. The most exciting part of all was when you took me in your hand. I'll never forget that."

And suddenly, almost as if she was unaware of it, her fingers trembled and then closed around the staff of flesh under her hand. He stirred and spoke. "I want to fuck you, Becky. Will you take me? Now? Not because I'm paying for it. I'll pay anyway. But only if you want it from me. Only if you want me to fuck you, now."

She wasn't smiling any longer. He saw a tremor at her lips as though she started to say something but couldn't find the words. Then without further hesitation she stood up and dropped her skirt, revealing shapely young legs and a small patch of pale red hair at the crotch. For a moment she was motionless. The firm-fleshed round belly, half-exposed below the brief blouse she wore, was rising and falling quickly. He raised his head and saw her mouth parted, expectant. "Becky," he said, and reached for her, his arms around her, his hands crushing luscious buttocks and drawing her down beside him on the bed. She was still watching him as he knelt in his nakedness between her thighs and lifted her calves, pushed them gently backward till her knees were almost touching her shoulders. Slipping into her, deep, deeper, he felt her tight but not too tight, the soft folds pulsating, the innermost flesh sticky and warm. Just once she moaned, faintly, and looking down at her he saw the dark blue eyes darker before they closed. Her arms were around his back and tightening.

Mildred, coming out of the bathroom, stopped on the threshold and smiled.

# 22

For days thereafter he felt a nagging desire to return to
Whore Street, find Mildred and Becky again, and repeat
the experience. But he held off. For one thing, he realized
almost as soon as he'd left them that evening that he'd let
himself get carried away by his need for sexual outlet, relief from the long period of abstinence broken only by the
one night with Hank Fisher and his two girlfriends. After
all, Mildred and Becky were prostitutes, and intercourse
with them courted the risk of gonorrhea or worse; he
washed carefully as soon as he got back to his apartment
and hoped uneasily that he hadn't picked up anything. Yet
the memory of his enjoyment lingered on at the back of
his mind as he plunged back into his work at the bureau.
He'd liked them as *persons* somehow, not as faceless,
anonymous streetwalkers who'd happened to cross his
path. Mildred and Becky, both so friendly and cheerful in
their cockney brashness. But he had to watch himself—
an affection of that kind could become a habit, dangerous
and expensive as well. Sexual loneliness had its pitfalls
for the unwary.

Nevertheless, after scrupulously avoiding their neighborhood for several weeks, the urge was too strong to resist one night as he walked home, and once more he found
himself on the same block as he crossed Mayfair. And he
did see them, together as always, as he approached the
corner where they first accosted him. But they were busily
occupied with two middle-aged men—Mildred, in fact,
had already linked arms with one of them, and the other
was looking lasciviously at young Becky.

They didn't see him as he passed by and he was glad
they didn't. Somehow he felt cheated or annoyed that
they hadn't been free, especially at Becky's little smile as
she looked up at her prospective customer. For a few

moments that he wouldn't soon forget, Brent had believed that smile belonged to him. He didn't want to imagine it any other way. And he realized, hurrying on, that it was best not to think about Becky or Mildred any more.

As it happened, this turned out to be easier than expected. Only a few days later, and for the first time, Jack Hawley invited him to dinner at his house in St. John's Wood, among other guests. Daphne Cortland was one of them.

For Brent the meeting was an event. They were not seated together at the table for eight but he had a three-quarter profile view of her without staring and she was a real beauty, English style—perfect body, golden hair and skin, upper-class accent and manners, violet eyes. She might be thirty or thereabouts, a very sophisticated, worldly thirty who'd been everywhere and seen everything, by contrast to Edna Hawley, who after eight years in London was still as middlewest American as Terre Haute. And Daphne Cortland's voice—smoky, insinuating, challenging —was most alluring of all. Taken together, her charms were the charms of a woman he could never hope to possess; she was out of his class; they were a world apart.

And out of the class of the others at table—a visiting Ohio college professor and his wife, an editor from the London *Morning Post*, evidently a bachelor, and a middle-aged woman who was a house guest of the Hawley's; Brent couldn't decide from her speech whether she was British or American. Sitting there only half-listening to her chatter beside him, he tried to follow Daphne Courtland's conversation with Jack Hawley and gathered she was the wife of a Guards officer on duty in the Suez Canal area. She brought her fresh Scotch and soda to the table with her. She smoked incessantly. She ignored everyone except her host and never once looked in Brent's direction.

It was the same after dinner; she occupied a corner of the living room, beautiful legs well displayed under the short skirt of what must have been a costly dress, with Jack Hawley still hovering, keeping her brandy snifter well filled, lighting her chain-smoked cigarettes. The college professor earnestly told Brent how lucky he was to be working in London at such an interesting time in history and wished he himself could stay on. His wife and Mrs. Hawley's house guest found each other congenial, while

Edna talked desultorily with the editor. Out of caution, Brent resisted his impulse to join the host and his seductive guest in their corner chat and was relieved when the professor's wife stood up, announced it was her bedtime, and brought the evening to an end.

At the door, after kissing Jack and Edna dutifully on the cheek and smiling brightly if vacantly at the others, Daphne Cortland looked at Brent as if seeing him for the first time. The professor and his wife, with the editor in tow, were getting into their rented car and waving goodbye. The house guest had already said goodnight and removed herself upstairs. Mrs. Cortland said, "Can I give you a lift, Mr. Brent?"

Why did it seem she said it with double meaning? "I don't want to take you out of your way," he said.

The dazzling smile, with slightly glazed eyes. "No trouble at all, really."

Edna Hawley shook hands with them both and Jack patted him on the shoulder. But was there a trace of jealousy or envy in his grin? "No use telling Daphne to drive carefully," he said. "She never does."

She had a two-seater white Jaguar with open top. It figured. And he saw what Jack Hawley meant—she was not only reckless, she was drunk. He felt a little drunk himself, drunk enough not to worry about a few hairbreadth misses on the road, drunk enough to feel a sense of elation at being with Daphne Cortland. The breeze unfurled the top of her skirt and he caught a glimpse of slender thigh as they sped through sparse traffic. Neither spoke a word, and it was ten minutes or more before he realized they were not headed into central London but away from it. He also realized he had not given her his address.

"Lovely night," she said then. "Too early to go home, don't you think?"

"I agree. Where are we going, by the way?"

"Anywhere."

He laughed. "I agree with that, too. Tomorrow's my day off."

"Your day off has already begun."

Something had begun. They didn't have far to go; Daphne Cortland's cottage in Surrey was only half an hour away. It was while she was pouring them a nightcap in her small, elegantly rustic living room that he realized neither had spoken on the last lap of their journey, in fact they'd hardly exchanged a word all evening. Already Jack Hawley's dinner party was receding rapidly into the past. It was still hard to believe so much had happened in so short a time.

Daphne, infinitely desirable in the lamplight, raised her glass and toasted him with a smile. "Welcome to my hearth and home."

He grinned. "Do you know that's the longest speech you've made to me since we met?"

She shrugged, beautifully. "Words are mostly useless, don't you think? It's only actions that count. Life is actually very simple. Either one does, or one doesn't. Shall we bathe and then sleep a while?"

He felt his heart thumping. "Excellent idea," he said. He could be as casual as she was.

The upstairs was a movie love nest: one huge bed filling almost all of the low-ceilinged room, with separate dressing rooms and bathrooms on either side. She pointed. "That's Jeremy's side. Being an American you probably prefer to shower. Afterward, you'll find me in my tub, waiting for you to soap me."

Under the shower he wondered about Jeremy and his tour of duty out there in Egypt with the Guards. Did he know his wife was spending evenings like this in England? He'd gathered from Hank Fisher that the upper-class British could be promiscuous, or at least have a steady lover, without affecting their marriages. The trick was to keep the liaison strictly separate, never mention it, never let it interfere with the routine of a proper marital relationship. Toweling himself after the shower he looked at Jeremy Courtland's closets, at the rows of expensive suits, the drawers of shirts and sweaters, the boot racks. Whatever the sources of the Cortland income, he had plenty of it; maybe they both came of rich families.

Wearing one of Jeremy's dressing gowns, he crossed the room and went into Daphne's bathroom. She was waiting for him, a rosy young Venus lying in a pool of scented bubbles, dainty knees and ankles floating on the surface, the blonde cloud of her sex peeping through the foam. For the first time he saw the breasts, as perfect as the rest of her. She smiled up at him, her chin just above water, a glossy plastic cap covering her hair. "Here," said the smoky voice, and she handed him a piece of perfumed soap.

The tub was half again as long as her body and a good two feet deep. Kneeling beside it, he passed the round, smooth ball over her glistening skin in slow, gentle strokes, first the throat and shoulders, then the armpits, afterward each breast, lingeringly, feeling her torso stir under his hands and watching the nipples harden as she closed her eyes in exquisite sensation. Minutes passed like an eternity of pleasure. Now he was giving the soft white belly prolonged attention, massaging slowly, feeling it give and swell under his delicate pressure, before dropping his hand to her feet and ankles and working upward, still slowly, pausing at each inch of her yielding flesh with his touch, kneading the backs of the slender calves, over and around the dimpled knees, the thighs that floated lazily weightless as his hand reached inward between them and found its way underneath the buttocks to draw her body toward him, caressing and squeezing their delicious contours until at last it held the golden delta, the ultimate goal, her crotch agape for his exploring fingers.

The soap slipped from his grasp, floating away as her thighs swung wide, wider at the touch of his fingers between the open lips. Gradually, infinitely tender, they pressed inside—first two fingers, then three forming a soapy wedge, feeling the pulsing tissues tighten deep inside her. He heard her dreamlike moan and felt her whole body tingling; involuntarily her thighs came together in the water and she opened her eyes. *"Wait!"* she gasped. *"Oh wait, my darling . . . Do you know what you're doing to me?"* Then he was lifting her onto the floor, drying her with the huge enveloping towel that hung on the rack beside them, and she was leading the way into the bedroom where she took a small vial from the bed-table and, sitting on the bed, soaked his penis with its sweet-smelling lubricant. He stared in surprise—surely they had no need for this. But a moment later he understood.

Standing again, she rubbed more of the lubricant deep between her buttocks, reaching behind her, then turned her back to him and knelt on the edge of the bed, the exquisite white and gold ass thrust upward, open, revealing the anal cleft. Her voice was small, tense, urgent, almost as if in pain. *"Take it!"* she whispered. *"You must, you must!"*

He needed no further entreaty. Without hesitation he moved nearer, opened her buttocks still wider with both hands, and for the first time in his life penetrated the most secret recess of a woman's body. She gave a low, anguished cry and thrust her body closer to him as he forced the narrow passage to the hilt. Never had he been held so tightly, a prisoner of her passion; she was rocking back and forth against him. And never, as he held her belly with both hands, swaying in rhythm with her motion, had he felt a woman's body so alive, so electric, so hot, had he been so excited by her excitement. He couldn't hold back his orgasm any longer, not with the stimulus of that half-hour touching her in the bath, and now this emotion that was like delirium for her. He knew she could feel him coming; her movements increased to frenzy; he was hurting her and she wanted it; all at once she collapsed and they fell forward together, still locked in the most intimate of all embraces, his weight overwhelming her, her scent intoxicating him, and the sound of her sobbing gratitude filling the room.

# 23

He had thought, in the days that followed, that Daphne would be easy to know well; that a woman who could give herself so completely physically on the first night she met a man was at basis simple, direct and uncomplicated in character. Certainly, he reasoned, David Brent was no great catch in Daphne's world—neither rich nor glamorous nor handsome in the conventional sense. And she was young enough to take her pick anywhere among the best of them—this was no case of an older woman seeking youth to reassure herself that life had not passed her by. So she had taken this chance acquaintance to her arms, to her bed, for reasons still obscure to him. Why not just consider himself lucky and stop wondering why? Daphne Cortland was everything that any man could want in a sexual relationship—beautiful, passionate and otherwise undemanding. As Daphne said, it was only actions that counted. She was a woman of very few words and a lot of action. Still, he wanted to know more about her life when she was away from him. He wanted to picture her in the context of the rest of her world. But something in her remained mysterious.

It was only gradually that the picture began to come clear. In the first weeks and months after their meeting and the glorious night in Surrey, they were together frequently, sometimes at the cottage in the country, sometimes at her chic little flat in Knightsbridge. He soon learned to let Daphne propose the date; he found that when he called her she was almost invariably either not at home or she told him she was otherwise engaged—meaning, she would explain with a little grimace of annoyance, with Jeremy's parents or her own doting father, a widower who lived at the exclusive Albany apartments. Unlike most

women, Daphne didn't want to be taken out to dinner or
the theater or night clubs. When she was with Brent the
occasion was for sex, insatiable sex, the most satisfying
experiences he'd ever had, always accompanied by Scotch
or brandy or both. Nothing deterred her lust for him; even
menstruation simply sharpened her imperious desire. It
was too exciting to become monotonous, yet he did feel
he owed her a little change from time to time, and he was
pleased when she accepted an invitation to dine with him
at Waldo's in Soho.

He'd discovered Waldo's through an English colleague
—it was small, discreet, excellent food, the friendly social
ambiance of a pub and, best of all, within his means. A
number of heads turned when he came in that evening with
Daphne, smashing as usual and wearing a new Paris dinner
suit that would have been more at home at the Mira-
belle. He'd hoped she would like Waldo's and he wasn't
disappointed; several times she murmured her approval
and glanced about the room. He never ceased to wonder at
her capacity for liquor: tonight, as customary, she had four
Scotches before they began to eat, and washed her food
down with an expensive Burgundy she selected from the
menu herself. Through all this, he had to ask himself what
they'd talked about, aside from his recital of life at the
bureau. Daphne talked mostly with her eyes, or with a
hand upon his hand on the table, or, once, since they
were sitting on a corner banquette, side by side, her other
hand at the same time lay on his lap, softly fingering the
buttons on his fly one by one. By the time they finished
eating it was after eleven and the earlier dinner crowd had
departed; now Waldo's was getting a fresh group of after-
theater people at the tables and mostly stags at the bar.

Waldo himself offered his best brandy, beaming upon
Daphne, and the talk at the tables around them became a
general exchange in which admiring glances were cast in
Daphne's direction. At one point, a youngish dark-haired
man sauntered over from the bar bearing a brandy in each
hand and insisted on their accepting it. Daphne acknowledged the gift with a brilliant smile but Brent decided,
after the man retreated to the bar, that he'd better get
Daphne back to her flat while they could still navigate, and
called for the bill. It was a long time coming, and while

they waited he excused himself to go to the men's room. When he came back Daphne was gone and so was the man at the bar.

Waldo, waiting with the check, said no, Madame was not in the ladies' room. Waldo assumed Madame was waiting outside with the other gentleman. At the same time Waldo managed to look both sympathetic and amused. Brent paid and left, knowing already there was no one waiting for him outside and realizing what had actually happened. The alcohol in him cushioned the blow, but had he any right to expect anything else, Daphne Cortland being Daphne Cortland?

He was learning. He didn't rush to Knightsbridge and beat angrily on her door. Nor did he call her next day from the office to inquire. Nor did he mention it, a few days later, when she called him to invite him to Surrey on the next weekend. She didn't mention it either, and by the time they drove down together in the Jaguar it seemed better all round just to forget it. And somehow, surprisingly, it gave a new edge to their sexual encounter that night. Daphne's life had a new dimension for him: other men. Several times, early in the relationship, he'd asked her about her husband, but her cool, evasive reaction soon taught him this was in the no-no category. She was more forthright in their intimate relations, refusing fellatio and flatly asserting that cunnilingus was no fun. But she did offer her breasts to his tongue; his sucking mouth at her nipples aroused her to such excitement that she climaxed in minutes, the first in a series of preliminary orgasms that built toward the final tear-flooded paroxysm. In such moments, all defenses down, the Daphne she withheld from him was suddenly honest and direct.

Lying face to face with him in the warm darkness, her brief whispered words had the quality of confession, though she offered no apologies and remained imperturbable. Only in these fleeting moments could he feel they were friends as well as lovers. Only in those moments did she tell him, little by little, what he should have guessed from the beginning: she was a hopeless nymphomaniac. Maybe after all he would not have guessed, because she was so good at drawing the curtain over the rest of her life, that a hundred men had fucked her, maybe more, maybe many more, before and after her marriage. It happened on the spur, at any hour of day or night—in bed, on the floor, on stair landings, alleyways, anywhere; they were men she had known or men she'd picked up or who'd picked her up, like the man bearing brandy at Waldo's. Brent wanted to know more about that night but he felt the lovely shoulders shrug as if to say it was always the same.

"Where did you go with him?" he whispered.

"Here."

"Didn't you have any regard for my feelings at all?"

"I knew you'd understand."

"Did he fuck you well?"

Again the faint shrug against his chest. "I don't remember."

"Did you take him in the ass?"

"I don't remember."

A pause. "Do I fuck you well?"

But already the other Daphne was receding. "Don't be childish," she said. "I want a drink."

It had to wait until the next time, when once again profiting by the post-coital frankness he asked her if Jack Hawley had ever taken her.

"Of course."

"And Jeremy never knew about any of them?"

Like all questions about Jeremy, it was not directly answered. Instead she said, a faint smile at her lips dimly discernible, "Jeremy is no innocent. He learned all there is to know at quite an early age, I suspect. When he was at Harrow his housemaster used to come to his room every night after lights-out and suck him off."

"Did it turn him into a homosexual?"

"How do you Americans say it?—he's AC-DC. And I think that's why he likes his foreign tours of duty. Which is not to say he doesn't have his little affairs in England."

"And you don't object?"

"Idiot, how could I!"

"When does he come home from Suez?"

"He has another six months. By that time we'll probably be fighting the Russians, won't we?"

"By that time we may be fighting the Germans."

"A pity. I rather like the Germans."

"From personal experience?"

"Rather. There was a young baron who . . ." She

stopped, possibly to tantalize him. "I don't think I'll tell you, it's too horrible."

"I thought you liked the Germans."

"Gottfried was frightful and wonderful at the same time. He hurt me terribly but I was coming like a machine gun."

He waited, but she said no more about Gottfried, and he knew it was no use pursuing it. Instead she asked one of her rare questions. "Did Jack Hawley ever ask you whether we'd seen each other again after his dinner party?"

"No, and I haven't told him. Have you been seeing him since?"

She shook her head in the hollow of his shoulder. "He only fucked me once, a couple of months before I met you. I think I frightened him. He's awfully conventional, you know. As a matter of fact I was surprised when he asked me to dinner. With his dreadful wife, and those dreadful people . . . *not* including David Brent." He felt her smile. "But now I think of it, I'm sure he asked me there to meet you."

"Me?"

"Men are so strange, darling. I think Jack Hawley introduced you to me because he felt inadequate, sexually inadequate, himself, and it was his way of compensating me, or Jack Hawley, or you, or somebody." She laughed. "Who knows, perhaps he's in love with David Brent but doesn't dare admit it, even to himself. Has he ever made the pass at you, my dear?"

"No, and I'm certain you're wrong about his homosexuality. You said he fucked you. Didn't he do a good job?"

"Why *do* men always ask that question? Well, as nearly as I can recall it, he has a good cock—long and thick, I mean—and not the vaguest idea what to do with it. He kept apologizing for coming too quickly, and promising he'd do better another time. *Fancy!*"

He laughed and kissed her smooth, warm cheek. It was their longest conversation about anything.

"And what about David Brent's cock?" he said.

"I knew you'd say that. What do you want me to answer? I'll say anything you like."

"Just the truth."

"I know why you're asking." Her voice was low and teasing.

"Tell me."

"You want me to excite you. So it will get big and hard again and come into me."

"Maybe that's partly why."

"So you can straddle my belly and take my breasts in your hands and rub it between my breasts."

"That, too."

"So I can reach up while you're doing that and cuddle your balls and squeeze them, but not too hard, and feel them tighten in my fingers. That's how I'll know you're ready. That's how I'll know you're desperate for me, you can't wait any longer for me." As she spoke he felt both her hands reaching down to hold him, the fingers following her words, drawing the scrotum downward, then sliding up the shaft already stiff and hot.

"You haven't answered me. How do I compare with the others?"

"Darling, don't talk. Kiss me."

The words took him back to their first night. *"Kiss me!"* she had commanded, and he had obeyed her ever since. As now, tasting her lips with their mingled intoxication of smoke, perfume and alcohol and crushing her slender shoulders to him; as now, straddling her body and caressing her breasts, bending to kiss and suck the nipples while she reached to clasp the straining penis in feverish fingers. It was she who spoke, a low, wordless sound, when he lifted it to massage it with her breasts. Now he was moving away from her to kneel between her thighs, bending again to kiss the warm, moist delta of hair about to be entwined in his own, but suddenly she rose against him, softly forced him sideways and down on his back, then with a single swift movement spread her legs, knelt over him, deftly guided cock into cunt and sank down on him in sitting position with a rapturous sigh.

Both were motionless, in the grip of controlled enchantment, their only sensation the throbbing of membrane deep in her clinging sheath. He lay there looking up at her in the pale darkness, sitting straight like a girl on her first saddle, almost afraid to breathe. But when he lifted his hands to her breasts again she began to move upon him, slowly at first, slowly upward and downward, from root to apex, almost losing him, sinking once more to the soft mound of hair below, and now with an exquisite circular motion, broken from time to time by abrupt swiveling twists that jerked a groan from him. He bore the ecstasy of it until he could bear no more, reached for her shoulders and drew her mouth back down to him for his kiss. Helplessly his haunches rose to her rhythm, up and down with the silver thighs, in and almost out and in again, deep, more and more swiftly now. She was riding him like a jockey in the homestretch, bouncing like cork on a wave, their bodies thudding together, his tongue seeking her essence in her panting throat, his hands clasping the buttocks that closed and opened as she rose and fell, his finger penetrating the secret entrance between them just as he flooded her, just as she pulled violently away from him once more, torso thrown wildly back, eyes closed, lost in the frenzy of orgasm.

He didn't know how long she stayed there after the paroxysm subsided, but gradually her breathing slowed and she bent toward him, letting him slip out of her as she kissed him, whispered: "You *are* nice, David," as an English girl might have said it at a proper tea party. He smiled and drew her down beside him. Through the venetian blinds wisps of moonlight came into the room. "Tell me about the baron," he said, holding her close. "What did he do to you?"

She hesitated. Then: "It was here in this room. We were still in riding clothes. I thought it would be the regular thing. After all, it was the first time with Gottfried. Plenty of time later for whatever pleased us most. I let him strip me—rather roughly, I thought, but I remembered he was German. I thought he would strip then, I wanted to look at him, but instead he made me lie face down on the bed, calmly bound my wrists over my head with one of my stockings and tied them to the bed. Then he pulled my legs apart, jerked them, really, and tied each one to the bedposts."

"Didn't you resist?"

The low tone, almost a whisper, seemed to tense as if she were reliving the scene. "I was a little drunk. And curious. And somehow he was hypnotizing me with what he was saying, rough hands but caressing voice, going on about a woman's ass is most beautiful when she's astride a horse and he wanted to see me spread naked that way. When he had me properly trussed he began to undress behind me and I tried to turn my head, but he'd fixed me so I couldn't see him, I only heard him kicking off his boots and tossing his clothes over the chair in the corner. By this time—I guess it was my helplessness and being naked in that exposed position—I felt myself getting wet. I wanted him terribly. Maybe it was just his newness and the—special circumstances."

She paused again, went on: "I didn't know what he was going to do now but I was fearfully excited waiting for it. I began to twist around in the bed, as well as I could. I arched my ass up toward him—it was the only way I could really move. He wasn't talking any more. And if he wasn't going to say anything, neither was I. He didn't keep me wondering any longer. But instead of his hands or his mouth or his cock I heard a sudden swish of air, like a cracking whip, and a leather thong struck me sharply across my thighs. I screamed, in surprise more than pain, but he only struck me again, a little harder and a little higher up. I realized he was using the handle end of Jeremy's crop he'd borrowed for our ride. I told him then he would have to stop, that he might like this but I didn't, to untie me and let me go, but he just kept on hitting me, moving the thong up just a little each time until he was stroking it across my ass. I was crying, of course, I couldn't help it, but after a dozen strokes I lost count, I was feeling something mingled with the pain—first just my skin very hot, burning hot, then a kind of excitement and desire that was all new to me. And he seemed to know just how hard to hit without cutting, without bringing blood, he seemed to know when I stopped sobbing with the pain but kept on crying in a different way, wanting him, begging him to come to me. He was muttering in German to himself, something vicious and passionate at the same time, as if I didn't exist or was a dog or a horse that had displeased him. But when he heard the change in my weeping he stopped, I heard the crop clatter onto the floor and felt the bed give with his weight as he sprang on to it and knelt between my legs. In a moment I knew I would feel him inside me, I could feel my ass quivering hot, I was pouring it down to take him, but it was his mouth I felt first, his tongue. He was licking me like an animal, right there where I taught you to take me—he was wetting me with his juices and mine to make me ready . . ."

A long silence. Brent drew her closer to him and ran his fingers down her back. "Here?" he said, and touched her there.

"Yes. He didn't need my little vial, but I would have taken him without anything, I would have let him split me open if he had to, I only knew I had to take him all the way, full-length, till I could feel his balls heavy in my crotch and his hand squeezing the front of me, hurting me in every way . . ."

She stopped again. At last she seemed unable to go on.

"And he took you."

She nodded, and he kissed her tears.

# 24

The return of Major Jeremy Cortland seven months later brought an immediate change in Brent's relationship with Daphne—temporarily, Brent assumed. But it was not only that which had altered the situation. Increasingly, Daphne had come under the sway of a West Indian combo called the Buccaneers, most particularly the singer with the band, Casper Hardy, a coffee-colored giant whose calypso rhythms were captivating London in a West End night club where Daphne, arriving alone, became a frequent visitor. By the time Brent found out where she'd been keeping herself, Casper had taught her to sniff cocaine; she called Brent one night during one of her highs and offered to introduce him to the habit, reacting with sullen indignation when he declined and spurning his warnings. Another night she called him to tell him Casper Hardy was in bed with her and to propose he might like to stop in and watch. Her mocking laughter echoed in his ears long after he'd hung up the phone on her.

But the most compelling reason their relations changed was impersonal: the international situation had darkened perceptibly and was casting long shadows over much of British life. The Nazi takeover of Austria was already past history. While the British people stood stunned and mute, Neville Chamberlain sold out Czechoslovakia at Godesberg and Munich. On the night Hitler invaded Poland, Hank Fisher phoned from the UBC bureau with an offer from New York proposing that Brent quit the *Trib* and join UBC as a radio correspondent at a salary half again what he was earning at the *Trib*. He would be Hank's assistant in the London bureau to start, subject to assignment to the Continent where events were heating up fast.

How could he refuse?

Jack Hawley, unflappable as ever, told him to go

ahead and grab the opportunity. And it was at that meeting, sitting in Hawley's office with the door closed, that Daphne Cortland's name was mentioned between them. Since the night so long ago that Brent had met her in Hawley's house, neither had brought up the subject, and it was Hawley who asked about her—was it perhaps because Brent was leaving the *Trib* and he felt he could abandon his habitual caution?

"How's Daphne?" He was trying to sound casual.

"I haven't seen her or heard from her in weeks, Jack."

"Reason I ask, I heard her husband's unit has been quietly alerted for special training in the north. I don't suppose that will make her very happy."

Brent looked at him. Either Hawley knew very little about Daphne Cortland or this was just an opening. He decided to be frank. "I suppose that depends on how well you know Daphne."

"Who knows her better than you do? From what I hear, you fucked her."

It startled him only for a moment. "So did you."

"Did she tell you that?" Brent could see the flush deepening to crimson.

"What difference does that make? It's true, isn't it?"

He was ugly with anger now. "I asked you whether she told you."

"And I'm not going to answer the question. That's between you and Daphne."

"What did she say to you, Brent?"

"If you think she told me, ask her. Don't get sore at me."

"She's a liar, whatever she said. You know she's a liar?"

"She's worse than that, in case you aren't aware of it."

"And what does *that* mean?"

"You've heard of Casper Hardy?"

"That nigger!"

"She's been sleeping with him. And he's taught her to fool around with cocaine. That was a while ago. I've an idea she's hooked by now."

Hawley whistled. "Good God, let's hope not."

"Why don't you call her and see her? Maybe you could do some good. I've tried. She only laughed at me."

"Well . . ." Hawley appeared to be giving the problem grave attention. "Maybe I will."

They left it at that, but Brent doubted Daphne would get any help from Jack Hawley. That night he made one more attempt on his own, but the phone rang without answer both at the Knightsbridge flat and the cottage in Surrey. Hanging up finally, he wondered when and if he would see Daphne Cortland again. Maybe she'd gone north to be near her husband. He hoped so. Maybe the deepening political crisis all around them would have its effect on Daphne as it was changing the lives of so many others. Few among Brent's colleagues doubted now that Britain and France would be at war with Germany within a matter of days—*world* war was on the way, with consequences too vast and too tragic to be yet comprehended by the untold millions of souls who would feel its terrible impact. And David Brent was in this position to bear witness to the grand drama to come—his words, his own voice, would cross the Atlantic and enter the homes of countless listening Americans, his fellow countrymen.

It was a sobering prospect, but at the same time he felt a rising excitement of anticipation, a sense of being fatefully drawn toward the very center of conflict by the challenge of a reporter's duty to the public he serves. With Hank Fisher coaching him in the techniques of radio broadcasting under the careful eye of the number-one man in the bureau, Trent Adams, he threw himself into his new job with total concentration, and after only two test recordings, less than a week after he was hired, he made his first broadcast to the network studios in New York. This alone was an exhilarating experience; more than that, it instilled the confidence that he could succeed as a broadcaster. The rest, as Hank told him, was just a matter of practice. And who knew but that soon he would be covering the story from the front lines in Europe?

But contrary to expectations, and in some ways a personal disappointment to eager-beaver newsmen, there were no front lines and no signs of combat in the months that followed. The phony war was on, replete with threats and warnings on both sides, busy with preparations for military action, but no action. Meanwhile Hitler went on with his methodical program of subjugation of eastern Europe, abetted by Stalin's Soviet government. Britain was curiously calm, and aside from small-scale, occasional, brief naval engagements between German and British units on the high seas, people seemed lulled in a sense of security despite the suspicion that the calm would not last. The feeling of anticlimax made Brent restless; waiting out this static situation behind a desk or sitting around a pub with print journalists was depressing him. Already he was caught up in the faster tempo of the radio business; he wanted big news to break from hour to hour. Compared with the way news was developing on the Continent, London had become a backwater.

Then, a few days before Christmas, Trent Adams called him into his office. "Our man in Rome is being transferred to Washington, Dave—how'd you like to replace him?"

Just like that. Brent felt a surge of elation. "Rome? But I don't know Italian."

"No problem. You can pick it up when you get there. Your French will help."

"If you think I'm up to it . . ."

"Of course you're up to it! In times like these, we rise to the occasion."

Hank Fisher was envious. "I did a hitch in Rome myself a few years back. What a town! And what women! You'll eat it up, fella."

"I hope you mean that literally."

They laughed together. Less than forty-eight hours later Brent walked into the Stampa Estera, Rome's press club, a full-fledged foreign correspondent with his own one-man bureau.

# FOUR

# 25

After the cold, fog and winter rain of England, he was in lotus land. Brilliant sunshine beat down on the ancient city, its narrow, crooked streets thronged with strolling, shopping crowds, all smiling and chattering as if they hadn't a care in the world. The war in Europe? That must be on some other planet. And besides, it was Christmas-time—*Natale!* From the terrace of the UBC office, actually a part of the penthouse apartment that served as living quarters for the correspondent, Brent overlooked a dazzling vista of the Seven Hills, covered with gleaming white villas shaded by umbrella pines and cypresses. Hard to believe that in one of those classic, sunny buildings Hitler's ally, Mussolini, was plotting and scheming his dark purposes.

And the women. They were everywhere, the embodiment of sensual southern beauty, gorgeous inducers of dreaming and idleness. Did the Italians ever have time to do anything except make love to these goddesses? Charlie Haines, Brent's colleague at International Press and first friend in Rome, explained the cause of the country's high birthrate: it was the four-hour siesta, when all business activity ceased, government workers went home for a long lunch, shops closed, and everybody got between the sheets, full of pasta and Chianti and desire. Of course. What else? Roman women were an unspoken invitation to sex—or, rather, they didn't have to say it, their bodies did the speaking: queenly, long-legged, deep-breasted, utterly feminine, with slumbrous dark eyes, thick black hair worn long or coiled, perhaps not the chic dress of the Parisienne, perhaps not the sophisticated talk, but proud, moving with animal grace and dignity and fully aware of their power to charm.

He did his first broadcast from Rome on Christmas

morning after attending the solemn high services at St.
Peter's basilica. He took as his theme the Pope's appeal for
peace and the likelihood that the warring governments
would completely ignore it. Stopping at the telegraph
office on his way back to the apartment, he cabled holiday
greetings to his mother and sister in New York, then settled down in the sunlight on his terrace with a long Scotch
in his hand and contemplated the view. He had never felt
more at home anywhere. It was as if Rome had been waiting for him, confident that he would, inevitably, like thousands of others, find his way to the city by the Tiber and a
new life.

He was learning that his new pal Charlie Haines was
two different people. Apparently neither suspected that the
other existed. On the job he was Haines of the IP—stern,
probing, dogged, the archetype of the dedicated overseas
news correspondent. He'd been with the Rome bureau
for eight years and resisted efforts to transfer him elsewhere to more prestigious posts. To this Haines, nothing
else mattered, or was even mentioned, while he was at
work. References to activities of the Other Haines—the
Hyde to Jekyll—were met with a blank look of dismissal
or puzzlement, as if he couldn't remember. But once out
of the office and off the assignment of the day, Goodtime
Charlie took over and Dr. Jekyll was forgotten. Glass in
hand, eye roving across cafe or restaurant, nose sniffing the
air for sex like a truffle hound, he was alive to every joy
of the sensual life. Memory returned: he could recall
previous carousals down to the smallest detail.

A series of bellicose speeches by Mussolini, mainly
directed at France, was keeping the news wires humming
and the microphones hot. Brent ran into his first censor-
ship trouble with the Italian authorities when he reported a
juicy rumor: Foreign Minister Ciano, shouting at the
French ambassador, was supposed to have demanded: "If
the Italian army crossed the French frontier tomorrow,
what could stop us?" "The Customs inspectors," replied
the Ambassador . . .

Fortunately, with Charlie Haines intervening at his
side, Brent and his network escaped sanctions, possibly
even banishment. But it was a sobering reminder that in
the present European atmosphere a reporter couldn't be

too careful what he wrote or said on the air. At the same time he had to fight for his facts against officials who would try to mislead him or manipulate the news. In that regard Haines quoted to him that memorable Latin dictum: *Illegitimi non carborundum* (Don't let the bastards grind you down).

It was the first time Haines had let a smile cross his face in weeks. The news had slackened again into still tense but more stable daily developments, and they were relaxing over dinner at Libotte's, a press-corps hangout near the Stampa Estera. Gradually Mr. Hyde was emerging; with each glass of *chiaretto di Garda* Charlie waxed more reminiscent of past pleasures of the flesh, more eager for new adventure.

Haines was fingering a small card on which Brent glimpsed a bold black feminine handwriting. "Can't make up my mind," he said. "Want to go to a party, Dave?"

"You know the answer to that."

"Kind of special party. Very aristocratic. And celebrities. Never know what may happen, who might be there. But I happen to know the hostess—old friend, in fact. Always invites me, and sometimes I go."

"And who would I be? A movie director, a millionaire, a prince incognito?"

Haines burst into laughter and clapped his knee; Goodtime Charlie was in full form. "You'll be yourself. In times like these we're the most sought-after guests in Rome—you'll see."

He was right. The greeting was cordial and full of respect. It was a magnificent *palazzo* off the Piazza di Spagna and the hostess, born American, was the Marchesa Fignoli, née Edna Johnson of Pittsburgh. She couldn't have been much over thirty despite her ten-year marriage to the Marchese, already, divorced and remarried to another rich American woman, but her exposure to sophisticated Roman high society showed in her elegance of dress and manner; her accent was British now and she spoke fluent Italian with her guests, most of whom called her Pupi. One look betrayed them—as Charlie had explained on the way down the Spanish Steps, they were a fast, decadent and titled crowd.

Apparently Pupi had given a dinner party for most of them, perhaps a dozen or so, an equal number of men and women. But there were several girls who arrived later, as Brent and Haines did. The ancient clock in the gilded ante-room read ten past eleven as they came in, early for Rome, Charlie said. Pupi glided up to meet them, arms outstretched to embrace Charlie and a glittering smile for Brent. She was tall and slender in a dress of some shimmering material that was slit halfway to her waist to display slim thighs. "A new recruit from New York by way of Paris and London," Charlie introduced him, as a liveried servant proffered a tray of Scotch and champagne. Pupi gave him a swift, cool glance of appraisal head to foot. "And attractive, too!" she murmured. "We must lunch together, David, so you can give me all the latest. Poor Paris! Do you suppose Hitler will invade France? He practically owns Italy already."

But she moved away without expecting an answer to her question, the glittering smile fixed in place for two more guests, a jaded-looking young man and a very blonde, very solemn young girl with huge, visionary eyes and a frail yet somehow provocative body. Brent and Haines moved on into the main salon with its ancestral paintings of Fignoli popes, cardinals, generals and admirals and frescoed ceilings dating, Charlie said, from the fourteenth or fifteenth centuries. Standing in a convenient observation corner, he itemized the people chattering and drinking in the center of the room.

"The tall guy with the spade beard, Count Andrezzi, otherwise known as Bobo, is the most notorious cocksman in Rome. Don't challenge me on that. I've seen it. The two women he's charming at the moment are both princesses, one of them Italian, the other German. Tschu von Tschurnitz has a brother in the Vatican involved at the moment in some delicate negotiations that I'd like to know more about."

"Choo-choo, or whatever you call her, is a knockout."

"You like blondes, eh?"

"I can love both fair and brown, her whom abundance melts and her whom want betrays, her whom the country formed and whom the town . . ."

"What the hell is that from?"

"I must be getting drunk, Charlie. I memorized that in college and I haven't thought of it in years."

"I'm drunk already and intend to get drunker. What with Libotte's wine and Pupi's Scotch I doubt if I'll make it to the office tomorrow but who cares?" He corralled a waiter and grabbed two more drinks off his tray. "Let's see, where was I? . . . Shall I proceed with identifying the rogue's gallery? Center in that group in the left corner is Adriana Colpuso, lesbian fashion designer and the leading Roman muff-diver. I seem to recognize a couple of her models here tonight: the tall dark one earns fifty a week strutting the platform, and five hundred on her back."

"The lesbian knows you're talking about her, Charlie —don't look now."

"They know everything. Never sell one short, son."

Brent saw the quick dagger glance turn away, black, malevolent eyes half closing in pure hostility. Why do they hate us—jealousy, envy, contempt? Beside him Haines had shifted his sights again. "Various gamblers, playboys, actors, females attached and unattached, a few I haven't seen here before, but on the whole a representative top-level congregation, gathered round High Priestess Pupi. Best to remain unattached ourselves for the moment, Dave, till we see what develops. Meanwhile, another drink, eh? . . ."

And another, and another, as they drifted along the outskirts of the crowd, a few polite words here and there but no lasting colloquy. Pupi swam by occasionally, making sure everybody was comfortable, flashing her smile. And gradually it seemed to Brent there were subtle changes in ambiance: the servants set up a bar at one end of the room, stocked it and then discreetly disappeared entirely. Somehow the tone of the conversation sounded more discreet, buzzed lower not noisier as it would have in New York or at any American party where there had been such steady drinking. He looked at his watch—already nearly two o'clock. No windows in the great room, but outside was the night, the city, the war, all forgotten in this human space turned in upon itself, feasting on the closeness of talk and bodies, confidential gossip, half-whispered compliments or malice, subdued laughter. He felt a little unsteady by now, though he wouldn't admit it to Charlie; it was time to stop drinking before his sight began to waver; he'd had just enough. Was he mistaken, or were there fewer people in the room than a short while before? But he hadn't seen anyone going into the anteroom on their way out.

He mentioned it to Haines, who grinned, nudged him slightly and turned toward the back of the room. For the first time he noticed a door behind them, less a door than a wide panel in the tapestried wall which stood slightly ajar. Even as they looked a middle-aged, distinguished-looking couple slipped through it and closed it carefully behind them. "Prince and Princess Puglia," Charlie grinned. "Let's just follow suit." He led the way.

They were in a broad, carpeted hallway that led into the far recesses of the palazzo. Arched entrances on both sides of the hall opened into a series of separate rooms from which issued a low, excited sound of movement, sighs, muted gasps, soft exclamations. Haines took a few tentative steps and stopped, beckoning him into the second archway on the left. To Brent's surprise it was an immense, luxurious bathroom, replete with red brocaded walls—as though padded to deaden sound—elaborate dressing table, full-length mirrors on both sides of the room, all dominated by a huge bathtub in antique bronze decorated with a frieze of nymphs and satyrs. Half a dozen people were standing a few feet from the tub, frozen in tense silence, their gaze concentrated on the scene before their eyes: a woman bent forward over the rim of the tub, her dress flung up over her back to disclose quivering white buttocks, and behind her stood the bearded Bobo Andrezzi, his magnificent physique naked, slowly thrusting and withdrawing in and almost out of her offered cunt. It was a moment before Brent recognized the woman, until her sharp, exulting cry echoed hollow in the bronze depths, the voice of Pupi Fignoli. But it was Andrezzi's cock that seized and riveted his attention as it appeared, sank to the big balls and reappeared in almost unbelievable length. Only once had he seen a penis as phenomenally long and thick: on photos of a Negro murderer seemingly caught at half-erection that had been passed around the *News* city room in New York. If either Pupi or the Count was aware they were being watched they gave no indication of it. The steady pumping continued as though it would go on all night, and Brent didn't doubt that it could, or that Pupi would welcome succeeding partners. The tiny beads of sweat on Andrezzi's forehead were the only sign of strain . . .

He felt Charlie's hand on his arm; it was time for further exploration of the Palazzo Fignoli. The other watchers, totally absorbed, were oblivious of their departure. In the hallway once more Haines waited, listening, then moved silently forward until he halted in front of another archway. A golden beam of light from the ceiling illuminated the tableau within. Surrounded by a group of witnesses, the frail young blonde with the huge eyes knelt before a dark-haired man Brent had noticed earlier in the evening. His trousers had fallen to his feet and the child-like girl was sucking his cock like a famished animal, while kneeling behind her, squeezing her breasts and urging her on with soft whispers, was the jaded young man she had arrived with. His words seemed to goad her to even hungrier efforts, taking the staff deep into her throat and closing her eyes in ecstasy, and Brent, glancing at the drawn face of her prey, suddenly realized where he had seen that face before; the man was an actor in minor screen parts, either American or British. He glanced at Charlie Haines as if for confirmation and saw him smile faintly and nod; he knew they were both thinking the same thing. Now the man moaned; he was nearing climax; the girl's pale hands that had been caressing his balls slid around his body to clutch the buttocks and pressed her fingers between them. Convulsively he began to double up, reached down to grasp the thick blonde hair that fell to her shoulders, clenched his teeth as he stiffened toward the final paroxysm, and she stayed with him, held him deep in her mouth, her head bobbing faster and faster till she gasped and gulped at last, and drank, the semen dripping from her lips.

A long sigh like relief escaped from the knot of spectators. For the first time Brent noticed the men reacting with visible movement, the women standing with them rubbing their bodies against them, reaching for their erections, falling into passionate embrace. Slowly, reluctantly, as if it gave her pain, the kneeling girl at last had sucked her partner dry; he released himself and looked down at her with tenderness as she fell back into the arms of the man who still held her from behind. Her eyes were still closed and her natural pallor was even whiter now, as though she had just survived a soul-shaking religious experience, and perhaps it was, to her. His soft whispering seemed to fill the room, comforting, reassuring, praising, and he kissed her mouth . . .

Once again they stood in the hall, Brent waiting for Haines to make the next move. He was listening intently, but except for murmuring voices farther down the hall the palazzo was silent. Charlie beckoned him in that direction, and cautiously they tiptoed along the corridor to the last archway on the right. Here the light was so dim that at first Brent could make out nothing but a circle of silhouetted bodies on the far side of the room. Little by little the picture resolved itself: a single lamp threw its rays toward the chair that was hidden by the circle of watchers until Brent and Haines approached and peered past them at the vision of Princess von Tschurnitz, totally nude, lying against the chair's tilted back with a faint smile on her beautiful face. She looked like a blonde Goya on a background of deep purple velvet, rich breasts standing from the voluptuous torso, the golden skin of her body, the deeper gold gossamer below. But the pose was more than the artist could ask: the thighs were spread wide, the legs straddling the velvet-clad arms of the chair, a position that yielded the body's innermost secret to the covetous eyes that devoured it. And her long, slim hands, indolently flung backward over her head, twisted slowly, sinuously together, waiting.

A movement in the shadows beyond the chair arrested Brent's eye: the tall, dark model Haines had singled out as one of Adriana Colpuso's fashion team was just slipping back into her clothing, apparently having just finished playing her part in the night's activity, and behind her, emerging into the light, was Adriana herself, fully dressed but her hair awry, lipstick smeared, still breathing a little heavily as though after strenuous exertions that could be imagined. But everything in her attitude said she was unsatisfied; barefooted, she moved like a panther, eyes gleaming, gluttonous lips parted, no longer aware as earlier of others watching her, talking about her, but avid only for the prize that lay open and still, spread-eagled, white legs dangling helpless from the chair's two arms. Swiftly the panther glided into the center of the room, turned to face the chair. Brent felt a tug at his arm and followed Haines into a position where they could watch in profile view. For a long moment the two women confronted each other, the princess utterly relaxed, Adriana motionless except for the slight heaving of her breasts under their garnet covering. Then their eyes caught and held, and Brent saw a look like fear creep into the princess' eyes; but it was fascination, too, and challenge, dread and desire both, mixed in what was to come, while the other face hardened, seemed to grow longer, almost wolf-like, the lips thicker, hungry hands working at her side. But when she crouched to her prey it was to the breasts her mouth went first, the long scarlet tongue flicking out like an animal's, curving around the pink nipples that grew in seconds to double their length. The pale hands, shining with rings, came down from the back of the chair to caress the hair of the woman who kissed her thus, and the emerald eyes closed in abandon.

Who could have said how long she loved the breasts? Time became timeless, to the watchers as well as the participants. Finally the curling, flicking tongue moved lower, lingered on the navel set like a small medallion in the porcelain bowl of flesh, licked its way into the hollows of the flawless thighs, nearer and nearer the golden delta. And in response the thighs moved wider in anticipation, the long legs, the dainty feet and ankles, swung impatiently from the chair arms, the fingers tightened on the crouching woman's shoulders. No sound disturbed the stillness of the room but Brent saw the watchers breathing faster, spellbound in the enchantment of the spectacle. For the whole mouth opened now to engulf the cobweb of flaxen hair, to take its textures between gleaming teeth and tug with utmost gentleness. And for the first time sound escaped the princess' lips, a long, expiring sigh of yearning as she lifted her bottom from the velvet seat and thrust the crotch forward. There was a last glimpse of cunt for those who watched, the aureate cleft gaping, pinker and still paler flesh as it opened to the full, and from deep in those recesses now flowed the ultimate response, the ultimate reward, as the mouth and plunging tongue descended and the sucking, biting, devouring began. Adriana was making her own sounds, a smacking, guzzling frenzy at first, then, parting the wet lips with her fingers, her lips and tongue closed on the clitoris itself, tonguing and sucking toward orgasm. It was swift in coming; she gave a whimper like anguish, the glorious body thrashed, a mermaid out of water, gasping for air, while below, deep in the crotch, her fluid gushed through hot twitching membrane and the driving tongue lunged on, relentless, lapping the last drop.

# 26

"You should have stayed," said Pupi Fignoli; "there was lots of fun later."

"I wish we had, but Charlie had other plans."

They were lunching together in the palazzo—not in some fashionable restaurant, as he'd assumed he'd be playing the host, but on the Marchesa's home territory. True to her suggestion she'd called Brent at his office and reminded him they were going to talk about Paris and London, in exchange for which she offered the latest Rome gossip. While that was under way, nothing was said on either side about Pupi's party. It was Brent who brought it up in the conventional way, telling her how much he'd enjoyed himself. He still didn't know whether she knew how much he had seen, or whether Charlie Haines had told her. He couldn't find out from Charlie because Charlie had lapsed into his non-communicative period again.

"And just what," Pupi was inquiring now, "were Charlie's other plans?"

He hesitated to tell her and she laughed, sounding very American. "Oh, come on, now, David—don't think you can shock me! I know what Charlie Haines is like; he's one of my oldest friends. And you and I should have an understanding right away: you can talk to me like one man to another—and don't spare the fuck, shit or any other word you'd normally use. Have I made myself clear?"

His turn to laugh. "Okay, it's a deal. And I admire your frankness."

"Life's too short to live any other way, David. If Charlie were here with us right now he'd agree. Unfortunately, his wife is back from her Swiss vacation. She keeps a close eye on his activities. Have you met Clare, by the way?"

"Not yet."

"A stunning girl, but strangely puritanical. That doesn't fit, in Rome, but"—she shrugged in Italian style—"I've given up trying to convert her. I'm afraid Clare will never approve of me. Do you?"

"Do I approve of you? Emphatically." He grinned. "Do you approve of *me?*"

"So far, yes. Of course I haven't seen you undressed yet, but I'm a patient soul."

They were interrupted by the footman in livery who came in bearing the second course—a fish glistening in white wine sauce garnished with little shrimp, served with an Alto Adige in a tall green bottle. They were lunching in what Pupi called her "intimate" dining room, but the frescoed ceiling was still about fifteen feet over their heads and the ornate furnishings of the room were in the grand style. As the servant poured Brent's glass his eyes flickered to his face a moment and the faintest trace of a smile touched his lips; then he bowed to the Marchesa and silently glided out of the room.

Pupi had noticed. "Don't be annoyed if Giordano seems a bit familiar," she smiled. "It's just his way. And I keep him on because he has a glorious cock."

"He's a handsome man."

She dismissed it. "Let's not talk about Giordano; I'm waiting to hear what you and Charlie did after you left my party."

"To be truthful, my memory is a little blurred because I was full of your marvelous champagne, Marchesa—"

"Pupi!"

"Pupi. Charlie had it in mind that he wanted to lay a lesbian—."

"He could have done that here."

"—that is, a lesbian that seems to be a special favorite of his. So we went to her apartment, woke her up, had her phone a girlfriend who came over, and we watched them make love—"

"I thought you said he wanted to lay the girl himself."

"Only after he'd watched her making love to another woman."

"So finally he did?"

Brent nodded.

"Well—go on. You laid the other one, right?"

He smiled. "She was willing."

"You like fucking lesbians?"

He raised his hands in protest. "Not because she was a lesbian. Because she was a woman. By that time I was ready to fuck anybody."

"And she cooperated?"

Again he smiled. "Fully. She must be AC-DC."

"And you," Pupi said, "are you AC-DC?"

"Homosexual? Definitely not."

"Don't you think it'd be more fun if you were?"

He looked at her. "Are you, Pupi?"

"I've tried it. I'm afraid it's not an acquired taste, at least for me." She laughed. "I'm just as straight as you are, David."

Giordano was back in the room, this time with a delicious fruit soufflé and a Chateau d'Yquem that was liquid gold. "To France!" Brent toasted.

"To Paris! I had a French husband before Gaetano, you know. He taught this little wide-eyed American everything she knows about sex—which is just about all she really knows about anything."

Brent remembered the scene with the bathtub. "What's your favorite position, Pupi?"

If she suspected he had been among the watchers at her party she gave no sign of it. "Dog-fashion," she said readily. "I can take it other ways, of course, but it's the only way I reach orgasm."

Her talk gave him a sense of elation, loosening his inhibitions at this first conversation with the Marchesa as it had loosened his tongue. He reached across the table and took her bejeweled hand. "It's going to be nice knowing you, Pupi—I just have a feeling."

"That's nothing to the feeling you're going to have after the coffee," she smiled.

The espresso was served with an Italian cognac called Vecchia Romagna, and afterward she was as good as her word. Swinging hands, they walked through the vast *salotto* where the party had gathered that night he came with Haines, and through the wall panel into the long, softly carpeted hall. But she wasn't taking him to the room where the bath was; instead she led him through the third archway on the left, into a luxuriously furnished room with gorgeous drapes over windows through which the afternoon light filtered restfully. The whole atmosphere was one of quiet and relaxation. The Marchesa paused inside the arch to close the door, and the silence was complete.

"Take off your clothes," she said, "and lie there."

She pointed to a velvet-covered couch at one side of the room against the black brocaded wall, more a table than a couch as it rose to about his waist. He smiled. "Who am I to disobey?" he murmured, and watched her eyes cover every inch of him as he disrobed—jacket, tie, shirt, shoes, trousers, socks and finally, facing her, dropping his shorts. He was at half-erection but her searching gaze didn't seem disappointed; on the contrary she smiled as if in approval but made no move to come nearer or touch him.

She spoke again in a low tone of command. "On your face," and gestured toward the couch-table. Slowly he complied, stretching at full length on the rich velvet, still asking no questions. She herself gave no sign of undressing. As he had noticed at lunch, she was wearing only a flimsy silk dress which barely covered her bra-less breasts, no stockings, and simple pumps on her feet. "Now let yourself go—completely," she said, her voice still softer.

He needn't have been told. The food, the wine, the quiet, most of all the velvet under his body combined to induce a state of total restfulness, almost a narcotic reaction, and he seemed only half aware as she moved to his side and laid her hands on his shoulders. He felt her fingers, cool, light as lace and strong, as they slipped across his back, moved upward to knead his neck, slowly, gently, pressing at the nerve-ends, squeezing, penetrating the hollows of his shoulders. He had never been to a massage parlor, let alone caressed in a room of such splendor, but nothing could be a more satisfying sensual experience than this, no professional hands more sure, no touch more aware of his body and its need. She was working along the middle of his back now, inch by inch down the spinal column, then moving back upward along his sides in steady, soothing strokes—soothing except to his belly where fire was gathering, his erection at the full.

She seemed to know that, too, as he heard the low, chuckling sound of her pleasure; for she was feeling it, must, this infinite sense of pleasure that was flooding his body and seemed to travel from her fingertips into her own body. Her hands had reached his buttocks now, grasping them with firmer touch, rolling them together only to spread them apart, so that waves of reaction were radiating downward along the backs of his thighs, down to his very ankles, anticipating her hands as indeed soon they came, squeezing the firm flesh and quivering muscle, following his sensation with the relief of touch. The sexual reaction was now so strong that involuntarily he pressed hard into the table, held it there until the high point passed without orgasm, then understood as he relaxed again that this was what she was doing: preparing him for special endurance when she should take him into her at last.

But that was not yet. Softly, lightly, the sinuous hands implied that he should give under their touch and turn over on his back. Again he obeyed her command, and now lay prone under her gaze. His eyes were closed but he knew she was devouring him with her look; and once more the hands followed, caressing his forehead, his cheeks, his chin, swooping downward over his throat, his chest, where fingers lingered at the nipples, arousing them to hardness as her own must be hard, tracing an outline of fantasy over his stomach. But while his genitals ached for her touch she swiftly, deliberately, passed them by to drop to the thighs, squeeze them with strong hands, the grip of the professional masseuse, then to caress the knees, run a single finger along the shin and bend even to the toes, pull each one in turn with tiny, gentle tugs. He let a long sigh escape him, and silently the hands answered, lifting his knees apart and moving up the insides of the thighs, little by little, seeming to creep in centimeters. He tried to open his eyes but could not, the emotion was too intense, the feeling was overwhelming. But the fingers were closer, they were almost there—and suddenly, as he heard her half-suppressed moan of pleasure, both hands seized and cupped the balls, the whole scrotum grasped and clutched as in a gesture of triumph, one hand moving upward then and clasping the throbbing column, claiming its own.

Simultaneously a wave of relief swept over him, but without the orgasm he would normally have achieved. The paroxysm was delayed again. Ah, she knew what she was doing, this subtle sculptress of the body, this magician of sex! Her methods, prolonging the pleasure indefinitely, were making the final culmination even more intense. And it was for herself as well as the man—she was assuring the prolongation of her own pleasure. Once more before his closed eyes he saw the naked body of Count Andrezzi, the magnificent Bobo, standing by the tub and driving his beautiful instrument steadily and skillfully in and out of the distended body thrust toward him, and once more he heard Pupi's muffled cry of gratitude sounding from the bronze depths. Tonight, by her sensual alchemy, she was making another man Andrezzi's equal. And he was ready for her, knowing even as the pressure of her fingers cunningly changed that her work was finished and his must begin. No words were needed as she drew away from him and he slipped off the couch into a standing position beside her, and there was no kiss. Even as he moved she had leaned forward over the couch, burying her face in the velvet cover still warm with the heat of his naked flesh. She had assumed the posture he had first seen in the bathroom, her body provocatively thrust upward and backward toward him. As easily, familiarly as though he had done it a hundred times, he lifted the short skirt and dropped it over her bare back, exposed the white waiting flesh, the slender thighs braced firmly against the couch, ready to receive his first uplifted stroke.

In the moment there flashed across his vision the memory of watching the mating of a stallion on a Carolina horse farm in this same position: the mare hot, steaming, sweating with anticipation, tail held aside; the great horse bellowing behind her, teased into rearing with the man-held whip, the huge prong swinging into its instinctive action. Just as it moved on the target the mare's vulva yawned open, twitching convulsively; and looking down now at the human body open before him Brent saw the wet cunt twitch, heard the hoarse whisper muffled in velvet, imploring, begging, *"Please . . . oh, please . . . now . . . now!"*

She more than took him, she sucked him into her, as swift, as deft as with her fingers, and in response he eased into the deep, steady plunges Andrezzi had given her, aware that never in his sexual life had he felt the power he was feeling now, the sense of endurance forever, the limitless control. Pupi had made this possible for him, had led him gradually to build and restrain this strength that gave him mastery. And she was still teaching him—answering his driving strokes with subtle movements of her hips, lifting to grind herself against him, swiveling, and most exquisite sensation of all, tightening her vaginal muscles as he slid inward, loosening as he drew away. How long they continued thus he could not know; he only knew it was longer than any that had gone before, longest of all. Time stretched out endless, or existed no more; he was losing track of where he was, who she was, who they were together—or were they one person? It had been so long since she took him into her he couldn't remember the beginning; there was nothing now but sensation, blinding, blissful, beyond even touch and feeling. The orgasm when it came was a synthesis of all the orgasms he ever had, beyond orgasms; something so full, so complete, it passed outward and above the sense of sex itself. Her shuddering groan of fulfillment sounded far away, somewhere in a sky of fleecy clouds, drifting as he was drifting into the universal peace.

# 27

Perhaps Pupi Fignoli had not been quite accurate in describing Charlie Haines' wife as "stunning," but Brent could see what the Marchesa meant the first time he met Clare. She was not a glamorous type, although good looks and breeding were evident at first glance. Probably it was by contrast to the overcivilized, oversophisticated Rome set that Clare made her special impact: there was something so fresh, so healthy in the direct, clear-eyed gaze of this girl from Wisconsin that she stood out like one in a million. And though she might not be dressed in the ultra-latest Roman fashion her natural American sense of style gave her a chic all her own, and a sex appeal that had Italian men clambering all over each other to get a second look at her: the tawny boyish-cut hair, the athletic young body, high-breasted and long-legged, smooth skin tanned by her ski vacation at Davos where only a few days before she'd said goodbye to her visiting sister and returned to Rome.

The fact was that Clare didn't like Rome, or Italy, or the Italians. Charlie said so frankly, joking about it. They'd only been married a year or so and he was ten years older than Clare, but she still looked like a bride— radiant, innocent, reaching for a new life. Her only friends were a few of the younger American Embassy types, though she didn't really need to be with them. She had her own self-sufficient life, studying Italian, experimenting in her kitchen with Charlie's favorite dishes, and content during the long hours her husband had to be away from her to read, to listen to records or write letters in the penthouse apartment.

Brent wondered what would be the effect on Clare if she ever suspected what sometimes went on in the Palazzo Fignoli.

Obviously Charlie didn't worry about it; in his working mood he had too many other things on his mind to worry about anything but the next European news scoop and the resultant rocket from IP headquarters in New York. Brent's tentative mention of his luncheon with Pupi, and what happened afterward, was met with Charlie's usual blank stare. That would have to wait until the Haines mood changed and Goodtime Charlie was back on the rails again; it was clear he just didn't want to hear about it now. But shortly after Clare returned from Switzerland he called Brent and asked him to dinner at the apartment, the first time he'd laid eyes on Mrs. Haines.

As it happened, Charlie was delayed at the office on a late-breaking story and Clare was alone when Brent arrived. Instantly, he felt, she accepted him, even liked him; or was it just because he was American and not one of her husband's Italian friends? No, it had to be more than that, unless he was deceiving himself: something he sensed in the awareness a woman has of a new man, a kindling visible in the eyes, almost a challenge, and certainly a basic sexuality in the encounter. She hadn't dressed up for the occasion; obviously such things didn't matter a damn to Clare Haines. The peasant skirt swung loosely but smartly over the slim legs, and the simple short-sleeved shirt clung to the full-breasted torso. It came as a distinctly pleasurable surprise to see that she wasn't as demure as he'd thought he'd find her in at least one respect: she wore no bra under the shirt. The imprint of her nipples was clearly defined, and for a moment her glance caught his eyes resting on the sight. At once she turned slightly away and her tanned cheeks colored even darker, but there was no hostility in her little smile, just a kind of wonder, or puzzlement, as if she couldn't imagine anyone being interested in such a normal thing.

Was it possible Charlie hadn't made her aware, *more* than aware, of her physical beauty? How much had he told her about his "other self?" Not much, judging from Pupi Fignoli's advance description of her as "puritanical." Nor had he found it necessary to warn Brent to watch what he said to Clare about her husband, assuming, correctly, as one sophisticated male to another, that Brent would be careful. As it turned out in the first half-hour of conversation, the talk was all innocent and Clare did most of the talking, delightedly recounting details of her ski vacation and the stuffy Swiss. Sitting opposite him beside an open fire—evenings in Rome are cool, even in summer, and the apartment was unheated except during the winter months—she was a portrait of youth and charm, knees crossed and bare leg swinging a slender, sandaled foot, her second martini in long fingers, wide, red-lipped smile showing perfect teeth, a boyish laugh. Brent watched and listened, trying to conceal a feeling that must show in his eyes, in spite of himself: a desire to take her loveliness in his arms and taste that vibrant young flesh, the lust for life in her laughter.

There was a pause while she mixed them a third drink. She glanced at the old Italian clock standing on the marble mantel. "I hope you're not too hungry—Charlie ought to be here any minute now."

"I'm a newsman, remember? I know how it is. Besides, I think I'd rather listen than eat."

She laughed, wide-eyed. "Listen to me? I'll bet I've been boring you to death!" She handed him his glass. "Tell me about yourself, David."

"I'd much rather hear about you."

Again her laugh. *"Me?* What about me?"

"Well . . . where you grew up, where you went to school, all that."

"Janesville?" It amused her. "There's nothing to say about Janesville—it's no different from any other midwestern factory town."

"College?"

"Colorado, but that mightn't mean anything to you."

"Somebody told me once it was full of pretty girls. He didn't put it quite that way."

"You mean we have a *reputation?* I didn't realize it."

"He said there wasn't a virgin left in the senior class."

She smiled, her skin glowing in the firelight. "Possibly he was right, although I doubt it."

A key clicked in the lock and Charlie Haines came in. Brent felt an instant disappointment; he wanted to be alone with this enchanting girl, especially as the conversation was just getting interesting. But he grinned as Charlie slouched across the room, seized a bottle of Scotch and poured himself a hefty potion. "Sorry I kept you fellas waiting, but at least I cleaned up the docket and I can take tomorrow off." He drained the glass in one gulp. "Ah . . . that feels better! Whatcha got for us in the kitchen, baby?"

"Chicken cacciatore, as promised. And I found some Grignolino at Gabrieli's—his last three bottles."

" 'At's my girl! My favorite wine, Dave, you're gonna like it."

"If I had a wife like Clare I wouldn't need any wine, or any dinner either."

They all laughed. "See, baby? I told you. Dave's your boy."

She was smiling quizzically at him. "Are you sure you didn't hoist a few at the Stampa on your way home?"

He raised his arm. "Swear to God, honey." But Brent didn't believe him; Goodtime Charlie was definitely coming back to life. They watched him pour himself another big slug and down it straight. "Well, what about you two?" he demanded.

"We've had three double martinis, Charlie."

"That's only a starter for my Clare. You wouldn't believe how this kid can drink, Dave. Never seen her drunk, to this day."

"Oh, I can get drunk," Clare said. "I just don't show it. But let's have just one more, David, shall we?"

"Well, just to keep Charlie company . . ."

It was a gay little dinner party, maybe the gayest since his Paris days. Goodtime Charlie was launched again, and after they'd knocked off two of the three bottles of Grignolino Brent was feeling pretty high himself. Whipping in and out of the kitchen with swift, lithe movements, Clare was cook, maid and hostess all in one. He marveled at her steadiness after the amount of alcohol they'd consumed, and told her so.

"She's got a hollow leg, that's the secret," Charlie said. "Show the man your hollow leg, sweetie!"

"I will *not* show him my hollow leg, or the other one either!" Laughing, she dodged back as Charlie tried to pull up her skirt. "What's the matter with you?" she demanded, almost seriously. "What is David going to think of us?"

Brent made no reply, but he couldn't repress the look of embarrassment that flashed across his face and knew she had seen it and understood his feelings.

They drank their espresso standing before the fireplace and he felt steadier, but the coffee seemed to have no sobering effect on Charlie. He leered at his wife, looking her up and down, then turned to Brent. "Think she's sexy, Dave?"

"That's not for me to say, Charlie."

"Only one trouble with my Clare—she needs experience, sexual experience. And she admits it. She's looking for another man."

She smiled tolerantly at her husband. "You're talking nonsense, dear—can't you think of something more interesting to say?"

In answer he set down his coffee cup and seized her in his arms, kissing her violently despite her resistance. Brent watched her body slowly relax, her arms go around his shoulders and her mouth return the kiss. Color flooded up under the tan; she seemed to lose herself, lose all control, become a willing instrument for his desire. One of his arms slipped down behind her and lifted her bodily, held her close to him.

"Come on, Dave!" he muttered, and to Brent's surprise he carried her into the bedroom.

It was dim in there as he followed, still embarrassed, reluctant, saw Charlie Haines lay down his lovely burden carefully on the bed, the peasant skirt forgotten halfway up her thighs. Now he was opening the front of the blouse and baring her breasts; still she did not speak or resist, but she was watching Brent as he looked down at her. Suddenly she smiled, spoke in a low, level tone.

"You see, David, I *can* get drunk."

"I want you to take Dave," Charlie said.

He waited for her response. Brent felt his breath come short.

Clare lay motionless. "No," she said.

"You don't mean it." Charlie spoke softly, eagerly; Brent could sense his excitement. "You know you want him to fuck you. You know you need to experience another man."

"No."

Charlie sat down beside her and took her breasts in both his hands. "You told me you wanted to try. You admitted it. Remember?" His hands were kneading her breasts in the dimness. "The night before you went to Davos . . ."

"You coaxed me to say it." She was almost whispering. "I said it to please you . . ."

His voice had a wheedling urgency. "But you admit you like Dave. He's standing right here, baby. He's ready, aren't you, Dave?"

Brent felt his face flaming. "Look, Charlie—don't talk like that."

"But don't you *want* it?" Charlie was saying to her. "You're a woman, Clare—I can feel your breasts wanting it. I know you want it, right now . . ."

"I want it," she said softly, "from *you,* darling Charlie."

"You don't care if Dave is here with us?"

She shook her head very slightly. "No, I don't mind . . ."

Fascinated, caught between embarrassment and lust, Brent moved back a step as the other man stood up; he watched him as he stripped off his jacket and dropped his trousers and shorts, bared the heavy, distended erection. The girl loosened her skirt at the waist and settled her body, opened her legs as her husband crouched over her and bared her crotch, watched her as she closed her eyes. "Sweet Clare . . ." he whispered as she took him in, slowly, little by little, as though to avoid hurting her, until at last it was sunk all the way and his rhythm began, answered with exquisite movement by her whole body, the legs as if unconsciously widening still further, the knees and ankles lifting, back, back, until the whole ass was bearing his steady strokes and her hands crept around his neck, drawing his head down for the long, long kiss that held while his cadence gradually increased, drove faster with his breathing, with her breathing, while Brent watched from the shadows, his own cock ready to burst with what he knew they were feeling. And then, for what reason he did not know, impelled by some irresistible instinct of togetherness, he moved silently to the edge of the bed, standing only inches away from them, and saw her hand reach blindly toward him, appealing, gripping, sharing, clinging till her long nails dug deep into his palm, her eyes still closed, her mouth gasping, locked in the warm, good kiss of married love, taking him with them into their orgasm.

# 28

Several days went by before he had any further contact with Charlie Haines. The memory of the climactic scene in their bedroom both excited and troubled him—troubled because his abrupt and emotional introduction to their most intimate relationship had left him with a deep and haunting attraction to Clare which in a strange way she had seemed to reciprocate while rejecting her husband's equally strange entreaty to yield her body to Brent. Now, days later, he could still physically feel the imprint of Clare's nails in the palm of his hand, even though, once their paroxysm had subsided, she withdrew it and clasped Charlie in both arms as he rolled to her side on the bed. So they lay, face to face, motionless, wordless, bathed in the wonderful afterglow of passion, forgetting everything within its blissful private world, and just as immediately Brent had felt himself become the intruder on sacred precincts, and had quietly left the room and let himself out of the apartment.

Since that night Charlie hadn't called him, nor had they met as they so often did while covering a news break, but he was reluctant to make the first move himself in light of the very special circumstances of an evening he would never forget. He felt it was not his place to appear to take advantage of the priceless intimacy they had bestowed. He was not willing so soon to confront the stern visage of Charles T. Haines, veteran correspondent, in his official role. For he assumed that Charlie had lapsed into his other self and would draw a blank if Brent even asked about Clare in a gesture of simple politeness. He was beginning to know Charlie Haines pretty well. Nevertheless, after the fourth day without either sight or sound of his colleague, Brent phoned the IP office and asked to speak with him; could be he was ill. But the answer was a surprise: Haines had been transferred to the Paris bureau on a temporary basis owing to the increasing threat of Nazi invasion and it wasn't known how soon he would return to Rome.

Again Brent was faced with a delicate dilemma: he wanted to find out if Clare had gone to France with her husband but hesitated to ask his office or call the apartment. He went through another three days of increasing uncertainty before the situation resolved itself, and then it did so by chance. It was mid-afternoon; he walked into the Cafè Greco for a *cappucino* and Clare Haines was sitting alone at a table against the rear wall. Or was she alone?— the flashily-dressed young Italian at the next table was leaning toward her, leering and low-voiced, saying something that was obviously offensive to her. As she looked away in a kind of desperation she saw Brent, and relief flooded into her face. Smiling, she looked at her wristwatch and spoke as he approached.

"You're late, David—I was just about to leave." And she held out her hand.

It was enough for the Italian. With something like a silent snarl he got up and walked out, avoiding Brent's threatening stare.

"This is my lucky day," she said.

"And mine." He took the seat next to her. "I thought you might have gone to Paris with Charlie."

"I wanted to but he wouldn't let me—too dangerous."

He looked into the eager blue eyes. "My guess is it'd take more than a war to scare you."

"I wish Charlie thought so."

There was a silence between them. To fill it he ordered coffee for them both, as her cup was empty. Then: "I never thanked you for a beautiful dinner."

Her color deepened. "And I never said goodnight."

"Anyway, I'm glad we're—I'm glad to see you again, Clare. I was afraid you might not want to see me any more."

"Why?" Her eyes widened, but they knew what he meant.

"I thought you might regret letting me stay as long as I did."

She shook her head slowly. "I don't regret it, as long as it didn't make you feel—well, left out . . ."

"And then there's Charlie. He didn't call me next day, or any other time. With Charlie, I never know how he's going to react to something, or just pretend to forget it. You know how he is."

"Yes," she said softly, "I know how he is."

Another silence, and again it was Brent who spoke. "Don't ever think I felt—left out, Clare. You made me feel part of something wonderful. If I never saw you again I'd remember it all my life."

"That's a sweet thing to say, David."

"Was Charlie upset about it, afterward? I mean, we were all pretty drunk, I guess, and he may have said things he regretted later."

Again she shook her head. "He meant everything he said. I'm sorry I couldn't agree to all of it."

He smiled. "You were wonderful about me. I feel it made me know you."

She was blushing again. "It's not the usual way of getting acquainted, is it?"

For the third time silence descended. They both sipped their coffee. Then: "Clare, I don't know how long Charlie's going to be away, but if there's any way I can be of help, UBC is listed in the phone book."

"Thank you, David."

"Maybe you'd like to go out to dinner, or the opera, or anything that pleases you . . ."

There was a teasing look in her eyes, in her smile. "You're wondering whether Charlie would mind if we saw each other alone. I'm sure he wouldn't mind, David. Quite the contrary."

He felt a wave of relief. "That makes me feel very good. Let's make a date right now!"

She laughed. "I'm in favor. Got any suggestions?"

"You name it, we'll do it."

"Charlie left the car, decided it was too risky to drive up to Paris. How would you like to take a spin in the country some day when you're free for a few hours?"

"How about tomorrow?"

And tomorrow it was. He was summoned by the beep-beep of the tiny two-seater Fiat under his window and found a radiant Clare behind the wheel, picnic basket lodged in the back compartment, a flask of Chianti peeking out of one corner. It was a gorgeous, sunny midwinter day, as mild as springtime back home, and they drove north toward Lago di Bracciano, a favorite spot of Clare's. Once out of Rome the roads were almost deserted, the countryside as green as summer. She wore a silk scarf over her tawny hair and a rust-colored cashmere sweater that clung closely to her body above a short dark-plaid skirt and hiking boots, making a picture so delectable he had a hard time keeping his hands off her. And as she drove, they talked. It seemed natural that he picked up the conversation from the point they had left off the first night they met, just when Charlie walked into the apartment.

"You were telling me about Colorado," he said.

She giggled. "I remember. The non-virgin seniors."

"Were you?"

"A non-virgin senior? I cannot tell a lie. Yes."

"Tell me how you got that way."

"Why do you care, David? It's the usual college-girl story."

"I still want to hear."

"I was living with three roommates who were all having affairs."

"So you figured it was about time, is that it?"

"Not quite. I was beginning to get the itch."

"I thought only boys got the itch, girls too?"

"Don't they ever! It got pretty bad at times, I can assure you."

He laughed. "Come to the point, what was he like?"

"Oh, him? He was cute. Dark hair, very dark eyes. He was built sort of like you."

"Athletic stud."

"Not at all. A very serious engineering major. He loved music, I used to go to his room and listen to Bach on his little phono."

"That wasn't all you did in his room, was it?"

"We necked it up, but I resisted going all the way."

"Until?"

"He was pretty suave about things, I guess he'd had enough experience to be patient. I suppose he could see I was coming around."

"I want to know just how it happened."

She grinned and glanced at him beside her. "David, you're being neurotic."

"No, I'm just a newsman. But if I'm embarrassing you—"

"You are, sort of. But I'm really trying to remember. It was so long ago . . ."

"Not that long ago. Besides, women never forget anything about these things."

Her low, exciting laugh. "Women never forget anything about anything."

"Clare, you're stalling again!"

"Not really. Well, I just gave up resisting one night and let him do it all."

"Do what all?"

"Like taking off my pants for me and pushing my legs apart. Poor guy, I was like a dead weight."

"But you got to liking it after a while?"

Her laughter pealed. "Don't we all? But I'm not going to talk about it any more. You're neurotic."

"If that's being neurotic I think it's the way to be."

They were laughing together and for a moment she dropped her gloved hand to his knee. "Oh, David, it's such fun being with someone unstuffy."

"Isn't Charlie unstuffy?"

"Only about half the time."

"And to think Pupi Fignoli called you puritanical."

He saw her smile fade swiftly. "She told you that? What does that bitch know about me except that I don't like her or any of her friends?"

"I suspect you've been to one of her parties."

"Correct, and it was a hateful experience. Charlie got drunk and tried to persuade me to join the others when they took their clothes off. No, thank you! I walked out on him, the only time I've ever done that."

The lovely young face clouded with recollection. He couldn't help remembering that she hadn't minded when David Brent saw her copulating but he wasn't about to mention the inconsistency. He didn't need to; Clare did it for him.

"I know what you're thinking," she went on, "after the other night at my house. And it wasn't because I was drunk, either. A woman will do anything when she's sexually aroused—I've learned that. She's just not responsible after a certain point." She added after a moment: "Besides, you're special. We're going to be friends, David."

"We're already friends," he said. "We always will be."

She smiled, her face calm and composed again, and suddenly on the rising ground in front of them Bracciano Castle came into view, a huge battlemented pile standing grimly against the background of hills covered with olive groves. Below, the lake was glittering silver-blue in the morning sunlight. She stopped the car by the road and they sat in silence, drinking the beauty of the scene like wine.

"Fifteenth-century," Clare said. "The Orsini family built it, but some other noble owns it now. Beautiful frescoes inside. Did you know the lake supplies water to the Vatican through an aqueduct that comes out on the Janiculum Hill?"

He grinned. "I didn't know. You seem pretty well up on your Italian history."

"What else have I got to do in my spare time?" she laughed. "C'mon, let's find a spot for the picnic." He took the lunch basket, she locked the car, and together they set off through the pine woods toward the lake. It was silent under the high umbrella of trees, the air filled with their scent. They followed the winding, narrow path until they came to the water's edge. Here it was almost oppressively hot; the stillness of high noon was absolute and the lake had a brooding quality. A curtain of lofty rushes stirred slightly in the wisp of breeze. He turned to the girl beside him, saw the tiny beads of sweat above her lips, the column of her bare throat. As naturally as instinct, he took her in his arms and kissed her, feeling her body yield to him and her shoulders tremble a little under his hands. Then just as suddenly they drew apart and, with unspoken assent, resumed their walk along the lake's edge. Neither of them spoke. There seemed no need to discuss it. For he knew now, and knew Clare knew with a wisdom surer than his own, that the moment was inevitable; in that instant they had surrendered simultaneously to the living beauty around them, the soft earth under their feet, the brooding stillness, the scent of the pines, and become part of it. Would it go on from there, beyond this woodland beauty, beyond the response to overwhelming nature? Would it become Clare and David without the need for spell, enchantment, drug? Had her kiss committed her? It was the unanswered question, even as now, like sister to brother, they joined hands with a single impulse and moved along the path together.

He spoke softly. "Do you remember reaching for my hand, that night?"

"Of course I remember."

"Why did you reach for my hand, Clare?"

"I only know I did. It was you, and you were standing beside me."

"I could feel your nails digging into my hand for days afterward."

She was smiling. "You squeezed my hand hard. Like this. And all the time I was coming, I felt you there. But it was confusing, David. A woman can't take two men at the same time." She gave him a swift look. "Or can she?"

"I'm told there are ways."

"Even if I got very drunk again and you took me, in Rome or anywhere, while Charlie was away—even then I would be thinking of Charlie when you came into me . . ."

In the long silence her words seemed to echo in the scented air. He stopped, still holding her hand, and they stood face to face.

"Do you want me to come into you, Clare?"

Her voice was low and troubled but their eyes held. "I think I do . . . I think I will . . . but not yet. I would have to love you, David. I've never loved anyone but Charlie before. I can't just . . . become a new woman overnight. But maybe I can learn. Maybe you can help me learn, teach me . . . I don't think it would have been possible if I—if that hadn't happened with Charlie and you that night. But now . . ."

She looked tremulously up at him and he put his arms around her, drew her close, so close he knew she could feel his erection throbbing against her body.

"I need a little time," she whispered, and they walked on together.

So it began—days and then weeks when he gave every spare hour to being with Clare. His broadcasting schedule was always uncertain: sometimes he did two or even three a day, then several days would go by without a newsbreak in Italy or a request from New York. He had to travel, too, as the news dictated, to Milan, to the French and Austrian frontiers. But always there was the daily phone call to Clare, the meeting when possible. She told him not even Charlie kept as faithfully in touch as he did. There was no indication when Charlie would return to Rome—his assignment was a day-to-day thing. And meanwhile Brent was giving Clare a life in Rome she had never known with her husband. They went to restaurants where she had never been, attended the winter season of opera and concerts, drove to the country on fine days when Brent was free, and always with the feeling between them that it might be the last time, that Charlie could be returning on a day's notice, or none at all, and this very special relationship would end.

For it was special—not since the day at Bracciano had he touched her but for the friendly kiss-on-cheek of greeting or parting. And he saw in her eyes the gratefulness that was gradually turning from affection to need, closer and closer to the verge of sexual surrender. They talked freely of everything but the act itself, and guardedly of Charlie.

"Do you tell him how often we see each other, Clare?"

"Not every time, no."

"And what does he say about it?"

"He doesn't mention you."

"Not at all?"

"No."

A pause. They were sitting facing each other by the fireplace in the Haines apartment, as they often did after returning from dinner or the theater.

"Doesn't he tell you he misses you?"

"Of course."

"Sexually?"

"Of course."

"And you? What do you tell him?"

She blushed slightly. "I tell him I miss him."

He didn't press her for more, sensing that here they were on dangerous ground. As their present relationship stood, Charlie Haines didn't exist, and it was unfair to bring him into the conversation, to remind her that she was another man's wife, to reawaken the sense of guilt or at least confusion that she must surely feel. He sensed it again as he bent to kiss her goodnight, felt it in the warm grasp of her hand on his arm as she stood up.

"You're a very patient man, David."

"I love being with you, that's all."

"I'm not fair to you."

He smiled. "Just be fair to yourself, Clare."

"I'm trying to be fair to Charlie, too."

"Which Charlie?" He couldn't help saying it. "The man who begs you to fuck me or the man who doesn't admit I exist?"

She didn't answer immediately and he was afraid he'd spoken coarsely. "Forgive the way I said it," he muttered, and took her unresisting into his arms. She was crying softly, he felt her tears against his cheek, but when she drew back he saw she was smiling. "You thought I was shocked at that word, dearest David—how little you know me, after all! I *love* that word, and all the words like it. And not only when you say them, darling, but when I say them." Again she moved close to him, his lips in her warm soft hair, her arms tightening around him, as though all at once the floodgates of her emotion had broken and every pent-up desire and secret of her innermost self was pouring through. "Charlie has nothing to do with it, not any more," she was murmuring through her tears, "he doesn't have to beg me to fuck you, I *want* you to fuck me, I lie awake dreaming of the moment when I open to you and I take you all the way, after so long . . . after so long! . . ."

"And will you take me now?" he whispered.

*"Oh, yes . . . please, please! . . ."* She took him by the hand and led him into the bedroom, this woman who in one moment, with total unexpectedness, after weeks of withholding herself, had suddenly become another identity, a statue come to life in his arms. She began to speak but he stopped the flooding words with his mouth, ran his hands hungrily down her back, over the whole body he'd coveted in so many hours of longing, felt her give and sway against him, almost swooning as his fingers closed on the rich weight of the buttocks, felt them yield and surrender to his touch. They were both panting, breathless, as their mouths parted. "Ahhh . . ." she whispered, "so good, so good . . . if you knew what those hands mean to me, like waking me from sleep, like raising a dark curtain that had been between us since that first night in this room, this same room . . . I wanted you that first night, dearest David, secretly I wanted you even while Charlie was fucking me, but I couldn't say it, not even when he pleaded with me, it

was too private, too new . . . because it happened all at once, I don't know how, I'll never know why . . . I felt it almost as soon as you walked in the door, before Charlie was with us, when we were alone . . . was it the way you looked at me? I was startled, startled at myself, and I felt my breasts reacting to you, I had to turn away to try to hide them because they were hardening . . . but I wanted your hands on them, your fingers playing with them, and then when Charlie came into me I felt you nearer, stronger than ever, I opened for him wider and deeper than I ever had, and he knew it, David, oh, he knew it, I could feel it in his kiss, and I knew that was why he told me to fuck you, because he knew it would arouse me and make me deeper and hotter for him, and it excited him, too, he wanted you to see him fucking me, to see my breasts when he took them in his hands, to see me naked before he covered me with his belly . . . oh, David, I wish there had been more light for you, so you could see him moving in and out, and my fingers touching his balls . . . but he was all over me by that time, I couldn't have seen you even if my eyes were open, his kiss was swallowing me up, but I knew you were there, darling, I knew you must be there, and my hand went out and caught you, and held you hard, I would have held your cock if you had given it to me then, but I was losing myself in my own orgasm, just the feel of your hand set me off, and Charlie felt me coming, that was what he wanted, that was what he always waited for, when I was helpless and throbbing, his signal to let go and let me have it all . . . he was hitting me with it, David, harder and deeper than he'd ever been, and just before he exploded I felt, just for a last instant, that *both* of you were fucking me, both of you were coming, until I blacked out and there was only Charlie when I opened my eyes . . ."

Her fresh tears scalded his face. "Clare . . ." he murmured to her, his lips buried in the soft flesh of her cheek, "I love you to talk to me like this, I want you always to tell me everything you feel, every beautiful word, the most naked, the most intimate thoughts in your mind, the most secret feelings of your body . . ."

"I've never said these things to Charlie," she whispered, almost as if afraid someone would overhear, "but suddenly, tonight, just as you were leaving, something inside me seemed to dissolve, I couldn't hold it back any

longer, like feeling moist all over, all at once, feeling my
legs wet and my skin flaming hot, fighting myself to keep
from trembling when you bent over to kiss me goodnight.
Because I could smell you, David, the very own scent of
you I smelled that day at Bracciano and kept with me ever
since, so intimate, so intoxicating I woke at night with the
scent all around me, believing for a moment that you were
near, naked, ready to come into my bed and lie beside
me, smother me with it, overwhelm me with the scent of
your body, your skin, your underarms, and let me bury
my face in your crotch hair, drink the heavy male
smell of you . . . will you let me drink you, all of you,
David? Soon? Now? . . ."

Her voice was low, husky with pleading, her hands
loosening his belt with soft, deliberate insistence, delicately drawing open his fly, reaching up to draw back the
shoulders of his jacket, unknotting his tie, and he in his
turn undressing her as they stood face to face in the lamplight, their smiles enveloping each other as they uncovered
mutual mysteries, her breasts freed at last for him so he
could devour them with his eyes, he at full erection before
her fascinated gaze. "You're beautiful," she said quietly,
"you're the most beautiful man I've ever seen. Like a
Greek sculpture reborn to life."

"No. You are the Greek sculpture."

Suddenly she knelt before him. "Like adoring the
gods at an altar," she said, "at some ancient ceremony of
sacrifice." Slim fingers grasped, rose and fell along the
slender column of flesh. "How strong he is! How lovely!
And mine. Soon he will be deep inside me, so I can hold
him there forever . . ."

In answer he drew her back up to her feet and they
kissed with bodies touching head to foot. He felt her
toes embracing his feet, her breasts warm and full against
his chest, their knees touching, their thighs quivering at
contact, his column long and hard against her belly. He
dropped his hands slowly along the arched beauty of her
back and took her buttocks again, slipping his finger between them to just touch the hot little orifice hidden there,
and her hands imitated his, her finger finding the same furrow; as she pressed it deep he trembled at the sensation
and felt her body tremble in response.

It was time.

They moved together slowly toward the bed, hands clasped, with solemn steps as in a sacred rite. Just once they turned on common impulse and looked deep into each other's eyes, saw there the steady burning flame of worship, body and spirit as one. Tenderly he laid her down on the dark blue counterpane and knelt between her legs, the bedspread cool and smooth against his skin. "I want you the way he took you," he whispered, "all of you," and watched, spellbound by her beauty, as her knees lifted, her thighs widened and the golden gorge lay open to his desire, the lips already puffed and glistening, thrust toward him with a movement like the yearning of her whole body. She took him with a long exhalation of her breath into his mouth, broken with tiny whimpering gasps as inch by inch he eased into her. Even before he reached at full length she had begun to burst with her first orgasm, and as suddenly his body answered her: he was powerless to control himself, try as he would in the moment of wild elation, knowing now that she wanted it this way, swift, violent, complete, their bodies impacting with solid smacking blows toward the relief that in the splendor of its fulfillment was only prelude to the slower, more exquisite joys that would follow.

# 29

A time unlike any other in his life, perhaps because they both knew it was stolen time, every moment they could spend together away from his work infinitely precious. The Roman winter merged with spring, with warmer sunshine, greener hills, and beyond to the north, somewhere, the war went on, the Nazi armies swept through eastern Europe and stood menacingly at the borders of the West. Each day Italian fascism moved closer to Hitlerian control, but 'for Clare and Brent Italy was still for stealing moments of loving and laughter, for sun-drenched luncheons on the apartment terrace, for secret hours of sex and music, for nights clinging naked together, half-waking to whispers mouth to mouth, aching with a desire that could never be satisfied for more than a few days. Could he ever have been as happy? More and more it seemed to him that he was becoming like Charlie Haines, wearing his professional identity like a mask, a cloak, only to cast them off each precious time he was reunited with Clare, forgetting the whole world outside to plunge into the utterly private realm where she reigned as insatiable mistress. It was a realm from which he returned only reluctantly to the daily routine of broadcasting. At the back of his mind, the very scent of his nostrils, the image of Clare haunted him until he could rejoin the reality of her presence. She had obliterated the past, but the future was not to be denied. On a day they were driving across Rome together the news blared forth from amplifiers all over the city: at dawn the German army had invaded Holland and Belgium; Hitler's proclamation declared "the decisive battle for the future has begun."

Involuntarily Clare leaned toward him and clutched his arm, burying her face in his chest, her shoulders

quivering. In response he slowed the car and pulled over
to the curb, putting his arm around her. "Darling, it's not
as though we didn't expect it."

She shook her head, blindly, as though refusing to accept the truth. But he knew, and knew she knew, that this
meant the eventual fall of France, and the return of
Charlie Haines to Rome. He tried to comfort her. "The
British and French will stop them, you'll see."

"You know you don't believe that! No one does. The
only question is how long the French can hold out before
they collapse."

He summoned a little laugh, but it sounded false to
him. "If you want to bet on it, I'll give you odds the
French chase them out of the country."

"You're just trying to reassure me." She straightened
up and rearranged her hair. "I'm all right now, dearest, it
was just the shock of it really happening. But what will
that crazy Mussolini do now?"

"Stay neutral, of course. The Italians don't want to
fight, not this time."

They had hoped for a quiet evening at the apartment
but that was impossible now; he left her without going
upstairs and took a taxi to his office. As expected, cables
requesting reaction reports were already arriving from
several news programs, and the overseas operator called
to say New York was holding a wire open for an immediate conference. It was after nine before he was free again
to return to Clare.

He could see she was making an effort to smile as if
nothing had changed and they both confined themselves
to trivialities while she served him supper. As always it was
delicious—thin strips of veal with a wine sauce and a simple salad. Afterward they sat in candlelight, facing each
other across the little table, and spoke what was really on
their minds.

"David, what is going to happen?"

"From everything I've been able to find out tonight,
the second world war."

"That isn't what I meant. I meant what is going to
happen to you and me?"

"Darling, I knew what you meant. I guess I'm just
trying to avoid facing it."

"Charlie called from Paris. He said the French are cocksure the Nazis will stop after they occupy Belgium and Holland. But he doesn't believe it."

"I don't either. Why should they stop?"

"He said this might be the last time he could get through by phone but he'd keep trying. He left tonight for Brussels."

"He's going to the front?"

"That was all he said—Brussels."

A silence. Then: "Still no sign of when he's coming back to Rome?"

"I asked him again. He just doesn't know. Nothing is certain, from now on . . ."

"As usual, he said nothing about me?"

"Nothing, David."

So the stolen time would continue, the shadows always in the background. But the shadows were growing longer with each passing day, as the Nazi conquest crept steadily over the face of western Europe. Brent saw much less of Clare now: his days were filled with hectic work —interviews, broadcasts, street demonstrations, coverage of speeches and government events, all tied to the mounting triumphs of Fascism. The time differential between Rome and New York, with the regular radio news programs taking air late in the evening, Rome time, further complicated his relationship with Clare; sometimes it was two or three in the morning before he finished and returned to the apartment, to find her dozing fitfully, hungry for his arms.

There was no further word of Charlie. Both Clare and Brent, at her request, tried to get through by phone to the IP office in Paris, but without success. He knew that secretly, trying to keep it from him, Clare was intensely worried about her husband, somewhere with the French army retreating toward Paris. Once, deep in the night, he woke beside her and found her softly weeping. "I'm sorry," she whispered brokenly to him, "I can't—help it. I had a terrible dream . . ."

"Charlie?"

But she was unable to tell him, unable to speak. He took her in his arms and comforted her as best he could until, at last, she slept again.

It was broad daylight when they woke. Sunlight as

hot as summer was pouring into the room. It was a few moments before Brent became aware of what had awakened them: a swelling sound of activity, excitement, the babble of talk in the street below, then sporadic cheers, the sound of a bugle and marching feet.

"Another parade?" Clare sighed, opening her eyes.

It was more than another parade. With growing premonition he reached for the bedside radio and switched it on.

The voice of Il Duce proclaiming that Italy had placed itself at the side of Germany. Italy was in the war.

There was no immediate change in Brent's professional undertakings, no sign of unusual activity at the broadcast studios where he did four reports to New York during the afternoon and evening. But the next day an arrogant Italian army censor was present to check his scripts, and the day after that the world spotlight was on another capital; Rome was only a backwater in the news.

Paris had fallen.

The official word came through on his office radio and he immediately phoned Clare, but the wires were clogged with the thousands of calls prompted by the news from France and he wasn't able to communicate with her despite repeated attempts during the rest of the day. Between the demands of broadcasting and coverage of official Italian reaction it was nearly midnight before he could get back to the apartment. He let himself in hastily and hurried into the salotto. A man was standing in the center of the room, glass in hand, looking at him in surprise, while behind him Clare stood up and remained rooted to the spot, as if frozen, her eyes large and dark with anguish, a fixed smile at her lips.

Charlie Haines said, "I see you have your own key."

He was wearing a dirt-stained war correspondent's uniform and looked twenty pounds thinner. A knapsack and some other gear were piled in a corner of the room. "Well, aren't you going to say welcome back?" Haines demanded, and swayed slightly; Brent realized now he was drunk.

"Charlie! For a minute I didn't recognize you." He moved forward and they shook hands. "How the hell did you get here?"

"U.S. embassy plane out of Bordeaux. Hitched a ride. Lucky to get out of that madhouse. Nazis will be there by tomorrow." He turned to his wife. "How about a drink for my old friend Dave?" he said, and followed her with his eyes as she went to the table and poured the martini out of the pitcher.

"How long have you been here, Charlie?"

He was still looking at Clare. "Only a little while. Hardly had time to sling my gear before you came." A brittle laugh. "Quite a coincidence, wouldn't you say?"

"As a matter of fact I've been trying to reach Clare on the phone ever since this morning, to ask her if there was any news of you. She's been very worried, naturally."

"And you do what you can to comfort her, right?"

Clare spoke for the first time. "I've been grateful for David's friendship since you've been gone, Charlie. He's been a consolation." Her voice was low, level; she was in control of herself now, smiling calmly as she handed him his drink. Only her eyes betrayed the strain he knew she felt, as if beseeching him with a strange appeal.

Haines said, "Well, here's to consolation!" and raised his glass in a toast.

"I'm glad you're back safe, Charlie," Brent said. "You must have had a time of it."

And he had. He'd covered the Belgian, British and French armies from the day after German troops launched their invasion. Sitting down now, motioning Clare and Brent to the sofa opposite, he recounted the tragedy as an observer who was there and saw—the swift collapse of original resistance in the Low Countries before the overwhelming power of the invaders; the blitzkrieg against Holland and the quick capitulation of the Belgian King; then the outflanking of France's vaunted Maginot Line, the routing of Britain's expeditionary force and the fall of Dunkerque, and finally the drive on Paris that scattered the French defenders before it and sent their Government into panicky flight southward, along with a rearguard of American reporters including Haines of the IP.

When he finished, nearly an hour later, interrupted only by fresh servings of drinks all around, his listeners broke their silence at last.

"It's a miracle you weren't killed or wounded," Clare said softly.

"Not quite a miracle—just luck." He looked at Brent. "You missed a great story, Dave."

"I wish I'd been there."

"No you don't." Again the ambiguous note in everything he said to him, a sardonic glint in the eyes. "It's no fun getting shot up by a bunch of Nazi bastards. At least nobody's bombed Rome yet." Now he turned his gaze on Clare. "God knows where you'd be tonight if I'd let you come with me. Aren't you glad now I turned you down?"

"I'm only glad you're back safely," she said quietly.

He went on as if she had not spoken. "After all, you're snug and comfy here—plenty to drink, regular meals, a big, soft bed! And a protector who has his own key."

*"Charlie, please . . ."* she began. He ignored her and went on to the table, poured himself another triple martini, sat down again and spoke, this time to Brent. "Did you give her a lot of protection, Dave? She looks like you did. I never saw her look more luscious. In fact, you two look mighty pretty, both of you, sitting there side by side. Well, go ahead, boy, put your arm around her, show me how it was! Did you lay her on the couch while I was away or did you prefer the bed, eh?"

"Charlie . . ." she began again, but he laughed and waved her off. Brent stood up and moved away from the sofa, tried to speak but could find nothing to say. He wanted to look back at Clare but kept his eyes on Haines, waiting for him to continue. But the other man was silent, and finally Brent spoke.

"Look, Charlie, let's be sensible. You've been under great strain and all of us have had too much to drink. If you want to talk to me about something, okay, but let's wait till tomorrow, when we're both sober, and sane."

The wicked grin. "You didn't answer my question, old friend—did you fuck her on the couch or on the bed? Or on the floor, maybe? In front of the fire on those chill winter nights?"

"If I remember correctly the last time we were together you *asked* me to fuck her!"

"All right, I'm asking you to show me how you do it, right now."

This time he turned, looked at Clare. She sat stiffly

upright, her face flooded with color, her hands working
in anguish, her eyes huge and bright with tears. She was
staring at Haines.

Brent said, "Thank you, Charlie, but you're out of
your mind."

In answer Haines sprang to his feet, walked deliberately to the couch, pushed Clare backward against the
cushions and said, "If you won't fuck her, I will," throwing
up her skirt to disclose her naked body to the belly.
*"All right,"* looking down at her, grim, challenging, *"let's
ask you which one of us you want—me or him!"*

Motionless, as if hypnotized, she lay there without
speaking. Brent stepped quickly to the couch. "Clare . . ."
he said, "what do you want me to do?"

He had never seen her so lovely, so helpless, the gold-
en thighs very slightly parted, the vulva open to the depths
beyond. She lay before them in all her beauty, making no
movement to cover herself, totally exposed, totally vulnerable, as the two men stood side by side above her,
immobile, powerful, waiting. Her gaze went from one to
the other and back in a kind of agony, like a splendid
young animal trapped and desperate. For a long moment
her eyes rested on Haines again, then went slowly, finally, back to Brent. And it was to Brent she spoke, each
word entreaty like a prayer, her voice a barely audible
gasp. "He—is—my husband," she whispered, and closed
her eyes in surrender.

Beside him Brent heard the hoarse chuckle and saw
Haines unbuckle his belt and loosen his trousers, as if no
longer conscious of his presence. There was nothing more
for any of them to say. It was Clare's decision, and she
had made it. Brent turned then and left them without
looking back.

# 30

The cable from New York came three days later. Brent was to be replaced by the UBC correspondent in France and transferred to the Washington bureau. He was startled by the suddenness of the order, but not really surprised: by this time he was getting used to overseas radio news practices, the extreme mobility of network operations abroad and abrupt shifting of reporters from one post to another. Personal considerations were coldly disregarded: if you didn't like this business, then get out. New York knew nothing, and cared less, about a girl named Clare and her relationship with David Brent, who remembered now that his predecessor in Rome had also been transferred, abruptly, to Washington; maybe they would meet there and compare notes about Charlie Haines, dual personality . . .

Because Brent had not heard from either Haines since the nightmare experience three days ago when he had turned away and left the apartment, left Clare lying in tears on the couch, her body bared, awaiting the man who was baring himself beside her. Brent could still hear her echoing words: *"He—is—my husband . . . ,"* could still feel the storm of jealous anger at his heart. Somehow, despite the shock that caught him unawares, he'd known, they'd both known, the crunch was coming, had to be faced. But to happen this way, so suddenly, without warning or preparation, was too much to handle, especially for Clare. At the crucial moment her courage deserted her, all her feelings of marital loyalty returned with the sight of her husband returning from his trial by fire, and she retreated into her former life; David Brent was all at once a dream.

Not that she wouldn't regret it, after their months of joy together; she would have her bittersweet memories,

191

as Brent would have his. But that was all that was left, he was sure of it as the days passed without a letter, a phone call—anything to assuage this soreness he carried around inside him. Twice he had seen Haines at press conferences since that night, and without seeming to make any effort to do so, both men kept deliberately apart, giving no more than a glance at each other without change of expression, without recognition. It was a matter of pride now; only Clare could break it, but she wasn't going to, not even a word of farewell was forthcoming—the situation was beyond her control, beyond her experience at this stage of her life. Later, maybe, somewhere, sometime, in a year to come . . .

Meanwhile he was left with a new burden of loneliness. He'd forgotten how to be lonely. In the midst of it, one of Cathy's bright, amusing little letters arrived from New York, and for a few minutes his sister's scribbled words lightened his disappointment. It would be good to see family again, his mother and, somehow even more so, Cathy herself. He hadn't known how much he missed them both, and soon would see them again. He wrote immediately, promising to let them know his date of departure as soon as he knew it. Then he lapsed into his mood of melancholy once more. The wonderful days spent with Clare were haunting him, and he didn't know how to cope with them. It was all so hard to believe, and he knew it was even harder for her; for all his jealousy and sadness, he felt no resentment toward Clare, only a hope that she wasn't suffering, only to hope for himself that his replacement would arrive promptly and he could get far away from the scene of his memories. The replacement, Ted Hurlbut, was on his way by boat from Lisbon after a hazardous roundabout journey. The hardest thing until he arrived would be to resist the almost overwhelming impulse to call Clare, even to go to the apartment if she wouldn't talk to him. But again it was pride that came to his aid. Perhaps he would write to her before he left Italy —but there, too, lay the danger of embarrassing her with Charlie if he intercepted the letter or caught her with it. There was no trusting what he might do.

He met the boat at Naples on a morning of brilliant sunshine. Italy had never seemed more beautiful—the bay shimmering with a thousand lights, Capri in the hazy distance, Vesuvius rising majestic above the shoreline. Surprisingly, he was able to get Hurlbut disembarked with a minimum of red tape, though the Fascist officers were sneering and arrogant as they stamped his passport and went through the contents of his dufflebag, his only luggage. The new Rome correspondent didn't look much older than Brent but he was wise in the ways of European politics and it was clear from his conversation on the way up to Rome that he could handle his latest assignment without difficulty. He'd also served a tour of duty in Washington.

"Lucky bastard!" he grinned at Brent across the jolting train compartment. "D.C.'s the prime spot these days —a madhouse of activity."

"Ever work in Italy, Ted? This is a madhouse, too."

Hurlbut rubbed his hands. "I'm ready. By the way, did Charlie Haines make it back to Rome?"

"Large as life." He felt a pang as he said it.

"Last time I saw him we were both hiding in a farm shed under bombardment." He paused, reflecting. "You'd think you'd get to know a man under conditions like that, but all the time we were at the front I never could figure Charlie. D'you know the guy well?"

"I can't say I do," Brent said. "I've tried, though."

"There must be somebody behind that grim facade, Dave, but I'm damned if I could smoke him out. I'll try again, in Rome."

"I wish you luck."

Hurlbut smiled. "Incidentally, what do I do about women in this here country? You going to put me in touch with something before you go?"

He thought of Pupi Fignoli. "I'll do what I can, Ted."

"You're a pal!"

He was as good as his word, but first they went through the routine of showing the new man the bureau procedures and putting him in touch with its news contacts: broadcast studio layout, post-office facilities, Italian and U.S. Embassy official sources and the half dozen British and American resident correspondents (although Haines was not around when they went through the Press Club and met the crowd at the bar). The day before Brent left for America he took Hurlbut to lunch at the Palazzo Fignoli, by prearrangement with the Marchesa, who was graciousness itself—and a bit more.

"How d'you do, how long is your cock?" was her formal greeting as she extended her hand to Hurlbut. For a moment he stood there astonished, then burst into a roar of laughter, bowed low and replied: "In repose, or stimulated?"

Pupi had a glass of wine in her hand, and behind her the butler offered two more on a silver tray. "David," she said, "I think your friend and I are going to get along."

"I had a feeling you would," Brent said.

"Count on it," said Ted Hurlbut.

The Marchesa was in fine form during lunch and Hurlbut was enchanted with her verbal sketches of Italy's leading politicos, all of whom, of course, she knew personally and several of whom had compromised themselves more than once at her all-night parties. "You must come to my next one," she told her new acquaintance. "Then I'll have something on you, too."

"Sounds fine to me, Marchesa!"

She turned to Brent. "I had hoped to see more of you during your stay in Rome, David, but I know the reason why you were so busy, so I forgive you." Her smile was brightly malicious. "I see Charlie Haines is back in Rome. I suppose it's just as well that you're leaving. Still, I'm sorry to see you go. I won't forget you."

"I won't forget *you*, Pupi."

Hurlbut was looking puzzled. "Something not good between you and Charlie?"

But Pupi changed the subject before Brent had time to reply. "We'll take coffee in another room," she said, getting up, "where I have something to show you."

"Another room" proved to be located in a part of the palazzo Brent had not seen, a marvel of Renaissance decoration and lush comfort. They sat around a richly carved coffee table in low, capacious armchairs surrounded by tapestries of nude nymphs and prancing satyrs. Almost immediately Brent noticed the penis on the half-horse, cloven-hoofed satyr in the central painting. He was bearing down on a supine nude with his prick distended at full erection and a demoniacal grin.

Brent laughed. "Is that what you wanted to show us, Pupi?"

She shook her head. "But I thought you'd spy it—everybody does. The face is a caricature of one of Gaetano's ancestors. Gaetano," she explained to Hurlbut, "is my ex-husband. He taught me about sex."

Hurlbut motioned at the satyr. "If he inherited *that* from his ancestor, you sure must have learned a lot."

Brent was studying the tapestries. "Are we supposed to find something else?"

The Marchesa smiled. "No, dear. But I won't mystify you any longer." She pressed a button at the side of the table and after a few moments a girl appeared carrying the tray of coffee and liqueurs. Both men tried to conceal their breathless reactions as the girl served them with quiet deference. She was dressed like a waitress and she was probably, Brent thought, the most beautiful girl he had seen in Italy—no older than eighteen or nineteen, with the face of a Madonna and the body of a nymph, a combination of purity and innocent sexuality.

Pupi was watching the two men. "Yes, this is what I wanted to show you. Elena is one of my prize possessions."

At the sound of her name the girl looked up, blushed faintly and smiled with a touching shyness. The Marchesa said something in Italian and she dropped a graceful little curtsey before she withdrew.

Hurlbut let his breath out. "God!" he said, "or should I say *Dio?*"

"She's the daughter of my head gardener at Monte Mayo—my country place. She doesn't speak a word of English but she doesn't need to. But there you see the classic beauty of Italian womanhood, unspoiled as a budding flower. My lesbian friends froth at the mouth when they see her, but I've warned them to keep off. Later, if that's what Elena wants, she can go that way. But she's utterly loyal to my wishes for as long as she stays with me."

They drank huge snifters of cognac with their coffee, on top of the copious wine drunk at lunch, and Hurlbut was beginning to show the effects. "They didn't tell me Rome was like this," he burbled happily. The Marchesa was feeling no pain, either. More and more relaxed, more and more free in speech, she had gradually opened her

knees so that Hurlbut, sitting opposite, could see that she
wore no underwear; she was visibly naked to the waist.
Once he glanced excitedly at Brent to see if he had noticed and was rewarded with a slight nod of understanding.
Pupi, either unconsciously or deliberately, seemed unaware of her nudity until at last she couldn't help seeing
Hurlbut's stare.

"Like it?" she said lightly, downing the last drops of
her cognac.

"Well . . ."

They all laughed. Pupi made no effort to close her
knees. "David's had it," she said. "Haven't you, David?
And he's also had the best Goddamn massage on the
European continent. I gave it to him myself. If you're a
very nice boy," she went on to Hurlbut, "I'll give you one,
too."

"I can't wait, Pupi."

"Well, there's no time like the present!" She stood up,
lurching slightly, and smiled down at Brent. "No, you can't
watch—not this time." And leaning to whisper in his ear
she added: *Wait for us here. My bon-voyage gift to you
is Elena. Handle gently . . .*"

He watched her take Ted Hurlbut's arm and steer
him from the room, but not before she pressed the table
button to summon the servant. Hurlbut looked dazed with
delight as they disappeared into the hall, then their footsteps died away and Brent was alone in the silence. He sat
down again, his eyes on the closed door through which
the girl had come with the tray, and for a moment he
couldn't believe what Pupi had whispered to him—was it a
wicked tease or did she mean it would really happen? As
the seconds ticked away he felt excitement rising in his
belly and loins, anticipation that was suddenly touched
with fear it was all a joke; maybe the girl wouldn't come
back at all.

But she came. The door opened slowly, almost timo-
rously, and as she crossed the room with the tray under her
arm she stared straight ahead of her as though no one
else was present. Brent was motionless, watching her set
the tray down on the table, pick up the cups and glasses
one by one with deft, quiet hands. Still she ignored him,
or rather, seemed oblivious to his presence. The lovely
face was a mask, a painting by Raphael; his gaze traveled

deliberately over the beautiful body outlined in the black, tight-fitting uniform with its lace collar—wide shoulders, tiny waist, the hips swelling gorgeously beneath, the curving slender legs in sheer stockings, narrow feet in simple slippers, and as his eyes scanned upward again, the breasts of a young Aphrodite, born for the sculptor's hands.

The table was cleared, the tray was filled, and just as she was about to lift it she paused, her whole body still, the marble-white bare arms poised as though holding an artist's pose, infinitely graceful and aware. She turned her head then, the huge black eyes were on him at last, as though seeing him for the first time, and the mask broke, softened into smile, showing the perfect teeth—a white flash of recognition, disarmed and disarming, fresh, ingenuous, direct as a child's trusting acceptance.

"You're the most beautiful woman I've ever seen!" He heard himself blurt it out, then remembered the words meant nothing to her. He smiled in the joy of looking at her, and saw her understand. Those eyes understood everything; he wouldn't even try to speak to her in Italian; they would communicate in this blessed silence.

He stood up and she straightened to face him, almost eye to eye, and the romantic phrase of a poet who loved Italy rang suddenly in his mind . . . "Divinely tall and most divinely fair . . ." But Elena wasn't fair, if Byron had meant it as blonde—she was fair in the total sense of beauty, her smooth dark hair gleaming with vitality, with the bursting intensity of youth expressed in every inch of this body. The smile died now but the cherry lips remained parted. She was waiting—not submissive, not expectant, but with the dignity, the composure, that the Marchesa herself might envy. He had the swift impression that he was looking at a thousand years of breeding, a living statue from an ancient age, that she might stand utterly motionless like this forever, like the frieze on a classic vase.

But Elena was all too real: he took both her hands in his and felt the warm pulsing blood beneath the skin, saw her eyes kindle with response as he drew closer, was standing now with their bodies almost touching, and their lips touched, she yielded, felt his arms go around her in the long, perfect kiss. Desire rioted in his blood; and still he couldn't believe this was happening; this girl was of the earth, earthy, it was glorious flesh he held in his arms,

warm and growing hotter through the thin covering of her
dress. It was no dream, but only the improbable, the impossible Pupi could have created the reality; what had he
done to deserve this rare diamond dropped casually in the
palm of his hand by an oversexed, scatter-brained American heiress? Again he faced the girl's glowing eyes, seeking some sign of reluctance, of rebellion against the will of
her mistress, but he saw only a desire like his own, an
eagerness to experience it all, a smoldering excitement
awaiting his every wish. Was Elena the willing sex chattel
of whatever friend designated for pleasure by the Marchesa? Looking at her now he didn't think so, but he was
equally sure this was not her first time: the eyes were too
knowing, almost avaricious of what was to come.

He stepped back and his gaze swept her from head to
foot and mounted again to her face. He made a slight gesture of adoration with his hand and she understood it immediately. With a beautiful lissome movement of her
shoulders she reached back, loosened the uniform, brought
it forward and dropped it to her feet. Her eyes never left
his face, seemed to be asking humble approval for the sight
he beheld. She was wearing a simple white bra and panty
over an old-fashioned garter belt, serving only to empha-
size the breathtaking body they contained. He could see
why the bra was necessary: with those breasts released,
even under a uniform, no male guest of the Marchesa
could concentrate on anything else in the room; as it was,
they threatened to burst out of the sheath that held
them. As if aware of everything he was thinking, Elena
reached back once more, still holding his gaze with her
eyes, and this time the bra slipped slowly off the hidden
treasures beneath; rosy nipples stiffened out of the darker
aeroles that rose and fell with her quicker breathing.
"*Bella* . . ." The word came as from another man speaking. "*Bella Elena* . . ." And she smiled softly, glancing
down once at her own beauty as though to make sure no
flaw would mar his fascination at the sight.

She was bending forward again, this time to slip off
the panty, and as she did, with a charming little shrug of
modesty, she turned away and stood with her back to
him, offering up a vision of perfection: framed by the
black garters and belt the sight of an ass so ravishing in
its perfection, so infinitely desirable in the undulant curve

of soft buttocks and the dark cleft between, that his hand
went instinctively to his straining cock and gripped it hard.
But she was to allow him only a glimpse before facing
him again, still bending forward, unhooking the garter belt,
peeling off the sheer black stockings as she lifted first one
leg, then the other, and dropping the whole delicate little
outfit in one heap with her slippers on the floor. Now she
straightened up to face him: naked female beauty incar-
nate, and he saw for the first time the fleece of soft dark
gossamer spread between her legs. She followed his gaze
and smiled, no shyness in it this time, the full, rich smile of
a young pagan, belied only by the warm blush that spread
from her cheeks down across her throat and breasts and
belly that rose and fell a little more quickly now. She
moved toward him, took his hand and placed it there between her legs where he was looking, clasping it closer
to her until his fingers felt the hidden sticky wetness.
Their eyes met again; in all this he'd spoken only her name
and *bella* . . . and once more he said the word again, with
the words that said everything he was feeling, directly,
simply, in her own tongue: *"Ti voglio bene . . ."* I want
you . . .

She answered him in silence, with her eyes, with her
quivering mouth, with the hand that clasped his hand and
led him through the door where she had come in and down
a short corridor to a room fitted as starkly as a chapel;
there was even a crucifix on the wall over the narrow
couch that was covered with a plain dark red blanket.
Was this her own room? He didn't look further; he only
knew his eyes were devouring this body that Phideas himself would have coveted. He wanted to bury himself in its
beauty as though it were the first and last time he would
ever hold beauty in his arms. And he watched her move
like a nymph reborn from a tapestry as she glided to the
door, closed it carefully, and returned to his side, her hands
helping him take off his jacket, loosen his belt, receive his
tie and shirt like precious gifts in her hands and put them
one by one on the narrow chair at the head of the bed. He
was naked now to the waist, and when he dropped his trousers and shorts they lay forgotten on the floor. Her eyes
were elsewhere, staring at the swollen column, its tip glistening with its own lubricant, the heavy scrotum tightened
and aware, and suddenly she laughed with delight, with

elation, as a child claps her hands at something wondrous
and desired, the soft peal of pleasure like music in the silent room—silent until she spoke; for the first time he heard
her voice, warm and rich like her body, low and intimate
like her little laugh. *"Bello . . ."* she said; it was her turn
to say it; and saying it she came to him with her arms
wide; they were around him; he was hard, throbbing,
against her belly, and it was time, time for them both, his
dream realized. The devastating beauty of her lay open,
waiting, cream white against the red covering on the narrow couch. She took him without effort, deeply, fully,
easily, and for a moment before he began his rhythm
both lay together transfixed. He was looking down at the
Mona Lisa eyes, and then he kissed them, gravely, softly,
feeling her whole body tremble with the feel of the hot
prong inside her, spearhead of his passion. Ancient Italy
was overwhelmed, was surrendered, in joy.

# FIVE

# 31

He was returning to a homeland caught up in the fever of world war. Because of military operations over a vast area, he traveled a circuitous route by plane and ship and then plane again, finally reaching Miami after crossing the South Atlantic and proceeding to New York by air on the final lap. He found the country gripped by the realization that American entry into the war was inevitable, while on the home front millions of aliens were registering under the Smith Act and its doctrine of guilt by association. Defense experts anticipated a great future for the Sikorsky helicopter, a radical new departure in air power. Franklin D. Roosevelt, in office for an unprecedented third term, was working behind the scenes with Winston Churchill in the Allied war effort and calling upon the United States to become the arsenal of democracy.

Cathy was at the airport, and to his surprise had brought her mother, despite her declining eyesight. She was stoic and strong, as always, and as always hid the emotion she was feeling at her son's homecoming safe and sound. But Cathy was the revelation: he had left her still thin and boyish, still a kid—now, standing at the entrance to the passageway from the plane, he scarcely recognized the handsome young woman, chicly dressed and with that look of awareness of her own attractiveness. Little sister was all grown up, and in the right directions, judging from the glances men gave her as he collected his luggage and hailed a taxi outside the gate. It was Cathy who took over from there, instructing the cabbie to drop Mrs. Brent off first at her West Side apartment.

Brent stared. "Since when are you two not living together?"

His mother laughed. "Cathy stood me as long as she could, but I guess we're both glad to have places of our

own. We Brents have always been independent souls—
look at yourself, David!"

"You could have mentioned it in a letter."

Cathy's impudent smile. "The Brents don't tell everything—look at yourself, David."

The drive in was an opportunity to catch up: Cathy's
steady rise from lowly receptionist in the ad agency to her
job as assistant to the agency's woman boss; Margaret
Brent living quietly but comfortably on the annuity left by
a mindful husband. Both were eager to hear the latest in
Brent's life in Europe after months of fear for his safety.

Cathy hugged his arm. "You're the only brother I've
got, you know . . ."

His mother squeezed his hand with both her own. "I've
prayed for you every day, David."

She kissed him tenderly as they let her off at the apartment. "How long can you stay before you go to Washington?"

"They've given me a few days, but it won't be long.
I'll find out tomorrow. But we'll have a good long talk before I go, I promise you that."

"Thank God you're in America again! Will we be
dragged into the war?"

He smiled at her. "I'm afraid so, darling. Call you
tomorrow." He turned to Cathy. "Know a good hotel?
I'm on expense account."

"I thought you'd feel more at home if you stayed with
me—I've got room."

"I'd like that. Lead on."

She gave the driver an address in the east sixties and
they crossed through twilit Central Park. "What you were
saying to mother, David . . . do you really believe we
can't stay out of the war?"

He shook his head. "It's inevitable we'll go in. There's
no use worrying about it, though. Let's hear about you.
You don't look worried about anything."

"I'll tell you all about me over a drink, sweetie. I
think we both could use one, don't you? And unless your
taste has changed, you'll be glad to hear I'm giving you
chopped sirloin and mashed potato for supper, okay?"

"You're quite a girl, to remember," he smiled.

"I remember more than you think."

Her apartment was small, well-organized and tasteful

—a big studio room with smaller bedroom and bath off one side and a compact kitchen on the other. There was also a portable bar, amply stocked, which Cathy wheeled over to the divan where he sat in regal comfort. She poured out two lavish Scotches and joined him, and for a time they sat silent, content to look at each other and sip their drinks. "I suppose," he said finally, "I'm wondering why a desirable girl like you wasn't married long ago."

She grinned in a way that touched his heart, a flash of the child she used to be. "I could ask you the same question, David."

"You first."

"It's really very simple: them that liked me I didn't happen to want, and them as I liked didn't linger. Oh, I tried them out—or they tried me out, whichever way you want to put it." She shrugged with a tiny sigh. "The one I cared the most for turned out to be queer. I guess it figures, New York now being the homo capital of the world." She laughed. "Be on your guard, brother!" More seriously she said, "I don't know why, but homos seem to like me. My boss is a lesbian. She's made me a standing offer to move in with her. I think she really expects me to do it one of these days. But I'm still hoping Mr. Right will come along in the meantime."

"Have you—did you 'try out' your boss lady?"

"Oh, sure. I mean we all have to find out, don't we?"

"And how was it?"

She gave a little shudder and grimaced. "A complete flop. Meaningless. I let her have her fun, but I might as well have been a display-window mannequin for all I felt." She gulped her drink and smiled. "Now it's your turn to tell."

"I've thought a lot about it, Cathy, but I think the main reason I'm not married is there just hasn't been time, as yet. I've been living on the run, virtually, ever since I left the country. And there's no sign ahead that I'll be living any other way for some time to come."

"But you've had your share of tryouts along the way."

He grinned. "But definitely."

She leaned over and lightly kissed his cheek. "Time to start dinner," she said. "There's the bottle. Serve yourself."

For a moment she stood over him, smiling down, then

she drained her glass and poured a fresh one to take to the kitchen with her. Brent said, looking up at her, "It's a little strange, in a way. I can't think of you as a sister any more. You're a person, now. My sister was somebody else."

"Would it surprise you if I told you I've been thinking the very same thing about you?"

He watched her as she crossed the room—the lusty young body moving with graceful purpose, head held high. She had a whole new life of which he knew nothing. She was a fascinating stranger. And they had only a few days to find out about each other—as much as either might be willing to reveal. On impulse he stood up and followed her into the kitchen where she stood facing the cupboard. He put his arms around her from behind, holding her waist, and kissed the back of her head, inhaling the warm female scent of her hair.

"What's going on?" she smiled.

"Just returning your kiss, stranger."

"It's about time. I've been waiting for that ever since the airport."

"Didn't I kiss you at the airport?"

"No. And I didn't kiss you, either. I felt shy, I guess."

They dined to the accompaniment of soft radio music and a bottle of Chateauneuf-du-Pape. Briefly and lightly he touched upon his experiences overseas, eliminating any intimate references to his relationships with women. It was an odd and troubling aspect of their conversation: he spoke carefully, as if she might be jealous. He had been ready when he first arrived at the apartment to hold back nothing, and felt then that she would do the same, but something somehow had changed their easy family give and take; he was wary, and felt she was too. They listened to the eleven o'clock news together, as she always did, Cathy said, in hope of hearing one of his reports from Rome. Then she got up and stretched luxuriously.

"Aren't you just a little drunk?" she smiled. "I think I am. Wine and whiskey, kind of risky."

"I feel very, very risky, and I'm not sure it's all from the wine and whiskey."

He was sorry the moment the words came out but she responded only with her lazy little smile, an enigmatic smile. She went to a closet and returned with blankets and a pillow; the divan was quickly transformed into a roomy bed. "Are you still a pajama boy?" she said.

"Strictly in the raw, Cathy."

"Naughty!" she said, and yawned. "I'll use the bathroom first, unless you're in a hurry."

She lowered the lights to a pleasant dimness and went into the bedroom, leaving the door slightly ajar. And still sitting motionless on the divan he caught glimpses of her undressing. Relaxed and casual in her movements, it was as if she were alone in the house, completely unaware that he could see her, or as if they both were little children again, unconscious of each other's bodies. As she stepped out of her dress her dark red hair fell softly to her shoulders; she loosened her half-slip and let it fall to the floor, revealing the statuesque lines of her hips and legs. Now she was clad only in the briefest of briefs and bra, and in a moment her rich young breasts came free and she was bending, humming to herself, slipping off the bikini panty. Was he mistaken as her hair fell forward, half concealing her face, that she smiled? The lamplight behind her was deceptive and he could not be sure. But her back was to him when she straightened and walked, silhouetted, into the full glare of the bathroom's brightness and he caught just a glimpse of white, curving back and creamy buttocks before she half turned with a saucy little movement and closed the door. A moment later he heard running water.

He was glad she couldn't see him now. In spite of himself, he was in full erection.

He had read about this but he knew now, only now, how it really felt: brother and sister, or mother and son! It was instinctive sex but the strangeness made it somehow deeper, closer. The strangeness, and the sin! From somewhere far inside his memory returned the echo of a childish voice, a little-girl voice out of the remote past: *Mama, why can't David take his nap with me?* . . . and another voice, high and sweet, trembling in the summer air: *But Davie, why do you want to see it? It's just like Cathy's* . . . Emotion shook him; he had never felt exactly this before. He was standing by the divan, wearing only his shorts, when the beam of bathroom light fell across the room again and Cathy said, "It's all yours, Brother."

He turned and looked at her. A silk nightgown covered her but revealed her too, the tapering limbs, the dark shadow between her thighs. And she could see him, the bulge of his erection under the shorts, he was sure of that, although her little smile betrayed nothing. She was humming softly; she turned back the coverlet on her bed and slipped between the sheets with a grateful sigh. "G'night, David," she half whispered, "sleep tight . . ." and turned toward the wall.

How long he sat on the divan, waiting for her to sleep, he didn't know. He only knew he must quiet this runaway tumult in his body before he was any nearer to her. Finally he felt able to walk past her bed and into the bathroom, carefully turning his body to conceal the erection that still rose stiffly under his shorts. It remained that way while he performed his ablutions, then he switched off the light before opening the door and found his way back to the divan, extinguished the last light in the studio room, dropped his shorts and crept between the covers of his bed. For a long time he lay on his back staring into the darkness while the involuntary riot within slowly subsided and fatigue, so long forgotten, gradually took over. Sleepily the events of the day passed before his mind in kaleidoscope but always the image of Cathy was renewed in the shifting pattern . . . the colors of her skin, the feel of her little kiss, the Gershwin tune she was humming before sleep, "Someone to Watch Over Me . . ."

He heard her voice again, but in his sleep, and this time it was no dream. He woke, startled, his heart beating against his ribs, a feeling like fear. "David," she was saying clearly and softly from her bed in the other room, "are you asleep, David?"—a faint note of pleading in the words.

He stirred in the darkness and half sat up, licking dry lips. "Cathy? What is it, Cathy?"

Without thinking he got up and walked half blindly, groping his way, to her room. It wasn't until he was sitting on the edge of her bed, her hand in his hand, that he was awake enough to feel the chill in the apartment.

"You're shivering," Cathy whispered. "Come under the covers. Oh, David, I had such a bad dream . . ."

Naked, he lay on his side, his back carefully turned toward her, feeling her body close to him but not quite touching, feeling her warm breath against his shoulder. He wasn't shivering any longer but his body was all alive again. "What time is it anyway?" He heard his own voice husky with sleep.

"I'm sorry I woke you, David, can you forgive me? I was so scared . . . I don't know why. But the dream is beginning to go away now. If you just stay with me a little while I'll be all right . . ."

"Of course I will. Until you're sound asleep again, Cathy."

Vaguely he was aware of the sounds of the city night. Half a dozen stories below them the garbage trucks were pounding their way through darkened streets. A car horn sounded somewhere farther away. A drunk was singing and chattering to his friend. Remotely distant, a police siren pierced the air and was gone. Beside him in the bed he was acutely aware of her breathing, slower and steadier now. They didn't speak any more but he could feel her gratitude like a gentle caress.

And then, against his foot, the soft, insistent pressure of her toes.

He didn't respond until he was sure she was awake and conscious of what she was doing to him. Every nerve in his body wanted to answer. He waited, patient and wondering, while his penis hardened and tingled, straining with instinct that would not be denied. *"Davie . . ."* she whispered, and her arm stole across his shoulder, her fingers nestled in his chest hair. So she knew, and wanted!

Almost violently he turned and took her in his arms; they lay utterly still a moment; the nightgown was up to her neck; she was nude and wet and murmuring to him with little crooning sighs. And he found her, slid into her, as their mouths found each other and their fingers bruised flesh. Suddenly they were one body, flaming, throbbing, cock soldered in cunt, nipples crushed under chest, the ultimate kiss, and all as natural as breathing itself. Yet he heard his intoxicated whisper of anxiety, foreboding: *"Cathy, Cathy, darling, what are we doing? . . ."*

Her hands slipped down his back and pulled him closer into her. *"It's all right, Davie, I'll see to that, just . . . give me—all—of—it . . ."*

For already he was moving on her, hard and slow, pumping belly to belly, squeezing her words into little jerking gasps, grasping her hips now with both hands as he felt her settle and widen, taking him deep.

"*Oh, Davie . . .*"

"*You haven't called me Davie since—God, how long ago . . .*"

"*Davie, do you remember—under the tree that day, who you showed me . . . when I saw you, and took you in my hand . . .*"

"*I do remember . . .*" Out of the misty past the image all at once came clear, flooded warm through his mind, quickening his blood and quickening the rhythm of his stroke.

"*I think I've . . .*" her words hot against his cheek— "*I've always wanted you, even before I knew—knew what this was . . . I've dreamed you doing this, like this, now . . .*"

"*You're beautiful, Cathy, little Cathy . . .*"

"*No, you're beautiful . . .*" Her voice rose suddenly, filling the air around them, exulting, her whole body shuddering against him, an anguish of joy. "*More than beautiful, because you're fucking me, faster . . . and faster . . . and we're coming together, now . . . now! . . . Ahhhh, Davie! . . . my brother, my love . . .*"

# 32

At his meeting next morning Sprague, the network news chief, was pitiless: the Washington bureau was hurting for bodies and Brent was expected in the capital by evening at the latest; no appeal. There was only time for the promised talk with his mother and a quick phone call to Cathy at her office before he was off again, bound for a new assignment, a new life. Her voice broke a little as they said goodbye.

But wasn't it best this way, after all?

The night with Cathy had left him with a deep sense of guilt, passionate and beautiful as it had been. Maybe guilt was not the right word, he thought—maybe it was just the premonition of consequences as yet not fully foreseen, fear that Cathy would in the longer run be scarred by a hopeless situation that could never be resolved. Already, in those few ecstatic hours together, they were in too deep, drifting out with a tide that could engulf them in the end. Yet in a strange way he could not reject the experience, would treasure it all his days. *Bliss was it in that dawn to be alive* . . . it was right that they should have been together.

The days and weeks that followed were so filled with work that it was easier to keep Cathy out of his mind than he had feared. Once again, as in London, as in Rome, he was having to adapt to new daily problems, new techniques, new professional relationships. The vast, institutional world of Washington loomed almost frightening around him, a far different and more complex setting than he had faced in Europe, and UBC's Washington bureau was by far the biggest staff he'd worked with so far, even though it was dwarfed by the headquarters setup in New York. At least the network was paying his room rent at the Statler, near the office, until he could find a permanent place to live. Meanwhile, he was learning the rules of the game, the American game, and its name was competition—intense, brutal if necessary, unrelenting around the clock—just as the political game on the Hill had its own rules. Underlying the veneer of patriotic attitudes, the pious speeches, the gladhand welcomes, was a total cynicism. The aim was survival—in Congress, to get reelected; in the bureaucracy of the agencies, to survive the periodic changes in administrations.

The UBC bureau, like the newspapers and other networks, had its own competitive struggles. There was a certain professional camaraderie in broadcasting but it was wary, suspicious, especially of the new man, the unknown quantity, with his overseas experience and his untested abilities. Brent felt it in the tentative smiles of the staff men at his level. And there was another element: the female talent as reporters, writers and editors. On the station's general assignment desk the gals were as intensely competitive as the guys. And of the half-dozen women on the Washington staff easily the most attractive was Lee Masters, an Iowa girl still in her twenties who was making a name for herself as one of the network's ace reporters. From the first time he saw her work Brent was drawn to her in admiration. And perhaps because she felt he was no threat to her job Lee responded to his open deference, cautiously at first, then with comradely warmth and frankness.

"I can learn from you, Lee," he said over their first drink together in a bar near the office.

She stared at him a moment, then laughed. "You're the first man in this outfit who ever said that to me."

"You know why that is—they're scared you'll beat them."

"Tough," she said.

"That's what I mean. You can be as tough as they are, and they don't expect that."

"They can expect a lot of it from now on," Lee Masters said. She grinned her wholesome Iowa, deceptive smile. "And so can you."

"Isn't news a kind of heavy game for you? I mean with your looks you could make it big in a lot of easier things—fashion model, actress . . ."

"What makes you think it's any easier there? Right her in Washington I have to peddle my ass—up to a point. How do you think I can wheedle stories out of these horny old politicians if I don't give them a whiff?"

He laughed. "Okay, but that's only part of it. You have to write the stuff after you wheedle it. And you're damn good, Lee."

"We ain't seen nothing yet, Mr. Brent. Wait till they let us broadcast our own reports—that'll separate the girls from the girls!"

He wondered about Lee's sex life. Outwardly she was a healthy, breezy, gregarious young female from the midwest who looked as if she just might possibly be still a virgin. What went on behind that brash poise was another question. Office gossip said she was having a very, very quiet affair with Bill Hurd, the news producer, but if so there was no visible evidence; Lee seemed to treat Hurd with the same cool, offhand manner she showed everybody else, including David Brent. Whatever the truth of it, David Brent knew one thing for sure: he wouldn't kick Lee Masters out of his bed. At the same time he had no plans to promote such a possibility. He'd have to be a lot more sure of himself on the Washington scene before he tested himself with Lee or anybody else.

Meanwhile he was succeeding in putting Cathy out of his mind. She hadn't written or called him since he left New York, and he sensed—he hoped correctly—that she realized as he did that it was better there was no communication between them to rake up the embers.

And Lee Masters was helping out. Through Lee he was introduced to Washington's night life—not, he discovered, a cafe-society life as in other big American cities. The true Washingtonians didn't go out for their partying to restaurants and night clubs. Everything happened at home, especially in Georgetown, where the younger, richer and gayer political set mixed their cocktail parties and dinners with equal parts of the Executive and the Legislative branches, including a generous portion of the print and radio media, all ages. Lee Masters got him the invitations by talking him up to her hostess friends as the coming news star in town—well, anyway, he was a new face from the broadcasting ranks and as such deserved to be looked at at least once. From there he was on his own. And as Lee conceded, he clicked, first time around.

Especially he clicked with Eve Terrell, a leading Georgetown hostess and wife of a senior southern senator. She could have been forty and looked at least ten years younger, compared with Vance Terrell's sixty-odd. And the Senator treated her that way, tolerantly indulging all her whims and paying no attention to the perennial gossip about her sudden, violent romantic attachments. To all such intimations Terrell responded with his usual courtly grace and an air of complete disbelief. Even in the face of the evidence, Lee Masters said, the Senator preferred to ignore the truth. She steered Brent to the Terrells' house for his first Georgetown party and abruptly left him alone.

Everybody was arriving at once. In a few minutes the big room was full of a cross-section of Washington, all of them talking at the same time. He drifted from one conversation to another, listening to scraps of the latest hearsay for as much as he could make of it, and accepting a first and second drink from one of the Negro waiters who circulated through the crowd. He was about to reach for a third when a slim-shouldered handsome woman with close-cut dark hair and a smile of practiced vivacity materialized suddenly, a cocktail in one bejeweled hand.

"You're the only man in the room I don't know, so you must be Lee's David Brent."

He grinned. "I didn't know I belonged to Lee, but she did me the honor of bringing me along. Do I address you as Mrs. Senator?"

"Eve," she smiled. "Didn't you bring Mrs. Brent along?"

"There's no Mrs. Brent."

"You never know, with Lee's friends. Actually you look to me like a man who's either had several wives or was smart enough to never get married."

"I admit I'm running out of time."

Her smile was cocky and he liked it. "Come on, Mr. Brent, you're younger than I am."

"Impossible."

She bowed. "I like that. I also like your laugh. When can I hear you on the radio?"

"Whenever I get a good enough story to put it on the air."

She waved an arm. "A lot of stories right here in this room tonight. Let me know which ones you want to meet and I'll introduce you."

"Can I have a raincheck? I don't want to cramp Lee's style."

"Now that's generous! No wonder she likes you."

"Does she? I'm flattered. She's a real pro."

"Don't you want to meet the Senator at least?"

They passed Lee Masters as they pressed through the crowd to reach the Senator and she flashed them a smile. She was talking very earnestly to a young Congressman who was listening just as earnestly. "Know him?" said Eve Terrell. "He has enough Defense secrets under his hat to keep Lee in news for a month."

"She knows just where to go."

"Don't you?" said the Senator's wife, and pressed his arm.

Brent left that evening with a warm assurance from his hostess that she'd put him on the list for her very next party. But he hardly expected to hear from Eve Terrell as soon as he did—a telephone call to his room the next Sunday morning, his day off, as he sprawled in bed with the papers.

Her impish laugh. "Are you alone?"

"Quite alone."

"Sure?"

"Sure. How did you locate me?"

"Have you forgotten you told me you were at the Statler? I'm disappointed, David—I took it as a hint."

"Whatever you took it for, I'm delighted you called."

Silence for a moment, then: "David, this is the most absurd situation. The Senator's speechmaking in Michigan and I'm free for the afternoon. I'm also depressed. I'm always depressed when it rains. What's your room number?"

"Eleven-forty."

"I think I'll come around to see you. Incognito, of course."

"All I can offer is room service."

"That's the best kind. See you shortly."

"Just give me time to shower and shave."

Stepping out of the tub he felt suddenly refreshed and renewed, as if Eve Terrell's phone call had marked the beginning of a new phase in his Washington experience, a sense of belonging. He dropped the towel and caught a glimpse of himself in the full-length mirror on the back of the door, stood there staring at his reflection as if recognizing an earlier, half-forgotten self. His body looked trim and powerful, white flesh glistening with steam, its muscles rippling with his movement, and he cupped the genitals in his hand and felt them warm and heavy. He was smiling. When he was a boy he could make his cock rise just by looking at it in a mirror. He still could; he felt it stirring and swelling between his fingers and heard the sheer laugh of exultation as if the image in the mirror alone had laughed, was challenging him to imitate it. Bowing, he threw a sardonic salute at his portrait: that was the real David Brent, not the humdrum workaday fellow from UBC so busy winning his D.C. spurs that he had no sensual life of his own. Well, he could pay some attention to this fellow in the mirror from now on. His bosses admired his work and told him so; he'd won the spurs. Now he could be his full self again.

Humming softly, he shaved and dressed with care, full of his old confidence again, ready to conquer.

When he opened the door to her she stood there smiling her impudent smile and wearing a raincoat that looked as if it had been made for her by Dior, a scarf over her hair that could only be Italian and a general air of grooming that must have been the product of a lifetime of money; then he remembered Lee had told him Eve was rich in her own right. He kissed her hand.

"You learned that in Europe," she said.

"Sorry about the rumpled bedcover—I passed up the maid this morning."

"As long as that's all you did to her I forgive you." She walked to the window pulling off her little black gloves and staring with distaste at the misty, dreary street below, then wheeled again in her abrupt manner and looked around the room. "I admit to having rendezvous in hotels before but this is my first upstairs visit to the Statler. Repulsive."

He laughed. "If I'd known you were coming . . ."

"You'd have engaged the royal suite, I know." She sat on the bed and doffed her scarf, swinging one expensively shod foot and smiling up at him. "Don't I get a drink?"

He opened the Scotch that room service had sent up and mixed two drinks with soda. "First today," he said, handing one to her.

"Not for me!" The black eyes sparkled wickedly. "In weather like this I always take a wee drap of brandy in my breakfast coffee."

"I'm learning all about you."

"I want you to." And over this drink and the next she told him—a Long Islander-born who always seemed to be somewhere else, went to school in Switzerland, had two husbands before the Senator—one a doomed alcoholic, the other killed riding a horse in Virginia—met and liked the widowed Vance Terrell on a visit to Louisville and decided, since Washington was the only place she'd never lived, to give it a whirl. Didn't regret a moment of it, or any other damn thing she'd ever done, and was enjoying her life. Was David Brent enjoying his?

"I am now," he said, taking her empty glass from her hand and putting it down beside his on the table, then lifting her off the bed and into his arms. It was a long, exciting kiss and after it was over she lay down against the pillows and said, "David, dear, I don't want to be a bore or waste any unnecessary time, but if you're going to make love to me I do want you to understand I'm not a call girl though I may have sounded like it on the phone. I did like you, really, from the very beginning, and I hoped you'd like me as much, and if you do I want you to tell me, David, and if you don't let's just have another drink."

He sat on the edge of the bed beside her and put his hand on her breast, felt it swell under his fingers. "You didn't have to say all that, but I do like you, can't you tell?"

"Now you're talking," she murmured in a way that made him laugh. It was all relaxed, friendly, comfortable, no tension or special effort on either side; suddenly they were like lovers long familiar with their intimacy. Yet the very casualness had its own subdued excitement—looking down into her eyes he saw desire smolder and quicken, felt himself harden to full length. He brought his other hand to her other breast and for a time caressed both very gently, just letting the weight of his hands communicate what his body was feeling. And she stirred under them, closed her eyes in the soft promise of it, until she reached down and loosened her skirt and said, "Rub my back, darling, the way you're touching me now."

She turned on her face and his hand found the warm, firm flesh of her thighs, pulling down the flimsy silk panty that was her only underwear, fingers roaming lightly over the bared buttocks, skimming the hot crevice with the tentative, tantalizing touch that made her squirm a little each time they went deeper.

"That's not rubbing my back."

"Sorry. Does it upset you?"

Her low laugh, half smothered in the pillow, shook her body slightly. "Of course it upsets me. That's why you're doing it and that's why I want you to do it."

"That's not all you want me to do."

Again the low, spreading laugh. "How'd you guess?"

"Us news people are just smart, Ma'am, that's all."

"I suppose you're fucking Lee Masters."

"Wrong. I've never touched her."

"But you'd like to."

"Wouldn't anybody?"

"Then who *is* fucking Lee Masters?"

He smiled. "Maybe nobody?"

"I'd never take a bet on that, if I were you."

"I don't know enough about her. I thought you were the authority."

"She talks freely, Mr. Brent, but she's the most discreet woman in Washington when it comes to her private life."

"Does she have a private life?" His fingers were sopping wet by now and her crotch was opening for him. "Anyway, why are we talking about fucking Lee Masters when we should be talking about fucking you?"

"I was hoping you'd change the subject." Slowly she turned on her back again and smiled up at him. "Why don't you just take off those pants of yours and let me have a look."

"Pleased to oblige," he said, and drew away from her, pulled off his jacket, dropped his trousers and then his undershorts and stood beside the bed, watching her eyes upon his erection. She looked at him for a long time before she spoke, softly, the amused smile at her lips. "I never see it without thinking what a miracle it is. That he can't speak and yet understands so much. Me, for instance —he knows all about me. Knows all about what I'm feeling right now. He can hear what I'm saying to you, too. And he's just—waiting, to perform one of his miracles."

"Don't make him wait too long."

"Ah, he's in no hurry." She reached with her small, slim hand and cupped the balls, ran her fingers along the distended staff, felt it throbbing at her touch. *"I'm* the one who's in a hurry." Skilfully she kicked off the clinging black panty and drew her skirt up over her belly with her free hand, still holding the rigid staff and drawing it to her as she settled back against the pillow and opened slender legs. "Now, sir, with your permission, we'll *both* have what we want, won't we? Of course we will . . ." Her eyes were closed and her voice sank to a murmur, almost dreamlike. "Right . . . here . . . ah, he knows the way, all right, he knows the way . . . Wait! . . . There . . ." Her guiding hand left him and her arms went around his body, embraced the smooth flesh of his back under his shirt, pressed and tugged at his skin. Their mouths met as he went deeper into her, felt her yield and open wider, urgent, hot. She was saying something into his mouth, broken like a sob, the long outbreathing murmur mingling perfume and the taste of whiskey; repeating it so he understood the words . . . *"you . . . know . . . how to . . . fuck . . . knew . . . you knew . . ."* Under his steady driving thighs he felt her legs drawing together again, tightening, wrenching, her belly rising fiercely against him, until she held him in a vise with all her strength, her knees crossed under his arching blows, her nails spiking his bare shoulders. And answering her fury of movement thrust for thrust, fighting to master the surging body beneath him, he reached and grasped her buttocks, crushing the offered flesh, heard at last the cry of release as he too was drained . . .

When she left him, an hour later and after a second, longer, thrilling simultaneous orgasm, she said, "How am I going to keep the rest of Washington from finding out about you, my little treasure?"

He laughed and kissed her. "As long as the Senator doesn't find out, I guess we're both safe."

"Oh, Vance . . . Vance doesn't care. He only wants me to be happy, the dear man."

"How's sex with Vance?"

"No problem." It was all she said about it.

# 33

It was a busy time—the busiest of his career so far. He supposed he could call it a career by now. His job was secure, his prospects bright; there was nowhere to go but up. By the accident of fate his voice, his natural poise, his sense of observation and his interest in people had fitted him for the role of reporter and commentator. It had been a logical step from the print media to broadcasting, a higher paid profession than newspapering and one in which a man's name became known more widely. His Washington reports were on the UBC national network, and his mail came from listeners all over the country. Already he had become one of the familiar faces at White House news conferences, in the halls of the House and Senate, and wherever the news of the day might lead him. He was on a first-name basis with government officials and the crowd of his press and radio colleagues, all scrambling after their piece of the action. And his talents were respected by his superiors at the station—as his first Washington winter wore into spring Bud Atkins, the bureau chief, called him in and awarded him a substantial raise in pay. He was also receiving an extra fee each time he contributed to a commercially sponsored program, enabling him to move into a small but attractively located apartment of his own when the network stopped subsidizing his hotel room.

Socially, his friendship with Eve Terrell had proved the entree to that other sector of life in the capital so essential for news contacts: the world of cocktail and dinner parties in the private homes of officials. And the Senator's wife was not about to let him forget he was the beneficiary of her sponsorship. Despite her own busy social schedule, she contrived to make time for clandestine meetings between them at which her insatiable sexual appetite could be indulged. More openly, she'd taken to calling him at his office, sometimes when he was just about to go on the air or was involved in hectic conferences; he didn't like this habit but so far had said nothing to Eve about it. But Lee Masters had noticed. She noticed everything that went on in the newsroom and once, by accident, had come in on the line while Eve was talking to him over another extension.

Across the big news desk Lee flashed him a conspiratorial smile but refrained from making herself known to Eve, quickly hanging up while Eve continued to rattle on: "Oh, I know it's last-minute notice and all that, but the Senator's just called from Cincinnati and won't be able to get back till late tomorrow, and since I'm already at Laurelton, alone, I thought you might come keep me company tonight—no party, just a quiet dinner for the two of us, I'll send the car around to your apartment and Henry will drive you out . . ." and so on, the warm, affectionate tone with just that touch of the peremptory command in it which could not be refused.

Laurelton was the Terrell country place on the Potomac half an hour's drive down the river. The countryside had just begun to green and the views from the car were beautiful, but Brent felt uneasy. It was his first visit to Laurelton and the first time Eve had sent a car for him; even the black chauffeur knew; had Brent detected just a trace of irony in the man's smiling greeting?

Now, finishing the dinner she had prepared herself, side by side at the end of the long candle-lit table, he said, "Isn't it a little risky my coming out here like this?"

She smiled. "But why?"

"I mean suppose the Senator made it back tonight after all? Wouldn't it look a little—I mean just the two of us like this?"

There was an edge of irritation in her voice. "Isn't a soul in the house but ourselves, David. Henry's gone back to town and the others have the night off. You'd find some nigger motel more to your taste, perhaps? Or is your position of eminence making you more cautious?"

"Now, Eve . . ." He laughed and kissed her hand. "I've had a heavy day. Just give me a little time to relax." He poured them another glass of the excellent claret she always provided.

"I love your laugh, David. So deep and rich. I'm so used to you now I feel you belong here, all the time."

"That's a sweet thing to say, Eve."

"And you know I mean it. We're more than just the slam-bam-thank-you-ma'am thing that goes on all over Washington. Well, aren't we?"

"You know we are." He squeezed her hand.

"I hear you have a secretary of your own, now."

The abrupt change of subject was characteristic. "Who told you that?" he smiled.

"Never mind. Tell me what she's like."

"Harriet?" He laughed. "Middle-aged and dignified, but she knows the ropes."

"I'm middle-aged."

"Aw, Eve, now really!" Leaving the dining room he put his arm around her and pulled her close to his shoulder. She had hardly eaten at all while he sat there filling himself with good food and drink. His fatigue was disappearing now; with a couple of bourbons he'd be able to carry on as usual, equal to it but not particularly wanting it as he had in the beginning. Only lately had he begun to resent this feeling that somehow he had become part of Eve Terrell's property; she had begun to own him. He hadn't planned it that way; in fact he hadn't planned it at all; Eve had done the planning, making everything easy and delightful, showing him his new world. And he was grateful, yes, but not to the degree she evidently expected.

Her voice at his shoulder. "Pensive?"

"Maybe a bit. Large day tomorrow."

"Becoming a big man in town, aren't you? Pretty soon too big for little old Evie."

"Don't tease. You know that could never happen."

"I like to hear you say it."

They were standing in soft lamplight in the sitting room at the back of the entrance hall, looking through tall glass doors across the darkening garden at the lights of Washington, a dull glow in the sky. It was time for the preliminaries to begin, and he knew now he was tired of them—the little bouts of simulated pique, the talking around it, the foreplay. Jesus, it was like a couple of school kids! Lately she had seemed to need him more,

to want to be with him all the time. He was getting too
far into this; it was becoming too much to handle.

"David . . ."

"Yes?"

"Put your arms around me, David . . ."

He was standing a little behind her and he leaned
forward and put his cheek against her cheek, reaching
from behind and taking her breasts in his hands. "You
want it now, darling?"

"David, you know something? . . ." her voice dreamy
singsong.

"What, darling?"

"When we're this way together I forget the difference
in ages."

"There isn't any difference, you know that."

"And I know you have younger women . . ."

"Eve, be fair. You know you give me everything I
need this way."

"You make it sound like taking vitamin pills."

She was touchier than usual tonight. "I don't mean
to," he said. "You know how I feel about you."

"How can I? You don't tell me."

"Of course I do. Everything." He suppressed a sigh.
"What are we fighting for? Let's not fight, darling."

"I'm not fighting you, you're fighting me."

"What nonsense." He breathed the words, kissing her
hair and drawing her still closer. "You need it right now?
I do."

"David, don't pace me, you're pacing me." He felt
her stiffen a moment.

"Eve, *please* don't talk foolishly."

The dreamy singsong again as she relaxed against
him. "I remember something . . . something dear, something precious . . ."

"Tell me . . ."

"Remember our first time, when I came to the hotel?"

"I remember."

"Nobody ever took me like that, not in years, you
were so *gentle*, why were you so gentle that day?"

"Was I?" He led her to the long low couch at the
side of the room and she lay down obedient on the cushions, loosening her clothes for him.

"You were so loving. And it was our first time."

"I felt that way."

"Am I good for you, too? Still?"

"Don't talk like that," he whispered. "The very best."

"You mean better than others."

"No others."

"When you love me that way I'd do anything for you."

"I know that."

"When you love me this way you make me feel like you never loved anyone but me."

"But I haven't. Not the way I feel now."

Her eyes were open but not seeing anything. "You made me feel it so much, that day."

*"Like now? And now? And now?"*

*"Yes, yes, yes . . ."*

But even as he fucked her deep and knew it was always the best, with Eve or with anyone, he knew it was the last time with Eve. He knew he would have to end it.

# 34

He lost no time making good on his pledge to himself. A few days later, leaving a Congressional hearing room, he ran into Lee Masters in the corridor, took her by the arm and casually invited her to dinner at the best French restaurant in Washington. And somewhat to his surprise, she readily accepted.

They had drinks first in the bar. She'd gone home to change meanwhile and reappeared looking stunning in close-fitting black, short-sleeved and short-skirted, displaying her blonde beauty to full effect and, as usual, attracting attention from all males within staring distance.

"You know," he said, smiling over their third martini, "six months ago I wouldn't have dared imagine being here with Lee Masters like this."

The drinks had heightened the healthy flush in her skin and enhanced the bright blue of her eyes. "You were just a recruit then. Now you're a D.C. veteran."

"If I've grown up a bit, Lee, it's thanks to your example."

"Me?" She laughed. "We hardly know each other, pal."

"Maybe nobody knows Lee Masters very well."

She had no comment on that and he continued, "But I've watched you operate. You're as smart a reporter as anybody in this town, Lee."

"You're pretty good yourself. And getting better all the time."

"I've noticed particularly how well you handle yourself in the newsroom. A good-looking gal, all those admiring guys, and you never show which one is your favorite. If any."

She didn't answer that one either, except with her eyes: they said, hinting will get you nowhere, Mr. Brent.

"Another cocktail?" he said.

"Are you kidding? I'm plastered already!"

But she didn't look it, threading her way through the restaurant to their corner table, male glances following her graceful progress as always, some nodding at Lee and looking a little curiously at her escort.

"It hadn't occurred to me—you know this place well," he said.

"Only because a State Department guy used to take me here."

"He around now?"

"He's an ambassador in Africa."

Once again her oblique reply—no name, no country. He didn't pursue it. The maitre d' was calling her Mademoiselle Masters and the wine steward hovered nearby. They dined well and expensively, and by the time they'd finished three courses and two wines they'd managed to cover domestic politics, the international situation and UBC's coverage thereof. He was struck by the impersonal way she discussed all of it, never committing herself fully on anything, especially the local bureau's operation.

He grinned. "You keep to the middle ground, Lee."

"That's the name of the game, hadn't you noticed?"

"We've been together now over two hours and I don't know a damn thing more about your personal life than I did when we walked in here."

With her brightest smile, lifting a glass, "Well, I like Burgundy."

"I'll keep it in mind."

"As a matter of fact," she said, "you're not so very confiding yourself."

"I didn't think you'd be interested."

"Why not? I'm not a nun."

He laughed. "Does that mean you have a sex life?"

"Well," she smiled, "maybe not as active as yours."

"Mine?"

"Come off it, Dave—don't try to tell me you're not having it good with Eve Terrell! Everybody else has."

"*Too* good, to tell you the truth."

She nodded, unsurprised. "Kind of wearing you down, is she?"

"I couldn't have expressed it better myself."

They laughed together and for a moment she dropped

her hand over his hand. "Poor Dave! And now you want
to get out of it."

"Well . . ."

Brandy was being offered on the house. The maitre d'
told Mademoiselle how glad he was to see her here again
and hoped she would come more often in future. Mademoiselle promised she'd do what she could about that—
maybe Monsieur Brent would help.

Monsieur Brent said he would try.

"Would you believe the coincidence," Lee said when
they were alone again, "if I told you that I'm in the same
fix you are?"

"You want to get out of it?"

"It's as simple as that."

"Who's the man?"

"You know him, Dave, but it could be anybody."

"I understand."

"And I like that about you. Most newsmen *don't*
understand when to stop asking a woman questions."

"I've learned from experience, Lee. Let the lady give
the cues."

In the taxi bound for her apartment, sitting close together, she turned impulsively and said, "I've been curious
to see your place, could we go there on the way?"

"We sure could." He changed the instructions and
sat back, taking her hand. This time she didn't withdraw
it, but moved companionably closer to him, murmuring, "A
good dinner, and I do believe I'm pleasantly loaded. How
about you?"

"Happy and serene."

She liked the little apartment, sublet furnished from a
Georgetown University professor on sabbatical abroad,
and she liked even better her first taste of Cordial Médoc.
"My favorite liqueur in France," he said, "but I couldn't
afford to drink it."

"That's life, Dave—you always get what you want
—but never *when* you want it."

Curled up at the other end of the couch, beautiful
legs tucked under her and bare arms golden in the lamplight, she looked irresistible. "Tell me," he said softly. "If
you want to."

"I don't want to hurt him, but he knows, now, I
want to break it off. At least he suspects it. So far I've

denied it. The problem is I don't know how to make the break. He's become such a habit with me, even though we don't live together."

"Why don't you live together?"

"He's married, Dave."

"Does his wife know about you?"

"He says she doesn't but she has a way of looking at me . . . Anyway he's threatened to give her up, and the two kids, give up everything, if I just say the word."

A silence. He saw the unaccustomed tears come suddenly to her eyes. "I *can't* say the word, Dave. Because I never intended it to go this far. You may not believe what I'm going to admit now, but he was my first man. I came to Washington just a little corn-fed kid from the Midwest, sexually speaking, and Bill was right here to coach me into it, diaphragm and all."

"Bill Hurd?"

She flushed and reached for her liqueur. "What difference does it make? We tried to keep it quiet but these things always get around eventually. If it hadn't been Bill it would have been somebody else. My curiosity was aroused. I was ready for it." She paused again.

"And how did you like it?"

A smile that seemed derisive. "So-so," she said. And more seriously, "But I don't want to marry Bill Hurd— and not just because it would hurt his wife and children. I've got my sights set on another kind of life. It's been a good experience, although I've hated all the sneaky business connected with it, hiding, running, never having enough time. But lately I've realized it's—well, it's just over, that's all. And I have to tell him, Dave, I've got to say it to his face. Because I'm not about to put it on paper—no way!"

"Tell him there's another man."

"But there isn't. He'd know I was lying."

"Try one."

The blue eyes flashed. "Say again?" she demanded.

"Find another man. Then you won't have to lie."

She looked at him, the ghost of a sudden smile at the corner of her mouth. She seemed to be calculating the situation as she would the possibility of a news angle. She said, "Give me a name."

"David Brent."

In a moment her laughter pealed, hard as crystal, made him wonder how serious she was about giving up Hurd.

"What's so great about David Brent?" she said. "What do I know about the guy, after all?"

"All right. If you've got a better offer, take it."

Again the laugh. "Offer? I get six a day, friend. What makes you think *you're* right for the job?"

"It's not a job. If you think it'll be a job with me, forget it."

In the long silence she appeared to be studying him, contemplative, perhaps studying herself, her own reactions. Then abruptly she leaned forward and impudently offered her mouth. "Kiss me, David Brent! I'll check you out."

He gave her more kiss than she expected, and when at last she withdrew from his arms she was gasping. She spoke in a half-whisper. "Was that you or the alcohol?"

"That's for you to say."

As with sudden resolve she stood up and slipped out of her shoes, and he too stood, facing her, put his hands on her shoulders, felt her breathing a little faster, looking up at him.

"You see?" she said. "I'm not as tall as you thought."

For the first time she seemed for a moment tremulous, vulnerable, the hard-nosed reporter transformed into soft and yielding flesh against her will. "My turn," he said, and kissed her again.

This time her whole body moved against him, head to foot; her strong young arms were around him, jerking him closer, and his hands slid down her back to her buttocks, holding them like treasure. "Ass . . . too . . . big," she said into his mouth. "No, oh, no," he replied, and for an instant their lips glued together were one smile.

She drew away and looked around her, rescued her purse from the table. "Where's the john?"

He pointed and smiled, watching her glide swiftly to the bathroom door and close it behind her, imagined her sitting on the seat, her skirt lifted, inserting the pessary which of course she carried around with her for quick unscheduled moments with Bill Hurd. And now it would happen to him! Involuntarily he touched his stiff erection, shifted it in his trousers, felt the deep excitement begin to stir in him, still not quite able to realize it . . . Lee Masters, the unattainable . . . Thanks to the dinner and drinks he was in control tonight, no shooting off like a kid overwhelmed by his fortune, too impatient for the prize he couldn't believe was in his grasp. Tonight he would make Lee Masters forget Bill Hurd; tonight he would make her want David Brent and want to keep him for herself alone.

She came out of the bathroom all flushed and serious, took his outstretched hand and let him lead her into the little bedroom. For a moment as they stood by the bed he reached to turn off the lamp but she stayed his hand, then still standing, facing him, she began to open the front of her dress. "Let me do that," he smiled, and drew her toward him. He sat on the edge of the bed and held her knees between his knees, reaching to slip down the top of the dress and unfastening the bra which held so much loveliness from him. Then as her breasts came free he buried his head between them, holding them in his hands, lifted his lips to the nipples, kissing and tonguing till they stood hard and high, and felt her body tremble helplessly under his fingers.

"Your breasts are beautiful, Lee . . ."

She looked down at him and shook her head. "They're too big. In five years they'll be ugly."

"Never . . ."

The dress dropped to her feet, leaving only a garter belt and stockings to cover her nakedness, exposing the triangle of dark blonde hair curling rich and thick in the glow of lamplight. And now it was there he buried his lips until she withdrew abruptly with a small sharp exclamation and pulled him to his feet. "Hey! How much of that do you think I can stand?"

The fragrance of her body was overwhelming him. He watched her lie down on the bed, still in her stockings and garter belt, and stare back at him, her eyes gleaming with challenge as she watched him strip down. He didn't try to enter immediately, but lay quietly beside her, locked in a double embrace, one leg extended over her warm thighs while his mouth sought her mouth for another kiss. He could feel his column crushed against her side, throbbing and wet with almost unbearable anticipation, while her arms tightened around his shoulders. But he was not hurrying this; he was going to make her ask for it, beg for it, to give it meaning beyond tonight, beyond many days ahead, a meaning she would long remember. And now she did speak, the words muffled at his ear, "You bastard, you've got me helpless . . ." her thighs drawing apart despite the weight of his leg. At last he knelt over her, saw her close her eyes in a desire that matched his own, and slowly, with infinite tenderness, his fingers parted her and found the way that opened for him as if reluctant and received him, inch by inch engulfed in yielding flesh that closed around him until she had it all.

He was motionless then, resting. He felt a long sigh go through her body and she looked up at his face so close to her, no longer the insolent smiling challenge in her eyes. It was as though everything he had felt—need, passion, the fever of desire—was concentrated now in the depths of her belly and, while feeling it a separate entity, they were free to think again. When she whispered the words they seemed to come from a long way off, so soft and wondering they were. "How can you hold everything back like this? He was always finished before I got started . . ."

"I don't blame him. You're beautiful and desirable."

"Sometimes . . . sometimes I seemed to come a little, but there was never time, he never gave me time . . . to go as far as I know I could."

"I almost came, Lee . . . a little while ago, just looking at you undress. But the drinking helped. It slows a man down, holds everything in suspense, for longer. And I don't want to come until you give it all to me, you know that. It isn't right to leave you hungry."

She had closed her eyes. Deep below, deep inside her, he felt her begin, and her lips trembled, her eyelashes fluttered, she turned her head to the side as he kissed her throat and murmured his understanding, a sound, not words. He felt himself stiffen, lengthen, but still he held quiet, while the folds of her tightened around him as her arms tightened on his back, and a low moan came to her lips and was lost in soft exhalation. Now she moved, responding to irresistible want; slowly her body shifted, twisted under him, urgent in its craving, not to be denied. It was time—time to answer her lust, her rhythm, and he rose on his elbows, kissed her forehead, swung into long, steady strokes, driving. Slowly at first, then quickening as she quickened, pulling out almost to the tip but never losing her, slipping back all the way, farther, to the womb's mouth. She was all liquid fire, he saw her making words that wouldn't come, knew she was somewhere else now he couldn't go, could never go; he had reached the molten core and she was lost in her own mystery. He was lunging, and with each lunge she cried out as if she didn't know she was crying out, as if it was another woman, a cry like a sob, forced out of her body like the impact of blows, his blows, that drove her to the final extreme, orgasm like a sunburst, her body shaking in convulsions, the tears streaming down her golden skin, while he in his delirium felt himself open to her from the guts and give, pour, empty the last best part of him into the fountain of her beauty.

# 35

In some ways it was like that last wonderful spring in Rome with Clare, when the secret of their relationship was woven like a thread of scarlet through the fabric of his days and nights. But Washington and the countryside around it, beautiful as it was, cast a different kind of enchantment—and here there were scores, hundreds of people who knew both Lee Masters and David Brent, so their moments alone together had to be coveted, snatched, fought for. The urgency of wartime, in which all things are forgiven, was lacking as background until the shattering surprise of Pearl Harbor transformed the capital and the nation as a whole, multiplying the number of broadcasts on all the networks and doubling Brent's work, as it did Lee's. Even then, they found a few hours here or there to get away—a stolen night at the Williamsburg Inn, a drive to the Eastern Shore. But most of the time they were lucky to have dinner together at a late hour in some hideaway not yet discovered by their news colleagues, and then the joy of sleeping together at his apartment or hers. Even that was often cut short by news developments in the middle of the night and urgent calls from the station, or further complicated by the necessity of rising at dawn to prepare early-morning scripts that would be broadcast on the daytime news programs.

From the beginning—since their first intimacy—Bill Hurd was a gnawing problem. Lee had played it carefully, waiting until Hurd had fixed their next rendezvous in the secluded bar where they usually met, before telling him she had decided their relationship was unfair to his wife and children and declaring that in any case she didn't want to marry him, or anyone else; it was the end of the affair.

"He just sat there, dully, staring at me," Lee said, recounting the confrontation later that night. "He was dumfounded. But it didn't seem to occur to him that there might be another man in the picture. At first he tried to laugh it off. He'd already had several drinks because I was late getting there, and after the first shock of what I told him he told me I was just a silly female who didn't know what she was saying. He said I'd forget all about it tomorrow and things would be just like they were before. But when I refused to drink any more with him he began to take me seriously and plead with me that he couldn't bear the thought of living without me, that he couldn't take it having to see me around the office every day, knowing we were no longer lovers. But he could see this had no effect on me, and he began threatening to commit suicide unless I agreed to marry him. He swore he'd go home and tell his wife all about us and start immediate divorce proceedings, and I had to tell him to go ahead—no matter what he said or did, nothing could change my mind."

"And then?"

"I just walked out of the place and left him there. I thought he might try to follow me but he just ordered another drink and turned his back."

"You realize he's bound to find out about us sooner or later. Probably sooner."

"I can't help it, Dave." She took his hands in her own. "Don't let it make any difference to us."

"Of course not! I'm just sorry you have to face the situation."

"Don't worry a moment—I can take care of myself."

And she could. He marveled that in the newsroom where she was in daily contact with Bill Hurd her demeanor was unchanged—alert, cool, always good-humored. But Hurd was showing the strain; his habitual gruffness had turned surly, sour, and his short-tempered outbursts when some small thing went wrong led to a session with Bud Atkins behind closed doors which quickly became the subject of office speculation that the boss had warned Hurd to cool it, or else. For weeks after the break with Lee he pestered her with nightly phone calls, sometimes in the small hours, but never seemed to suspect that when she didn't answer she wasn't at home. Once when Brent was sleeping there Hurd appeared in the hallway and hammered at the apartment door until the super came at the behest of the neighbors and persuaded him to leave, threatening to call the police if he didn't.

Inside the apartment, naked in Brent's arms, Lee smiled and went back to untroubled sleep.

By contrast to the difficulties with Bill Hurd, Eve Terrell gave no trouble at all. Several days after Brent's visit to Laurelton she called the station and left her number, but when he didn't call back he didn't hear from her again. Perhaps, that night at Laurelton, she had felt with a woman's sixth sense the new direction of his feelings. By now, she must be sure of it. Maybe she too had changed direction; wasn't that her track record?

Brent got his confirmation the next time they ran across each other at an embassy reception. He saw her on the other side of the room in animated conversation with a tall young Argentine attaché who listened with special attentiveness. She caught Brent's eye and gave a little laughing wave of her hand, greeting and dismissal in one gesture. Had her heart skipped a beat? If it had, she didn't show it. If it had, it had probably skipped before in the same situation and she was used to it by now. The Senator's wife took life in her stride. . . .

And the next time Brent ran across the Senator, that dignitary bowed and smiled with what was certainly genuine friendliness.

The same afternoon, however, when he returned to the station to prepare a broadcast for the evening news spot, Bill Hurd called him into his glass-enclosed office.

"Can it wait till after air, Bill? I've got a piece to do."

The producer was pale and tight-lipped. "No, it can't wait, Brent." He closed the office door and they stood looking at each other in the middle of the room.

"What is it, Bill?"

"You know goddamn well what it is." His voice trembled.

"I'm sorry. You'll have to explain what you're talking about."

In the moment Brent felt really sorry for him. Hurd was in pitiable shape, the worst so far. For days he'd been coming to work unshaven, in unpressed clothes, dirty shoes, snarling at his underlings, hypercritical of the broadcasters. Now he centered it all on Brent. "You thought you were going to get away with this, didn't you?"—he spat the words, clenching and unclenching his fists.

"Get away with what, Bill?"

"You stole my woman, Brent, and I'm going to see you're fired out of here."

"I still don't know what you're talking about—"

Hurd was shouting. "You think you can come in here like a big-time foreign correspondent and take over this station and everybody in it! Well, by Christ I'm going to show—"

He stopped abruptly, looking over Brent's shoulder. The door had opened quietly and Bud Atkins was standing on the threshold. Brent heard the low, level voice before he turned.

"That's enough, Bill. Dave, will you leave us, please? And close the door behind you?"

Going out into the newsroom he saw the startled faces all looking at him. Stoddard said, "What's up with the guy now, Dave?"

He answered him with a shrug. Stoddard probably knew, anyway. They'd all know soon, if they didn't already. One of them probably had seen him with Lee going into his apartment, or hers, and couldn't resist dropping it to Hurd. He was glad Lee was not in the newsroom right now, although she would have passed this off with her usual cool.

He felt a little shaky himself but hoped he looked composed. After all, they'd both known it had to come. "And so what?" Lee had said.

Anyway, he had a broadcast to write. He went to his typewriter in the far corner, took out his notes and glanced at the clock. Just once before he began to write he looked over at Hurd's office. Bud Atkins was talking calmly. Hurd sat at his desk, his head in his hands . . .

"We've seen this coming for quite a while, well before you came to the staff, Dave."

Atkins spoke quietly. The evening news shows were over and the newsroom seen through the big glass partition was almost empty.

"I'm not going to ask you any questions, because I don't need to. Bill Hurd is going on an extended vacation

—call it a leave of absence—beginning immediately. He wasn't talking too much sense in there with you but, aside from his feelings about the girl, there's a residue of bitterness in him that's part of what's wrong with him. You see, Hurd is not a broadcaster—just doesn't have the gift of it —and he's been watching younger men come along and take over the choice jobs and the money and public position that goes with them. Instead of accepting himself at his own solid value he's persisted in envy and jealousy of people like yourself—a trait of immaturity that he's never gotten over. Then along came our little glamour girl to further complicate his already unhappy marital situation— or did you know about that?"

Brent shook his head.

"He has the kind of wife, nice girl that she is, who hates the news business and wishes she was back in Indiana with the good steady, small-time breadwinner she should have married in the first place, somebody in a bank or running a store. Instead she finds herself trapped, in a town she detests, with a tortured, highly ambitious guy who's eating his heart out in the radio news business and chasing a girl who, inevitably, would leave him far behind."

Atkins paused to refill his pipe. Then, "It'd be a different matter if Bill were equal to it. If he could handle the situation without cracking. Office romances are none of this company's business, and that's really why I asked you to come in here tonight. As long as you understand, and Lee understands, that any personal relationship you may have must not be allowed to interfere with the quality of your work, then it's strictly your own affair—you should pardon the expression!" He grinned over a poised match. "That's all I wanted to say, fellow, except maybe to tell you you're doing a solid job for us, and New York knows it as well as I do."

Brent stood up and offered his hand. "You're the best boss I've ever had, Bud."

The grin again. "Stick with me, kid—there's a hell of a lot of action ahead."

# 36

Like all decisions made in the hectic days after Pearl
Harbor, this one came with brutal suddenness. Lee Masters
was assigned to a newly created war desk in Hawaii and
was to leave immediately for her new post.

Brent heard about it even before she did, and went
at once to Atkins' office.

"Is it true, Bud?"

The bureau chief nodded soberly. "I suspected both
of you would be upset, Dave, but it was out of my hands
from the start."

"And this is in direct consequence of the Hurd business? Somebody's afraid of a sex scandal?"

"Not even indirect consequence. You have my word
for that."

"Nobody's trying to separate us, just to be on the safe
side?"

"I told you, Dave. Nothing to do with it."

A pause. Could he believe him? Was he lying? He'd
probably never find out the truth of it. And what difference
did it make, now? There it was.

"How long will the assignment last?"

Atkins shrugged. "In times like these, everything is
indefinite, you know that."

"How about getting me transferred to the same area?"

Atkins shook his head. "We've got other plans for
you, Dave."

"Such as?"

"I'm not free to tell you as yet, sorry. There ought
to be word on it soon. But don't worry, you'll be. . . ."
He stopped and looked up. Lee Masters stood in the doorway.

"Am I interrupting, Bud?"

"Come in, Lee. We were just talking about you."

239

Brent watched her as Atkins outlined the job—
watched her face change from shocked surprise to tense
concentration to a growing expectancy and, as Atkins
finished, a look of jubilation. "You'll headquarter in Hono-
lulu," he was saying, "but we especially want you to
cover all women's units wherever they are—army, navy,
marines, nurses."

"That includes combat areas?" Lee said eagerly.

"Wherever the story is."

There was a silence. Color had filled her cheeks and
she was breathing a little faster. She turned to Brent. "Isn't
it great, Dave?"

"It's not a game, Lee. You'll be risking your neck
every day."

"It's the least I can do."

Bud Atkins was smiling. "It won't be dangerous as all
that. Nobody's going to let a gal as pretty as you get hurt."

"I don't want to be a pretty gal, Bud. I'm a reporter,
period."

"Just be careful."

Suddenly Brent felt left out of the discussion. Lee
pulled up a chair and leaned over the desk, oblivious of
anybody but her boss. "See you later," Brent said.

She didn't seem to hear him . . .

And now, little more than a month later, she was
gone. They were days full of briefings, interviews, preparations, and a new Lee Masters emerged—more vigorous,
more dedicated than he'd ever seen her. That is, when she
had time to let him see her, usually late at night when she
collapsed into bed with an exhausted sigh and was almost
immediately asleep. And, characteristic of the current Lee
Masters, their leave-taking was brisk, unsentimental and
soldierly. He had to admit she looked dashing in her war-
correspondent uniform, but a last, passionate embrace at
the airport where he saw her off for the West Coast was
out of the question; the girl who had been his lover existed
no longer. They were colleagues, professionals caught up
in the vortex of war. Nobody's life could be the same as it
was even months ago; to long for those days now was an
act of disloyalty to the present.

Lee had warned him she expected to be too busy to
write him as she'd like to. Her notes, when they came,

were brief and factual, full of the fascination of her new assignment and the nearness of war. And in turn he kept his own letters to a minimum, feeling that a personal relationship like theirs no longer had any importance amid the vast conflict that was submerging the whole world. Already, under the Atlantic Charter of Roosevelt and Churchill, American arms and war supplies were being ferried to Britain, and without official announcement American troops were being moved eastward as well as west. Brent's new assignment, whatever it was to be, had not yet come through; he'd stopped querying Atkins about it after weeks of impatient waiting.

But God knows there was enough work in Washington to keep him fully occupied. He tried to keep his mind on his job and his memories of Lee out of it, but sometimes, late at night, the images of their lovemaking returned irresistibly and he lay awake for hours, remembering. The inevitable result was a sexual longing for a woman, any woman, that came near to overwhelming him. Finally it did.

He admitted defeat after a third whiskey at the Press Club bar one night at the end of a day of exasperation covering a House debate. Hugh Jenkins of the *Star* had been joking about the Washington underground's most famous pimp aand the stable of young and willing amateurs he provided at any hour. Before leaving the Press Club Brent made a point of jotting down the phone number, only half seriously. But now, getting out of the taxi in front of his apartment house, he knew he was out of control. The drinks had done it—for the first time since Mildred and Becky in London (Christ, how long ago it seemed!) he was going to buy and pay for sex.

Motionless in the night air, he watched the taxi's tail lights glimmer and disappear, feeling the breeze off the Potomac cool at his head. Downriver a barge hooted its mournful fog note. A train lumbered distantly across the bridge toward Alexandria. In the park across the street the breeze murmured like a secret, ruffling the trees. It was the kind of night that moved him sexually, troubled him, and he felt excitement slowly beginning to stir through his body. His watch dial gleamed in the pale dark; he hoped it wasn't too late. Tonight the apartment building lay somberly asleep; Wednesday, Friday and Saturday were the busy nights. The elevator hummed softly to his floor.

On the phone he said, "Mr. Pussy? Hugh Jenkins gave me your number."

The cautious Negro drawl. "Yes, sir, you want some company?"

"You have somebody?"

"It so happens that way, yes, sir."

"Just one. I'm alone."

"I onnerstand, just one. I'll bring her up there myself."

He gave him the address and the apartment number. "Quiet coming in, Mr. Pussy."

"I know, yes, sir. About twenny minutes."

Time for another drink before they came. He poured himself a Scotch and water, went to the locked drawer in the bedroom and unlocked it, took out the box of snapshots he hadn't opened since he left Rome. One by one he glanced over them until he came to the set he'd taken that far-off day at Torre San Lorenzo with Clare. Snapped in the dunes in the stillness of high noon, she looked at him now from the photograph: squatting nude in the sand, her knees apart.

The buzzer startled him out of another time and place. He shook his head as if to clear the mist of memory from his eyes before crossing the room to release the downstairs door, listened to the faint whine of the rising elevator and the footsteps in the hall.

"Hi," the girl said, expressionless. She stood there beside him without moving while he paid Mr. Pussy; the tip for her would come after services rendered. Then the man who brought her went back down the hall and Brent closed the door. In the silence the girl smiled mechanically, a little wary or tense. How new was this to her? She could have been sixteen, or even a well-developed fourteen. Her fair hair was smooth and straight to her shoulders and she was wearing what they all wore, a leather jacket and tight bluejeans that made her taller than she probably was. He smiled gently. "What's your name, honey?"

"Sarah Lou."

"How old are you, Sarah Lou?"

"Don't you worry about that part."

"You've been to Mr. Pussy's place before?"

"A couple times. You in the gov'mint?"

He laughed. "We all are, right now."

She looked puzzled but didn't question it.

"Call me Dave," he said.

"Dave," she repeated obediently. Her low-keyed monotone had a curious, soft charm, like her pouting mouth and little-boy hands.

"Would you like a drink?"

"Sure." She followed him to the liquor cabinet.

"What are you wearing under those cute pants, Sarah Lou?"

"Nothing much."

He felt his erection stiffening again. "I'm kind of a big guy for a kid like you."

"I can take it," she said.

"Maybe you're bigger than you look."

"That's what they tell me."

He handed her a drink and poured another for himself. "Your boyfriend waiting for you somewhere?"

She widened china-blue eyes. "There's no hurry."

"You like it here?"

"It's okay."

"You like me?"

"Sure."

"Sure, Dave."

"Sure, Dave."

They sat close together on the divan, their drinks on the coffee table in front of them, and he dropped one arm around her shoulders, his fingers very lightly and steadily brushing her breast. The nipple rose immediately and she dropped her head back with a little sigh.

"Tired, Sarah Lou?"

"Maybe."

"Had another man tonight?"

"No."

He asked no more questions but from time to time he glanced at her in the lamplight, saw her aware of his look but not returning it. Suddenly she spoke, still without looking at him. "What you thinking about, mister? You going to do something strange to me?"

"No."

"Then what you thinking about?"

He smiled. "Well, before you came I was thinking about a girl I knew in Italy. But now I'm thinking about you."

"Italy," she said. "Oh, my."

"I used to look at her when she was naked. I'd like to see you naked, too."

"Any time you say," she said.

"There's no time like now, right?"

She turned to face him and a faint blush began in her smooth young cheeks. "Right," she said.

Sitting forward, she peeled off the jacket and tossed it over the nearest chair. She was wearing a dark red T-shirt underneath and he helped her pull it over her head. Beneath that she was wearing nothing.

"Sit back and let me look at you, Sarah Lou."

The clear skin of her torso was slowly suffusing with the blush now deep in her cheeks. She had pretty shoulders and nicely shaped bare arms. The breasts were heavy but still high, with pink areoles, fresh and firm with her youth. Impulsively he leaned and kissed them, catching the stiffened nipple with his tongue. "Hey . . ." she said in a small, astonished voice, moving away from him.

"Hey what, Sarah Lou?"

"Nobody ever did that."

"They'll learn. Make you feel good?"

"Maybe."

He smiled and cupped both breasts in his hands and lifted them very gently, feeling their delicious weight. She was looking at him with large, solemn eyes. "You're a pretty girl, Sarah Lou. I'm glad you came to see me tonight."

"Yeah." She looked unused to gentleness, dropping her eyes then to his crotch, and his own glance followed hers—his erection was plainly visible under the trousers. Shyly, she averted her gaze with a touching movement of her head, and once more he bent to kiss her breasts, left and right, then again and again, one to the other, until her torso squirmed with the sensation, his mouth salty with her taste.

"Lie back on the cushions," he whispered, leaning to slip off her moccasins and squeezing her slim, naked feet in his hands. Under the lamplight from the end table he saw her lips tremble slightly as he loosened her belt and slowly drew down the jeans over her hips and thighs and knees. She was wearing the flimsiest of pale blue panty and as he pulled it down and off he bent to kiss the warm young belly as it rose and fell under his lips. Again her body stirred, as if in surprise. Her eyes were watchful. As he lifted her knees to move her thighs apart he saw how his gentleness had excited her: the lips half hidden in the mass of dark blonde hair were open and distended; she was wet and beginning to flow.

He stood then and stripped, saw her eyes holding him with their wide, cautious look, almost a sense of fear in her gaze, as though it was all happening to her for the first time, or in a way it had never happened before, and this excited him even more, so that he felt himself bigger than life, huge and heavy as he knelt before her on the couch, felt it give way under him and bear them both down.

Her mouth tightened as in pain. "Hurting?" he whispered as he penetrated little by little, felt the hot folds give and close around him. Slowly she shook her head from side to side, her eyes closed again, patiently, as if waiting for him to finish with her and let her go. Afterward he couldn't know how many times he struck into her; he was losing control because all at once the body beneath him was Clare's, then fading and merging with Lee's, and with this a longing came, a sorrowing, beyond the loneliness for a woman, any woman, that had brought this anonymous girl to his arms. Unexpectedly he felt himself contract, and burst, as her body braced to take his final thrusts. And in the moment their eyes caught and held. He was not taking her with him in orgasm; he saw in her eyes only an obscure perplexity—a sympathy?—nothing more. He wondered if she saw in his a lust betrayed, not by her, by himself; and his sadness; and his shame: she was only a kid.

# SIX

# 37

The overseas job Brent had coveted so intensely came through at long last. Already key battles had been fought with the Axis, in the Pacific, North Africa and Italy. While Brent remained in Washington covering the Roosevelt White House and developments in Congress, combat correspondents were on the scene at Midway, the Coral Sea, Guadalcanal; American forces swept across Sicily and landed at Anzio on the Italian mainland, chasing Mussolini into exile. To all Brent's entreaties for transfer to a war zone, a sympathetic Bud Atkins had the same reply: "You're commercial, Dave—the sales department wants you here where they can sell you. So it's out of my hands."

Brent's frustration at confinement to the home front despite his foreign experience finally became so bitter that he flew to New York to inform Al Sprague personally that he had decided to resign, effective immediately, to join one of the other networks. "I'm fed up with the runaround and I'm not taking it any longer!"

To his surprise the notoriously tough network news chief caved in. And on a warm autumn morning two weeks later Brent boarded a flying boat at New York's marine terminal, bound for London.

The British capital was a city under siege twenty-four hours a day. By light and dark the RAF and the Luftwaffe fought for domination of the skies. By day the British air fleets roared across the Channel; by night the Nazi blitzkrieg descended on southeast England in a horror of fire bombs and high explosives. Already American planes were in action alongside their allies; American ground forces, first landed in Northern Ireland, were building up their strength in the home counties, training for what would eventually be the invasion of western Europe. It was a world of blackouts, fire wardens, dispatch riders, underground shelters. For radio war correspondents, operations headquarters was London's Broadcasting House and its labyrinth of basement studios where, to catch the New York news programs, transmissions were scheduled around midday and midnight. Here David Brent joined the staff of UBC correspondents still headed by Trent Adams, though his old London friend Hank Fischer was covering the other war somewhere in the Pacific.

Outside, London was eerie in the total dark, but the British bore it stoically as they did everything else. The cabbies developed a sixth sense in dealing with the problem, although after dark few were on the streets and finding a taxi was a major undertaking. During air raids all movements except ambulance calls ceased. The wailing of their sirens between bursts of ack-ack from Hyde Park became a familiar if macabre sound. Yet life went on as always behind blackout curtains and shuttered storefronts, though by morning those once-happy habitations and those shops and offices might be lying in smoking ruins, and fresh bodies added to the toll of many thousands of casualties taken to hospital or morgue. It was the biggest reporting challenge David Brent had yet faced—too big to cover in all its appalling detail, too vast in its implications for the listening world to be chronicled except in broad generalities, especially with the time limits imposed on radio.

But at least the world of the British Establishment, by tradition tight-lipped and resentful of publicity, had come around to more accommodating access to the press and broadcasters, especially the Americans whose aid and sympathy were desperately needed by their embattled cousins; the task was made easier for Brent and his colleagues in their daily round of visits to their information sources in government, and to their contacts with military and police authorities. But it was a long day, every day, particularly if as so often your night's sleep had been blasted awake repeatedly by enemy action and you went to work bleary-eyed with fatigue, your only consolation the fact that you had not joined the night's casualty list like your neighbors across the street or around the corner. No place in London could be called safe, not even down in the Tube which served as air raid shelter night after night for the numberless poor—whole families, bringing babes in arms and household pets with them. And even the infants seemed infected with the contagion of courage, seemed to understand and exhibit the fortitude that was everywhere around them, enduring the long nights without a whimper.

In his regular twice-a-day reports to New York— sometimes marred by maddening static that distorted short-wave quality—Brent tried to tell the story of a dauntless people facing the supreme test in countless incidents of individual bravery and compassion. Night after night he trudged through the blackout to Broadcasting House to deliver his late-evening summary of the day's events, then joined the weary little crowd on line at the underground cafeteria for a late supper of powdered eggs and Spam accompanied by watery bouillon or tea. The talk around the tables was low, dispirited; another day of survival achieved; another one to face tomorrow. Yet no one doubted in the ultimate victory—you could see it in the tired tenacity of these British faces, crouched over their miserable food in this miserable eating place, hanging on. You could see it in the quiet efficiency of government at every level, most of all the military, from RAF marshal to girl dispatch rider—calm and cool, equal to every crisis, confident that in the end Jerry would pack it in; it was just a matter of time.

More and more, as the months passed, the British story became the American story. Supreme Headquarters had been established under General Eisenhower, American Air Force bases were in full function under Tooey Spaatz, a U.S. documentary film unit was already at the work of compiling history as it was made, and training areas for the invasion were set up along England's south coast. As dreary winter evaporated in the warm spring air, the guessing game began: what date would be chosen for the land assault on France?

America waited and wondered, too, most especially the families of the steadily increasing numbers of American soldiers, sailors and airmen overseas. To Brent's surprise and delight a long, affectionate and cheerful letter arrived from Cathy without any reference whatever to their night in New York and no surface indication that their relationship was any different from the ordinary affections of sister and brother. But underlying the entertaining small talk, the little jokes and the gag admonitions to be sure to wear a steel helmet at all times, he could sense a deep and abiding concern that by any name could be called love. He replied in kind.

From Lee Masters, somewhere in the Pacific, no word.

# 38

The war in Europe wasn't real—it was romantic illusion. So it seemed to Brent that gentle spring in the English countryside. Far above this landscape of soft green hills and pink hawthorn, tranquil village and budding copse, Allied aircraft swam soundless through the skies, trailing their exhaust like banners of peace. It was all a false impression, of course: the southeast counties were swarming with invasion preparations, more American troops and materiel poured into the base camps every day, the sealed coastal harbors were crowded with U.S. naval units, and those planes overhead were carrying the air war across the Channel, unloading their tons of bombs each day in a relentless softening operation against Nazi targets in France.

But to the newcomers on British soil—young, spirited, virtually all of them without previous combat experience—it was the great adventure, with off-duty fun to sharpen the expectation of glorious deeds to come. And the dreamy weather conspired with them: not within memory had England seen so dry and perfect a spring. To top it off, not only were the local girls cheerfully available to the GI's but WAC's, nurses and Red Cross girls were arriving from the States to supplement the fighting forces, converting Nissen huts into female dormitories and setting up infirmaries and canteens.

Brent was spending two or three days at a time away from London now, driving a UBC car or catching lifts by air to the new American bases for interviews and color stories, then returning to the capital to broadcast his impressions. It was on one of those side trips, standing at the bar of a pub in a Kent village where he was lodging for the night, that he met Judy.

The pub was crowded, mostly with people from the

nearby USAF base mixed in with a few locals of both sexes, and the decibel count was high. The sweating proprietor and his wife were doing their best to cope with the demand, assisted by what appeared to be the village idiot, smiling foolishly to himself as he washed glasses. Gradually over the hubbub Brent became aware of the conversation between the young American officer and the girl in the Red Cross uniform perched on a bar stool between him and Brent. It was an argument, good-humored but persistent, and well sprinkled with Scotch whiskey: was Adolf Hitler German or Austrian? The girl looked around her as if seeking a ruling and saw the war correspondent's patch on Brent's shoulder. Suddenly she grinned, a wide, impudent, attractive grin, tugged at his sleeve with strong, tanned fingers.

"I'll bet *he* knows! Sir—Mister—whatever—is Hitler German or Austrian? I say he's German, am I right?"

"Now don't start bothering people," the lieutenant said. "We'll check it out tomorrow."

"We'll check it out right now! War correspondents know everything." Large brown eyes stared up at him in appeal.

Brent smiled. "He was born in Austria, at Braunau. Germany was just across the river."

The lieutenant chortled. "That makes him Austrian, just like I told you, Judy."

"But I'd have to add," Brent said, "that he became a German citizen about ten years ago."

Judy was triumphant. "So he *is* German, I was right!" Impulsively she half rose off the stool and gave Brent a warm, resounding kiss on the cheek.

It didn't please her companion. He scowled and muttered, "Whichever he is, he's a bastard."

Brent laughed. "Actually his father was a bastard, but by the time Adolf came along his father was legally married."

The girl was smiling up at him. "I knew you knew everything. What's your name?" And when he told her, "I'm Judy Raymond. You're the first War Correspondent I ever met. Bob's one of those know-it-all's they put out at West Point."

"He's right, in a way, you know. Hitler *was* born in Austria."

Resentment was plain on the lieutenant's face; it was their argument, not this stranger's; he didn't care to be comforted by a temporary uniform, even when it carried the assimilated rank of captain. Abruptly he took the girl's arm and swung her around to face him, and just as swiftly she pulled away from him and turned back.

"I want to buy you a drink, Mr. Brent!" She motioned to the woman behind the bar and slapped a pound note on the counter.

"Let's go, Judy." The lieutenant stood up but she ignored him.

"I have to get back, Judy."

"*Now* I remember," the Red Cross girl was saying to Brent. "I've heard you from Washington on the Fort Wayne station."

The officer moved behind her and spoke again. "Are you coming or not?"

"G'night, Bob," she said, not turning her head.

He didn't look at Brent as he wheeled and left.

"Your friend's pretty sore," Brent said.

"He'll get over it."

He handed back the pound note with a smile and said, "I hate to be the cause of a quarrel between two nice young people."

"Young?" She laughed. "How old are *you*, for instance?"

"Old enough, Judy."

"Bet you're not thirty yet!"

He didn't follow up on that and she didn't persist. "Anyway," she said, "Bob's just jealous. It's the same whoever I talk to."

"Then he's in love."

"Love!" She tossed off the word with a little laugh, dismissing it. "He may be in love, but *I'm* not. And if I was it wouldn't be with some little shavetail, I'll tell you that!"

It was easy to see why. Already she had her pick around here, from shavetails to colonels and back. For the first and maybe the last time in her life—and she knew it—she was riding the giddy, exhilarating crest of a seller's market, and all the buyers were competing for Judy Raymond. He heard it in her voice as she told him about the girls in her unit; about the exciting trip across the Atlantic that brought her to the wonderful world of men at war, or soon to be; about her anxiously protective mother and father back in Indiana who were against the whole idea from the start and wrote her every day.

Suddenly she stopped, almost out of breath, and gulped the rest of her drink. "I'm doing all the talking," she protested, "and you're just listening!"

"And looking," he smiled.

"At what?" she demanded.

"At about twenty years of pretty girl, full of life and ready to take on the whole goddamn German army, pleasantly crocked with Scotch whiskey and very, very attractive to the man standing next to her."

Her color deepened under the tanned cheeks. "Is that all?"

"There's more, but maybe you don't feel I know you well enough yet."

She gave him a sly little smile. "What did you mean —take on the whole German army?"

He laughed. "I meant in battle, not bed. I'm not expressing myself too well tonight—this is my third or fifth or seventh drink, anyway too many. I'm tired, Judy."

"You're not allowed to be tired; don't you know there's a war on?"

"Better than you, I'd guess. That's the advantage of being a correspondent—we get to see things where Red Cross girls can't, bless their hearts."

"Tell me about it. Please!"

He did, a little, while she listened wide-eyed and silent. About London under the blitz. About Italy in wartime. About Paris before that. And as he talked the memories flooded back into his mind and he felt himself relaxing, really relaxing, for the first time since he left Washington—no, since Lee Masters went to Hawaii. He'd heard from a UP man recently arrived in London that Lee was serious now about a navy fighter pilot. Curiously, the news had affected him much less deeply than he would have supposed.

Judy said, "Is that all?" and drew him back to his monologue on the French Riviera; he'd been talking about Cannes while thinking about Lee and her fighter pilot.

"That's all for now, Judy. Look, can't we go outside for a breath of air? I've had it with this place to-night."

She knew the area. In cool starlight they walked through the already blacked-out village until the road narrowed to a lane, meadowland on either side. Her quarters at the base were in the opposite direction but she was in no hurry to get back there. "Anyway the bus doesn't come for the last pickup till eleven; there's plenty of time."

He took her hand. "I'm glad we met, Judy. Lately I'd forgotten how nice it can be—just taking a walk with a girl."

"Are you married, David?"

"No. And I'd tell you if I were."

Quiet enveloped them. There was no breeze tonight and the trees hung still with their spring blossoms. A warm scent of new grass pervaded the air. Then they heard the faint sound of singing somewhere distant; he recognized the distinctive Negro accent, a lonesome, wistful spiritual. He'd noticed a black sergeant in the pub as they left, with a white local girl, and asked about it.

"Everything's fine," Judy smiled. "The locals won't go out with Negroes but if they say they're American Indians, right away they're in like Flynn."

The lane curved and narrowed still further; it was darker in here between two rows of trees and rougher underfoot, and he put his arm around her to steady their steps, surprised to find her waist so slight when the rest of her had seemed so solidly strong—wide shoulders and broad hips. The warm young flesh was firm under his hand and she wasn't resisting.

His head was clearing. "I'm not drunk any more. How do you feel now, Judy?"

"I feel just great."

Almost involuntarily he leaned and pressed his lips to her hair for a moment, a gesture somehow so friendly there was no sex in it at all. She smelled as fresh and clean as the grass under their feet, the hair soft and thick. Just afterward they heard a girl's low, excited laughter only a few feet away. "I guess you're not the only one who knows this road," he said.

"Hedgerow humping is in full swing," Judy said, and giggled softly in the dark beside him.

"Do you ever get any leave from your outfit? If you can come up to London some time I'd like to show you around."

She reacted with her whole body. "I'd *love* it. Promise! We landed in Portsmouth and I haven't seen London yet."

"It's promised. Just let me know at UBC, Broadcasting House."

"D'you think I could find some stockings, and some underwear? Stockings are just not possible to find and I won't wear WAC panties."

He was amused. "What's the matter with WAC panties?"

"You wouldn't ask me that if you'd ever *seen* them! Bloomers! Khaki-colored and stretching from the waist to the knees."

"So you just go without?"

"I have a couple of beat-up briefs but that's all I've got left of my own."

"I was hoping you'd say you just go without."

"Why?" she said softly.

"I dunno. Guess I just wanted to picture it in my mind."

They had stopped by a broken gate at the side of the lane and stood for a moment in silence, breathing the perfume of the deep countryside. Almost imperceptibly she drew a little nearer to him so that they were facing, their bodies almost touching, his hand still on her waist. When he spoke it was almost a whisper. "Has the shave-tail ever seen those briefs?"

"Yes . . . Well, I don't know if he actually *saw* them . . ."

"But he helped take them off."

"Yes."

"Was it here?"

"Near here."

"You like him that much?"

She seemed to hesitate. "It's wartime."

"Will you kiss me, Judy?"

"I want to."

"I want to kiss that smile I saw in the pub. I want to kiss you because you're an American. And because you're from Indiana. And because you're beautiful."

"Not beautiful, David."

"You heard what I said. Smile, Judy, even if I can't see it in the dark."

He kissed her smile, and put both arms around her, pulling her close to him. Desire burned in him like flame; she was the first woman he'd had since Sarah Lou. Still gripped in each other's arms they half staggered through the gate and into the deeper shadows where the grass was long and damp and soft under her body. She lay there waiting for him as he dropped his trousers and shorts, kneeling to her then and finding the briefs and drawing them off. Helping she pulled her skirt up; he thought he saw her eyes widen and glow.

She was as wet as the dew under her bare thighs. She took all of him. And she whispered, her arms around his shoulders, *"I've never had a war correspondent . . ."*

Driving back to London next day he remembered the encounter with tenderness. He had been more than a lover last night—he had become a trophy. And he smiled to himself: with support like Judy's from the distaff side, how could the United States Army fail?

There was a letter awaiting him at the UBC office. It was in his sister's handwriting and postmarked San Francisco. For all that it implied, it was brief.

Dearest Davie,

I hope this note will reach you safely and that you yourself are safe and well. It is just to say that the opportunity for a better job came up in California, and I decided to take advantage of it for several reasons. One was the emotional situation with my boss in New York which had become too trying. I know you will agree that under the circumstances, I made the best decision. Mother made the move with me, and we are very snug—and smug—in our old-fashioned apartment. She prays for you every day.

I love you.
Cathy

# 39

David Brent landed on the Normandy beachhead in the wake of the U.S. 1st Infantry Division, covered the advance on Paris with broadcasts transmitted from a mobile army truck and rode into the liberated French capital with General Leclerc's 2nd Armored on the heels of the fleeing Germans. Swept along by the tide of wild jubilation that engulfed the city, Brent would remember the next three days as a crazy mixture of hard work and drunken dissipation, alternating between long talk and interview sessions at the microphone, and forays into the streets of Paris to be hailed, seized, embraced and lifted to French shoulders as a war hero simply because he wore an American uniform.

Waking in late morning of the third day, finding himself in bed with a girl he was sure he hadn't seen before, in a Montmartre apartment he couldn't remember entering, he lay staring at the ceiling (consisting of a mirror bearing his reflection) and trying to piece together the whole mad sequence that began some time before dawn on Liberation night after he'd finished his first series of broadcasts on the scenes he'd witnessed during Leclerc's triumphal entry.

So tired he could hardly move and so hoarse he barely could whisper, he'd tottered through the crowds into a bistro full of joyous French, somewhere in the Opéra quarter, and drunk a series of brandies which the patrons took turns buying for him despite his protests. Was it a big man with a short beard or a little man with a long beard who stood next to him at the *zinc?*—he couldn't remember. But he did remember he was wearing an ancient beret and tossing off glasses of red wine in rapid succession in honor of the rebirth of his nation. Brent was feeling much better now and asking happy questions such as "Just why *is* Paris the best city in the world?"

"That's easy," the man told him. "You eat well and you don't have to take any shit from anybody."

It was daylight when he left the place and at some point afterward fell in with an American Army captain (captain or major?) and two French Résistance types in a bar off the Champs-Elysées for more brandy. Still later, the streets again thronged with smiling faces, one of the Résistance types disappeared and the other guided his two American comrades to the House of All Nations, last of the grand old brothels remaining from the Belle Epoque of the 1890's. Here the captain (Bert, Herb or Buck?) was set upon by six whores while Brent and the Frenchman, drinking from individual champagne bottles and ensconced in armchairs, watched the writhing mass of twenty-eight arms and legs on the huge bed, the captain pinned securely in the midst of the heap, one girl seductively kissing his mouth, one sucking his nipples, one devouring his cock, one squeezing his balls, one biting the insides of his thighs and one tonguing between his toes, while the captain, not to be outdone while being done, massaged the array of crouching crotches on either side of him. The object of the game was to see how long he could last before orgasm, and as Brent remembered it the captain astonished them all by his endurance. He finally exploded, was skilfully sucked dry, showered with laughing congratulations all around, and then it was Brent's turn on the bed.

How to recall his reactions to the human, multiple-jet douche now let loose on his naked body? Dimly through the cloud of hangover he remembered successive waves of soft pleasure as little by little the tension rose. It was only the brandy soaking his system which enabled him to hold out as long as he did; coming at last, lifting his body violently off the bed, he remembered grasping two pairs of naked shoulders and jerking them down on his heaving chest with a shout of pure sensual frenzy which delighted Henri in his armchair (*Henri*, that was it) and set the captain off into paroxysms of laughter. Henri's turn now, a practiced past master of the whorehouse art. The two Americans watched in silence—this time it was a contest for the honor of France. The girls felt it; no more badinage among them as they bent to their cheerful task; the minutes stretched; comfortable under their ministrations, Henri glanced at the audience and winked. Soft lights burned around them in the heavily decorated room; from the hall beyond the door slippered feet hurried past discreetly, amid whispers and low chuckles, leaving the scent of perfumed bodies. Already Henri had survived longer than either of the Americans, perhaps both, laid end to end; but the climax was approaching now; they heard his subdued breathing go out of control, come sharper to gasps; saw him lift his body and mutter something. Whatever he said the girls melted away, only one of them remained; his choice lay back on the bed and spread for him, took him while their eyes held, grave, unwavering, and uttered a little yelp of triumph before their mouths locked and he struck into her for the last time . . .

There was a noble lunch that day in a black-market dive off the Marché St. Honoré. The Résistance man was known and loved; efforts by Brent and the captain to pay the check were rejected with indignation by the *patronne*. Oddly, the brothel session and the food had cleared his mind. Brent felt fresh and normal again, heading back to the Hotel Scribe, headquarters for correspondents where UBC's Paris office consisted of three adjoining bedrooms. Only Trent Adams was there, busy at his typewriter. No questions were asked. There was brief discussion of story possibilities and it was back to work until suddenly, after his third broadcast of the evening and a drink at the Scribe bar, exhaustion overtook him and he barely made it to his room before passing out.

He was not to be left in peace. Shortly after midnight the thunderous rapping at the door announced the captain, alone this time, alert and rosy-cheeked with slicked-down hair and freshly pressed uniform, and all ready to go again, a newly opened bottle of champagne swung in his hand. Buck (he knew his first name by now but kept forgetting to ask his last) hustled Brent out of bed and into a cold shower—very little heat anywhere in Paris—while plying him with reviving champagne. Since last seen, Buck had been reconnoitering, had discovered Suzy Solidor's night spot, claimed it as his home away from home, and cunningly tracked down Brent to share his find. The place was rocking with post-Liberation gaiety, Suzy leading the lusty choruses. Over more champagne she visited with the two Americans at their table and later introduced them to an elegantly dressed French couple who eventually took them in tow, driving them to an equally elegant apartment on the Ile St. Louis where another non-stop Liberation party was in progress.

It was a duplex, crammed with exquisite antiques and crowded on both floors with chic young men and women, all but two or three in civilian clothes. Buck and Brent immediately became the center of attention, were kissed and toasted by both sexes, and singled out for part-ners by two seemingly unescorted girls, one a model, the other a film starlet. Brent drew the starlet, a wide-eyed, deliciously pretty blonde in couturier clothes who spoke highly accented English with some difficulty and called herself Odile. He was aware that his French was in the same category, but with Odile very little talk was neces-sary: she could say almost anything with those lovely grey eyes. He looked around at the opulent surroundings.

"It's a beautiful place, Odile."

"You want to see it? Come." She took his hand and led him through the mob, up a winding staircase to the second floor and into a long, broad hallway which led through a series of salons overlooking the river on one side and a formal garden on the other. Gray light filtered through the lush portières; dawn was breaking over the city. From where they stood at a French window looking down on the Seine the party noises in the house seemed suddenly distant.

"Who owns all this?"

She shrugged and smiled softly, murmuring a name that meant nothing to him. "But they are not here so often, they live—everywhere . . . South America, Switzer-land. You didn't see him—Corrado, when you arrived?"

"Maybe I did. But after I saw you I stopped look-ing."

She laughed. "That is very sweet. Kiss me, I want to taste you."

Kissing, he held her until she trembled prettily and drew away, breathless. "Enough . . ." She looked up at him with her fawnlike eyes. "You Americans are very serious. I think you mean it."

"Try us. Any time."

"And now you have conquered Paris. Are you not proud?"

"Odile . . . tell me. How was it living here under the Germans?"

"Under?" Her smile again, gently amused. "The Germans were correct. But now we don't have to think about them any more. Now begins a new time."

"Shall we begin it together? Today?"

"You and me?"

"You and me."

"Why not?" she said, and came to his arms again. Suddenly he was hard against her belly, knew she felt it.

"Where?" he whispered. "Where, Odile?"

In answer she led him to a door across the room, opened it and drew back from the threshold, smiling. "Not here." Two men, naked, broke an embrace and turned startled faces toward them as Odile softly closed the door against the scene.

"This way, perhaps . . ."

He followed her into the adjoining salon where a door to an empty bedroom stood ajar. This time they went in and Odile slipped the lock shut behind them. The room was on the garden and they looked down at it together for a moment before she closed the drapes, shutting away the dawn. But he still faced the curtains. "Paris . . ." he whispered, as if to himself, his eyes suddenly full of tears. "I just realized I'm in Paris again." And then without turning, speaking to the silent girl who stood behind him: "Once in a museum I saw a picture of a man, half-dressed, standing by curtains opening on a Paris dawn. And behind him lying on the bed is a nude girl, with her eyes closed, her clothes scattered over the floor. I can still see every inch of that glorious young body—her hair, her throat, her breasts, her legs. That picture haunts me, and whenever I think of it I ask myself the same questions: is he about to close the curtains or has he just opened them? Have they already made love, or are they about to? Is she asleep, or waiting?"

"Like this?"

He turned at Odile's soft words and saw her lying naked on the bed. Her clothes were scattered over the floor and her eyes were closed.

She was waiting.

He felt his heart leap; he was living the picture, a

dream become real. This girl of Paris knew what he was
feeling, was making it come true for them both. And at
the same moment, walking slowly toward the bed, he
heard the sharp repeated knock at the door and Buck's
voice: *"Brent—that you in there, Brent?,"* low but hoarsely
urgent.

"What is it, Buck?"

*"Trouble!* We gotta get out of here, and goddamn
quick. We're in a den of collaborators, Brent! We can't
get caught with this bunch. Undercover type downstairs
just tipped me—there's a maquis raid due any minute."

A sickening dismay gripped him with the words. He
turned back to the girl, saw her eyes staring open now
and full of terrified awareness. "Odile—is it true?"

She sat up, the beautiful breasts falling forward. "Take
me with you! If they find me here when they come . . ."
Buck's voice sharper behind the panel. "You coming or
not, Brent? I've warned you—" And as Brent opened
the door to him the girl sprang off the bed and raced into
her clothes. The captain glanced at her. "She's in it, too,
like mine. They're all in it."

*"Take me with you!"* she pleaded. "There is a way
through the garden to the quai, we can get out safe that
way . . ."

The buzz of talk and laughter from below, the clink
of glasses and somebody playing piano grew fainter and
faded as they followed her along the hall to a dark narrow
stairway at the back of the house.

The quai was deserted when they came out. Morning mist lay along the river and the incredible beauty of
Notre Dame lifted above them. Odile between the two
men, they hurried through the deserted street to the
Tournelle bridge and crossed to the Left Bank where the
girl left them, promising to join Brent at the Deux Magôts
cafe in an hour. They watched her disappear into the war-
ren of the Latin Quarter, walking rapidly and furtively as if
stalked by unseen pursuers.

"That's the last you'll see of your little girlfriend,"
Buck said. "Her next date's with the maquis. They're waiting to give her a hair cut and shave. Free."

"I don't want to think about it."

The captain chuckled. "Plenty of other live stuff

around. Acres and acres of it. Let's head for Montmartre."

"I want her story, Buck. I'm going to the Deux Magôts."

"She'd be crazy to be seen in a cafe. I tell you she's one of them."

Brent remembered the terror in her eyes. "She said she'd meet me and I'll be there."

"You don't want her story. You just want to fuck her."

"No, I don't want to fuck her—not now."

They were walking slowly up the quai toward the Place St. Michel. The skies looked as if the sun might be out today. Soon, in a matter of days maybe, perhaps a few weeks, Paris would rally its indomitable strength and begin to look normal again. It always had before, hadn't it? But could it ever be again the Paris that he first knew —with Tanya, with Claudine?

A wave of nostalgia swept over him. The brooding shadow of war lifted for a moment, like the spire of the Sainte Chapelle, frail and imperishable. Maybe Odile wasn't guilty of anything; maybe she was just—hungry, like everybody else around here, like these black-shawled, shivering women creeping out of their houses and crossing the square to do some miserable little job for a few francs of sustenance.

With Buck sitting beside him, he waited in the Deux Magôts for nearly two hours.

The captain was right. Odile didn't come.

# 40

The thrill of the Liberation ended. The war went on. Allied troops penetrated the Siegfried Line and then were stopped cold by powerful Nazi resistance. Each day David Brent attended the Army news briefings at Paris headquarters, then covered the latest developments in his broadcasts to New York. The French capital was still gray, cold and wanting for every human convenience. But at the Hotel Scribe, in the heart of the city, the febrile gaiety of wartime went hand in hand with gin and whiskey at the Scribe bar, and life was a romantic adventure by contrast to the daily tidings of suffering and death from the front lines. Here at the bar, from early morning to late night, men and women officers and correspondents mingled with that reckless surrender of individual responsibility which war brings, heedless of next day's dawning, helpless in the hands of a common fate. Periodically their assignments took them to the battle sectors, from which they returned as to another world to taste the joys of blackmarket living and liberal rations of liquor and PX luxuries, while in the streets outside the army messes half-starved Parisians waited after each meal to raid the garbage cans.

It was at the bar of the Scribe that Brent first saw Loren Stevens and found her as beautiful and brilliant as her reputation as the leading woman newspaper reporter attached to Paris headquarters. But there was something aloof and haughty about Stevens—self-impressed by her own abilities or spoiled by adulation?—which put him off, and after a couple of efforts at conversation with her Brent gave it up as hopeless. But the stunning body encased in her smart khaki uniform, the long blonde hair neatly coiled at the back of her neck, the challenging look in the dark blue eyes framed by the perfect oval face con-

tinued to arouse him every time he saw her. As far as he
could tell, nobody else was any nearer Loren Stevens than
he was, although high-ranking SHAEF PR officers took
turns giving her a try. When Brent saw her at the bar or
passed her in the hotel corridors she acknowledged his
presence with a very slight smile and very slight flicker of
those long eyelashes—nothing more.

About the mysterious and haunting Odile, Brent's al-
most-conquest on the Ile St. Louis, there was no further
news. He was not even able to confirm whether or not
there had been a maquis raid on the house where they'd
met. He went so far as to query the police prefecture about
it, in the guise of seeking information for broadcast, but
met with a polite but firm shrug. If they knew something,
they were not about to confide it. Intelligence officers at
SHAEF assured him they had no information about any
such raid—which didn't mean it hadn't happened. A
French correspondent familiar with the cinema world during the Nazi occupation met his questions with a sly
smile, professed ignorance of Odile's existence but offered
to introduce him to several starlets of his acquaintance
who'd be grateful for the chance to have dinner on the
Army at the Scribe.

At least Buck, his companion on the Ile St. Louis adventure, was not around to kid him about Odile. The
captain's outfit had moved out and was now operating
somewhere around the Dutch-German border. Except for
brief trips to the battlefronts to check temporary situations
—which bogged down like the rest of the Allied line—
Brent had seen no heavy action since the drive through
Normandy. He was chafing to get out of Paris for a longer
period; Trent Adams promised to fix it for him as soon as
possible, but so far the opportunity had not presented itself. Meanwhile, though there were plenty of chances for
sexual diversion all around him here, nothing provocative appeared on the scene to compare with Odile's al-
lure, and only the arrival of Judy on a weekend leave
from her Red Cross clubmobile outfit brightened the picture, if all too briefly.

It was a special joy to introduce her to Paris, even in
its current melancholy, shabby state; to watch her wide-
eyed wonder as they walked together down the Champs-
Elysées and through the Tuileries. Hand in hand they

strolled through the mist-laden Luxembourg Gardens, found a student cafe near the Pantheon that actually had some cognac to offer with their weak and bitter coffee, raw and scalding as the cognac was. In the little shops off the Avenue Wagram they searched for blackmarket stockings and panties for Judy, as promised, and were able to find a few pieces of lingerie the Germans had overlooked. Later, in Brent's room at the Scribe, Judy luxuriated in a real bath, let him dry her glistening young body with a real peacetime bath towel, and sat on his bed with her feet up as he slipped the new stockings on her.

"Now the panty," she commanded.

"Not yet."

Gently he pushed her shoulders back on the bed, dropped his trousers and shorts and bared the erection that was already straining for her. Grasping her legs under the knees, he widened her thighs until she lay open to him.

"I've wanted you," she whispered. "Ever since that night . . ."

"Nobody else since then?" he smiled, looking down at her. "After all, it's wartime."

"I won't lie to you. There were, yes . . ."

"The lieutenant?"

"Yes . . ."

He was entering her, the eager flesh convulsing, gripping him.

"Who were the others, Judy?"

But she was beyond answering now. Her eyes closed, her mouth trembling. Her hands came up to draw his shoulders closer and her belly heaved under him, her thighs shook with the impact of his steady strokes. *"Oh, David . . ."*

For a moment, in the ecstasy of coming with her, a strange shadow fell across his mind: he was a little boy again, peeking through the keyhole, and his father stood naked between his mother's outflung legs, clad in silk stockings like this girl he clasped now in his arms, like this woman's body that surrendered its loveliness to the male, both of them lost and anonymous, and eternal.

They deserted the Army mess that night to dine in a little blackmarket place he'd found near the Palais Royal. Again, as he had since Judy arrived, he avoided St. Germain des Prés and Montparnasse. There had been moments when his nostalgia for his first Paris days was overwhelming but he'd fought off the desire to walk those streets where he'd walked with Claudine and Helen; to see the dirty, blistered and beloved walls of the little hotel in the Impasse des Deux Anges. And yet he'd agreed to meet Odile at the Deux Magôts—a rendezvous that was never held. Was it because she was a Parisienne and truly belonged there? Was it because she was Claudine? . . .

He was silent walking back to the Scribe with Judy, and she seemed to understand his silence. Her hand clasping and unclasping inside his hand, she said softly: "I'll never forget this, David—finding Paris, with you."

"You've helped me find it again, Judy."

"This is our last night. Can I come back?"

"I'll be waiting."

There was a message under his door when they reached the room, in Trent Adams' handwriting: *Assigning your special SHAEF group leaving for Ardennes 5 A.M. Good luck.*

It took him only a few minutes to throw some clothes together in his duffle bag and set his watch alarm. Judy lay in bed watching him. When he turned out the light they were naked together, and he wondered if she was thinking, as everybody was thinking in this war, that maybe it was the last time for one of them. But neither spoke the words.

# 41

In the gray winter dawn outside the hotel he didn't at first recognize the bundled-up figure sitting straight in the back seat of the command car. It was Loren Stevens. Two other command cars and a jeep were waiting at the curb. The PR major in charge of the correspondents' group waved briefly at them as he climbed aboard the jeep and they took off through the fog-shrouded boulevard.

Three huddled figures sat in the back of Brent's vehicle—Loren Stevens in the corner, Brent next to her and, next to him, a correspondent whose face was unfamiliar. It was close quarters, and unavoidably they were jammed in against one another. Up front were two Army people—the driver and a rifleman escort, who occasionally muttered something in muffled Brooklynese to the man at the wheel. Even if it had been decipherable the correspondent next to Brent wouldn't have heard it; he was sound asleep in his corner and snoring lightly, exhaling a heavy alcoholic breath.

Loren Stevens sat staring straight ahead, and Brent thought he could feel a tension in her thigh even under her overcoat, as though she held herself as far away from human contact as possible under the circumstances. Twice, as the little caravan barreled through the suburbs and headed eastward into the countryside in growing daylight, he turned and smiled at the set, concentrated face beside him, rewarded only with that slight flicker of eyelash that meant recognition and no more. This was a totally different girl from his impression at the hotel bar. He made no further effort. They drove on in silence.

By Chalons, at high noon, the sleeping correspondent woke for the brief lunch and rest stop, introduced himself as Hal Walters, representing a string of small midwestern papers, and promptly went back to sleep again as the

journey resumed. Loren Stevens sat stiffly straight, staring
out at the endless bleak landscape and saying nothing.
Only during the lunch break had she broken her silence
to join the other correspondents in clear, clipped tones as
they questioned the major about the purpose of his expedition. But the tour conductor said merely the trip had been
laid on to permit selected news people to interview General Bradley at Eagle Rear, his headquarters in Verdun;
he either knew no more than that or had been forbidden
to specify.

It was a long, grueling journey, and the silence made
it seem longer. Walters snored gently. Brent turned to the
woman next to him and said, "I wish I could relax like
that, don't you, Stevens?"

"I'm perfectly relaxed," she said. "It's just a question
of getting enough sleep at night."

There was implied censure in the way she said it. He
grinned, glancing at their companion. "You can't blame
him for living it up a little. It's probably his first Paris."

"He's not in Europe to see the sights."

Again he smiled. "Don't you ever see the sights,
Loren?"

"There's a time for everything."

*"Everything?"* He couldn't resist it.

She was aware of the intimation. "That's what I
said."

End conversation. He didn't pursue it—what was there
to pursue? The miles rolled past and Walters slept on.
From time to time Loren Stevens shifted her body slightly
and carefully, as if to avoid the slightest impression of
conscious touching, but Brent began to sense her weariness.
He glanced at her and saw her eyes were closed at last,
her head nodding. He drew his left arm back and put it
around her shoulders.

"Lean this way, Loren. Take a nap."

Immediately she opened her eyes and straightened up.
"Thanks. I'm not sleepy."

He withdrew his arm and smiled. "In case you change
your mind, the offer stands."

He took a nap himself—on Hal Walters' oblivious
shoulder. It was almost dark and they were on the outskirts of Verdun when he woke up. Loren Stevens was
applying lipstick to her mouth, holding up a pocket mir-

ror in the dim light, but she quickly put it away when she saw Brent was awake. He grinned. "You'll wow 'em at the mess, Loren," and for the first time she permitted herself a small smile.

"That's more like the girl I know at the Scribe," he said. "I thought you'd left the smile behind."

"We're not standing in front of a bar now, Brent. We're working."

Hal Walters sat straight and blinked his eyes. "What town is this?" he said. "And what time do we eat?"

Brent saw Loren throw Walters a glance of only faintly concealed scorn that said, is that all you think about, eating and sleeping? Then she went off to the separate women's quarters and wasn't seen at the mess later. Obviously she'd made better arrangements. Brent busied himself meanwhile querying several field correspondents just returned from the front below Aachen. Their unanimous opinion was that Allied forward progress was definitely stalled and would remain so for the rest of the winter; no story there. And when the general's briefing next morning failed to change that prospect essentially, Brent realized the trip from Paris was just a PR stunt designed to give the restless media something to do.

He felt a wave of disappointment and frustration. The prospect of returning shortly to Paris to resume the routine round of daily broadcasts far from the battle sectors appealed to him not at all. He wondered how Loren Stevens felt about that. As the briefing broke up and the correspondents gathered in small groups to compare notes Brent looked in vain for her trim shoulders and golden hair among them—until he heard the unmistakable voice at his elbow, even and cool.

"Brent—I want to talk to you."

She led the way to an empty corridor off the briefing room and spoke in careful undertone. "We're being flimflammed. They're planning a series of attacks—maybe a concerted offensive—and they're telling us just the opposite."

He looked at her. "How do you know?"

"I had dinner with a staff officer. He's a friend and he wouldn't lie about it. Of course he'd deny it if anybody else asked him."

"Why are you telling me, Loren?"

The dark blue eyes held his. "First because you're not print competition. The *Times* guy is sniffing around the edges but he won't get any evidence. Second, because I want to take a jeep and go up there, and they won't let me have a jeep alone."

"And you want me to join the party."

The eyes were glowing. "You mean you'd turn down this chance to break the story for radio?"

He grinned. "You know I wouldn't. Where's the jeep?"

Suddenly his heart was zinging—action at last, after so long! Loren dropped the word that they were heading back to Paris, quietly obtained the travel documents for both, and they slipped away while the others were still at lunch, heading north toward the front lines.

They reached Division headquarters at nightfall, taking turns at the wheel and driving fast. They were at Regiment, settled, by ten-thirty. Brent had noticed before that the nearer you got to the front the less red tape there was to restrict your movements, and this area was no exception. It helped that Loren was known personally to some of the officers they met. Still, he was surprised how readily they all assumed that these were two favored correspondents who had been let in on the secret operation to be launched within eight hours of their arrival. A bunk was found for Loren at the field hospital and Brent bedded down with a Signals group in what had been the town hall.

"*Just in time!*" Loren exulted in a hoarse whisper as they said goodnight outside her tent. Even in the dark he could see the repressed excitement in her eyes, her whole body, tired as she must be. And her handclasp, the first she'd ever given him, was fresh and strong. Twice he was challenged by sentries as he walked back through the battered streets; everybody was on edge before the attack. The silence of the December night was broken only by the occasional passage of a buzzbomb overhead, like an outboard motor on a frigid northern lake, and the muffled boom as it crashed somewhere deeper behind the lines, bringing random death to the countryside.

Jump-off was set for first light, but a full hour before that recon aircraft were up and circling over the target area. By the time Brent and Loren reached Battalion HQ a dozen tanks had clanked past them on their way up, the big 240's far in the rear had loosed their barrage, rocket batteries blazed out at the enemy and the infantry were moving warily, doggedly forward. Nobody noticed the two correspondents who joined the advance; everybody had his own job to do now. The noise was earsplitting, overwhelming. Brent glanced at Loren Stevens moving along at his side with steady footsteps, saw her face pale and taut under the borrowed helmet, the nostrils dilated, lips parted, all of her thrilling to this moment of total involvement, all of her violently alive at the edge of death. This was what she had come for, to see the way it really was: the thunder of battle, the dizzying excitement, conditioned anger against the unseen adversary and, under it all, the deep, unreasoning fear.

The unseen adversary was both hidden and silent. No answering fire came from his positions up ahead; or had he abandoned them during the night, or had he fled under bombardment? No, there must be some resistance: the first American wounded passed them on the way to the rear, some walking, helped by medics, one lying bloody and unconscious across the hood of a jeep as if flung there by an explosion, a white-faced driver at the wheel steering carefully; he could have been seventeen years old.

As abruptly almost as it had begun, the noise around them died down and ceased. It was suddenly so quiet you could have heard birds singing, but there were no birds. The company column was trudging along a narrow shell-pocked road, Brent and Loren a few yards behind the last squad. Only the sporadic rattle of machine-gun bursts sounded somewhere off to the left, like target practice. The big guns were silent; no more rockets; no air activity above, and the tanks were nowhere to be seen; maybe they'd veered off to one flank or the other. They came to the ridge of a gentle incline now and started down; a dozen beat-up houses came in view, clinging together to make a wretched little village. That would be the place called Heidrich they'd talked about at Signals last night, already it had changed hands twice in recent weeks, but maybe this time would be the last. Brent looked at the backs of the infantrymen slogging ahead of them, the plodding, reluctant walk, the slung rifles, occasionally a turning head, the face wan and somehow lost under the big helmet, shoulders too slender for the heavy gear, heavy boots beat-

ing the frozen ruts. They had not looked at the wounded
when they passed, but now there were no more wounded,
only this silence of barren fields on both sides of the road,
and a rising wind in the blank gray sky.

The head of the column reached the outskirts of the
village, stopped, seemed to hesitate, sent scouts ahead,
took the O.K. sign and moved on in. By the time Brent
and Loren were halfway through the single street the forward units were already in open country again and heading down the incline toward the woods beyond the village.
Brent looked up at the shattered houses on either side of
the little street, gaping with shell holes from previous combat, windows smashed, eaves hanging crazily. Whatever
was worth anything inside had been looted long since; if
any civilians had survived the seesaw battles they'd long
since fled from the area; not even a stray dog remained.
The quiet was eerie; for an instant of inner recognition
Brent seemed to hear the ghostly cries of children playing
in this street. Involuntarily he half turned and glanced behind him. Just afterward he heard the keening of the shell
overhead, and the blast of its detonation shook the whole
village.

*"Cover!"* The shout came from up the street as the
column broke and scattered. Brent turned swiftly; Loren
Stevens stood transfixed, frozen. He grasped her shoulders
and pulled her with him to the nearest doorway just as a
second shell burst, nearer; it was enemy fire, zeroing in on
the village, probably from 88's screened in the woods below. He was still holding Loren's shoulders, felt them trembling with shock. Up the street there was a confused shouting of orders and, again, a shellburst, this time a little
farther away but powerful enough to shake the hulks of
houses all along the street, empty now except for two
motionless bodies lying in the gutter a few feet from the
sheltering doorway they'd tried too late to reach. Brent
looked back at Loren, still shielding her with his body,
still striving for control of his own shocked nerves.

"We'd better stay put for now, it's suicide out in
the street."

She nodded, steady again.

"We may be in for a counter-attack." Even as he
spoke a fourth explosion rocked the street, then two more
in quick succession. He pulled her further inside and

slammed the rickety door, looking around at the dark, dank hallway. At the far end what seemed to be a stairway led down.

"Stay close, Loren."

Together they groped their way to the stairs and cautiously, step by step, went down into the cellar, finding to their surprise that it seemed little damaged and neatly arranged, as though it might have been used as a child's playroom, with a stone floor and thick stone walls without windows.

"Here, use this." She handed him a tiny flashlight she took out of her shoulder bag.

"Women think of everything."

"They have to, for their own protection."

He flicked it on; she was smiling. "You all right now?" he said.

"Speak for yourself, Captain."

"Captain? We're not prisoners yet."

"Has it occurred to you we may be at any time now?"

As she spoke another blast hit the center of the village. The whole house shook above them and dust sifted down through the board ceiling. Then for the first time they heard small-arms fire somewhere down the incline toward the woods.

"I don't like the sound of that at all, Loren."

He doused the flashlight. They were standing facing each other so closely that he felt her breath on his cheek, warm and quick. "Maybe I'd better go up and have a look," he said.

"No." Her hand on his arm. "You'll get yourself shot or blown up. Let's stay here till it's quiet again."

Two more bursts in succession. "That may be a while."

"We could be worse off, Captain. And by the way, thanks for dragging me off the street—for a minute I didn't know which end was up."

"For a girl with an end like yours, that could be serious."

They were laughing together. "We're back at the Scribe bar," she said.

With the aid of the flashlight they explored the place, finding a half-gutted candle in an old metal holder and, surprisingly, a box of unused candles under a bench against the wall. Another discovery followed: a small door opened into what appeared to be a child-size toilet that, by some miracle, actually still flushed.

Loren chuckled. "We're fixed up for the weekend."

"Don't push your luck. That might have been the last water in the tank."

Overhead they heard a series of sudden, sharp explosions, unmistakably mortar shells. Brent shook his head. "They're closer, unless that stuff is ours." But there was no sound of men or vehicles in the street above and no further small-arms fire within earshot. It was cold in the cellar but at least they were out of the wind. Side by side they sat on the bench, backs to the wall, still in their overcoats. This time when he put his arm around her and pulled her closer for warmth she didn't resist.

There was nothing to do but wait, and listen.

"If this goes on till dark," she said after another flurry of shelling, "we can try to make it back the way we came."

"And get shot full of holes by both sides? No, we'll wait for American voices and then let them know we're here."

"I guess you're right." She shivered and moved still closer to him. "Maybe if we lighted a few candles we could warm it up in here?"

"Only when we have to. We don't want to be seen by the wrong people."

"It's not fair," she said after a moment. "We should be allowed to carry sidearms."

"You good with a revolver?"

"Not bad. I'll show you some day, if we ever get out of this."

"Loren, there's a lot of things I'd like you to show me if we ever get out of this."

"We're back at the Scribe bar again." He knew she was smiling.

"I mean it."

"Name one of the things."

"I'd like to see you with your hair down."

She laughed, a low soft laugh in the dimness, leaned forward and with a swift graceful movement loosed the knot at her neck and let the long strands fall to her shoulders. "Okay?" she said.

It was irresistible. He leaned and buried his face in her hair, took it in his hands, let it sift through his fingers.

She didn't draw away, but said. *"What* are you doing?"

"Warming my hands. Here—warm yours." And he opened the front of his jacket and drew both her hands inside, against his bare skin.

She was startled. "Where's your undershirt?"

"Never wear one."

"You'll get pneumonia, you nut."

"Never mind that. Am I warming your hands?"

"I have to admit it."

He could feel the chill leaving her fingers as she relaxed them. Very slightly they moved and then were still, almost like a caress, and he felt the reaction begin deep in his belly. "Your hands feel good, Loren."

"You're well made. Did you know that? I guess you do."

"You sound like an artist, or a doctor."

"I was pre-med before I went into journalism."

"When do I get to warm my own hands?"

She gave a little covert laugh, impulsively withdrew her left hand to unbutton her tunic and let him slide his hand over her breast. "How's that?" she said.

"Like entering the world of Loren Stevens."

It was a beautiful breast, round and full and high, born to be cupped and kissed, but his hand lay there unmoving, feeling the heat of her blood flow into his own, feeling the tension of her strong young body abate under its gentle weight. A kind of peace seemed to settle over them both, as though the strain of this past hour was dissolving in a fatalistic acceptance of their plight.

"Strange," she said in a low voice. "I'm not scared any more. If this is the way we go, we go. Or tomorrow we'll be looking back and laughing."

"You're a brave person, Loren."

"It's not courage. I asked for this, and now I've got it, how can I complain? And if this turns out to be the last little while of my life, I only want to use it well. Why should—"

In the midst of her words a tearing, grinding shock flashed through the street, rocking the house above their heads, shaking the very foundations and sending them both sprawling off the bench and onto the floor. The blast threw them into each other's arms, her skirt somehow ripped open at the side to bare her thigh to his blindly clutching hand. Just afterward the swelling rattle of machine-gun fire, punctured by the deeper bark of tanks and armored vehicles, burst from the slope below the village. For a moment they lay there in the cellar stunned and speechless, but this time Loren was not trembling: a fierce exhilaration gripped her body and her mouth sought his mouth in frenzied abandon. At any minute now another shell might finish them both; the end was soon coming whichever way it went, in death or mutilation or rescue; but the girl in this instant of wild defiance in the darkness was clawing away her clothes till she was naked from the waist down, seizing his belt with both hands and tugging at his trousers with a frantic urgency. Everything else seemed suddenly far away: the sounds of battle, the tottering house above unreal, as in a dream. There was only Loren and the feel, the odor of woman, white body supine and spread-eagled on the disarray of clothing, open to him and wanting, urging him to take her offering against fate, enclosing him in her arms, her thighs as he centered and struck into her depths, felt her yield and give it all with a glad groan of surrender. Up there in the street now the roar of motors for the first time, a confused shouting—theirs or ours? it didn't matter, there was nothing but Loren, her mouth, her hair, her body twitching with orgasm again and again, until at last he too burst and gave it all and lay like a dead man upon her.

How long was it before she stirred beneath him and he opened his eyes? Her eyes glowed in the faint light, answering, and her arms tightened around his naked back; she made a little sound of tenderness. Where were they and had this happened to them? Slowly he became aware of the silence. The silence! The guns had stopped, and the shells, and the roar of motors. But there were voices in the street, American voices, still tense and cautious, the voices of men who had just come through alive. "You hear that?" he whispered, hearing the relief and exultation in his own words. "You hear that, Loren?"

She offered her mouth to his kiss, his lingering kiss.

"I'll go up and take a look," he said, reluctant to draw away from her as he moved, feeling himself hardening even as he withdrew.

"Be careful!" she whispered after him.

He dropped his coat over her and pulled on his trousers and boots. Just once at the foot of the stairs he turned to look back. Two thin rays of light from new chinks in the ceiling gave pale illumination to her golden hair. She was sitting up, coiling the strands of hair at her neck, a small comb in her mouth that she'd produced from nowhere.

"Women think of everything," he said, and smiled.

"In case of emergencies," she said.

He walked down the hallway slowly. The door to the outside was still shut as he had left it. Carefully he opened it and peered out: helmeted infantrymen were scattered through the street, perhaps as many as platoon strength, apparently regrouping under instructions from an officer at the far end. No one saw Brent immediately. As he stepped outside he heard the *whoosh*.

The shell burst just opposite him in the middle of the street.

# 42

He missed reporting the Battle of the Bulge, the horrors of the Nazi death camps, the German surrender and the Nuremberg trials. For nearly five months David Brent lay in a hospital at Liege recovering from the crippling shell-fragment wounds he suffered in the village of Heidrich at the moment he stepped into the street from the house where he'd found shelter with Loren Stevens, who was unhurt. Three American infantrymen were killed and four wounded by the same blast.

A series of surgical operations and subsequent rehabilitative treatment by a team of specialists, Belgian and American, almost completely restored the use of his left arm and leg, leaving him eventually with only a slight limp but otherwise healthy and strong again. But anxiety made his enforced immobility hard to bear; at first every instinct urged him to get out there and into the thick of the story. But the long hospital stay gradually changed him, quieting his impatience to resume his active life. And he had Anne-Marie to thank for this, at least in part.

She was a Belgian girl of good family who worked in the hospital as a physical therapist, not because she needed employment but as her individual contribution to the war effort. She was also something of a beauty, with her slender body, graceful movement and soft brown hair to her shoulders, framing the open brow, gray eyes set wide apart, and full lips parting in a warm smile. Brent didn't notice at first, when the pain was almost continuous, how attractive she was. But as he improved little by little and his treatments were largely entrusted to Anne-Marie alone they became friends, in that oddly impersonal-personal relationship between helpless patient and ministering nurse fostered by a long convalescence.

Having spent two years studying in England before the war, Anne-Marie had no problem with English. Their conversation became a jumble of French and English. Each day, during their morning session, they further improved Anne-Marie's English, and in the afternoon Brent's French. Similarly the girl brought him delicacies from her mother's kitchen to supplement the hospital diet, while Brent's PX card and food packages from his family in New York helped augment Mme. Berenger's meager supply of staples like coffee and sugar. It was only after Loren Stevens' visit that Brent wondered whether Anne-Marie's feelings toward him might be more than normally kind.

Loren had been at his side during the first tense hours after the shellburst when, with three other grave casualties, he had been rushed unconscious to the nearest field hospital, barely kept alive by repeated blood transfusions. All seriously wounded were later removed to base hospital and, subsequently, Brent was taken to Liege for special surgery. By that time Loren was back in Paris at the insistence of her bosses, but she kept in touch with brief letters to Liege before rejoining forward units of the 1st Division for the climax of the fighting in Germany. Only once was she able to visit the hospital in Liege, just after the Nazi surrender. The reunion had a quality of strangeness.

What made Loren different now? Was it because she looked tired and depressed, greeted him almost perfunctorily as he lay in bed, seemed to resent Anne-Marie's presence, even temporarily, in the room? Was that why she didn't bend to kiss him and spoke with restraint, even after Anne-Marie had left? It was a short visit—Loren said her driver was impatient to get back to his unit—and only after she'd gone did Brent come to the conclusion of what was wrong. This was not the girl who shared that nightmare with him in the cellar at Heidrich. Their intimacy was an accident of war, a crazy something that couldn't have happened under any other circumstances. It was the excitement of danger that had so aroused Loren Stevens, kindled the unsuspected flame that for a wild, brief moment transformed her into a fiercely passionate lover. Now the metamorphosis had faded; the orgasm of combat was over. Peacetime had taken command, and for Loren Stevens there was only the dull-eyed routine of a civilian future in a drab city back home: the thrill was gone and would never return.

Later, after Loren had left, Anne-Marie had come back to the room to say goodbye till tomorrow, found him staring at the wall with a baffled look, seemed to understand at once what disturbed him.

He forced a smile. "What d'you think of her?"

The gray eyes under their long lashes were thoughtful. "She looks just as you described her, David, but somehow . . ."

"Go on. Please."

"She was disappointed? Do you say, let-down?"

He reached for her hand and drew her into the chair beside the bed. "Exactly. Tell me more."

.. She smiled faintly. "I hope it was not because she did not find you jumping around, all fit and ready to . . ." Again she hesitated, her hand still in his hand.

"Ready to run away with her?" He shook his head and smiled. "No. What she's feeling isn't a personal thing at all. It's just that the war is over and she—well, she didn't want it to be."

"But you say she has a successful career in America."

"Yes. But I'll bet that as soon as she gets back to Paris she'll ask for transfer to the Pacific theater."

There was a silence. Both suddenly looked down at their clasped hands, as if noticing it for the first time. But Anne-Marie made no effort to withdraw her hand. She went on, speaking teasingly, "But you, David, how did *you* feel about her?"

"Just now? The way you did."

"No, I mean before. Before you came here. Before you were wounded."

For the first time, he told her about the cellar in Heidrich. Her steady gaze held his eyes without surprise, almost as though she knew what he was going to say before he said it. After he finished she spoke again. "And when you saw her just now, did you want this to happen again, just here, like the cellar?"

He smiled. "I didn't think that far ahead. And even if I had, the leg is still in this goddamn sling. I can't move off my back, as who should know better than you?"

"Poor David. It won't be too long now before you are *ambulant* again. It must be very hard."

"Only lately, Anne-Marie. And then only when you are near me. And sometimes it's hard even when you're not here, just thinking about you."

She started to speak, then stopped. He saw the puzzlement in her look. "Hard," she said in a low voice. "I was not making a play on words, David."

"Believe me, it's not a game. It's only to be expected, isn't it? Surely you must have seen it."

"Yes, I have seen it."

"I try to keep up appearances. I try to hide it from you. But now, when you touch my leg, or even my arm, it starts and I can't help it."

Her hand stirred in his hand and he looked away from her eyes, saw her hand move tentatively from his loose grasp, watched it move to the edge of the sheet that covered him. Just once she glanced up at the door, as if to be sure it was closed. The hospital was quiet; this was the quiet hour of the afternoon and even the traffic on the boulevard was quiet during the post-lunch period. Brent closed his eyes and lay perfectly still. He didn't want to inhibit her impulse by the slightest word or movement. Now he felt her hand creep under the sheet, touch the waistband of his pajamas and with practical skill loose the string knot and lay open the fly. Then the long cool fingers flicked down the length of his penis to squeeze the scrotum with a quick, sure tenderness, returned inch by inch to hold the hot distended column in a softly closing fist.

"*Ahh . . .*" the long gasp escaped his parted lips little by little; his head went back against the pillow; his eyes opened to the softness of her eyes. "You needed this, I know," she whispered. "You should have asked me . . ."

"I wanted to ask you . . ."

"But it was better to wait until you felt strong again . . ."

"It was so long, Anne . . . Anne . . ."

"It will be better now." She was jacking him with slow, pliant strokes and he was watching her breasts tighten under her blouse, her eyes calm and intent. "I wish I could see your breasts now," he whispered, and heard her whispered answer as to a child, "Yes, yes . . . the very next time."

"Will—you do—this for me—every day?"

"Of course, David . . . whatever you ask."

*"Darling, darling, Anne-Marie . . ."* He turned his head as the agonizing ecstasy rose to climax, saw her free hand come up with a handkerchief before he closed his eyes, lifted his buttocks off the bed in a supreme straining movement toward her bending body, and felt her hand tighter, and tighter still, both hands clutching him now, as the great wave of spurting relief washed over him and his lips found her willing mouth.

Afterward, every nerve in his body felt at rest. He lay utterly motionless, feeling his heartbeat gradually slow down to normal again, and watched Anne-Marie move about the room, washing out the handkerchief she had used to cover him, hanging it neatly to dry on the wash-stand, straightening her skirt, smoothing the bed sheets and then—as though suddenly aware of him once more— smiling the cool smile of a professional nurse.

"Better now, *n'est-ce-pas?*" she said.

"I feel like a man again. How do *you* feel, Anne-Marie?"

Her smile was faintly puzzled. "But very well, thank you."

He studied her. "Come here and sit beside me a min- ute." And when she obeyed and he took her hand in his, "You did a beautiful thing for me. Do you realize how grateful I am?"

"You don't have to say it, David. As long as you feel relieved, I am satisfied."

"It wasn't the first time you've done this for a pa- tient?"

"Oh, no. I have done it before."

"Many times?" He was beginning to understand.

"Several times. It is normal therapy in some cases."

"Normal therapy?"

*"Mais oui,* David! You have just told me you feel bet- ter."

"Did you kiss them, too?"

She smiled. "Why not? But not all wanted that . . ."

"I see," he said, and wondered that he had not seen before.

She stood up and adjusted his pillows, made sure that the books on the table were within his reach, looked at her watch. "And now I must leave you," she said.

"It won't be too long before I have to leave *you*, too, Anne-Marie . . . and then it's back to America, for good."

"Not for good. Surely you will come back to visit Europe."

"Who knows?"

"But you will write to me sometimes, yes?"

He nodded. She was standing in the doorway, smiling back at him and wagging her fingers in that quick little gesture he knew so well. And he knew he would always remember her just like this.

It would be too late now. Though I kept too
much distance... and then I must in America, for myself.
Maybe for you. Surely you'll come back to mind
sharper."

"I will never."

"But you will have to make distinctions, yet..."

He nodded. She was standing in the doorway, smiling
tears that never were going on against, in that room. He'd
tidied up these up only. And he was quite wondering

# SEVEN

# 43

The war that supposedly ended with Adolf Hitler's suicide and the defeat of Japan was not really over. So far as America and Europe were concerned, it merely spawned a new and perhaps more ominous conflict called the Cold War. Typical of the situations it created was Russia's blockade of Berlin, a move that was countered by a British-American airlift of supplies to the stricken city which eventually resolved the issue. The Marshall Plan was launched to rescue the tottering economies of postwar nations and their anti-Communist governments. Meanwhile, the state of Israel was born.

The Cold War raged in domestic politics as well. The House Un-American Activities Committee, with eager assistance from Whittaker Chambers, put Alger Hiss on the road to prison, where he joined American Communist leaders. Senator Joseph McCarthy singlehandedly prosecuted the State Department, and a Hollywood studio dropped production of a movie about Hiawatha because his peace efforts among the Indian tribes might have been construed as communistic.

With traditional resilience, Americans embraced the postwar era in new fields of activity. The computer age was ushered in at the University of Pennsylvania. On property donated by John D. Rockefeller, Jr., in New York City, the United Nations organization prepared to move into its permanent headquarters. Electric blankets and tubeless tires went on sale, and dry ice was used to seed the clouds and produce rain. Religious ceremonies in the schoolroom were outlawed by the Supreme Court, long-playing phonograph records were introduced and the craze for bikini bathing suits began. In tests in which the U.S. Air Force was especially interested for future combat duty, the Bell X-1 broke the sound barrier for the first time.

Most of these developments, foreign and domestic, were reported as they occurred by David Brent, seated at a microphone in a network broadcasting studio in midtown New York. It was his next assignment upon his return from Europe.

New York was a new life—growing public recognition, sharply higher financial rewards, entrée to the city's social and intellectual circles. He was now assigned permanently to the New York staff under a recently appointed News vice-president. The Washington staff had also been shaken up—Lee Masters, for example, who'd married her fighter pilot, was now with the San Francisco bureau; Brent sometimes caught her on the evening national news, as blithely sharp and effective as ever.

His own programs went on at 5:30 and 10:30 P.M. six days a week. He read a news script written for him by others and he was learning, as other men have learned in the course of a career, that often the most lucrative jobs are the easiest to perform, the least paid the most tiring and time-consuming. In consequence of his new duties he enjoyed a freedom, a prestige and income that ten years before he could only have fantasized. The ignorant kid who once ran copy for the *News* was now the man of the world become man about town, the seasoned correspondent with front-line war scars to prove it, the familiar face in countless American homes.

For a time he reveled in it all, acquired an East Side brownstone, a low-slung Jaguar for weekend excursions, membership in a convivial club and cultivated his taste for expensive wine. Attractive female companionship required no effort; it sought him out. And he played the field, from Park Avenue society to the Broadway theater, to the "in" restaurants and night spots. Actresses and dancers, models and playgirls—he tried out all the types and tasted the ambiance of every scene, along with the favorite among his men friends, the New York and Hollywood director Chad Newsom, a veteran of night life on both coasts. It was in long conversations over lunches with Chad that both men discussed the basic differences between them: Newsom the happy hedonist, Brent's bouts of pure pleasure-seeking alternating with moods of serious thought that reflected on his past life and found it spiritually aimless. It was hard for him to put it into words, but Chad diagnosed it for him with typical bluntness: "You've been hustling too long, baby—you want to settle in, look to the future with a wife and children, God help you!"

Chad came up with the facts, as usual. Brent's professional situation seemingly provided the right setting. But finding the right girl was something else again.

It was characteristic of his relationship with Chad Newsom that they should have met on a junket to the Bahamas. Brent's secretary had the information, pointing out that the station brass was specially anxious for him to go on this one.

"Not interested, honey."

"It's in Nassau." She was looking at the memo sheet. "You'd be relieved of your Friday and Saturday shows and you wouldn't have to be back till Monday afternoon. All you have to do is be polite to the sponsor."

"The sponsor?" He looked up from his desk. "What sponsor?"

"Only Slater-Morrison, only the oldest sponsor we have. Mr. Slater Senior is the host."

He hadn't met the Slater-Morrison people, just a couple of rubberstamps from their agency. Slater Senior should definitely be cultivated. He'd better go. He could spend the weekend lying on the beach. He'd go in to Tripler's in the morning and get some resort clothes, a conspicuous gap in his growing wardrobe. "All right," he said. "Tell them to count me in."

The plane was half an hour on its way and the two stewardesses were getting dinner ready when Chad Newsom introduced himself. About thirty guests were on the stag flight, all working their way through their second or third drinks. Brent had never even seen a picture of Chad Newsom when the broad, grinning face introduced itself. "Dave!" He stuck out one hairy hand, the other clutching a huge martini. "I heard you'd be on this but I wouldn't believe it till I saw you."

"The pleasure's mine, Chad."

"Why you hiding back here all alone, baby?"

"Just catching my breath."

"Hey, you look different on the tube, you know? Like older, stern. But they cream with that smile!"

"That's part of the gimmick, I guess."

The grin spread again. "I dig you, Dave, I do. I watch your shows. I'll never forget what's-his-name but I like you better, honest."

"What's his name is on CBS now, haven't you caught him?"

"I haven't caught CBS yet." The laugh was half a bellow.

"What about yourself, Chad? What brings you here?"

"I directed their new batch of commercials." He turned and shouted up the aisle at a stewardess. "Nancy! Mr. Brent needs another drink." When she came up to take his glass Newsom patted her shapely rump. "Be good to him, Nancy, he's special."

The girl flashed her smile. "That's what he says about all the boys, Mr. Brent. I'm beginning to think he's queer."

They watched her move back up the aisle; she was well above average airline looks. "You approve?" Newsom said. "I picked both these chicks, they've been on junkets with me before."

"What's the program when we get there?"

"These cats are all Slater-Morrison vice-presidents, I guess you know that. Young Slater is the one up there in the second seat."

"He gave me the official hello."

"He's a swinger. It's his old man runs the company, he's already in Nassau with some of the directors. This is their annual board-meeting shindig, like they did Palm Desert last year and so forth."

"Slater-Morrison is very big in TV."

"Only the number-two or -three client, that's all. Why are you here? Why am I here?"

"I'll tell you why I'm here, Chad, and Slater-Morrison better get used to the idea. I'm here because I want to sleep in the sun for the next two days."

"Crazy," Newsom said. "We'll have a gas. They've got business sessions all day tomorrow, all we have to do is be on tap for the dinners tomorrow and Sunday, O.K.? In between we'll make our own scene."

"Like what, Chad?"

The grin. "Like I've got plans."

He sauntered back up the aisle and Brent watched

him go. Chad Newsom was instantly likable, a brash, gutsy spirit out of the world of entertainment who could laugh at himself as well as anybody else.

Nobody came to bother Brent during dinner, served with a good Beaune, and he was sound asleep when they began the descent, wakened by Nancy gently shaking his arm and giving him a warm, damp tissue for his eyes. He felt suddenly rested and refreshed; sometimes a nap could make you feel better than a long night's sleep. Young Slater, the swinger, staggering slightly on the plane ramp, blew a strong breath in his direction and waved good-night. The air was soft and breezy under a sky full of stars, he could feel it envelop his body like a caress. Half a dozen limousines were waiting to take them to the hotel with smartly dressed, British-style black drivers saluting as they opened the car doors. His room opened onto a balcony over a curving stretch of beach, the Atlantic lapping lazily at the sand. Christ, what a night to be without a woman! He was standing looking out across the water when the phone buzzed discreetly by his bed. "Dave? Chad. You want a belt before beddy-byes? One flight up, in four eleven."

The door to 411 was open for him and Chad greeted him with a fresh martini in hand. Behind him, sitting deep in a white chair, was Nancy. The other stew, as dark as Nancy was blonde, turned from the balcony and gave him a little wave. Both still wore their uniforms but had put aside their caps. Both were nursing drinks. There was a bottle of bourbon, among other bottles, on a table near the window. Chad said, "Nancy remembered your brand."

"This is great," Brent said. "This is all great." Sue was pouring him a drink. "I'll bet you two kids are tired."

"Not from serving the dinner," Sue said, "just from fighting off the customers."

"We almost didn't make it to the room," Nancy said. "We had eleven offers."

"About average for the flight," Chad said. "In Palm Desert we had Bobby Slater on our hands for the first night but tonight he was too drunk to get it up, a new record for him."

"Thank God," Sue said.

"She's had Bobby, you see," said Chad.

"Up to here."

Brent laughed and kissed Sue's cheek. "Don't worry. I'll behave."

"I don't mind," Sue said, "you're nice. Slater's a slob."

"Just one thing," Chad said, "keep the decibels down tonight, the very ears have walls around here, this is Nassau."

"Relax," Nancy said. Brent liked her indolent voice. She kicked off her working shoes and threw her legs over the side of the chair. "Chad, baby," she snapped her fingers, "break out the joints."

"Yeah, how about you, Dave?"

"Never refuse."

Actually he didn't care for the stuff, but maybe because he'd used it so little or he'd always had it with mixed drinks. Tonight he felt like anything and everything, whatever came along. Slowly the drifting smoke, the smell, began to fill the room. He liked it, like understanding it for the first time. Puffing it very slowly and holding it deep, he sat on the edge of the big bed with Sue between him and Chad and looked at Nancy's knees. Outside the sea hissed against the beach; it must be well after midnight. A huge moon the color of eggnog was hoisting itself into the cobalt sky. He liked that too, and he liked listening to Chad's description of putting Bobby Slater to bed in Palm Desert so Bobby Slater's father wouldn't hear him in the next room. And finally he liked the way all their voices, even his own, sounded slightly remote, the laughter fragile, musical. They were all smoking, he had his third and the others their fourth, or had he lost count? The bourbon was helping it along; he felt deliciously relaxed, as though he could talk and drink indefinitely, for days. New York dissolved in the smoke haze. Chad had taken off his jacket and thrown his tie around Nancy's neck. Some time later he was knotting it around her throat and slowly pulling it tight. "Feel it?" he was saying to her, "Feel it? Feel it?" She was laughing, a faraway, brittle sound, and Nancy was standing up, smiling, unknotting the tie and slipping out of her shirt under which she wore nothing, her movement like slow-motion film. Everything was slower and better now. There was a contest—Sue was standing next to Nancy, both stripped to the waist and slowly pivoting for the audience, modeling their breasts: Nancy's low-slung and faintly golden and desirable, Sue's higher and bold with very red nipples. After that, time dissolved into no-time, they were all four naked, a tangle of twisting bodies in the bed, shaking the bed with their helpless laughter, then suddenly quiet and serious. No sound at all, only the universe of flesh, warm, smooth and distantly exciting, lascivious tongues, endless erections, Chad now going to work on Nancy's body, all of it, while Sue and Brent lay quiet, watching her devastated reactions, Chad turning suddenly and taking Sue again, Brent with Nancy in his arms again. Had they slept? It was dawn and cool. The girls offered a dip in the sea, just on the sperm of the moment, Nancy said, but Chad forbade it . . .

He woke, alone. The girls were gone, Chad was gone, he was back in his own bed, the odor of Sue's body still on his hands. Still caught in the spell, he got up and showered and put on the new trunks he'd bought in New York, went out on the beach. The sun stood high, he could feel its heat glowing in every inch of his body. He stared at the curling green and white water. Right now in New York it was probably snowing. Around him people were heading to and from the outdoor bar in front of the hotel. Some of them recognized him, of course, and were pointing him out in low voices. A woman said from under a floppy beach hat, "Hello there, Mr. David Brent!" and he nodded and smiled, moving away a little nearer the water to avoid further conversation.

He could use a pick-me-up and some food. In the beach elevator, just before the door closed, he was joined by Bobby Slater and two of the Slater-Morrison group who'd evidently been for a swim before lunch. "Hey, Dave, we going to see you at the dinner tonight, right?" and so on. He wondered if Bobby Slater had ever taken part in one of Chad Newsom's little orgies and concluded that he had, probably in California last year with the same two girls. Remembering Nancy and Sue at dawn, he felt a small pang of jealousy, but why?—did either of them mean anything much to him? But he disliked Slater with his bland, Papa's boy manner and his bulging alcoholic eyes; for that matter he was learning to dislike the whole milieu of broadcasting's executives, network and agency yes-men, spineless flatterers and hangers-on. But you tolerated them if you were on the talent side. They were a necessary part of the game. Like Nancy and Sue, who'd also learned to tolerate them, even competed for them. They must have known half a hundred like Bobby Slater and gone to bed with most of them. And hadn't Nancy and Sue competed for him as well? Hadn't Sue tried to show him she was better at everything than Nancy in those soft, wild hours when they had changed partners again and again? When women were aroused, really aroused, did it matter who the man was?

He ordered lunch in his room beside the balcony, looking out over the beach, deserted at this hour. A warm breeze wafted in from the tranquil sea. No word from Chad yet today, and he was glad of it, grateful to be alone. Grateful too that the girls weren't around, either. He wasn't sure he was equal to another all-night session. One glimpse of Sue or Nancy, of course, and he could change his mind.

He smiled ruefully. Music sounded with an insidious West Indian beat from somewhere in the depths of the hotel. Doubtless they were rehearsing for tonight's festivities; he didn't look forward to the occasion. More food, more liquor, and maybe, if he knew Chad Newsom as he thought he did, new girls. How much longer was he going to slip and slide over the slick surface of his life, with girls in Nassau, or New York, or London, or Rome or wherever? Yet wasn't that the easiest way, the least complicated way? Slam, bam, and so-long, au revoir!

No. He might have thought so once, but now he knew that wasn't the way, it wasn't enough. He wasn't the same David Brent any more; he was another David Brent, quite new.

He liked him. He wanted his respect.

# 44

Back in New York, lunching at Sardi's with Chad, he told him about a new friend.

"I think she'd like you, Chad. I know you'd like Alison."

"Alison? Alison Chandler?"

"Now tell me you know her. You know everybody."

The director grinned and shook his head. "No, but she's in the columns a lot and she was pointed out to me, that's as near as I got. Hey, you get around, man! You got yourself something there, I mean like rich and a dish and a swinger, so I hear it, all wrapped up in sable and mink."

"Want to meet her?"

Chad rubbed his hands. "If you think I'm worthy."

"She's giving me a birthday party Saturday and I can bring anybody I want."

"I wouldn't miss it."

Brent thought from the beginning that Alison Chandler would be a different experience. Different, that is, because he hoped the friendship would be more important than the sex. They'd met at the Plaza for a charity thing where he'd agreed to hand out the door prizes and Alison was chairwoman of the party. Either he liked her a lot immediately or it was too much champagne; anyway he asked her to lunch at "21" next day and they exchanged self-portraits over a corner table.

She was slim and darkly attractive, vivacious and soignée. She looked to be in her mid-thirties and her forthright manner reminded him of Eve Terrell, the Senator's wife. (Curious how, as time went by, likenesses and personalities seemed more and more to repeat themselves.) Twice divorced from socialite husbands, coming herself from a socially prominent family, Alison had New York securely in her little handbag, and Brent soon found

himself her most favored escort. She had tickets to everything—the opera, the ballet, the latest play openings. Together they indulged a mutual delight in fine French food.
And the first time they went to bed together, in her spacious Fifth Avenue apartment, they discovered a sexual
harmony almost too good to be believed.

For the birthday party everyone was in evening
clothes except Chad, who wore his customary Hollywood
uniform of light sports jacket, open collar and nondescript
trousers. It didn't seem to make any difference to the
dozen or so guests; ten minutes after he walked in with
Brent he was surrounded by an eagerly listening, laughing group and Alison was saying to Brent, "They like your
friend. At first I thought they might not. But then they
don't get a chance to meet someone like him every day."

"I should have warned you, Alison."

"Don't be absurd, I'm just sorry I haven't met him
before this."

"I haven't known him long, but he's a chum already.
I think I needed a chum, a male, that is."

She was laughing at him. "You're a ladies' man and
you know it, don't try to pull the bedclothes over my eyes.
Chum!"

They dined by the soft blaze of bayberry candles in
tall silver holders and Emerson, Alison's butler, in white
gloves, had an extra man in to pour the claret and the
champagne, both of distinguished vintage, as were the
cigars Emerson passed around after the women left the
table. Chad Newsom insisted on joining the ladies immediately, and Brent could hear gusts of uninhibited female
laughter coming from the living room while the gentlemen
drank their brandy at the table.

"He's going to have to learn some manners," Brent
said to his fellow guests.

"Not at all. He's very amusing." The response came
from Alison's Uncle Seward, all his WASP frostiness mel-
lowed by alcohol by now.

Still defying custom, although well aware of the situation, it was Chad who stayed on after all the others except
Brent had said their goodbyes and left. "Hey!" he said, as
the three of them sat in the living room with their renewed brandies, "we didn't sing 'Happy Birthday.' "

"Thank God," Brent said.

Chad was in top form; Brent had never seen Alison so charmed. "Chad, you're divine!" She took his hand in her hands. "Why haven't we met before this?"

"Because you're a lady, baby, and I'm a bum."

"I don't know what you're talking about. You're a distinguished director, I've seen several of your plays and movies. What's he talking about, David?"

"He's not a bum, he's just a roughneck."

"But *I'm* a roughneck, Chad—David can tell you that."

Chad was shaking his head. "You're no roughneck, but I could teach you to be a roughneck."

Her laughter pealed. "I can't wait, when do I start learning?"

"Like tonight?" He grinned wickedly at Brent. "Shall I come along for the ride?"

Alison said, "It sounds like an indecent proposal to me," and let go his hand but leaned to kiss his cheek. "Not tonight, Chad dear, but I'm interested."

"Call Artists Service and leave a message."

"Artists Service. I'll remember the name."

It was midnight when Chad left them, blowing Alison a wicked looking kiss from the elevator. When the door closed and they went back into the apartment she said, "Phew! That man is a human tornado. Was he actually suggesting what I thought he was suggesting?"

"And what was that?"

"Going to bed with us?"

He laughed. "You've got an overheated imagination, Al."

"Come on, you know he was."

"You didn't sound too highly offended."

She giggled. "He's incredible, David, he really is. He'd have laid me on the dining-room table if I'd asked him, you know he would have."

"I wouldn't know."

"Of course you'd know, you're as naughty as he is."

He put his arms around her; they were still standing in the hall. "Are you trying to make me jealous? All right, I'm jealous." They laughed and kissed just as the butler came in.

"I'm so pleased, Emerson," Alison said without a trace of embarrassment. "Everything went so well tonight."

"Is there anything else, Miss Alison?"

"Nothing. I hope you gave them champagne in the kitchen."

"Yes, indeed."

They watched his dignified departure and Alison said, "What would I do without Emerson?"

"It's too awful to think about."

"Mother keeps demanding him. After all, he does belong to Mother."

"How can he resist Florida, at this time of year?"

Her eyes were full of happy malice. "I'll tell you how, David—Emerson has a gentleman friend."

"I'd never guess it."

"A hairdresser, and his job is in New York, so you see." Suddenly her face was serious. "I suppose I could get along without Emerson, but could I get along without you?"

He laughed. "You could forget about me in an hour and you know it."

"No, you could forget about *me*, that's what I'm afraid of. With all the girls around . . . Tell me, who was the best-looking girl here tonight?"

"After you?" He considered. "That quiet one who sat next to your Uncle Seward."

She chortled. "I'm safe there! Sandy's a loner." With which she dismissed the subject, took his arm and led him across the room to the fireplace. Smiling, she reached up and took a little gift package out of a vase on the mantel. "For you." She handed it to him.

The box was from Cartier and the cufflinks were square with tiny rubies. "Happy birthday, David," she said. "I almost forgot your present."

"You shouldn't have! Isn't that what I'm supposed to say? But I'm going to level with you. Secretly, I'm so glad you did."

"Sit still." She was extracting his other cufflinks and putting in the new ones.

"We could hear you all laughing it up after dinner. What was Chad saying?"

"Telling dirty jokes, of course."

"That explains the laughing. You mean Sandy was actually laughing too?"

She gave him a sharp glance. "You liked Sandy."

"Liked her? I don't even know her last name."

"And you're not going to get it out of me." She handed him back his other cufflinks. "There."

He admired them under the lamp. "You're a sweet one, Alison."

She bent her head and kissed his hands. "You deserve much more than a pair of baubles."

"What, for instance?"

"Anything I have, any time."

"I think you mean that."

"I do mean it, pal, just try me."

He laughed and put his arms around her. This was getting too serious. He was thinking, but not telling her, of Chad's story about the guy who met the girl at the Park Avenue party and she took him to her own place, an immense triplex across the street, where she showed him her late husband's wardrobe—dozens of suits, hundreds of ties and shirts, mink-lined overcoats, handmade shoes, and said to him, "I want you to have all this," then lay down on the bed and opened her legs as wide as they would go, she was nude under her dress, and said, "Now, kiss me." "Well, go on," the guy's friend said. "When she said that, what did you do?" And the guy replied, "Oh, I had to have some of the suits altered, and the shirtsleeves were a little long . . ."

Alison saw his smile. "What's entertaining you now?"

"I'm looking forward to making love to you."

"Then what are we waiting for?" She took his arm and they walked together through the foyer and down the hall to her bedroom, a scene of feminine magnificence. They stood there in the doorway a moment, arms around each other's waists, and Alison said, "I wish you belonged here, every night. How about it, David Brent?"

He knew she wanted him to say "Are you proposing marriage?" or other words to the effect but he only smiled, and sensed at once her shock of hurt and pride. Neither spoke after that: the business of sex was at hand, and even as they stripped and fell to the bed together he felt her denying her body to him, even as she took him into her. In the subtle lamplight her face was a mask; her arms lay at her sides and her body was motionless, a challenge. For a long time he too was quiescent, as if waiting for the moment of perfection, mastering his impulse to thrust, to drive; if she could hold back, so could he, hot and deep and desirable as she was in his possession. But gradually his blood quickened, he felt himself harden and lengthen inside her, felt her for the first time respond if ever so faintly, a tremor in her loins, a tightening of the folds. And her arms stirred, her fingers lightly touched his body— a touch, no more. That was when he sought her mouth and kissed her inert, unresisting lips, feeling her arms lift and come closer then, the fingers rest lightly on his buttocks, the mouth open delicately, enough to receive his tongue. He was moving now as her thighs widened under his weight, striking with a careful, controlled rhythm, withdrawing to the tip, and she was breathing faster, her warm breath in his mouth. She was melting under him, forgetting where she was, forgetting who she was, and her arms came up and around his shoulders as her belly rose to match his swinging blows, forcing her rhythmic moans and signaling the approach of the orgasm he knew so well. Her nails dug into the skin of his back and her lips tore away from his mouth as she gasped deeply for breath; they were coming together as they always did. It was here; he felt the fluttering deep in her vagina, the agony of reaching, holding, fulfilling; and in that moment, even as he gave her everything he had, even at the instant of his own bursting, flooding power, she was not what he wanted; the image of Sandy, for no reason he knew, was in his mind . . .

# 45

It was Chad Newsom who brought it all up again, over a week later, tramping down the hall into the newsroom and walking unannounced into his office.

Brent grinned from behind his desk. "What's up, baby?"

"You don't return my calls."

"Busy, Chad, busy."

"You don't call her anymore, either."

"Her?"

"Come on. Alison."

Brent looked at his watch. "Can we have lunch on that?"

"Now you're making sense."

They walked over to Romeo Salta's and ate beef marrow and drank Bardolino. There was the usual fuss over getting them the best table and between courses they obligingly signed autographs for the customers.

"Ever come here with Alison?" Chad said.

"I was wondering when you'd get back to Alison."

"Look, I'm only trying to help."

"Help with what?"

"You know with what."

"You're speaking for her, right?"

The goatish laugh. "Would I do that to a friend? You think I see Alison?"

"I thought you might. She thinks a lot of you."

"Sniff again, Brent. I'm out of her class. I'm a wild man."

"So's she, in her polite way."

They both laughed at that. Chad said, "Okay, little darling, I'll tell you something. I've seen her. She called me the other day."

"And she wanted to know about me."

305

"I told her I hadn't seen you or heard from you and no, to my knowledge you weren't fooling around with some other chick."

"Is that all?"

"That's all about you." He was grinning. "These things happen, you know? I was with her for half an hour and already she was hinting if I had any grass on me, she'd never tried it."

"And you just accidentally had some."

"We were up in her apartment, the old queen served dinner to us and she told him to get lost."

"She told you Emerson was queer?"

"I told *her*. Don't put me on, Dave, the guy's a leaping faggot. Five'll get you ten he's hemstitching a boudoir cap right now."

"So you smoked a couple."

"Yeah. And she got to talking pretty good—about you, not me."

"Press on."

"How you think she wants to marry you and how you're right."

"I assumed she knew, and this confirms it."

The other man's eyes narrowed quizzically. "You ever tell her about my bag, Dave? Like the Nassau gig when I went down on those two kids?"

"Absolutely not."

"Okay, here we go. She wanted that and I gave it to her, she blew her mind. I mean it was nothing to me. You know dolls like this, it's curiosity, it's a change. And I was glad you two weren't with it right now, you know? So you wouldn't maybe plug me for what I did."

Brent smiled. "Never, Chad. I need you."

"You *need* me?" The grin was vast.

"Let's say we need each other."

"Man, we do. Above and beyond the greatest quim we ever saw, right?" He laughed. "Unless you've found something female better."

"Nobody, Chad. But I'm looking . . ."

"To get married?" And when Brent nodded, "I've told you before and I tell you again, any cat foolish enough to do that is out of his skull. Like I did it twice, when I was still wet behind the ears, but never no more."

"I know what I want, Chad. I'm a grownup now."

"Don't get too grownup, you'll stop having fun."

"You have to think past the fun. You have to think long haul."

There was a pause. Newsom studied him under heavy eyebrows. "So I tell Alison you're not going to see her any more?"

"For Christ's sake, Chad, don't make it any worse. Just say I'm in a busy period and I'll call when I'm out of it, O.K.?"

"And there's no chick in the wings?"

"I wish there were. But if I find the right one, friend, I'm going legit."

"Alison won't qualify?"

"Alison's going to be able to take care of herself. You're the best proof of that. And many happy returns, Chad . . ."

It was their last lunch together for some time. Brent heard nothing further from Alison Chandler and made no effort to call her; it seemed best to let matters lie for the present. But the haunting image of Sandy refused to leave his mind, surging up at unexpected moments, even in the midst of a news broadcast, or at night in the moments before sleep. How to find her and exorcise this delectable little phantom was becoming a problem, but he literally didn't know where to begin. That night at Alison's they'd only exchanged half a dozen words and brief smiles, and he didn't even have a last name to go on. But he remembered the smile in the lovely narrow face, and the steadiness of dark eyes that seemed in the moment to appraise him, to ask a question.

By merest chance, suddenly the problem was solved. He was passing the Brook Club on his way to an interview appointment when he almost collided with Alison's Uncle Seward coming out. He made the most of it, stopping abruptly and greeting the older man who obviously didn't recognize him.

"David Brent, Seward—we met at Alison Chandler's dinner party."

The frosty smile. "The birthday boy! My eyesight's not as good as it was."

"I shouldn't blame you. The only person there I knew by name was our hostess."

"And your friend—Newsom, wasn't it?"

"Of course! I forgot Chad. He was even more of a stranger than I was."

"Very amusing fella, Newsom. We were all impressed with him."

"And he was impressed with all of you, especially the ladies present. Even more particularly, the girl who sat next to you at the table—was it, er, Sandy?"

"Sandy?" He blinked. "Ah, yes, Alexandra Webb. I was glad to see her. She doesn't go about very much, you know." He looked around him. "Well, I must be off—late already." He waved and departed, stiffly but rapidly. Brent grinned. So much for Chad Newsom.

The unexpected encounter with Seward seemed suddenly to galvanize his latent feelings about the girl at Alison's dinner table. As if he'd seen her only the night before, her image for the first time came into focus as a whole. Visually there was the promise of the young, vibrant body clad in the simple, smart dinner dress, smooth-skinned and full-breasted, the coppery hair thick and shining with vitality. But beyond and beneath this outward view was his impression that somehow she was holding herself in check, restraining an urge to proclaim her beauty, her personality, until now withheld under tight control. But why? What would be the motivation for this quiet modesty, almost a shyness were it not for the ease and poise with which she handled herself amid the inanely cheerful small talk all around her? Twice, no, three times their eyes had met, but he was several places away from her and on the opposite side of the long table, too distant to exchange any words. Still, her look had lingered, somehow an oasis in the vacuum of chitchat, and her eyes told him she knew he was responding in kind. But surely there were other men who felt about her as he did, responded to the searching, faintly enigmatic gaze, the sudden lovely smile.

Well, he'd soon have some answers to his speculation. He knew he could find her now. In the busy New York street he hastened his step and smiled like a man with a secret.

She was listed at an address in the East Sixties but there was no answer when he called from his office in late afternoon. He tried again a few minutes after his early evening show. Her calm, quiet voice was suddenly and vividly remembered. She didn't say hello—simply the word, "Yes?"

"David Brent here."

A silence, then a low, musical laugh. "What an odd sensation. I was just listening to you on the air."

"I'm flattered. How did I sound?"

"Sound?" Again the murmured laugh. "Why, fine. As usual."

"Then you watch regularly."

"Just since Alison's party. I must confess you've weaned me away from another station."

"I'm even more flattered."

A pause. He was waiting for a cue. "One more viewer for David Brent," she said. "That's not interesting. It would be more interesting to know why David Brent is calling Sandy Webb."

"He'd like to see her again."

"My turn to be flattered, Mr. Brent."

"David."

"David."

"Shall we have lunch one day? Or are you free at lunchtime?"

"How nice! Quite free."

"Would you like to choose the place?"

He could hear the remembered smile in her voice. "I'm afraid I don't get around that much. You choose."

"The Argenteuil? Twelve-thirty tomorrow?"

"I look forward to it," said Alexandra Webb.

Why was his heart beating a little faster when he put down the receiver, and what was it about this girl that persisted in stirring something in him that had not been there before? He was glad he'd thought of the Argenteuil because they were unlikely to meet Alison there—a little off the track for the Beautiful People but excellent French cuisine and impeccable service. As it turned out, it was only a couple of blocks away from Sandy's office.

"You're a working girl?" he said, surprised, as they sat over Kirs at a corner table. "I thought you were one of the idle rich."

She smiled. "You must have got that impression at Alison's. As a matter of fact I almost didn't go. Don't misunderstand—Cousin Alison is a perfectly O.K. person but just not quite the right group for me."

"What's your group, Sandy?"

The dark eyes opened wider, almost challenging. "Me," she said.

"You mean you're your own best companion."

"Something like that. But don't misunderstand, I'm not a hermit."

"There must be quite a few boys around who see to that."

She nodded, her soft gaze holding his eyes as if she was fathoming things in him he didn't know himself. "But it's not quite so simple," she went on. "I guess it has partly to do with a so-called proper upbringing, a stuffy family that limited me to the suitable young men, the men they wanted me to feel safe with, protected, married—" She paused, smiling. "The trouble was, they bored me silly, all of them, until I tended to retreat into myself. And here I am, twenty-six years old, unmarried, and boring *you* with my self-analysis."

"I gather I'm not a suitable young man."

"Would it surprise you," she said, "if I confessed I hoped you would call me?"

"I'm glad to hear that, because I've thought about Sandy Webb every day since the first time I saw her."

"I can't imagine why."

"For all the obvious reasons, and some others I haven't figured out yet."

"That's the interesting part."

He smiled. "I'll let you know when I find out."

The mussels arrived, the Montrachet was poured, and it was evident from Sandy's comments that she knew her food and wine. The grilled salmon Béarnaise launched her into reminiscence of meals consumed in the Vosges, and other happy culinary experiences.

"Who do you work for, Restaurant Associates?"

She laughed. "I wish I did! Actually I schedule models' appointments for a fashion agency, isn't that glamorous?"

"You'd make a great model yourself."

"Thank you. I know women consider that a high compliment, but they wouldn't if they knew you have to work like a dog. Anyway, I've about had it with my friends up the street. One of these days soon I'm going to quit."

"What will you do then, Sandy?"

She dropped her head back against the banquette and

half closed her eyes. "Go back to my old life. Loaf. Sleep late, wander the museums, listen to music, cook simple, perfect dinners for myself and read in bed."

"What a waste," he grinned.

She turned to look at him, her face flushed and wistful. "Waste?"

"Reading in bed."

They laughed together. "Don't you like to read in bed, David?"

"You forget I read for a living, my dear. By the time I'm ready to sleep I'm too tired to read."

They had a half bottle of Chambertin with the Roquefort and an old Armagnac with the café filtre, and he was pleased to see that apart from her heightened color and a tendency to speak a little more rapidly she seemed still coolly poised.

"You approve of the Armagnac, Sandy?"

"I approve of it all, including my generous host. And I'm just drunk enough to quit my job today, provided you take my arm and very carefully hold me steady till I get back to the office."

"Not until you agree to lunch with me in the country on Sunday."

"I've been hoping you'd suggest it."

They had been together a little over two hours and he felt they were friends in a way he could never be with Alison Chandler. Leaving her at the elevator, he walked slowly back across town with a sense of quiet conviction he'd forgotten he was able to feel about a woman. He knew now why he'd longed for this girl after their first, almost perfunctory contact: she was an answer to everything he had been feeling, groping for. There was something inevitable, almost as if preordained about the meeting, and he was ready to believe there had been telepathy between them since that night, thé more so because he still knew so little, factually, about her background, her past, her life. The excitement came from knowing all that was unnecessary; it would come with time. Only two days before they would be together again! . . .

Sunday dawned clear and mild, one of those perfect days that could come to the Northeast as suddenly and miraculously as the first spring birds, mild as May though April was just beginning. Sandy was waiting at nine-thirty

and already, even with the swift movement of the car, the
sun was hot overhead. He was driving with the top down,
impatient for her to feel the full force of the power coiled
under that gleaming silver hood, trying to remember to
hold back on the accelerator. The Jag wanted to go, to
pass everything on the parkway, as if expressing the exhilaration straining in his own body, the throttled speed
waiting, challenging, the call to escape and freedom, with
her. They spoke little, and he wondered whether this
would be part of the pattern they were even now setting for
a future together. Veering off into a quieter Westchester
road he dropped one hand to the hands folded in her lap
and felt her fingers close around it, aware and warm and
confident, the sign of certitude, the gift of knowing what
he knew, and telling him so.

He found a grown-over lane in the wilderness of the
Mianus Gorge and, still holding hands, they left the car
and walked through woodland just wakening to springtime.
Between them was the silence of an understanding so unexpectedly complete that words were unnecessary, super-
fluous. At the same time he had a strange sense of déjà
vu, and it was Sandy's soft little question that identified the
memory. "What are you thinking?" she said. "I mean
*really* thinking . . ."

"About a time like this in the woods, years and years
ago, so long ago it almost seems unreal, now. I was in college and a professor's wife took me for a drive in the
country. She stopped the car and we got out, and like the
innocent little freshman I was I still didn't suspect what
she was doing, what she wanted." He smiled. "But I soon
found out she was all prepared—a blanket ready in the
back of the car and a hidden spot under the trees . . ."

"Was it—was she your first?"

"Almost. The other times were kid times, but she was
the first woman." He turned to look at her. "And what
were *you* thinking, Sandy, while we were walking a little
while ago and you were so silent?"

"About countryside, like you, David. In France. An
inn where I stayed a few days, a few summers ago. A
simple place. The blankets felt rough and good. In the
morning there were voices and happy breakfast noises
downstairs. There was a brook outside. I can still hear it."

"Were you staying there alone or was there a man?"

"I wish you could see that village, David. And walk like this in the fields. Very old country churches, that the tourists don't know about but have one beautiful thing inside, one piece of art that hasn't been taken for some museum or sold abroad, maybe the tomb of a crusader and his wife. Picnics with wine . . ."

"Outdoor lovemaking."

She was smiling. "The wheat stretched away for miles. And there was a castle on the hill."

"Were you alone, Sandy?"

"Wouldn't it be nice if we could go out in the country in France some day, together? I think we'd do well, don't you? Of course I'm just fantasizing." She turned her smile up to him again. "I spend a lot of my time fantasizing, about one thing or another. I guess you don't have time, David, but I sometimes think fantasies are more real than reality. And better."

"It's because you retreated, Sandy."

"Maybe I'm happier that way."

"Maybe it's because you haven't really tasted reality . . ."

"Oh, I've tasted it, in my fashion. But it didn't seem to mean very much."

"You can't just taste it. You have to gulp it."

She gave a wistful little laugh. "You're making me thirsty, David." For an instant her fingers gripped his hand with such force he almost winced, then she dropped his hand and said, "And hungry, too. Isn't it time for lunch?"

It was after twelve. He put an arm around her unresisting shoulders and they sauntered back to the car like comrades.

They were expected at the Crémaillère where he'd made the reservation the night before. With the trout they drank a Coteaux du Layon, with the quail a Chateau Pétrus, and with the Brie a Clos de Bèze. After some deliberation they decided against dessert, a concession to the cholesterol problem, but yielded to a snifter of Marc de Bourgogne, after which Sandy pronounced the meal the best she had ever eaten in America, acknowledging that the French wines were responsible at least in part, of course.

Over coffee he said, "How's Alison these days?"

"David, I don't see Alison three times a year. I assumed you'd know much more about her than I do."

He smiled. "How much is there to know about Alison that can't be learned in a very short time?"

"Many a true word is spoken in earnest," Sandy said, and they both laughed.

"On the other hand," he went on, "I suspect it would take quite a while to know all there is to know about Alexandra Webb, wouldn't you agree?"

"Especially since Alexandra Webb doesn't know all that much about herself."

"There's mystery in you, Sandy—something hidden, or maybe unawakened, waiting."

"If there is, it's a mystery to me, too, David."

"I'm not sure I want to know what it is. Because it's what attracts me to you the most."

"Mystery or no mystery, anything that attracts David Brent to Alexandra Webb can't be all bad."

Again they laughed together. He paid the check and they went out arm in arm into the cool, clear afternoon. If she had questions about his relationship with Alison Chandler she'd given no sign; it was part of the calm, steady core of her, the self-sufficiency that shone quiet and sure from her eyes. Did she know, fully, what he was feeling for her? They barely spoke a word to each other on the drive back to the city; her head back against the seat, her eyes closed, she breathed deeply. "I've had too much wine," she said.

"No one can have too much wine."

"It makes me sleepy when I want so very much to stay awake."

"Why so very much, Sandy?"

She didn't answer, and when he glanced at her he saw the enigmatic little smile that said no explanations were necessary. They were off the parkway by now and in town again, and still her head was back, her eyes closed. When he drew up in front of his house and she opened her eyes at last she seemed unsurprised, following him out of the car and standing on the sidewalk, waiting, while he locked the doors. She took his arm going up the stoop as if she'd done it a thousand times before, silent and secure. In the hall she waited while he locked the door from the inside, then, still without a word between them, followed his grave gesture and preceded him up the short flight of stairs and into the rear bedroom.

The curtains were drawn against the afternoon light but the faint warmth of earlier sunshine still pervaded the room. For a long moment they stood facing each other before, simultaneously, they came together in a kiss; their arms locked around each other's shoulders and her handbag tumbled against his leg as it fell to the floor. Their mouths held, timeless, until at last she gasped for breath and drew away. Reluctantly he let her go and stood motionless, watching, as she slipped out of her shoes, unsheathed the dress with a shy, gentle movement and slipped off her stockings with an awkward little lurch against the bed. Now she wore only bra and panty, her nude shoulders smooth and golden. She saw him look down at the coppery shadow seen through the thin covering between her legs and smiled. "Yes," she whispered. "Your turn now . . ."

And he undressed for her, all the way to the last garment, the shorts barely concealing what her steady gaze was doing to him. His low laugh was troubled. "I guess I'm embarrassed . . ."

"Why? Because of the wonderful thing happening to you?"

"Yes."

"The Greeks said that when it happens the god of love is entering your body."

"I believe it."

With a single movement she loosed her bra and stepped out of her panty, her hair falling forward over her face and covering one eye. "Now you," she said, still bent toward him. She watched him comply. A sigh went through her body as she lifted her head again. "I could never look at you enough . . ."

"You've looked at me enough already. The god of love is impatient."

She smiled and they lay down on the bed together, not touching except for clasped hands between them. The sounds of the city Sunday discreetly entered the room. What was it that made this girl so different from all before her, or was it the change in him?

When at last he came into her it was so tenderly that he felt he had never known such tenderness in himself.

Beneath him she lay serene, complete, the goal of all desiring, and they were together without moving, coming to each other without moving, as if they had never made love before to anyone. As if they had always made love like this.

# 46

They were married exactly one week later by a justice of the peace in Lambertville, New Jersey. Until they returned to New York that night it was a secret from everyone they knew, in keeping with their mutual belief that a wedding is strictly a private ceremony. The following day Brent was back behind the microphone as usual without having missed a single program. A honeymoon was out of the question: the outbreak of war in Korea had put UBC News on a crisis schedule.

The day after his walk in the woods with Sandy, U.S. ground forces landed in Korea, and Dan McCurdy called him into his office.

"I suppose the old fire horse hears the alarm bell ringing and you're raring to go, Dave, right?"

"Well . . ."

The news chief smiled. "We recognize your combat experience would be very useful to the network, but you're just too valuable in your present job. I may decide to send you out there later, depending on how it goes. For now, like it or not, I'm going to have to keep you here."

Habitual attitude told him to protest, but all his instinct said: be grateful. He shrugged and accepted it. Once before, on the Washington staff, he'd protested to McCurdy's predecessor and won assignment to the warfront. But this time he knew it would mean losing a new life with Sandy Webb. And he wanted that life, wanted to succeed in it above and beyond any other challenge. Lying in each other's arms last night they had talked into the dawn, and he'd learned this girl symbolized everything he'd so long subconsciously wished for: reason, order, regularity, a nearly miraculous matching of two very different temperaments. In the highly volatile world situation

317

now developing he couldn't be certain that McCurdy wouldn't change his mind any day and order him to Korea, with the danger and long separation that would entail. But at the least he could make sure of Sandy while there was still time. If she was willing.

Five minutes after he left McCurdy he was calling her at her office on his private line. "Can you talk, Sandy?"

"Up to a point."

"All I need is a yes or no."

"I see." He heard the smile in her response. "In that case I think I know what you're going to say."

He tried to keep the exultation out of his voice. "You always know everything. Would you happen to know how long the legal preliminaries would take?"

"Two or three days at most."

"Look into it, will you?"

"I will."

That was all. When he finished the late-evening show and went home, she was waiting for him.

The ease with which he adapted to their new life-style would have surprised him if it had all not seemed simply fated, inevitable. Even so, there were moments when suddenly he saw himself as in a mirror, a former David Brent playing the role of another man. Role or reality, he liked it, welcomed it, fell into its rhythms as naturally as breathing, step by step with Sandy at his side. She gave up her job immediately after they were married and devoted herself to redecorating the brownstone, bringing in her piano and pieces of family furniture from her own apartment, and buying supplementary things with her own income from the trust fund left by her parents, lost two years before in a sailing accident off Bermuda, their bodies never recovered. There were still other relatives in Sandy's life who had to be duly visited and as duly entertained—once. All were cut from the same mold, old New York connections which Sandy had gradually severed after her parents' death, maintaining only the barest minimum relationship for good manners' sake. These amenities out of the way, there was only the problem of Alison Chandler.

Alison had surprised him, but not Sandy, by the grace with which she accepted their marriage, sending a conventional little note of congratulations to them both and appearing all cheer and charm at the single cocktail party Sandy gave as a housewarming.

"Does she mean it?" he asked Sandy afterward.

"Of course not, darling."

"Well then, *why?*"

"Because it's the thing one does."

"That night at her dinner party I asked her about you. She called you a loner." He smiled. "I guess you are, in a way."

Her eyes seemed wider, distant, for a moment. "Perhaps I *was*, but I'm learning not to be, thanks to David Brent."

"You're a quick study, Mrs. Brent."

"There's still a lot I don't know about myself, I'm sure of that."

"Good! We'll discover it together . . ."

They had invited Chad Newsom to the housewarming but he was directing a picture on the West Coast and couldn't make it. Typically, he had phoned Cartier's and instructed them to get in touch with Mrs. Brent and give her something she needed for the house. The first day Chad was back in New York he taxied directly from the airport to Sixty-fifth Street for lunch with the newlyweds and escorted Brent to the studio afterward.

"What you say, Chad?"

"Little brother, with something like that there's nowhere to go but down!"

Brent laughed. "For something like that I don't need direction, not even by Chad Newsom."

"She's gorgeous, Dave. Like one of those silver nymphs they put on car hoods, long and slim."

"That's what I thought the first time I saw her. And that's what she looks like lying there naked. But when I take her, she's all ass. Don't ask me how she does it, Chad, or what happens to her when she comes. Maybe because it's all new to her, because I've awakened her to sex for the first time . . ."

Newsom stared at him. "You mean you're the first—?"

"I don't know. I don't discuss my women and she doesn't discuss her men, and we're not about to start. But the total adoration she gives me, that's part of it, too. I'm the only man in the world. I'm the only man that ever made love to anybody."

"Women are good at making a man feel that, baby."

"Faking it? Not this one, baby. I know a faker when I fuck one."

"Just a clean-cut American boy, right?"

"Newsom, you're reading my thoughts. I'm beginning my life again, starting out fresh."

"Settling down. Kids."

"Right."

"And goodbye dolls. Goodbye Chad."

"You think so? The first boy is called David C. Brent."

"C. for Chad?"

"Chadwick."

The director lunged at him and kissed his cheek. "I love you, you social climber!"

"Slob, you got lipstick all over me."

"Try Kleenex."

It was raining lightly when he got home after the late evening show. As usual Sandy had a light supper waiting for him in the alcove—tonight a quiche accompanied by chilled Sylvaner served in her old Alsatian goblets. "What did you think of Chad Newsom?"

"I liked him. And specially because *you* like him. He's awfully direct, isn't he?"

"He thinks you're wonderful, Sandy."

She smiled. "It's nice of him. But as long as you think I'm wonderful I don't care if nobody else does."

He was looking at the imprint of her breasts through the sheer blouse she was wearing. "Wonderful," he repeated. "And beautiful." He drained the last of the Sylvaner and took her hand across the little table. "Let's go upstairs, shall we?"

In the bedroom they undressed swiftly, her skin flushed and flushing deeper. Naked, they were alone, not one of the city's million eyes could see them. Her face was flowerlike in the soft light, her eyes huge and wondering, their kiss more reverence than lust. Each thing they did now, each movement, each whisper, had the sacredness of ritual. Even at the last, when everything in each of them flowed out and into the other, the meaning was greater than they were. The low roar of the city at night died away and was lost.

The wine, the silence, the rain. He loved her for the man who may have loved her first and any others along the way that he would never know about, and he loved her for all the beautiful girls he had ever known and ever seen because he wanted everything that she was and had been and wanted to give her everything of himself, now and always. He was shaking her with his power and she received him purely. The earth was shaken with his power and the earth was his.

# 47

The New York life settled in, became routine, expectable. Old tensions of pressure and uncertainty subsided; Brent's daily job became an almost automatic exercise, stimulating enough to hold his interest but never tiring, because he wasn't making the small-hour rounds any more; his hours away from the office were as regular as those in the newsroom. Not that they weren't full of pleasurable variety: with Sandy as his guide he made his acquaintance with the world of art and artists, with the Philharmonic concerts and their roster of conductors and soloists, Off-Broadway and Off-Off-Broadway theater, little undiscovered restaurants on the West Side, in the Village. But the best times were home times in Sixty-fifth Street, especially Sandy's Sunday brunches for members of the UBC news staff and their wives and girls. Nobody connected with Brent's programs was excluded, from Dan McCurdy down the line through editors, writers, control-room technicians, secretaries, researchers, a few couples each Sunday partaking happily of Bloody Marys or spritzers or whiskey sours with the hostess' justly admired omelets and croissants from the Versailles patisserie around the corner.

For Brent, the peace after the guests departed was the best time of the week: listening to Sandy's Schubert impromptus at the piano, her hair shining softly in the late afternoon light from the rock garden behind the house, or looking up from a book to watch her reading with her horn-rimmed glasses balanced distractedly on the tip of her small straight nose, her nearness in the silence almost unbearably sweet. Some mornings, rain or shine, they took long walks together in the Park, hands brushing, swinging, gradually holding with tight clasped fingers, then lunch at their accustomed table at the Tavern on the Green before he left for the office, and tending to wander, not caring if they found the nearest way or the nearest street, pausing at a corner, the traffic whirling past, to laugh together at something pointless or absurd, all the sights and sounds of the city around them like a celebration: tasting New York.

She had given him the deep sense of continuity, sequence, repose, that somehow he had hungered for without realizing what had failed him through the hastening, turbulent past. And with it a sense of family, left somewhere far back along the way. Maybe that was why the miscarriage hit so hard, struck him deeper even than Sandy, who smiled it off with characteristic grace, who took it as a piece of transient bad luck that couldn't happen again. The doctors agreed with her: she was healthy and without organic weakness anywhere. But eight months later it did happen again, and this time the advice was gloomy, prognosis poor for any eventual birth.

He marveled at Sandy's steady courage in reacting to the situation. As she would have said, it was the thing one does. Not talking about it was also the thing one does. Instead, you led your life as before, at least on the surface of things, and tried to ignore the sense of loss you knew you both felt. Maybe they were drinking a little more; he became aware that he was, but he couldn't be sure about Sandy. She faced long evenings during his seven-hour absence at the studio, and two or three times when he found her waiting for him as always after his late broadcast she seemed almost artificially cheerful and affectionate, her color higher, her eyes unnaturally bright, her speech lucid but rapid. Seeing her this way stabbed at his heart and he almost turned away, but not turning away was the thing one does. And time would heal the wound—or would it? Their nights had been full of peaceful, dreamless sleep, restoring the body for the day to come; now each lay awake or woke to know the other stared sleepless into the dark, hearing the endless minutes tick away.

They tried to overcome it on vacation in the islands, but found after the first few days of change that they were lonely and lost in memories of life together in New York. He fretted over radio and newspaper reports of events he should be covering himself; Sandy sat for hours on Half Moon Beach gazing at the tepid, surfless water, her book unread at her side. This getting away was only running away, left them even more depressed. In briefly spoken agreement they decided to cut short their holiday and return to their normal active life, the affection of friends, the familiar tumult of the city. Things went better then; it was good for him to be back on the air and busy, occupied; Sandy tackled the Brahms intermezzi; Chad Newsom blew in again from Hollywood and the Sunday brunches gaily resumed. But as with the first miscarriage, nothing was said to anybody about the new misfortune, not even to Chad.

They were putting up a pretty good front, to the world, to their friends—perhaps to each other as well? And yet the feeling lingered like some obscure malaise; it had changed their relationship in subtle ways they were still discovering, even in their sexual attitudes—no longer the frank, free sense of abandonment. In their most intimate moments together, naked in each other's arms, something held him back—fear of hurting her physically? conscious of awareness in her eyes that she too was different now?— and the best of the orgasm was spoiled. Ah, she wouldn't say so!, but was she simulating her own climax to meet with his before she was ready, before she reached the ultimate consummation? Afterward, still clasping her body close, he felt the tug of disillusion somewhere deep within him, felt it too in her as slowly he withdrew: they had come almost to the peak and failed, or rather he had failed to bring her with him all the way; it was failure for both.

Without mentioning the medical history, Brent finally talked to Chad Newsom about his altered feeling toward Sandy and the reciprocal change he felt in her. It was rare these days to be alone with Chad, a brief unscheduled meeting over coffee between shows across the street from the UBC studios. The director listened gravefaced, for once without interruptions, then reached across the table, grabbed Brent's hand and kissed it.

"So what else is new? Look, little brother, don't you know this happens to every marriage? Nothing stays the same, I don't care how beautiful you both are—and you are—you're humans like the rest of us. The novelty's got to wear off. The games get monotonous. But it's no tragedy, baby! you just adapt! You don't expect so much. Sandy's a wise kid, she probably knows better than you what happens only she won't say it, no woman will. So figure she's feeling like you and give her a break, give both of you a break. Take the pressure off. Kick up your heels and whistle! Show you understand and know she understands." He shrugged and grinned. "What am I telling you you don't know already, a smart fella like you? It's the same old story the whole world over—the only cure is change your luck now and then." The grin widened. "Lotsa nice stuff around, like always! Say the word, Davey boy, and I'll set up something . . ."

They laughed together. Brent said, "Thanks, I'll let you know, Chad," and left it at that. But the little talk lightened the emotional burden he'd been carrying too long. Chad was partly right, of course, even without knowledge of Sandy's troubles. Never in Brent's whole life had he sustained an intensely intimate relationship as steadily or for so long as in his marriage to Sandy—not with Claudine in Paris, not with Daphne in London, or with Clare in Rome or Lee in Washington. Had he expected it to continue without fault or blemish indefinitely? He didn't believe in resolutions, but going home after the late show that night he pledged himself to try for both their sakes to put this feeling of estrangement behind them.

His sense of making a new start carried over into the next Sunday's brunch, which somehow seemed the gayest of them all. Chad was there with one of his sex-kitten protégées, and Ed Kirk, director of both Brent's shows, with his sassy little wife, plus the usual diverse group of news staffers at several levels and one newcomer from the Boston station, a black reporter named Lyle Ashby just assigned to broadcast remotes for the early evening program. It was Kirk's opinion that Lyle Ashby was going to go a long way in television news, with his intelligence, commanding looks, like a youthful Sidney Poitier, his deep, musical voice and natural camera presence. To Brent he seemed even more a magnetic figure in the confines of this room where now he stood totally at ease among his new colleagues, his powerful body towering over the other men present and his gentle smile charming the women.

"Ed says you sing, too," Sally Kirk was chattering at him.

"I studied for a while, but I like doing news better."

"You're good at it," Brent said.

"Coming from you, that makes me feel proud." There was no trace of flattery in the quick warm smile.

They asked him to stay on after the others left, and as dusk deepened into dark Lyle joined in another drink. It might have been his fourth or fifth—Brent himself felt pleasantly high—but Lyle was as steady and smooth as when he arrived. He looked at Sandy's Steinway with admiration. "Do you both play?" he said.

"Only Sandy. I wouldn't be able to find middle C."

"There's a lot of music in Boston—good music, I mean, in people's homes. I'm going to miss it here." He looked at Sandy. "Wouldn't you play something?"

She smiled. "If you promise to forgive me . . ." and she sat down at the keyboard and played the Schumann *Warum* and a Chopin nocturne, music beautifully performed and somehow suited to the quiet mood that followed the clattering party voices of a while before. Listening, dividing his glances between Sandy's gracefully bent head and the fixed, rapt gaze of her guest upon her as she played, Brent wished he could feel this music as they did, felt somehow inadequate to the moment they both savored. When she finished, let the last chord linger in the silence, Lyle Ashby said simply, "That was beautiful, I am so grateful, Mrs. Brent."

She gave a little laugh. "I only answer to Sandy, Lyle. Anyway it's your turn! If you give me a tune I know, I can accompany, after a fashion."

There was no false modesty about him. He went to the piano and after they found his key sang three spirituals, the last ending:

*Doctors and lawyers, he had 'em to remember*
*That he was born on the twenty-fifth of December.*
*Little boy, how old are you?*
*I'm twelve years old.*

Singer and pianist were motionless as the notes died away. Lyle Ashby seemed very moved. Brent saw tears in Sandy's eyes. He waited before he spoke into this special stillness.

"You may have missed your true career, Lyle. You may have *both* missed your true careers."

Sandy was looking up at Lyle. "We must do this again. Could you bring some of the songs you studied?"

"I shall, Sandy. You're a perfect accompanist."

After he'd gone Brent said, "I wish I could feel music the way you two did."

She smiled, a kind of exaltation in her eyes. "It's a special kind of kinship, David."

He had an odd impression that Lyle Ashby was still in the room.

# 48

Lyle Ashby was very promptly making a name for himself. Audience reaction to his field reports came quickly and was highly favorable, and the news staff liked him as a person as well as admiring his work. Several times Brent complimented him on the quality of his reporting, and once jokingly said, "I'll have to watch you carefully, Lyle —you'll be taking my job next!"

"No fear of that, Dave. What you do you do better than anybody around, and you always will."

Lyle became a regular at Sandy's Sunday brunches and one day was even coaxed to sing a song or two with Sandy's accompaniment for the assembled guests. A few nights later, at supper with Sandy after the late evening program, Brent said, "Did you catch Lyle on the early show? He seems to get better all the time."

She smiled. "He thinks so, too. He said tonight he's gaining in confidence."

"He said tonight?" He looked at her.

"He was here for a while. He dropped in on his way home."

He felt his throat tighten and a sharp pang in his stomach. "He dropped in? Just like that?"

"Why, yes." She was perfectly calm. "Was there anything wrong in that?"

"Of course not. I just wondered why you hadn't mentioned it sooner."

She gave a half-puzzled laugh. "I wasn't trying to keep it a secret, David, if that's what you mean."

"No, I didn't mean that at all. I guess I'm just surprised he could walk in here so casually without . . ." He paused, lamely.

"Without asking your permission, David?"

He felt himself flushing. "Maybe he should have asked *your* permission."

She was smiling in a way that irritated him further. "Oh, he did. He called and suggested it."

Brent put down his napkin and drank the rest of his wine. "And what else did he suggest, or can I be told?"

There was a long silence. She was looking at him steadily and he had trouble meeting her eyes. Finally she said evenly, "I played for him and he had a drink—no, two drinks—and he spoke very warmly about you. And then he left."

"How nice." He couldn't keep the sarcasm out of his voice. "And what did he have to say, so warmly, about me, if I may ask?"

Again the long pause. When she spoke again there was a tinge of deeper color in her cheeks. "You're angry, David. Whatever for? I had no idea you were—"

"Not angry," he broke in. "If you don't see anything unusual about it, I guess I shouldn't, either."

She went on as though she hadn't heard him, "I had no idea you were so—conservative, David. Is it because Lyle is a Negro? Surely a man as sophisticated, as civilized as you are—as I hope I am—doesn't allow racial prejudice in his life. If I thought that, I certainly wouldn't have opened the door of your house to Lyle Ashby." Her voice hardened slightly. "I would have met him somewhere else."

"*His* house, maybe?"

He regretted it instantly, saw her eyes glisten with sudden tears and watched her rise from the table. "No, don't, Sandy . . ." He reached for her hand but she drew away from him with an abrupt gesture. "I'm sorry," he said, "I didn't mean any of this, I must be tired or . . ."

But she had left the room, her supper unfinished, her wine untouched in the glass. It was their first quarrel of any real consequence, and all because he'd been stupidly uncaring and thoughtless, because of a gut reaction—jealousy? fear?—he hadn't been able to control when it caught him unawares. He had hurt Sandy in a part of her he didn't know, couldn't anticipate. Implicit in what he had said to her was distrust and accusation; he was ashamed of himself.

The door to their bedroom was closed but not locked. He knocked softly without receiving a reply and opened it. She lay fully clothed, face down on the bed, and he sat down beside her, gently turned her over until she faced him, her eyes dry but somber with a pain like disappointment. "Listen to me, my darling," he said. "If ever I believed in anything, it's the right of every man and woman, married or unmarried, to be completely free to live their own lives, to follow their own individual impulses, without domination or interference from anyone else. Downstairs a little while ago I violated that belief by questioning a perfectly innocent and natural action in your relationship with a good friend to both of us. You were entirely justified in reacting as you did. I don't know the reason for my own reaction, I guess it was purely physical, but I know I hurt you, and all I can say is it won't happen again. I love you, Sandy."

It was only as he said the words, bending to kiss her mouth, that he became aware his hand had slid between her knees and was lightly moving back and forth between the warm, smooth thighs until finally it grazed the soft, tangled cleft that grew more tender with his touch. She was nude beneath her loose skirt, the secret signal that she had wanted him tonight, and the wetness under his fingers meant that already, so quickly, she was aroused. Eyes closed, she was lifting her head to receive his lips in the kiss of forgiveness, and as quickly he slipped out of his clothes and entered her yielding body. But why did just then the memory of Lyle Ashby's visit flash across his mind with the pang of fresh discovery, mingling unwilled anger at the image of black man and white girl caught naked in driving embrace? The vision stirred him to overwhelming excitement; suddenly he was lunging, swelling, beyond all control, and this woman he gripped in his arms responded as though herself overwhelmed by orgasm. In the wild moment the thought overtook him—was she too seeing a vision?

Afterward, lying apart and silent, linked only by clasped hands, their bodies slowly returned to calm. He had never felt so spent, so exhausted, as though in giving so much, as she had given so much, each had defended all that was so precious to them together.

Next day, passing Lyle in a newsroom corridor, Brent

nodded a cheerful greeting and received a smile in return
that revealed nothing but cordial warmth. Just afterward
he wondered if his own salute had seemed forced or arti-
ficial. Still later, at the staff conference on the day's news
schedule, there was opportunity to chat with Lyle but
Brent avoided it. Was the other man also avoiding the
contact? At any rate he made no effort to approach Brent
as the meeting broke up. On the early news program he
called Lyle in from police headquarters on a narcotics
story, and even in the midst of all the technical problems
in the studio, preparing to switch to the next spot, he felt a
little pang: would he find tonight that once again Lyle
had "dropped in" for a visit with Sandy? Between programs
he usually phoned Sandy at home, but tonight he found
himself deliberately refraining, while insistent anxiety
gnawed at him and grew. With an effort, he laughed it off
as neurotic nonsense, finally dialed the number, and almost
immediately remembered that Sandy was having dinner
tonight with the Howards across the street.

The intensity of his relief surprised him, and with it
returned the memory of his reconciliation with Sandy and
its dark sexual undertone. He put it out of his mind and
went back to work. When he got home after the late
show she was already asleep. A little note on the hall table
explained she'd been too tired to wait; his supper was
ready for him in the kitchen.

Once again the haunting anxiety overtook him: this
was the first time she hadn't waited up for him. But the
note was signed "Love," and he reproached himself for his
reaction. She didn't awaken when he slipped into bed beside
her, gently kissed her cheek, and was soon asleep himself.

Lyle Ashby wasn't mentioned again by either of them
until Sandy phoned Saturday afternoon to say Chad Newsom had phoned and she'd invited him for Sunday brunch
with, presumably, the girl or girls he had in tow for the
moment. The news gave him a lift—he'd been missing
Chad and needed to laugh with him again.

"And who would you like from the office, David?"
she said, as she always said.

"Well, Lyle, of course." He paused and waited. "Or
have you already asked him?"

Her reply was coolly ambiguous. "We haven't talked
about it. Will you tell him or shall I call him?"

"You call. Don't you usually?"

She didn't rise to the bait, or was it that she didn't even notice the little jab of sarcasm? Again he was annoyed at his own irritability, yet at the same time the creeping anxiety returned, a feeling of uneasy anticipation, almost of tension as the time neared and the first of the guests arrived.

It was a successful afternoon. Sandy looked radiant in black velvet slacks and a clinging, cream-colored silk shirt. Chad Newsom devoured her with snapping eyes and gave a long, low whistle of admiration which amused Sandy. Not that Chad's friends were less attractive in their own way— two Broadway dancers from a show in a rehearsal and a black musician, Hobe Mackey, who went to the piano after two drinks and stayed there, coaxing out familiar tunes in a subtle style. Two graphic artists from the News department and a girl who lived with one of them filled out the list; oddly enough, it seemed to Brent, Lyle Ashby was last to arrive.

Was there a wariness in his greeting? Somehow today he seemed different, guarded, despite the ease of manner and the broad smile. Sandy was in the kitchen when he came in and for a moment he scanned the room quickly as if seeking her with special concern, then he relaxed and they moved immediately toward each other as she came back into the room. Brent was watching, but if there was a special warmth to their meeting he couldn't detect it in either face: the hostess was equally gracious to all.

Gradually the party divided itself: a group around Hobe's piano, the rest centering on Chad Newsom and his nonstop patter. The tempo of talk and laughter increased as the drinks were poured and poured again. By the time Sandy served brunch it was four o'clock, Hobe's music was louder and faster and Chad's stories were rock-bottom dirty, all of which seemed to suit the general mood. As host, Brent moved back and forth from Chad's circle to the piano, keeping all glasses serviced. If Sandy had wanted to play or Lyle to sing they gave no indication of it today. For the first time Lyle was drinking steadily, Sandy looked definitely high and Brent himself had lost count of his Scotches. He felt good about them all; whatever had been bothering him about Lyle Ashby drifted away in the cloud of fraternal benevolence that hung over the whole room. One of the artists and his girl were kissing on a couch, one of the dancers was sitting beside Hobe Mackey at the piano with her arm around his shoulders, and Chad was pawing his own date like a friendly grizzly. He looked up and grinned as Brent came by.

"Look at these knockers, Davey! I'm in love with them."

"And with reason."

"You got an extra little corner we could hide away for a couple minutes?"

"No."

The girl pouted. "You're a meanie, Davey."

"Never mind, Bonnie, we'll find something," Chad said.

Grinning, he lumbered over to the piano. "That's it, Hobe! Time to move it." He clapped his hands and addressed the room. "Everybody out now! We kept these good people long enough . . ."

The music ceased. In a semi-daze of handshakes and embraces all around, the guests took their leave. Lyle Ashby too stood up to go but Sandy said, "Please, Lyle, not yet."

Brent smiled at him. "Stick around, it's early," and the two men stood waiting, not speaking to each other, while Sandy said the last goodbye at the door and came back to join them. The room was suddenly very quiet. Sandy breathed a deep sigh of relief, dropped onto the couch and motioned to Lyle to sit at the other end. "Peace at last," she smiled. "Now I can enjoy a drink."

Brent poured for all three and afterward, still standing looking down at them, he said, "I'm glad the others have gone, much as I like them, and I'm glad we're alone. Because I want to make a little speech to you both. And I'm just drunk enough to tell you how I really feel."

Sandy smiled, a little strangely. Lyle Ashby was expressionless but his eyes never left Brent's face. Neither spoke.

"The other night my wife and I had a little falling-out, Lyle. The reason was you. I suppose I was being jealous—what other reason could there be? But I was dead wrong, and I want to apologize to both of you." He looked now at Sandy. "I want you to be free always to see anyone, to be with anyone you wish. I don't want our marriage to have anything to do with it, ever. Marriage is only a device to tie us into the system. Aside from its legal usefulness, it should be ignored."

He felt light-headed, exhilarated. He swayed a little on his feet as he turned back to Lyle Ashby. "You've become one of our best friends, Lyle. I hope you're going to keep on being just that. I guess you know how much I like you. I hope you like me."

The other man spoke for the first time. "I don't have to say how much, because I think you know, Dave."

"I won't try to say it for Sandy. She can speak for herself. But I hope you are friends because you were meant to be, and whether I happened to have been there or not."

Lyle's steady smile was upon him. "We're glad you were there."

Sandy said, "We don't know what we would have done without you."

They all laughed a little, yet he felt a faint tension between them, he on one side, the man and the girl on the couch on the other. And he noticed that each had said "We." He went on, impetuously. "You approve of her, Lyle?"

"I will go further than that." All at once his face went grave and tender. "I will say frankly that if Sandy was not married to you, I would think seriously of asking her to become my wife."

The deep, warm voice seemed to echo in new quiet. Brent turned to look at Sandy but the smile froze on his lips; it was as if he was no longer in the room: her gaze held Lyle's, rapt and fascinated. With a movement that seemed irresistibly strong and infinitely gentle, Lyle reached to where she sat and covered her breast with his hand. It remained there, unchallenged, for a long moment, and she lifted her head and closed her eyes, breathing more quickly. It was withdrawn only when she rose, abruptly, almost defiantly, to face her husband. As though unconsciously, her hand was touching the breast where his hand had been.

"David . . ."—he heard the word low and urgent, somehow unreal—"Lyle and I . . . Yes, we've talked about it . . . He wants . . . We both want . . ."

She stopped, color burning over her skin. Lyle was

suddenly standing beside her with the utter stillness of a pointing animal, his arm around her, his eyes proud as he faced Brent in the silence. And Brent heard himself reply like another man speaking, the words strangely far apart, dropping one by one through the heavy air. "Why . . . of course. Of course. Didn't I just say . . ."

He looked away from Lyle and at Sandy, her head high and her eyes shining, knowing she had forgotten him in the flood of helpless desire, thinking as his eyes swept her body that she had never looked as lovely as in this moment. I never made you so beautiful, his mind was saying, and a feeling like despair broke in him.

"This is as it should be," he said aloud to her, the words spoken with a kind of desperate insistence. "Because you want it. Because it's right."

A long pause, all three motionless. It was so quiet he could hear the ticking of the little French clock on the mantel over the fireplace. He said then in a voice he fought to hold steady, "You can stay here, Lyle. I'll go to my club."

Swiftly he turned from them and swiftly walked to the front door. There was only silence behind him. He opened the door and stepped out on the stoop; the street was nearly empty. He closed the door and stood breathing deep gulps of the darkness, alone.

# 49

There was a noisy crowd at the bar, the usual Sunday night gathering of lonesome bachelors and husbands un-eager to go home, but he couldn't face the small talk and inevitable questions about the news. He went straight to the club office and arranged for a quiet room, retiring there at once. The thought of another drink sickened him; he'd had far too much already. And it was liquor that had precipitated the scene with Lyle and Sandy. Better thus! He sat down on the edge of the bed and stared at the wall. Better it had happened now, resolved the suspicion and un-certainty, than to simmer for weeks, months, until it boiled suddenly into emotional crisis and brought them all face to face with decision. This way it could end as abruptly as it began—a drunken night of lust, a one-time ecstasy they both had to get out of their systems.

He switched off the lamp and lay back on the bed, closed his eyes. *Civilized* . . . He spoke the word through clenched teeth and his fists closed. He had done the civilized thing, they all had. He could see them naked in their fierce embrace, *now*, the great black body shiny with thudding power, her breathless, whispered words, her gold-en arms around him in the supreme surrender, taking him endlessly, endlessly . . .

He sat up choking with nausea, the room unsteady, wavering in the dark, the walls bearing down. He felt the sweat start out on his shoulders and arms; he was ill, he knew only that and the rest fell away. He struggled to his feet as the retching began, stumbled toward the bathroom and stood in front of the basin until the sickness drove him to his knees and he vomited into the toilet, gasping, his eyes shut; a sound like strangled coughing and at last the vile stuff was all out of him, a relief like exhaustion.

He could sleep now. It was as if he'd cleansed himself of the humiliation he'd felt standing there before Lyle and Sandy, seeing them wanting him to go, waiting for him to go. And yet somehow it had all seemed inevitable; he was startled but not really astonished—Sandy's reaction was part of the mystery he had felt in her from the beginning; it could just as well result in a closer, deeper relationship than they'd had before. Lyle? Lyle had followed his instinct; he wasn't the first man or last to want Sandy with all his heart . . .

Sunlight streamed through the window; if he had dreamed during the night he remembered nothing. Even the shock and sickness of those hours before sleep seemed at first like something that had happened to someone else. But he knew, as he dressed and went down to a late breakfast, that gradually it would all come back to be faced again. He was shaved by the club barber and bought a shirt at Brooks on his way to the studio, arriving in the newsroom in ample time for the daily news meeting. He saw from the board that Lyle Ashby was listed for a Long Island remote and presumably was already out there working on it. There were no personal messages on his office list. But he would not call Sandy. He would wait.

The afternoon job was routine, and likewise the early show. Still no word from Sandy. The Ashby spot was late developing and not available until mid-evening, when it was recorded for broadcast on the 10:30 news. Brent listened to the voice as it came over before the show— deep, calm, self-assured as always. And the footnote to the show—deep, calm, self-assured as always. And the footnote to the Night Editor: *"That wraps it up, Jay—See all you folks tomorrow."* Wasn't there a trace of haste, elation, anticipation, in the words as he signed off? Would he be going straight to Sandy; were they together already? Once again he resisted picking up the phone and dialing the number. The next move would have to come from her.

Deliberately he stopped at the corner bar on his way home and lingered over two drinks. Was he making her wait and wonder, or was he afraid that when he opened that door tonight she would not be there? His footsteps quickened as he walked down the block and then quickly up the stairs of the stoop. A light was burning in the hall;

as he let himself in and came into the living room Sandy looked up from the book she was reading and smiled. "Hi," she said. "Aren't you a little late?"

"Sorry." He heard his tone stiff and wary, in spite of himself. She got up then and he waited for her embrace, some word of affection, anything that would bring them back to status quo, but she passed him, still smiling, on her way into the kitchen. "Creamed ham, is that all right?" she called back over her shoulder. "I put some Chablis on ice."

"If you don't mind I'll have a drink first. Something for you?" He went to the bar.

"Nothing, thanks. I drank too much last night."

It was all she said. Evidently it was all she was going to say. Not a word about why they hadn't communicated during the day, just the offhand smile, the small talk about the food and wine, which she barely touched, the cool composure that withheld everything she must know he wanted to hear from her. After his drink he had three glasses of the Chablis and mixed himself another Scotch as they came back into the living room. She was silent now, still silent as they faced each other in their customary chairs; he felt an unbearable tension and spoke. .

"You've always been honest with me, Sandy. I know you were honest with me last night."

"Yes. I was, David," the words low and steady.

"Did he stay all night?"

"No."

"What time did he leave?"

"I don't know, exactly. Some time after four o'clock."

"Did he fuck you?"

"Yes."

"How was it?"

His voice echoed harsh. For a moment she didn't reply. Then, "David, what kind of a question is that? And why are we talking about Lyle? What do you expect me to say? I have nothing to say. What happened is between Lyle and me. We didn't try to conceal it from you. We could have. Lyle is not like that. And neither am I, as you know."

"Have you talked to him today?"

"Yes."

"Have you seen him?"

"Briefly, yes. He stopped in about noon."

"By briefly you mean how long?"

"I don't know exactly. Perhaps an hour."

"Did he fuck you?"

She hesitated. "Yes. David, why are you torturing yourself with these questions? How will it change anything? What happened has happened. I've faced the fact and I can't help it. I'm sorry if it hurts you, but I'm not sorry it has happened."

"And it's going to go on happening?"

Again the faint hesitation. "Lyle is in love with me."

"Are you in love with him?"

There was a long silence. Fighting to control himself, he went to the bar and poured another drink. *"Well?"* he said. His back was still to her. *"Well? Are you in love with him?"*

"I don't know." It was almost a whisper.

"Are you going to see him again?"

She looked at him wonderingly. "Of course. Do you expect me not to?"

"Tonight?"

"No. Tomorrow, perhaps, if he's free. Tonight . . ." She paused, tremulous for the first time.

"Well, go on!"

"He knows I had to see you tonight, talk to you . . ."

*"Talk* to me! I had to drag it out of you before you'd say a word."

Large tears stood suddenly in her eyes. "You think it's easy for me? Don't make me cry, David, you know I hate to cry. I didn't know this would hurt you so much. After the things you said to us last night . . . how could I have known you would take it so hard?"

"But you did it," he said, his voice savage. "You knew what you were doing."

"Yes. *Yes!* Don't ask me to regret it! I'm not going to lie to you."

"And you're going to do it again."

"Not here. Not in this house. He can never come here again."

"And you think I'm ever going to sleep again in the bed where you were with him?" He felt himself out of control, jagged, jeering. "How many times did he come?"

"Don't, David, please . . ."

"Come on, tell me, how many times? . . ."

"I don't know, how could I know?"

*"How could you know?* You know, ah, you know! Every woman knows. Now you're lying to me, don't say you're not lying to me—"

"David, please, please . . ."

"And when he was here today, when you fucked him again, did he take you on the bed upstairs—our bed? *Well?"*

She was shaking her head, her cheeks wet with tears. "No. Here . . . On the couch . . ."

"And you were ready for him, right? No pants under the skirt. I know now why you were already wet when I touched you the other night, begged you to forgive me for snarling because he came to see you. You were wet for *him,* still wet . . . or did he fuck you that night? Tell me!"

"No. *No!* Last night was the first time." Her voice broke. "Why do we have to keep on with this? What difference does it make when, how, where! It happened. It will happen again. There's nothing any of us can do about it, can't you see that?" She was weeping openly, heavily, all defenses down, her shoulders trembling, and seeing her this way the storm of fury in him all at once turned to anguished pity, to shame of his own cruelty to her. He moved to her side and reached down to hold her, ask pardon for his bitterness, but she stiffened abruptly at his touch and drew away, murmuring *"No, no, no, no"* through her tears.

"Let me love you, Sandy, let me love you now," he whispered, pleading, "we'll make it all all right, we'll put it all behind us, like a nightmare, Sandy, like a dream . . ." But already he knew she was blind and deaf to him, silent and withdrawn. Slowly he straightened up and for a long time stood motionless beside her. When at last the heavy sobbing ceased she raised her head and looked up at him like looking at a stranger.

"Go to bed," he said quietly. "I'll bunk down here on the couch tonight . . . tomorrow we'll talk like sensible people."

She shook her head with a sadness that touched his heart. "Not tomorrow, David. Not until I know. Right now I don't know anything except what I feel. Today after we—today when he was here, I promised I'd come to him as soon as I could. Please let me go now, David. And be patient. I'll call, when I know . . ."

# 50

He had thought she would call him the next day, but no call came. He waited through the morning but the phone in his study didn't ring at all. Her own phone, in her upstairs dressing room, rang several times during the morning but he didn't answer it; she knew he never did, and if she wanted to reach him at the house it was always on his own phone. Once again he was spared a face-to-face meeting with Lyle Ashby, who was not in the newsroom for the daily program meeting. Brent didn't know how he'd handle that encounter when it came. Perhaps today would be like yesterday: no call from Sandy and no sight of her till he found her waiting for him at the house after the late show. But he wasn't hopeful for that; she had taken a weekend bag with her when she went to Lyle's apartment last night.

What she had been doing since then he tried not to think about.

Several times during the afternoon and evening he phoned the house without answer. He went so far as to note down Lyle Ashby's number from the newsroom telephone list, but pride or obstinacy restrained him from calling her at his apartment. When she still didn't answer at home after the late evening show he called Chad Newsom; he wanted desperately now to talk to Chad, but was not surprised when there again no one answered; a night owl like Chad would never be home until the small hours unless engaged in sexual activity, when he wouldn't answer the phone anyway. When he did reach Chad, late next morning and still no call from Sandy, the director was just walking out of his apartment to drive to Boston with his producer for an out-of-town opening and would be tied up there for a week.

"What gives, old friend? You're low."

"Nothing to talk about on the phone, Chad."

"Sweet Sandy?"

"Yes."

"The musical chum?"

"You're quick."

"Not quick—I thought I saw it Sunday. How bad?"

"I don't know."

"What does she say?"

"What I just said—she doesn't know."

A brief silence. "Wish I could help."

"I just wanted to see you, that's all."

"This is the worst possible time—the guy's honking at me from the street."

"I know, Chad. Call me when you get back?"

"Patience and fortitude, fella." He was gone.

Another phone call, for the first time to Lyle Ashby's apartment. He sat listening to it ring—six times, ten times, a hollow, mocking buzz—until he realized that even if she was there alone she wouldn't answer. Of course! They probably had a code for Lyle's calls from the outside: three rings, four rings and she would answer. He slapped the receiver so hard into its cradle that a piece of the plastic instrument fell off and flew halfway across the room.

An hour later, walking down the newsroom corridor to his office, he saw Lyle Ashby come out of the network studio and turn in his direction, the sauntering, easy stride, an athlete's grace in bearing. The hall was empty, the confrontation inevitable. For a moment as they drew near their eyes met in direct gaze—Brent saw recognition, pride, and a strange, inarticulate compassion. Surely it was up to Lyle to speak, to seize the moment to say whatever he would say, must say! Then, eyes unfaltering, both men passed without a word, without a nod. Brent felt the sweat in the palms of his hands.

He stood it for the rest of the week, making no further attempt to reach Sandy, hoping that each night he would find her back at home, awaiting him. There was no sign in the house that she had come to pick up any more clothes or any other possession. At the office and on the air his routine relations with Lyle Ashby were the same as always, on the surface; inside himself he felt an agony of apprehension, marveled at his own control in switching to an Ashby remote, speaking his name without a tremor of hostility. Each night, his work finished, he toured the bars on his way to the empty house in Sixty-fifth Street—P.J. Clarke's, Moriarty's, a half dozen other watering places along Third Avenue. By the time he reached the house he was sodden enough to fall into bed and call it a day. Even so, it wasn't easy to get to sleep; he lay in the big lonely bed drunkenly going over and over his life as a husband: *who was Alexandra Brent? What had gone wrong between them that had led to this? What would happen now? . . .*

He woke Sunday morning after a heavy pub trek that lasted till after four. Sandy had been gone six nights but it was still strange waking up without her, her breath on his cheek, one slender knee nestled warmly in his belly. His eyes opened painfully and focused on the clock across the sunlit room—after eleven and he was still as tired as if he hadn't slept at all. Once more the jealous fear gripped his heart, broke through the deadening hangover; it was maddening not hearing from her, a call, a note, anything to break this pitiless silence!

A whole day without the distraction of work. He sat at a counter for breakfast in a hamburger place over on Second where people stared at him, ready to open a conversation, and the faggish cashier-proprietor began, "Well, this *is* an unexpected pleasure . . ." taking his money. He turned and left without acknowledgement.

He bought papers and magazines at the corner and went through them all until mid-afternoon, limiting himself to one Bloody Mary and hardly knowing what he was reading. He was looking listlessly through the *Times* magazine when the phone rang in his study and he raced there half stumbling.

"Brent here."

"Are you free to speak a moment?" It was her voice at last, polite and toneless.

"Quite free." He tried to match his response to her calm.

"I thought we might have dinner somewhere, if you're not engaged."

"Of course. Shall I pick you up, or do you want to meet here?"

"That won't be convenient. It's best to meet at the restaurant."

"As you wish. Do you have any place in mind?"

"I'll be near Per Bacco, if that's okay for you. About seven?"

"Seven is fine. Sandy . . ."

"Yes?"

"It's me. *David*. You're talking like a stranger."

"Oh, I'm sorry. I can't manage differently at the moment."

She had hung up. He sat at his desk numbed by her coolness; it had been a business conversation. If this was their phone talk, what was their reunion going to be like? But what did she imply when she said, "I can't manage differently at the moment"? His heart jumped, then settled in the pit of his stomach again—hope turned to fear, the old dread of losing her.

He shaved, showered and dressed carefully, choosing a blazer and tie he knew she liked. Outside, the city turned somber gray in Sunday's semi-lassitude. He walked to the restaurant to use up the intervening time.

Per Bacco was in the twenties near Lexington, a quiet, cozy place off the beaten track. They'd often used it for lunch to escape the business crowd in midtown. Now, sitting at the bar and keeping an eye on his watch, he ordered a Bombay and tonic and felt his rising tension come under control. By "convenient" did Sandy mean she was somewhere in the neighborhood, possibly at a cocktail party with Lyle and some of his friends? Wherever she was, she was late for the appointment—fifteen, then twenty minutes late. Suddenly his panic returned, fresh and agonizing: was she just not coming at all? Then she was at the door, slim and summery in something simple, swinging a shiny handbag and wearing patent leather pumps. The way she moved toward him always went to his heart.

"Hi, Mrs. Brent."

He stood up and caught one of her hands and they stood for a moment smiling at each other. "You drink with me at the bar?"

"Perhaps we'd better sit down," she said.

He led the way to the table they always had here, a banquette in the back of the room, and she ordered a chilled Tio Pepe.

"Since when are you on sherry?"

"I like it."

The words had the same odd quality of diffidence he'd heard on the phone. "Does your friend like sherry?" he said.

"Actually he drinks very little of anything."

"How is he, by the way?"

In the silence she looked startled or wary. She said finally, "You see him every day."

"I see him, but he doesn't speak to me."

"He says you don't speak to him, either."

"What is there to say?"

Another pause. Then, "He would like to say he's sorry."

"Would he now!" He stifled a sardonic laugh.

"He realizes what he has done. And I realize what I've done. We both . . ." she hesitated, as if looking for a word, then found it. "We both respect you deeply. We didn't want you to be hurt—"

"Never mind about Ashby," he broke in. "The only person I'm concerned about is you. And why you've done this to me, to us . . . *why*, Sandy?"

The waiter came with the Tio Pepe and they waited until he was gone. She said in a low voice, "I told you that, before I went away. Because we—because I couldn't help it. Have you forgotten what I said?"

"You said you were going to make a decision. Have you made it?"

"Today, David, yes."

He took her unresisting hand in his own and held it, spoke softly. "What are you going to do, Sandy?"

She answered him looking absently across the restaurant, like a woman thinking aloud, like a woman frozen in a spell, her hand perfectly still in his hand, as though she was totally unaware of it, of him. "Tomorrow," she said slowly, "I'll come to the house and get my things."

And that was all. In the moment, withdrawing his hand, he felt numb, stricken, knowing only that no further effort to contend against this finality was possible. But hadn't he known it to be inevitable from the beginning, since that first night she had sat at the piano and played for the voice that filled the room, the eyes that never left her face? And what could he do about it then, or now?

The restaurant was beginning to fill up. A couple sat

down two tables away, the woman recognized him immediately and whispered to the man, who turned around, staring. The glass of sherry stood untouched.

Brent said tonelessly, "Do you really feel like having dinner here?"

"I think I'd rather not."

He paid for the drinks and they left together without speaking again. All at once he felt a queer sense of relief; the ordeal was over; the rest of it couldn't be any worse. Strange how their last minutes were not at all what he would have predicted, no storms, no tears, just silence between them, their bodies carefully not touching. For a moment they stood motionless outside the door while his mind repeated it blankly: *this is the end of the story of David and Sandy.*

Arrangements had to be made, but later, on another day.

The taxi saw them, slowed at his signal and stopped at the curb. As he opened the door for her he wanted to say something, anything, but no words came; he felt limp and lifeless. Just once she looked at him from the cab, but the light was so dim he couldn't see the expression in her eyes. As he turned away he heard her give the driver Lyle Ashby's address . . .

He was sitting dully at home, fairly drunk, when the phone rang in his study. It was Chad Newsom, feisty and cheerful.

"That you, boychik? Just got in. Your party over?"

"No party tonight, Chad," his voice thick and slurred.

"Oh-oh. Sandy with you?"

"No. And she's not going to be."

A brief pause. "Since when is this?"

"This is since a week. She gave me the final word tonight."

"You talked to him? Or him to you?"

"No. There won't be any of that."

"Does everybody know?"

"Not yet. I figure three or four days for it to get around. And I don't think I can take it."

"So then what?"

"I don't know what."

"I know what."

"I wish you did."

"I do. You go to the boss man tomorrow and you announce a vacation. I'm leaving for the Coast Thursday and you stay with me at Malibu."

"You're going too fast for me, Chad."

"Think about it. You want me to come over there now?"

"Thanks, but I'm not up to it."

The raucous chuckle. "I'll get you up to it! You want me to call Sue and Nancy? They're in town."

"I appreciate the thought, Chad, but not tonight."

"Listen, I remembered something, this house over on Lex near you, most gorgeous hookers in New York, a swimming pool yet. They got mirrors, electricity, the works. We go as many as we can, all included in one price. How about it?"

"Not if there's electricity."

"You're insane. They'll do wonderful things to you."

He pretended to laugh. "Right now I don't know whether I'm AC or DC. So goodnight, Yogi Bear, you're all heart."

# EIGHT

# 51

It was his first visit to Southern California. From all he'd heard and read, he was not prepared to like it. Coming off the breakup with Sandy he was not prepared to like anything, least of all the prospect of remaining in New York. But Dan McCurdy was prepared to understand. Did he already know about Sandy and Lyle Ashby? With McCurdy you could never be sure.

To Brent's considerable surprise the news chief nodded sympathetically at the recital of fatigue, ulcer symptoms, even boredom; after all, Brent hadn't had a real vacation in two years, needed a change from routine and a rest in relaxed surroundings. No problem about replacement—he'd bring on Welby from Chicago. "Enjoy yourself, Dave, I've half a mind to come with you! And don't hurry back, we're well fixed here for the time being. Just sack out on the beach somewhere and forget your troubles . . ."

*Forget your troubles:* was that another hint that McCurdy knew? And wasn't there a gleam of wholly uncharacteristic compassion in the small cold eyes as they shook hands? Well, if he didn't know yet he'd know any minute now, and who gave a shit whether or when or who?

It took less than forty-eight hours to close the house and talk to his accountant and get out of town. The principal aim in the meanwhile was to keep Sandy out of his mind. He was already loaded by the time he reached the airport and he had his first sound sleep in days on the flight to L.A.

It was Oz, with pollution. On one side the distant blue Pacific, on the other, shimmering in the white light of noonday, the high-rise buildings poking their glass penthouses, through a blanket of pink smog. Chad met him in a cream-colored open convertible and took him for a drive

351

through Hollywood and the surrounding area before heading for the beach, grinning, gesticulating, completely in his element in a way he never was in New York. Brent felt like a tourist and gawked like one—first a drink on the sun-splashed terrace of the Bel Air, then an easy, rolling promenade down Sunset, through Beverly Hills, a glance at some of the houses, all ochres and cinnamon browns and Spanish patios, another drink at the Polo Lounge, Chad clacking about the movie colony like a tour guide, free-associating as he went along about past, present and future and about everyone he knew or had ever known. Except Sandy.

"You'll like the women out here, baby . . . something in the air's good to them, gives them a taste like burnt orange . . ." and the wicked grin again: "I got plans for you, dear heart."

"I'm willing to believe it."

The dull ache was easing a little; he'd had it for so long he couldn't remember when it began and didn't want to. Chad Newsom with his frightening perceptiveness gave him a quick glance, laughed and dropped a hand to his knee. "Better already, I knew it." He was wearing a bright blue shirt open to the waist, white silk trousers and yellow sandals. A medallion hung from his neck on a long chain. Brent looked him over and smiled.

"I see I'll need some clothes, Chad."

"Sure. Malibu has everything."

It had. In addition to the sun, sand and gentle surf there was Chad Newsom's beach house with its broad deck, living room and two bedrooms decorated in Japanese style, and a spacious kitchen where Chad indulged his passion for pasta. Brent sat on the deck staring at a spectacular sunset while the singing host prepared his own version of fettucine Alfredo and uncorked a bottle of Barolo.

"Beautiful, Chad!" he said across the table.

"I raise my glass to you."

"And mine to you."

On top of two more drinks before dinner the wine carried him over into pleasant semi-drunkenness. There was a silence until Chad said, "You want to talk about it?"

"I don't think I do. Not yet, anyway."

"What you doing with your house?"

"Nothing, so far."

"How long you stay with me?"

"They're being very lenient at UBC. Maybe they'd like to get rid of me."

"Then fuck 'em. You know you can stay right here in this house as long as you want."

"Thanks, old friend."

"Think of me like a former mistress—everything still there except the urge, okay?"

For the first time in nearly two weeks he slept that night without dreams and without interruption, waking refreshed and strengthened to a clear hot day. Sunshine arrived on schedule out here and stayed steady until time to depart in favor of starlit skies. Wherever you looked was a movie set: palms ranged along a golden strand, the suntanned girls from television commercials scampering across the beach, the plastic men. Was David Brent himself the same man who left New York yesterday? Already, so quickly, he felt a change beginning. He was new, refashioned, becoming part of an accepted unreality, joining these others who no longer questioned it at all. He had thought, had feared, that leaving everything behind would mean a naked loneliness in alien surroundings. Instead he found himself caught up in a kind of enchantment, at home in the pagan air, acclimated at once in a sensuous world forgotten since childhood.

And Chad Newsom was helping him achieve the metamorphosis, filling the moments of uncertainty with gusts of laughter, hearty reassurance, making a difficult transition easier. He drove in with Chad that morning and sat on the studio set watching him direct a scene from a TV documentary on women's fashions. Afterward Chad came up and introduced him to a girl who'd played a bit in the scene in a bathing suit.

"I found a lunch partner for you, Dave. I can't make it today but she'll steer you to Chasen's—take my car and pick me up about four, O.K.?"

She was very young, an ash blonde with wide-apart china blue eyes, a broad nose and a rich, curling smile that was well aware of the spectacular body. She told him about herself across the table—Hope Andrews, a beginning actress from San Diego and a protégée of Chad's who felt very grateful to him for opening the right doors to her in Hollywood.

Brent smiled. "I'm afraid I'm wasting your time, Hope —I have no doors to open."

"Oh, no!" The eyes flared very wide. "You don't understand. I've seen you on the box. I'm a fan!"

"A pretty kid like you watching news?"

"I heard you on radio, too, from the war. My father used to kick us out of the room when the news came on." The curling smile. "I hated you back then. But I've got a thing for you now, ever since I watched with Chad the first time."

"I hope he didn't go away jealous."

The laugh was as extravagant as the smile. "Chad Baby's never jealous. It would cut into his bed time."

He looked at her. "You're very young and very grownup, Hope. Are you all like that around here?"

"Most," she said.

"Do you share Chad's bed time?"

"Didn't he tell you? Chad broke me in."

"How long ago was that?"

"Years," she said, and giggled like the ninth grade.

She wanted a brandy after lunch and he joined her. "Tell me more about yourself, Hope."

"Well, I don't wear underpants, you mean things like that?"

He laughed. "But you wear a bra. If you didn't somebody would call the fire department."

She glanced down at her breasts; even with the bra the nipples were prominent. "It took me ages to get used to these. When I was thirteen they got so *heavy*. Everybody stared."

"But you're glad now."

The smile again. "They pay off."

"But why no underpants?"

"I should. I really should. But, the hell with it. I hate them, even when I get sand in my quiff."

Her young laugh rang out over the room. Men at nearby tables turned around to look at her, smiling.

"You attract a lot of attention, Hope."

"From those cows over there? They're looking at you, not me."

He shook his head. "When they look at me they glare. Right now they're mooing."

"Some day they'll moo for the right reason, when

my name is up in lights. I'll be a star then, like you. And I'll sit at this same table with a boy fifteen years younger than me and I'll tell him about the first time I ever came to Chasen's with David Brent."

"Will he have as much fun as David Brent is having right now?"

"More. He'll be feeling me up while we're eating."

"By that time women won't be wearing any clothes to feel up under."

"I'm crazy for clothes," she said, "and then I can't wait to get out of them. You should see the closet in my apartment."

It was an open invitation, she was there waiting for him, a nymph out of the new Arcadia, the young fruit on the bough. It was a prospect uncomplicated by passion or purpose; maybe that was Chad's intention, to give him this girl like a pill, something to drive away the haunting hurt of Sandy. For an hour Hope had been hinting, cock-teasing; it wasn't long ago that talk like hers had fiercely aroused him. Yet up to this moment, so far, he had no erection, no urge to touch and hold.

"I'd like to see that closet," he said.

She lived in one of those dirty-yellow two-storey apartment dumps in an anonymous street off Sepulveda with a tired little swimming pool in the rear. The place had a drowsy, neglected look, with a narrow hall and creaking stairway. But her one-room apartment was cool and dim, the bed neatly made and the coverlet freshly laundered. There was no further mention of the closet. Undressing her she smelled of new-mown clover and grapes on the vine, food and drink in a summer meadow, and still, even kissing her, the sexual part of him failed to respond though all desire was there.

"You kind of like me, I can tell you really do," she said.

"More than you can tell."

"Come over here," she said, and sat on the edge of the bed while he dropped his trousers.

"Now lie down"—the whispered command as she bent her head and showed him what Chad Newsom was teaching her, took him in her mouth, her cunning tongue working, slowly at first, then more swiftly, arduously, feverishly, her breath hot and quickening, to no avail. She stopped then, lifted her head to look at him as he lay watching her with tenderness, her lips wet and very red, her words breathless—"What is it, darling?"

He heard his own hoarse whisper. "I don't know. It's never happened before."

She gave a small wry laugh. "I'm clumsy. I'm still learning."

"No, you're everything a man could want."

"You'll see, I'll learn."

He smiled over his feeling of shame, a dim panic echoing somewhere inside him. "You've done enough, Hope. It's me. I'm just . . . I want you very much, please believe that, but somehow, just today . . ."

He put his hands on her shoulders, the gorgeously tanned body was youth and strength and life; once he had thought this was all there was to want, in and of itself; now he knew it was no longer enough. He closed his eyes and saw Sandy the night she left him; he couldn't even pretend this was Sandy.

Hope Andrews laughed softly and got up, her breasts swaying in beauty. "Later," she said. "Later, darling."

She crossed the room and switched on the music station.

# 52

"Well?" Chad said, on the drive back to Malibu.

"Yeah!" He forced enthusiasm into it.

"That's my Hopie."

"I didn't realize at first you put her up to it."

"Least I could do, luv."

"I'm grateful. You know I am. I know you think it's the solution for me."

"The only one."

He couldn't bring himself to tell Chad what had actually happened; anyway the girl herself would do that. He'd left Hope touched and baffled, still believing it was her fault, asking when they would do it again. Like a loyal servant she wanted to make good her promise to the boss, and perhaps, in the generosity of her profligate spirit, to help Brent out of his embarrassment. But he knew it was more than embarrassment: for the first time in his life he was gripped by the fear of impotence.

Casually over dinner he suggested to Chad that he hadn't had time to see his doctor before he left New York.

"So?" The ears were up. "Something wrong?"

"I've outwaited my regular checkup. You know a good man?"

Newsom studied him. "You worried about Hopie? Clean as a whistle, caro!"

He laughed. "Look, I'm no hypochondriac. I thought you might recommend somebody you use yourself."

"Edelman's your man, right here in Malibu. We all love the guy. He's a GP, urologist and part-time shrink wrapped up in one ball—hold that, two balls! And he needs 'em both to keep up with the field around here . . ."

Dr. Nathan Edelman's office, at first glance, bore out the impression of an active life: a smashing redhead at the reception desk, golf clubs and a brace of squash rackets

357

against the wall, expensive originals hanging in his consulting room. He came forward with both hands outstretched and a vigorously warm greeting—fortyish, clean-shaven. In half an hour, with the aid of two nurses and a radiologist, he completed what he called a prudent physical, pronounced the patient in apparent excellent health, dismissed his efficient aides and said: "Now tell me, David, what's *really* disturbing you?"

It was hard to resist the evident sincerity of his concern. He was also a good listener. Brent found himself beginning with full details of the encounter with Hope Andrews and from there going all the way back to Lyle Ashby's first meeting with Sandy, where he stopped.

"Painful," Dr. Nathan Edelman said gently.

"Yes."

"I'm glad you've been so frank. I see a good many people who aren't. And as a longtime listener of yours —ever since the London blitz, in fact—I'm pleased to learn you're even better without a script." He had a sunny smile. "As to what you've just told me, I know what you've been going through, believe me. And I'm pretty sure what happened yesterday is directly attributable to your wife's posture of rejection. I can't be certain—beware of a physician who says he's ever absolutely certain of any prognosis—but I'd call what happened yesterday a temporary thing. Remember that, after all, this is a fairly common complaint, especially for men with highly active sex lives. So don't start anticipating failure the next time around; that might only prolong the condition." He smiled again. "I know it's easier for me to say this than for you to do it, but if the New York situation seems irretrievable it would be best for you to try to put it out of your mind and out of your life, for good."

"I can't face the thought of going back to my job there."

"You have to return soon?"

"Within about a month, at the latest."

The doctor put a compassionate hand on his shoulder. "Then you have time to delay the decision for a while. Relax and let Chad do all the worrying."

"That nut? He doesn't know the meaning of the word."

They laughed together. "You know," said Dr. Nathan Edelman, "Chad Newsom may just be the healthiest specimen I've ever encountered."

He was sipping his ritual evening cocktail when Chad blew in from work. "How are you, son?"

"Honorably discharged."

"You like the guy?"

"Just talking to him makes you feel better."

"Prognosis?"

"Relax and let you entertain me."

The director rubbed his hands. "It's what I wanted to hear. I'll lay on a session for tomorrow night."

"A session?"

"Never you mind, sweets. Some people you'll like."

"Hope Andrews?"

He shook his head. "Not yet a while, for her. This is a party for adults."

"Have you seen Hope?"

"Yeah. She sends her best."

"Did you two talk about me?"

He grinned blankly. "Why would we do that?"

They had, of course, and by this time Chad knew it all. And why not? It didn't seem to matter now; anyway Chad dropped the subject.

"You amuse yourself all alone today?"

"Can't you tell? I worked on my tan and forgot my troubles. I even came up with a story idea for you."

The host poured himself a drink and came back to the porch. "Press on, dear boy."

"I haven't worked out much of it yet beyond the general subject and the title—*American Royalty*."

"Provocative."

"A kind of panoramic look at the individuals from every walk of the national life who really control us—not just Government; in fact *outside* Government—the unreachables from industry, labor, science, education, the rich old aristocratic families, their myriad interconnections, their endless tentacles. How and where they hide out, a look at their private lives . . ."

"Could make a series."

"It began to percolate when I was watching your

documentary take shape yesterday. I've always liked documentaries—I mean as a form, a vehicle, able to investigate, penetrate what really goes on, just how the big decisions are made and by *whom,* behind our backs, without even arousing our suspicions, or with total arrogance, total contempt for the poor little bastards that live under invisible domination . . ."

The black eyes sparkled. "Man, that's exciting. You do something for me? Get an outline on paper when you've worked on it awhile so I can take it in and show it to some people who could do something with it?"

"Why not?"

"And see if you can work in the jet-set bunch, the internationals, you know—the glamour group?"

"Like TV and radio and Hollywood."

*"American Royalty . . . I like it!"*

He thought about it next day on the beach, a long, lazy day, turning it over in his mind, making random notes as the outline began to take shape. It was late afternoon before he realized that today for the first time he'd hardly thought of Sandy or New York at all; the memory was drifting away from him like a bad dream dissolved by daylight. He showered after a last dip in the sea and dressed in linen slacks and a light blazer he'd picked up on his way from the doctor's, ready now for what the evening would bring. He was sipping his first drink of the day, a long, cool rum Collins, when Chad and the guests arrived in two cars.

They were a mixed lot and it took a while to form his impressions; hard to tell at first which of them already knew which others. They were all high already, and calling for more drinks as they piled out of the cars carrying boxes and hampers of catered food selected by Chad at Scandia. The host didn't bother in the confusion to introduce Brent, who concentrated briefly on introducing himself as they did to him, first name only. But he gathered that the two men were typical Hollywood—a smooth-talking agent they called Jack and a short, bull-necked, bald film producer named Harry. None of the women were actresses but all four were lookers—as the cocktail chatter of small-talk continued it developed that Inga, the tall, lissome Swede, was a model; dark-eyed Luisa a Mexican dancer, the brown-haired colleen type with the saucer eyes was Denny, a secretary; and the one who looked oldest—maybe in her late thirties—was Vivian, ex-wife of an actor and in some indefinable way the most arresting woman in the room. Possibly it was the contrast of her languid, ultra-sophisticated attitudes and the smoldering intensity in the eyes.

For that matter Brent felt they all, men and women, were repressing a tension, a sense of anticipation, each in their own ways, that built slowly through the veranda supper of hot hors d'oeuvres, cold salmon in green sauce and vegetable salad, with a superb Paul Masson Chablis as good as any Chablis Brent had ever drunk in France. The Swede, however, stuck with the Carlsberg beer, "for stamina," she explained across the table to Brent with an alluring grin. The joints weren't brought out until after the iced coffee was consumed and the company went back indoors, out of sight of any eyes from the beach.

"From a fresh shipment just over the border," Chad said, passing the box around. "Full strength."

They all partook, tasted and pronounced the weed highly acceptable; in a little while the room was hazy with drifting smoke. It was the first time in months Brent had tasted the stuff, and wouldn't have been able to judge it strong or weak; he just knew a delicious lassitude began to creep through his body while at the same time all his senses were heightened. He looked around him with approval: Chad had cunningly arranged the furniture in a circular pattern so that they all faced one another around an open space of soft carpeting, sitting back comfortably on the two low couches and deep easy chairs. Cassette music from two concealed speakers, low with an insistent rhythm, sounded in the background, just loud enough not to be obtrusive. And hovering over them all, moving from one to another with another light, another drink, was the host himself, master of the revels and creator of special effects like the little object he had in the palm of his hand about the size of a deck of playing cards which he was refusing to explain, yet, to curious questioners.

"All in good time, children . . . the night is young."

Brent glanced over his shoulder. Through the apertures over the porch door he could see that darkness had fallen but he had lost the sense of time by now and it could have been midnight or nine o'clock or three A.M.; nothing like that mattered. What mattered was these people around him, these women in thin, soft clothes whose bodies seemed to breathe sensuality as they lay back against the cushions in careless or unconscious poses, seeming to offer themselves. There was less talking in the room, a subdued excitement in the murmured words. Denny, her white skirt halfway up her thigh, listened with an enigmatic little smile to whatever Jack was whispering to her; he leaned forward, one arm around her shoulders, and their mouths met in a lingering kiss. Gracefully in the indirect light, like a girl on a stage set, Luisa rose from her seat beside Harry and began a slow, dreamy dance around the circle of carpet, kicking off her sandals as she moved, as if alone under the moon on a beach or in meadowland. Chad crouched at Inga's feet, his chin on her bare knees, talking low and earnestly; indolently, she seemed not to bother to listen, her eyes closed, her head back. Only Vivian sat upright now, staring across from her deep armchair at Brent with a look he couldn't fathom, at once challenging and guarded, wanton and withdrawn. And for the first time he felt a tingling warmth begin in his crotch, slowly spreading downward between his thighs.

"Luisa!" Harry's husky undertone. He sat forward, his bald head suddenly catching the light, the muscles working in his jaw. "Let's see it, girl, you know what I want to see . . ." and in answer, swaying past him, whirling faster in her circular movement, the dancer dropped her outthrust arms to catch her spinning skirts and throw them upward, disclosing the naked flash of thighs, ass and belly glistening with the faint gauze of sweat, the dark bared mass of curling hair glimpsed and then covered again, her breathless light laughter echoing as she dropped back onto the couch and Harry's reaching arms.

Chad was applauding and the Swede opened her eyes. Glancing at Jack and Denny, Brent saw the agent's hand between the girl's plump knees that opened willingly to his touch. He looked back at Vivian again, but she wasn't staring at him anymore, she was looking elsewhere, at Chad who was standing behind Inga's chair now and softly massaging her temples, her cheeks, stroking her throat. His fingers moved downward again to her shoulders, squeezing and kneading with expert's skill; she closed her eyes again with a grateful smile. The fingers reached her breasts, brushed the rising nipples with a floating touch, feeling her stir, her body lengthen, her head come back for his bending kiss. Watching, Brent saw him reach into his pocket, heard a faint whirring sound, barely audible, as the hand resumed its caress. Eyes still closed, Inga spoke in a whisper as her whole body reacted to a new sensation. "Chad . . . what are you doing to me?"

"You don't like it?"

The low, husky little laugh. "I didn't say that."

"Then be quiet. Enjoy." The hand holding the tiny vibrator moved to the other breast, carefully, tenderly, with exquisite gentleness, and afterward down across the belly to rest in the crotch. Her thighs twitched and came closer together. With his free hand he reached to draw up the skirt that lay furled across her knees, drew it up above her waist until she lay exposed and unresisting. Like Luisa she was nude under her clothing, long and slender, a creamy suntan, the blonde triangle itself like a sunburst of gold hairs, opening and yielding to the vibrating fingers that closed around it. "Ah, God . . ." she murmured, and after that some words in Swedish, and again in English: "Chad, you—want to—kill me? You want I—have nothing left? . . ."

He laughed and withdrew his hand, bent again to kiss her while her arms went up and around his neck, holding him hard, Inga oblivious that her body lay naked and open to the room. Brent, watching, felt himself breathing faster and automatically his hand went down to his hardening column. Jack and Denny were oblivious too; her head was back against the cushions now and his hand, his whole arm, was deep between her open thighs under the skirt. Luisa, her dark beauty flushed, turned with a startled intake of breath as Harry suddenly left her side, bolted across the space of carpet and fell to his knees before the Swedish girl, plunging his bald head between her thighs and into the crotch itself, his hands pushing her knees wider apart, his tongue sucking her depths.

"*Yeah* . . . go, man!" It was Chad's hoarse whisper, breaking the spell for Denny and Jack, who turned now to look. Luisa was watching, her lips parted in a smile. Brent

glanced at Vivian, saw her rise then and move as if fascinated toward Inga and the man who plundered her body.
There was no resistance; only a guttural moaning filled the
room as Inga writhed and twisted, eyes still closed, unaware that all the others were watching, Vivian closest of
all, looking directly down at her. Now Chad moved to
Vivian, stood beside her watching, his arm around her
shoulders, pulling her almost roughly against him. Brent
saw his hand drop inch by inch along her back, lower still
until it reached to massage the swelling buttocks, then with
an abrupt movement it gathered the clinging skirt and
drew it up nearly to her neck, revealing what was to
Brent the most exciting body in the room: the long,
curving lines of a racing filly under the burnished skin,
voluptuous yet slim, mature yet somehow fresh as a young
girl's, a body molded by years of lovemaking under the
hands and lips of masters of the art. Just for a moment
Chad held her nakedness revealed, and just for that moment his satyr's smile flickered toward Brent. Then he let
the skirt fall and took Vivian impetuously in his arms,
bending her backward for his ravenous kiss.

Brent looked away, caught the Mexican girl's eyes
upon him, large and luminous and inviting, the pupils dilated with excitement. Her mouth was forming words in
silence, luscious words, lascivious words, and he rose and
went to her, sat down beside her on the couch, let his gaze
travel slowly over her body. She was wearing a bare-
shouldered dress that held her young breasts tightly imprisoned, and he loosened it now so he could draw it downward to her belly. The breasts were pear-shaped, not as
large as Inga's but ripe and full. His eyes devoured their
beauty, then looked back at her red-lipped smile.

"You like, David?"

"Now I've seen all of you." And he bent to take the
strawberry nipples in his mouth, first the left, then the
right, then the soft flesh between them. She winced and
shivered at his tender little bites but didn't draw back. He
assuaged the tiny hurt with his tongue and ran his hand
down over her body to the half-bared thighs.

A cry like agony rang over the room: Inga in orgasm.
Brent looked up and saw the blonde body convulsed by
Harry's last thrusting, draining swallows, saw Chad stand-

ing again behind the couch, his hands on the Swedish girl's breasts, soothing, comforting, while he murmured: "Yes, yes, my darling . . . it's good, it's good . . ." Her eyes were still closed but her face was relaxing now, resuming its calm with a new and grateful serenity. Reaching out, her fingers caressed the head of the man who lay still between her thighs, as if comatose. But there was new movement now—Jack and Denny, both naked, their clothes left behind them on the floor, embraced standing in the middle of the room, then Denny lay down at full length on the carpet, the first time they all had seen her fully unclothed. Jack stood above her a moment, his erection swinging free, his eyes gloating over her white skin, the deep breasts receding into her chest, the pubic delta almost a flaming red, brighter than the auburn locks that fell away from her forehead. She was raising her legs, drawing her knees back, far back, as though to show the watchers her most secret treasures, and a crimson blush spread downward from her face to her throat and shoulders, over her breasts and belly, like a bashful schoolgirl at her first medical examination.

Jack knelt between her thighs and she closed her eyes, trembling a little as his fingers explored the open cleft. Was this her first orgy? For Brent it was the first orgy in which he himself was taking part, and he knew now that Nathan Edelman had been right; his impotence was temporary only. Watching the couple on the floor he felt his staff throbbing, straining for action, ready to burst with its desire as he saw Jack sinking slowly, carefully into the girl who lay beneath him, then lying full length on top of her and quite still, their heads side by side on the carpet, Denny's arms creeping up to clasp him closer. The others were all watching by now: Harry had withdrawn from Inga and turned around, still sitting on the floor, cradling his large, stiff cock in both hands. The Swedish girl had opened her eyes and lifted more toward a sitting position, one hand lovingly touching Harry's bull-like shoulder. And Chad, leaving Inga, rejoined Vivian beside the couch where she stood transfixed, looking down at the couple on the carpet.

Jack had begun to fuck, swinging deliberately, steadily, in and out of the warm recesses that took him deep. And

Denny, her mouth half open, her face seraphic, answered his thrusts with matching rhythm, her arms tightening around his back, neither the man nor the woman conscious any longer of the presences around them. Still seated with Luisa on the couch on the other side of them, Brent felt the Mexican girl's fingers stealing toward his crotch, opening his fly button by button, and at last grasping the hot, rigid flesh in her little fist. He held her close and kissed her mouth for the first time, a long, unwavering kiss that rose in intensity until she seemed to be sucking all of him into her, the fingers grasping him tightening to pain. *"I want you,"* her tongue said into his mouth, and she drew away, undid the back of her dress with one swift motion, pulled it over her head and dropped it behind her. She sat facing him, naked and smiling, and her hand tugged at his shirt, at his belt, urgent, impatient.

He obeyed. Standing, peeling off the shirt and dropping his trousers and shorts, he saw that others were impatient too. The room was full of whispers. The real business of the night had begun. A hushed silence broken by Inga's cry of release had given way to preliminary pairing off: Denny and Jack, Brent and Luisa, now Harry was taking the Swede by the hand and drawing her down to the carpet beside him. All were nude by now except Vivian and Chad, playing his role as host to the last necessary moment, benevolently surveying the room as if to make certain that his guests were well bestowed before taking his own pleasure, as Vivian stood beside him now, enigmatic smile at her lips, almost absent-mindedly loosening her dress at the throat and letting it slip down to her feet, the magnificent body fully revealed at last. Chad sank to his knees, grasping her around the buttocks, his fingers tightening on yielding flesh, penetrating the dark chasm between, while he buried his face in the softness of her belly, drew back his head to tongue the downy aperture that opened for him as she spread her legs to hold her balance against his tender onslaught. But she didn't take this for long; she drew him up, urgent hands pulling at his shirt, his belt, as Luisa had done to Brent, a passionate woman's impatience to drink the full cup of sex.

Even as the Mexican girl waited naked beside him, Brent could not take his eyes off Vivian and Chad, who stripped swiftly and stood before his partner with his thick cock fully distended. Her turn now to sink to her knees, hands coming up to cradle his balls, tongue curving around the long, hard shaft like a famished animal's, mouth opening wide and wider to take it deep into her throat, her crouching body raptly intent in an attitude of total adoration. Of all of them, Chad was most in possession, eyes gleaming with elation as he glanced over the room—at Jack increasing the pace of his stroke into Denny, at Harry plunging roughly into the blonde, spread-eagled body of the Swedish girl, finally at Brent and Luisa, tense at the edge of the couch. "What are you waiting for?"—he barked. Chad's sardonic grin seemed to light up the room. "Take her, Dave, before she knifes you!" And in answer Luisa lay back on the couch and opened her legs to her partner, showed him the wet red depths that entreated him, the heaving belly, the quivering thighs. Brent looked down at himself, saw himself stiff and pulsating with desire that could no longer be denied. "Venga," she was whispering to him, "*Venga! . . .*"

He entered with one thrust, bracing his feet against the arm of the couch that sank under them, took them into its cushioned luxury. Her arms went around him and her eyes closed; the hot breath she poured into his mouth had a strange, exotic taste, like the mingling smoke-and-perfume odors that filled the room around him, the fumes of wine and alcohol, the endless beat of the music that seemed to come from nowhere and everywhere. Fucking her he looked at the two naked couples grappling, sighing, clinging on the floor, and again at Chad and Vivian, lying now on the other couch. One of her tanned legs hung curved and wanton, swinging off the side of the divan; one hand loosely caressed Chad's head. He had her thighs spread as wide as they would go and he was sucking her, softly, subtly, but before she closed her eyes to give herself up completely she looked once across the room and caught Brent's glance and held it. It was a look of infinite comprehension, bearing all the world's wisdom of sexual desire, and it said as clearly as if she had spoken the words: *It was you I wanted, didn't you know, why didn't you understand? . . .*

A sudden sound like a sob: Denny was beginning to

climax. Harry, his shoulders shining with sweat, grunted in rhythm as he struck into the Swede. Under Brent the Mexican girl settled and opened further, took him even deeper into the burning excitement of her body.

Brent smiled and kissed her eyes; he was whole again, riding easy.

# 53

They left just before dawn, after a naked swim off the beach. To Brent the water seemed to cleanse his body of more than the night's accumulated male and female secretions: the taste and feel and sight of Denny and Inga and Luisa began to fade from his mind. But the memory of Vivian, her look, her touch, the perfume of her beauty, would not fade, clung to him even as he woke seven hours later. He was alone; Chad had slept at his apartment in Hollywood after helping drive the guests to their respective addresses. Another perfect day, warm, sunny, somnolent, a day for luxuriating in recollection, of lingering over the choicest moments of that long night's celebration, the festival of sex.

To his surprise, the expected hangover had not materialized. Instead he felt a deep sense of well-being, was utterly relaxed and able to contemplate the night's events far more clearly now than when he witnessed them. Seen with this clarity they took on a look of permanence, like Grecian figures on a frieze, anonymous and beautiful, a moment in human history. Some of the things he had seen and taken part in last night were depraved by any standard of behavior, yet he felt no sense of wrongdoing. How was it Hemingway had phrased the issue?—immoral is what you felt bad after, moral what you felt good after. Judged by that viewpoint, what he had done, what they had all done, was moral in the most immediate sense. Provided the others felt today as he did, and he suspected they did. Certainly they were of a single mind about most of their acts, and their parting at dawn was as gay, as cordial— and in a curious way as impersonal—as their meeting. Still only first names were used; nobody asked prying questions: the prying had all been physical! And from the beginning of the evening, it had been orchestrated by the

369

masterly control of Chad Newsom—a succession of classic rituals, drinking, dining, smoking, the initial climax of four couples paired, then the lull for repose, for recuperation, followed by the series of free variations all carried out with the greatest of goodwill, culminating in a sweet, unforgettable exhaustion and the goodbyes of intimate friends presided over by the Professor of Ecstasy.

Intimate friends . . . who might never see one another again yet were bound inextricably together by total physical experience, to be remembered perhaps for a lifetime. Could such an experience be repeated by the same group with the same exquisite result? He suspected that Chad would never risk it. And yet there was one there last night Brent wanted to see again, know again, and not only for the beauty of her body. Vivian's eyes haunted him, from their first glance as he introduced himself soon after her arrival, to their last glance as she said goodbye and climbed into the car next to Chad . . .

He was making himself a light brunch when the phone rang. Chad, probably, or the studio demanding to know where the hell he was. But even as he reached for the phone a flashing intuition crossed his mind. Vivian said, "Have I wakened you?"

"No, but I'm twice as wide awake now."

"I thought I might stop by."

"I wish you would."

"In a little while then?"

"Sooner than that."

He heard her low, seductive laugh and she hung up. All at once he was tingling with anticipation. He'd finished shaving and just put on some fresh clothes when her little Fiat convertible raced up and screeched to a violent stop about eighteen inches from the house wall.

Brent smiled. "Do you always drive crazy?"

"Is there any other way?"

She stepped out, immaculately groomed in a pale blue shirt and brown pants. Strolling into the house she said, "I see the furniture is back to normal."

"I pushed things around a little, in your honor."

"Consider me honored. Could you also push a rum punch or something like that in my direction?"

"I could and will."

The great dark eyes confronted him with a glint of amusement in their depths. She looked even more attractive in pants and he mentioned it.

"At parties like last night," she said, "the proper attire for the ladies is *always* a full skirt."

"I have a lot to learn fom you, Vivian."

She smiled. "Just stick around."

They sat opposite each other in wicker chairs on the sun deck and sipped long drinks. "Would you describe yourself as a party veteran?" he said.

"Well . . . I'm an old friend of Chad's. Make of that what you can, and probably will."

"Did you sleep with him after you left here?"

Again the languid smile. "I don't see how I have any right to regard that as a personal question. The answer is no. I have a little house of my own in Palisades and that's where he dropped me off."

"I'm glad to hear it."

A pause. "Why?" she said.

"Just a proprietary feeling I have about you."

Another pause, her face a study in calm. "After you saw Chad Newsom fucking me? And Harry Bernard sucking me? And Jack Lewis taking me from the back?"

"I'm sorry. I still feel proprietary."

"I guess I'll have to consider that a compliment, David."

"You seem to know these people pretty well. Have you been to parties with them before?"

"Not last night's kind of party, no. But Harry's well known in Hollywood. He gets around. In fact my ex-husband was in a picture Harry produced."

"Would I have seen your husband in the movies?"

"I assume so." She told him his name and he sat straighter.

"What happened to the marriage?"

"Not that it would matter to you, but he's a drunk, and a liar, and a sadist."

"Nobody complained about a bit of S and M last night," he said.

"You may remember Harry didn't try it on me. Inga loves it, or so it would seem."

"He really went to work on her."

"She's used to a punch or two. I've seen her in a restaurant hiding a black eye." She smiled. "That didn't keep you and Inga from getting together."

"I tried them all. It was the thing to do, wasn't it?"

"It seemed to be the general idea, so I arrived prepared. How did you like Inga, by the way?"

"She looked great, but I didn't come. She's a little too roomy, if I could put it that way."

Her burst of laughter was fresh and lusty. "But it was a different story with Denny, right?"

He shrugged and smiled. "Who could resist that cheerleader energy?"

"Could you mix us another drink, by the way?"

When he came back with the drinks he said, "Forget the girls for a minute. What about you and the men?"

She replied without hesitation. "I've had Chad before. He's irresistible once you let him in, I'll say that."

"I heard you tell him."

Was it a blush that faintly showed through her tanned cheeks? "I'm sorry," she murmured. "After a certain point I don't know about what I say."

"And Harry?"

"I wonder if any woman can resist a really great tongue, once she allows it to start. Anyway, he got to me." She made a lovely shuddering motion. "I can still feel it, like being lost in the clouds."

"Did Jack Lewis really take you from behind?"

She shook her head. "He doesn't want that, I'm sure. He's no sodomist. He just likes the position with a girl." She sipped her drink and looked at him. "But Harry almost caught you."

"So you saw that, too."

"Last night I saw almost everything, except when I was climaxing."

"Harry completely surprised me, because I was concentrating on Denny and close to orgasm myself. He came out of nowhere. At first when I felt this sensation behind me I thought he was trying to get at Denny in some way, like when he and Lewis were both working on Luisa. Then I felt this tearing, ripping, burning feeling and I kicked at him before he could do any more. As soon as he realized I was having none of it he gave up."

"I gather you have no homosexual tendencies."

"No more than the normal male. What about Harry, or is he just playful?"

She gave a small, resigned sigh and smiled. "Harry's a little bit of everything, I'm afraid."

"He was certainly the star of that last free-for-all on the floor. I've been trying to remember just what who was doing to whom but it was too complicated and I was too far gone by then. But I do recall wondering why I hadn't seen any girl-on-girl the whole night."

"They finally got to it. Inga took Denny home with her this morning. Luisa was her first choice but she refused, indignantly. I doubt if our little secretary made it to her job today. Inga's probably breaking her in about now."

"And you?" he said.

She shook her head. "I've had my innings over the years, just to be sociable, but I never went that road."

"I'm glad."

Again her enigmatic smile. "Why?"

"I'm just glad."

"I should think homosexuals would try for you a lot, David."

"My turn to ask, why?"

"They'd want to kiss your mouth. As I did."

"I've been lucky, I guess. Except for an incident many years ago, when I was in college—and last night, with Harry—they've let me alone."

A silence. She sipped her drink and looked at the sea. They could hear the cries of children playing down the beach. "What are you thinking?" he said.

"Just remembering. You really want to know? How I looked across the room at you and Luisa when Chad went down on me. You were fucking Luisa but you looked at me. Do you happen to remember that?"

"I'll never forget it," he said softly.

"Now I call that a compliment! What was your impression of young Luisa, by the way?"

"A hot little tamale."

They smiled together. "Chad's latest discovery," she said. "He's teaching her to give head, which is not exactly a Latin specialty."

"She's learning fast, judging from the job she did on her teacher last night. I'd guess Denny could use some instruction, too. Did you see her with Harry?"

"She was overmatched. Harry's just too big for beginners."

"Do you like to suck, Vivian?"

Again the barely discernible blush. "I like it all."

"So does Inga."

"She's Chad's favorite, did you notice? Every time I looked around he was taking her or she was taking him. At one point she tried to pull him off Denny just as Denny was coming."

"I saw that. Dirty pool."

"Chad consoled her. He gave it to her where she likes it best—in the ass."

Another silence. He took her empty glass and refilled it and his own. The sun was no longer straight overhead and shone milder, lambent over the water. The beach was always quiet at this hour. Vivian raised her arms over her head and stretched luxuriously.

"When you do that," he said, "it thrusts your breasts upward and I remember how beautiful they were when I first saw them naked last night. What did you like last night?"

Her eyes held him. "Didn't you notice? When you finally came over to me and took my hand, and kissed me, and put your hand on me, here, very gently, and I said, 'It's about time . . .'"

"I wanted to take you into my bedroom, to get away from the others, but you said it was against the rules. You said, 'How about right here?'"

"I remember. I wasn't drunk any more with anything, by that time. I'd wanted you from the beginning, and there you were, my last man of the night."

"Is that why you wouldn't fuck Chad again?"

"Of course. I told him he hadn't done a sandwich yet and he'd be much happier with a sandwich."

He saw it again: Jack Lewis on his back, in Inga, and Chad on top, also in Inga. Vivian smiled. "The field was clear for you and me . . ."

"I didn't think I was equal to it," he said. "I'd come three times, thinking each time I was saving you for the end. And then when I was with you at last I was afraid I couldn't execute. Maybe you knew that, Vivian. Maybe that's why you took me in your hand while we were standing there. Is that why you took me in your hand that way?"

"Of course."

"You knew what it would do, didn't you? Not because it was it, but because it was you, it was your hand."

"Of course, David."

"And when we lay down and I entered you it was all I could do to keep from flooding you right away."

"I was already flooding you," she said, very quietly, her eyes still holding him.

"Why? Why so quickly, after all we'd both done?"

The faintest of shrugs. "Because we liked each other. Because of your gentleness. Because, right then, and for a little while, you were my man. It was as though the others weren't there at all. It was as though we were alone."

"I felt that way, too," he said. "You made me forget what was going on around us. After everything that had already happened, you still made me feel special. How did you manage that, Vivian?"

"I didn't manage it. I just couldn't help it. Even in the last round, in that mass of tangled bodies on the floor, I was trying to reach you again. But somebody, first one and then another, kept getting in the way."

A silence.

"There's nobody in the way now, Vivian. We're not on display any more. We don't have to join in."

"Ever," she said.

"Ever."

She was looking at him almost as if she couldn't believe the understanding between them was possible, yet he knew it was because he knew what she was feeling, knew what they both were feeling, in this moment of recognition.

"You don't know what you are doing for me, David."

"Ah, but I do. Because you're doing it for me. Don't you believe that?"

"I want to believe it. With all my heart."

He smiled. "You've already got mine," he said.

# 54

Chad Newsom looked thoughtful over his pasta. "Tired?" Brent said.

"Tired? Naw." He brushed it aside like a small boy denying the obvious.

Brent laughed. "You were up all night running the show. You have a right to be bushed. You've done a full day's work on top of that, while all I've done is lie around."

"Yeah?" The eyes glinted. "Don't jive me, baby. I dropped in on Vivian on the way home to bring her some flowers, and what d'you think?"

"She told you she'd been here today, is that it?"

"Yeah. And I get the scene, boychik. You can lose the details. What surprises me is you had anything left so soon after all the nightwork." He grinned. "I guess you're like me—the more you get the more you need."

"Vivian told you this?"

"Vivian told me nothing! That's what I don't understand. She's never lied to me before."

"Vivian wasn't lying, Chad. She came back here today and we talked for about three hours. Period."

The other man stared at him. "That's just what *she* said. I figure you agreed on the story. But why? I'm *family*, Davie, remember me?"

"I've never lied to you either. We talked. That was it."

A pause. Newsom studied him. "All right, say I believe you. What bothers me is Vivian wouldn't let me touch her. I was just checking, you know? Couldn't understand her attitude."

"Like you say," Brent said, "the more you get the more you need. And you didn't get enough last night."

Again the sardonic grin. "So maybe I felt like a quick blow job, is that a crime? She wouldn't give. And you wanna know why?"

376

"Tell me."

"Tell *you*? You tell *me*, man . . . what you do to that woman? Her answer was you. David Brent. So talk, Goddamn it! In ten years of knowing Vivian I never heard her speak of a man like she spoke of you. What went on here today?"

Brent shook his head, smiling. "You've got it wrong, Chad. What went on here today wasn't anything like your little gathering last night, with all due admiration for your efforts. But what I'm most grateful for, and always well be, is that you've made it possible for me to meet Vivian."

There was a silence. Finally: "So it's like that, is it? I was only looking to distract you from your troubles, *bello*. I didn't expect something like this . . ."

"Neither did I. And neither did she."

"How do you account for it? Here's this totally jaded, totally disillusioned gal who's been through every experience, emotional and physical, throwing herself to the dogs, taking on anybody and everybody that asks for it, trying everything, sniffing the dust, orgies . . . and then suddenly, like overnight, like in the old song, she turns me down and says can't we be friends. What *happened* between you two?"

"I don't know, Chad. I've been trying to explain it to myself, but I guess it can't be explained, doesn't need to be." He gave a small disbelieving laugh. "If somebody had told me, only two days ago, that tonight I'd be feeling like this, I'd have thought they were crazy. Yet there it is. Ever since I began to realize the change in Sandy, I've been struggling to get control of myself again. Everything in my life went sour when Sandy left me. But it wasn't only Sandy's leaving, so calmly, so abruptly—it went deeper than that. I began to believe that what she did was prophetic for me, for my life. With Sandy I thought I'd grasped the real nature of happiness at last. When my relationship with her collapsed, like a casual snap of the fingers, leaving me with only an empty memory, I began to believe that my unconscious search for the ultimate sexual partnership was doomed—whether by destiny or by my own nature or both. I guess I'd never fully understood how vitally necessary this sense of partnership is to me. Without it, I lost interest in everything else—my job, my feeling for people, the growing attraction I had to writing as a new career."

He paused. Chad Newsom, food and wine forgotten, was listening intently.

"Then I threw it all up and came out here to you, Chad. I'll never be able to repay you for the way you stepped in and took over, for your efforts to cheer me up and set me on my own road again."

The gentle grin. "Pish-tush, baby. All you needed was a change."

"I needed much more than that. I was in despair. I don't know why I deserve such a turn in my luck, but once again, in some strange way, a woman has come along who seems to fulfill my deepest need, maybe offers me my last chance to achieve the full sexual understanding I've been seeking from women ever since my childhood. And it's all happened so quickly! I'm still dazzled. But I know that if somebody new and beautiful and desirable walked up right now and said take me, I'd react exactly the same way Vivian did to you today . . . Thank you very much but no thank you. Because of Vivian."

In the silence Chad Newsom lit a cigarette, looked at him through a slow puff. "Don't get any false hopes, Dave. This too shall pass. Remember all the dames you've told me about—you've had a million of 'em and you've survived every one, just like you've survived Sandy."

"No, it won't pass. This is real and lasting. I'm sure of it. And no matter what you may think, as much on her side as mine. Vivian said today she wants to be part of the world again. If she has anything to give me, she said, it's only mine by right, because whatever I am I woke something in her, right here under your roof, that she thought was dead. And if I have anything to give Vivian, it's to help her keep that reborn something alive, by living again myself."

Chad smiled. "My friend, you were born to love many women and overcome many obstacles and do a variety of things well. Don't kid yourself that Vivian will be the last love in your life. You thought Sandy would be the last, and bang! she was gone."

" 'Bang' is the right word."

"That's why I said it. You woke her up. Then she got the feel of Olympic cock and said goodbye to you."

"It wasn't only the way he fucked her, Chad, I'm certain of that."

"Basically, it had to be. For a woman as young and alive as Sandy it always is. What makes you think it could be anything else?"

"He loved her. She responded to it."

"You loved her too. But you weren't black and you weren't as big and you couldn't prolong it for two hours."

"How do you know this about Lyle Ashby?"

"It comes with the franchise."

"Whether you're right or wrong, it doesn't matter now. It doesn't even hurt to talk about it."

"All that doesn't mean Sandy might not come back to you one of these days, of course."

"Too late, Chad. I can't visualize it any more."

A long silence. Both men sat motionless. Outside, a foggy dusk was enveloping the sea; soon it would be dark and damp.

"Chivas Regal?" Chad said.

"I'll skip it for now. I want to work on that outline."

"You rat, you're going straight on me!"

"Something like that."

"When do you get together with Vivian again?"

"Tomorrow and tomorrow and tomorrow."

He laughed. "Wouldn't it be more convenient to just move in with her?"

"We've discussed the possibility."

"And if you do move in, will you two kids accept my invitation to the next party?"

"As observers, maybe. Not as participants."

"You're gonna have an awful lonely sex life."

"Maybe you just wouldn't understand that."

"Davie! You're no fun anymore."

"But I'll always love you. Won't that suffice?"

Chad Newsom grinned at him. "I suppose I'll have to make do somehow."

# 55

The house in Pacific Palisades lacked some of the location advantages of Malibu but it was theirs alone, a retreat into total privacy. They wanted it for Brent's work and they wanted it for themselves. In the months following the move from the beach house their only visitor was Chad Newsom. *American Royalty* was purchased soon after Brent moved in, and now he was rejoicing in the discovery and development of a talent for both fiction and dramatic writing which led to magazine publication in *Esquire* and *Playboy* and a movie script about Hollywood titled *Women, Money and Weather* which was quickly accepted and already in the preliminary stages of production.

Two major problems in Brent's previous life were resolved without difficulty: he obtained a release from the remainder of his broadcasting contract with UBC, and he completed by mail and phone the necessary negotiations for Sandy's divorce. The decree was promptly granted and she was quietly married to Lyle Ashby.

Aided by Vivian's advice and experience, Brent dealt with the social side of the Hollywood success game by the simple formula of playing hard to get. They declined all invitations to parties, previews and premieres and courteously turned away the blandishments of film and literary agents. Brent preferred to negotiate directly with editors and producers, and when necessary he called on Chad Newsom to run interference for him. He was guided by the director's astute judgment in making his literary deals, always with the prospects of a movie sale in mind. But not even Chad could share the intimacies with Vivian that had once been his for the asking. That phase of her life was over; the new Vivian reigned with the reborn David Brent in the peace of a small house and a garden that was her passion in his working hours, trespassing forbidden.

Their life-style paid off in terms of the movie colony's respect, and Brent soon found himself an established image, perhaps even better known to the general public now than he'd been as a newsman. But within the walls of their house they lived only for themselves, in a total mutual devotion. It surprised and pleased him that Vivian's interest in cooking revived; she dug out recipes for dishes she hadn't thought about in years and prepared them expertly in her simple kitchen, then served them in the candlelit dining nook for two with the wine of his choosing. The air-conditioned "cellar" built into the garden shed to hold his bottles was a special delight to him, and he laid the foundation for a gourmet selection of California vintages.

"Sometimes it frightens me," she said across the little table during one of their dinners, "all this secluded happiness, this blessed quiet. I ask myself what I've done to deserve it all—and you, while outside the world is in such a mess, full of lonely, desperate people at each other's throats, full of noise and violence and confusion . . ."

"The usual condition of things," he said, and smiled. "Maybe I'm so accustomed to it, after all those years of reporting it, that I hardly think about it now as something immediate or special. You see what California has done to me? I'm selfish and lazy and I'm forgetting my responsibilities as a citizen of the world. It must be the sun. Every morning I wake up to the light of a golden universe. How could anything be wrong anywhere? Impossible!"

"Not tomorrow. The man says rain for the next three days. My garden will be grateful."

"Rain! That's a switch. This drought has gone on for longer than I can remember." He sighed and put aside his napkin. "It's all luck, sweetheart. Like you and me. The luck of fate. Let's be very, very thankful. How did Alfred Housman put it?—*And oh 'tis comfort small, To think that many another lad has had no luck at all . . .*"

He took her hand and they went into the living room. Vivian called it the Crunch—not large enough to be a parlor, not small enough for a den. She was wearing a sarong and sandals, her tanned shoulders bare, her hair drawn back to her neck, her naked body outlined under the flowing silk garment. As always, she mixed his brandy and soda and brought it to him in his own chair. One breast escaped from its covering when she leaned over him and he enclosed it in his lips as he took the glass, holding the nipple until she drew back, trembling. "The rain," she whispered.

It was pattering on the roof, dampening the leaves in the garden. "The immortal headline in the London *Times*," he said, quoting. "Fog shrouds Britain—Continent isolated. That's Hollywood, darling. We're Britain—the rest of the world is isolated. What *we* do, what happens here, is all that matters. And you know, after a while we believe it!"

"Isn't that the point of *Women, Money and Weather?*"

He looked at her. "Yes, I suppose it is."

"Then you do care, you see?" She smiled and glided across the room; he loved to watch her move. "Music?" she said.

"Let's listen to the rain instead."

There was room for her in the wide easy chair and she snuggled in next to him, her legs lying on his thighs, her skirt halfway to her waist. It was a familiar ritual; she sipped from his glass, and his free hand roamed across her bare ankles and calves and knees. "You have perfect knees," he said.

"How do you know?"

"Chad told me."

She laughed a little and kissed his chin. "How many perfect knees have you seen in your time?"

"Name any even number."

"You've forgotten more perfect knees than I could count. What is it with you and women, David?"

"You mean what *was* it. What is it with you and men?"

"I like them. I mean in the aggregate. It really doesn't matter whether they have perfect knees."

"Chad still wants us to join one of his parties at the beach. He asked me again today."

"He never gives up, does he? I hope you didn't encourage him."

"I told him what I've told him before—that it's up to you."

"You're teasing! You know all that's finished with us."

He grinned. "You just admitted you still like men."

"Every time I open my big mouth I put my foot in it."

"Now that's a position we haven't tried!"

"I'll do my best, whenever you say."

"Right now?" He got up, laughing, and put his drink on the table. "Well?" he said, looking down at her. "I'm waiting."

"You don't want a girl. You want an acrobat."

"Don't grumble. Do it."

"I don't know whether I can. I'm not double-jointed, you know."

He stood watching her while she straightened up, leaned forward in the chair, took one foot by the ankle and tried to lift it to her mouth. The sarong got in the way. She pulled it up above her waist and tried again. This time as she bent forward the leg came up and slowly, straining inch by inch, she drew the foot toward her mouth. The movement split her thighs apart and thrust her naked crotch forward; he had never seen her so open and helpless. "*There!*" she exulted. "I'm doing it . . ." She held the position a moment longer, watching his fascinated gaze, then dropped her leg, breathless. "Next request?" she said.

He shook his head. "No more requests. You'll never find an encore for that one."

"Don't think I don't know what you were up to. How long have you been planning to spring it on me?"

"I just thought of it."

"Oh, no. You didn't care whether I could put my foot in my mouth or not. You just wanted to look at me, admit it."

"I admit it."

"And it was ludicrous."

"It was beautiful and exciting."

"Prove it."

He opened his trousers and proved it. "I wish I'd had a camera."

"We'll be making home movies next." The sarong was still furled above her waist, the belly cream-white where the tan line ended, and below it, nestled in the mass of soft hair, the still open lips that seemed reluctant to close again. "Come over here, my little depraved one."

"Depraved but wonderfully happy," he said. She was

leaning far back in the deep upholstered chair, her knees up, her thighs opening, and he was stepping out of his trousers and shorts to kneel at the edge of the chair. She was wet and slick as he moved into her all the way, his body lying against her breasts, his head beside her, her hands coming around his bare thighs to pull him closer. Twice, at long intervals, he moved slightly within her, feeling the tremor run through her body in response; afterward, for a long time, they were both motionless except for the rise and fall of breath against breath.

"You're very deep," she whispered, and he felt the sheath that held him tighten and then relax again.

"Who taught you that?"

"You've asked me before. I taught me that."

"You do it a few times more and I'll be through for the night."

"Not you." The sheath tightened once more.

"It's the most exciting thing you do. Have you done it to other men?"

"Of course. I was famous for it." He kissed her smile.

"Who was your best lover?"

"I've told you, I didn't have lovers, I had sex machines, like Chad."

"Didn't you love your husband?"

"For a little while, yes. But he didn't love me, he loved himself. Like all actors. David . . ."

"Darling?"

"My legs are tired. Can we go to the divan?"

She gave a little sigh of loss when he came out of her and they went to the couch across the room. Gently he slipped the sarong off her shoulders and dropped it to the floor with his shirt. Now, both nude, they embraced once more before he lowered her to the divan and entered her body again. "Why does it always seem like the first time?" she whispered, taking him, feeling his rhythm begin.

"Because I'm not a sex machine; I love you."

"For my body."

"For your body, yes, and for your brains, and for your spirit. For all of you together. You're asking foolish questions, and not for the first time."

"I can't think very well when you fuck me like you're fucking me now."

"How is it different from any other time?"

"It's always different. It's always new. That's because it's you, isn't it?"

"Because it's you and me."

Her arms round his shoulders tightened. "I want to come, David, but I don't want you to come, yet. Will you hold back for me? I want to come so bad."

"Come, sweetheart."

"I—can't—help it. I need you so much. I—need you —always . . ." She lay quietly, keeping everything deep inside her, but he felt the helpless fluttering, kissed her panting breath, gripped her shoulders hard. Under the lamplight her eyes rolled and closed, her mouth grew smaller, tears welled up and streaked her cheeks, while he fought the pressure to let go, to come with her. But like her he wanted to go on, endlessly into the night, holding the spell that held her, keeping the special enchantment that had begun with a foolish game, a jape, and suddenly became the essence of their communion.

She was still, as if exhausted. He released his grip and lay inert upon her, resting and waiting. He had his second wind now; he had survived her orgasm without losing control. It was a familiar crisis; he knew he could stay with her, match her pace indefinitely, as stiff and wanting as he was at the beginning. And she opened her eyes with a look that meant she knew too, that meant she could begin all over again, mounting higher and higher through level after level, knowing he was with her all the way.

"Shall we go upstairs?" she whispered.

She walked ahead of him like a naked princess, and his eyes caressed her: the proudly held head with its crown of burnished hair, the wide shoulders and slender, swinging arms, her back narrowing to tiny waist then widening sharply again to the marble-white buttocks that swayed indolently with her walk, last the swelling thighs tapering into long, slim calves and dainty ankles. The bedroom, bathed in pale darkness, was just as he had seen it on his first visit except for the low king-sized bed which replaced her narrower bed when he moved in. He'd asked her that day, joking—and the memory flashed across his mind in this moment—how she'd managed so many male visitors in such cramped accommodations, and learned that in all her affairs she'd never yielded her body in this house, the one inviolable possession she still claimed as her own.

No words were spoken as she swept aside the bed-spread and lay full length on the black linen sheets, reaching to take his rigid staff in her hand and draw him down with her. But he was not ready to reclaim all of her as yet; he crouched beside her and covered her breasts and belly with his kisses, one hand roving lightly over her thighs, his fingers coming to rest at last in the damp, mossy delta where they met. His touch was like a sign. She gave a deep sigh of happiness and opened her legs to him once more. For a long moment he knelt be-tween them, his head bowed as if in adoration of not only her beauty, the beauty of this woman, but of all beauty, of all women.

Outside the rain fell softly, steadily. Their mood was all tranquillity now. Entering her, beginning the long, slow, easy thrusts, his movement was less exertion than repose; beneath him her body scarcely moved. Only her hands played over his back, her fingers tracing his spine from neck to buttocks, and further, between them, flicking the inner-most hot furrow so that, involuntarily, he leaped inside her.

"David . . ." her voice low, soothing, utterly relaxed. "Can we do this forever? All night, and all tomorrow, until we die, kill each other, sweetly, quietly, like this . . ."

"Of course we can. Do you doubt it?"

"Sometimes it all seems just too good, too wonderful to be real, having you, having what we are together . . . Ever since the night at Chad's I've had this haunting little fear that comes and goes: life is being too kind, life is not this kind, for anybody . . . it lulls you, builds you up, content, serene, smug . . . and then . . ."

"And then?"

"Someone is waiting around the next corner with a bag of wet sand. You've been tricked. You've been be-trayed, by yourself, by your own good faith and trust . . . And suddenly it's all gone, like water trickling through your fingers, it's all over, and you're back where you were, alone, hungry, remembering the pretty balloon that burst in your hand."

As if in answer he quickened his rhythm, felt her swift intake of breath, her thighs spreading a little wider beneath him. "Don't talk about it," he whispered, kissing her forehead, "don't think about it. Those are bad dreams, darling, they pass and they're forgotten. All we have is what we are now, in this moment. Nothing else is real, not the past, not tomorrow until it comes, just this time of being together and knowing what we have together."

"No, the past is with us always. You can't cast it off, David. It won't go away. As long as we can remember, it will be there. It lives because it has lived in us, become part of us. And after we die, even then, somewhere, in somebody else, in something, it will be alive. Maybe in something you've written, or something I've said to you. The past is living right now in all the women you've known and left behind you, David—in Sandy, in the girl you loved that spring in Rome, your little *amie* in Paris, your war-time women. Your past is living, already, in me, and my past is living in all the men I've known and had . . ."

He stopped moving and lay motionless on her, looking at her eyes in the pale dark. "You said that was all finished for you."

"That doesn't mean the memory is gone, how could it be? Most of all the worst of it—the drug stupors, the nausea, the dildoes I let them use on me, the table game . . ."

"The table game?"

"My first experience with special sex. I was very young, very impressionable, eager to learn and obedient to the man I was with. There were two other couples, I hadn't met them before. We went to a place just south of Sunset for dinner, a sort of club, very quiet and discreet, with private rooms. A high table covered with a green baize cloth that hung all the way down to the floor and over the laps of the people having dinner. They button it to the back of your chair and it fits close to your body just about under the chest."

"Go on."

"Can't you guess? There were two professionals, a man and a woman, waiting under the table. The dinner proceeded and they went to work. The first member of the party to show emotion loses for their couple. The scoring was by elimination. The last couple that didn't betray anything unusual going on got the dinner free."

He had resumed his rhythm, holding her closer. "Did your couple lose?"

"We didn't win, because of me. Of course it was my first game. I'd never been sucked before. David . . ."

"Darling . . ."

"When you go faster like this I can't think anymore . . ."

"I don't want you to think, I want you to feel."

"I excited you . . . what I was saying . . ."

"Yes. I could see you there that night. Just a kid, just beginning . . ."

"I'm glad I excited you. I didn't mean to excite you if . . . *oh, David* . . ."

He could feel her orgasm beginning and knew that this time he could let her come to him without losing his control. He slowed his stroke but struck harder, deeper, as her knees came up and her hands gripped his buttocks, pulling him toward her with each stroke. He was driving, ploughing to the length of him, withdrawing to the tip; the sense of his power was intoxicating him. And she felt it, her whole body beginning to vibrate under his plunging weight, lifting to follow him, stay with him every inch of the way, little panting gasps escaping her narrowed mouth, a straining, a frantic reaching, mouth to mouth now, and then with one great heaving sigh she flooded him and fell back as if exhausted, whimpering her ecstasy into the pillow. The sheath that held him pulsated like a heart, contracting, expanding, quieted at last. Both their bodies were glistening with sweat. "Dear God," she whispered, seeming to come back out of a distant cloud, "you've never been so close to me."

"I'm always close to you."

"Not that way. Not like tonight. You are inspired. How can you hold back, to give me so much joy?"

"My turn next." He smiled and kissed her damp throat. "And I'll take you with me."

She shook her head. "I've nothing left. You've taken it all. And given me everything."

"I want to look at you," he said. Very tenderly he withdrew from her, reached for the little bed lamp and switched it on. The rosy glow enveloped her body, all languid curves and contours, beautifully at rest. And she turned and touched him, took him in her fingers, said, "You're like steel. How can you still be so hard?"

"The better to love you."

"I'd kiss him now, I'd suck him, if I could lift my head."

"You are not to lift your head. Anyway I couldn't stand it. I want to come to you while I'm holding you in my arms, while I can feel all of you. I want to smother you under me." Smiling, he reached for the other pillow, lifted her hips and slipped it under her so that the gaping crotch lay offered and fully visible, saturated with its own dew, raised and ready. Now he could give it to her kneeling, lean to kiss her breasts, watch the changing colors of her face while he loved her. Now he knelt before her, gently spread her knees apart, sank slowly, deliciously into her again, saw her slender hand come up and cup him. "You're not too tired?" he whispered, and she smiled.

"I lied to you. Please never stop."

"It is promised."

Overhead the rain beat a tattoo on the roof, gurgled into the gutters under the eaves like a brook splashing. It was mood music for the most exquisite hours he had ever spent with her, a mood that had twice risen to exaltation in Vivian and again was rising in him to excitement of an intensity he had never felt with any woman before this night. And she knew what he was feeling, answered him with her eyes that never left his face, with her hands that reached to him, tugged with long slim fingers at the hairs at the base of his belly as though unconscious of what she was doing. For a long time he lay almost motionless inside her, felt her secret flesh awaken and begin to palpitate around the buried shaft.

"Don't," he said softly.

"I can't help myself."

She was coming alive again, fresh and strong. Her body seemed to undulate, her flanks stirring restlessly, her nipples rising hard and deeper red. And he bent to take them in his mouth, first one, then the other, while her hands came up and around his neck, holding him close to her breasts as he tongued her. He had begun to move in and out of her, slowly at first, as if the body beneath were so fragile a thing the slightest roughness would injure it. But he knew better than that: she had taken him violent before tonight and gloried in it, begged for it, in other moods, given it back with all the fury of her strength aroused. But tonight was loveliest of all, he knew she knew it; an overwhelming tenderness was in her eyes, dark pools of light that gave him all of her. More than the beauty of body and blood that surged like tidal waters under him, swirls and eddies of physical sensation, she was giving him her inner self—devotion, patience, loyalty, everything man needed in woman, now and always. And it was her eyes, her look, not the richness of submission alone, that stung him, galvanized him into fierce possession. His rhythm quickened, deeper, harder; if he was hurting her now she made no sound. But for the first time her eyes closed in an agony of need, and he too closed his eyes with the onset of this rapture that seized his body like electric shock, then broke the tension as he felt the womb itself open to his final spurting lunge and heard her ringing cry fill the room like a shout of triumph and pain.

# 56

He woke to the sound of rain, no sunshine visible. What time was it? He was tired, deliciously tired, too relaxed to open his eyes again, to care about anything but sleep.

"Darling . . ."

Vivian's voice. He turned in the wide bed to touch her but there was no one there. Slowly he opened his eyes once more, saw her fully dressed and standing in the bedroom doorway. "What time?" he muttered.

"After ten, and still raining. I'm going down to buy some food, back in a little while." Her light, springing step as she came to the bed, leaned down and kissed him. She smelled clean and fresh and beautiful. For an instant he squinted up at her radiant smile. He had it made.

"Sleep," she said. "You've earned it." And she was gone.

Gratefully he turned back, sprawling, one knee raised against his chest, yanked the pillow under his head and closed his eyes in content. His brain, like his body, was half numb. How good to sleep. Nothing but sleep. No broadcast, no phone, no deadline. Just rest and remembrance. Just Vivian. The perfume of her body was still on the warm sheets . . .

It was the last he knew until the bell rang. Perversely, insistently. His body refused to accept it, refused to listen. Who the Christ would be calling so early? He wouldn't answer. It would go away. But it wouldn't go away, continued to ring. What the hell time was it? He turned savagely in the bed, blinking his eyes, reaching for the phone to leave it off the hook. In the same moment he realized it wasn't the phone, it was the downstairs bell, somebody at the door. Well, fuck them. He'd wait them out.

Somebody knocking now. Where in God's name was

391

Vivian? Then he remembered she'd gone down to shop. Had she locked herself out? Cursing softly, he stumbled out of bed and down the stairs, saw the clock on the landing: ten past eleven.

He opened the door to two men, one in police uniform. "Mr. Brent?" said the other one. "Can we speak to you for a moment?"

Suddenly he realized he was standing there naked. The two men should have been amused at this but they didn't show it. "Come in," he said. "With you in a minute." His shirt and trousers were lying on the divan and he slipped them on. His two visitors waited in silence.

"Sorry. I was sound asleep. What can I do for you?"

They looked at him with a kind of stolid compassion. "There's been an accident," the spokesman said.

A cold terror blanked his brain. He heard himself say, "What?"

"Mrs.," the man began, and started again. "The lady who lives here, according to her license . . ."

*"Is she hurt? Where is she?"*

A pause, as if each of them was expecting the other to tell him. The officer said, uncomfortably: "She succumbed, sir."

The word didn't ring true. "You're saying she's dead."

"Yes, sir. We're sorry to tell you that."

In the long silence Brent stared at them, then turned abruptly and went to the garden door, standing with his back to them. When he spoke he heard the word, dull, flat, unreal; from someone else's mouth, not his.

"Instantly?"

"Yes, sir. That's what the ambulance man—"

"How . . . how did it happen?"

The officer again. "We didn't see it, you understand. According to two witnesses Mrs. . . . the lady was coming pretty fast down the incline to the boulevard when a little kid ran out chasing his ball. The road surface shows she braked hard and skidded across the slick. The car hit a fire plug and turned upside down. She never hit the kid . . ."

"Where is she now?"

The other man spoke. "Still at the hospital. We told them to hold the . . ." He started again. "We can take you there, if you wish."

The words fell like leaden objects. For a moment he was paralyzed, unable to think or act. Then he said, "Thank you. I'll get a pair of shoes . . ."

She had been taken out of the emergency room and was lying on a stretcher in an empty hallway, covered by a white sheet. The officer stood at his side while the intern drew back the top of the sheet. There was no visible injury. Already her face was pallid and waxen. Her eyes were closed. Perhaps someone had closed them for her.

"We'll have a report," the intern was saying briskly, "but it's not complete yet. I assume you'll be notifying a funeral director. And now if you'll excuse me . . ." He hurried back into the emergency room, a busy man.

The officer handed him her purse and said, "The car keys are inside with her other papers. I'm sorry, sir."

"I appreciate your help."

Brent watched him go back to his routine duties, his step quickening a little as if relieved to have concluded this latest brush with sorrow.

There was a phone booth at the end of the hall and he caught Chad Newsom just as he was leaving the studio for lunch.

"Vivian was killed a little while ago in an accident."

A brief, stunned silence. Then, "How?"

"Her car. You know how she drives."

"Are you hurt?"

"She was alone."

"Where are you, Dave?"

He told him.

"Wait for me. I'm on my way . . ."

Chad Newsom did it all—the funeral arrangements, the burial plot, the newspaper announcement. Brent sat in the Palisades house and stared into the garden. Next day, when the Los Angeles *Times* published a brief account of the accident it mentioned her former marriage but said nothing about David Brent. She had, literally, no family closer than distant cousins. They were not heard from. Burial was supposed to be private, with one limousine following the hearse to the cemetery, Brent and Chad Newsom sitting silently together in the back, but when they arrived half a hundred persons were gathered to escort the coffin to the grave. Among them were Harry Bernard and Hope Andrews, but not Vivian's ex-husband.

After the interment a woman came up to Brent with tears staining her face. Chad explained that this was the lady whose little boy had run into the street chasing his ball. Brent heard her say something about "this awful thing," thanked her and turned away.

It was only when it was all over that the full impact hit him. He found himself unable to make decisions of any kind, and at Chad's insistence he closed the Palisades house and moved back to his old room at the beach. There, sitting most of the day on the deck and staring out to sea, ignoring the phone and unable to do any work of his own, he struggled within himself to regain control of his shattered nerves. Usually, by the time Chad returned from the studio in late afternoon, the better part of a fifth of whiskey or rum had been consumed—he was alternating between the two on alternate days. There was wine during dinner and cognac afterward. By nine o'clock he was either asleep in his chair or had staggered to his bed and passed out.

To all this, Chad responded as if it wasn't happening. The first few days he tried patiently to get Brent to talk about it—Vivian's death or whatever else had thrown him into the deepest depression of his life. Brent just shook his head and attempted a smile. Twice Chad brought him story suggestions from producers who'd failed to reach the house by phone during the day. In both instances he faced a blank wall; Brent said he'd simply lost interest in writing for either film or print. He wasn't watching TV or following the newspapers; each night Chad found the mail copy of the *New York Times* untouched outside the front door. Books he would normally have read eagerly lay unopened on his desk.

A week had gone by when Chad said across the Sunday breakfast table: "I picked up some mail at Vivian's house on my way here last night. There was a letter addressed to you, but last night, as usual, you were in no condition to read anything."

"Sorry, Chad. You know I'm grateful for everything you're doing for me, and her."

"Here it is." He held out the letter. "It's from a law firm."

"Tell me what's in it, will you?"

"Christ, you can read a letter, man!"

"Just tell me what it says."

"As you please." He opened it and scanned it. "It's from her lawyer. Did you know Vivian left an updated will?"

"Why should that concern me?"

"She happens to have left her estate to you, that's all! The house and the alimony capital she was living on."

Brent was silent. Exasperation rose in Chad's voice. "Didn't she ever mention it to you?"

"No." He could not hold back the tears that welled suddenly in his eyes and he got up and went out to the deck. Chad followed him and put an arm around his shoulders. "Don't feel upset, baby. I cry myself sometimes. It's good to grieve. It's the first time I've seen you grieve."

"Chad. Let me alone, will you?"

"You can't go on like this, fella. You're copping out. Nothing can bring Vivian back, you know that. Life continues without her, just like it will someday when you and I are gone. The longer you stay this way the harder it is to climb out of it. Listen, will you let me suggest something? Will you have a talk with Nat Edelman?"

"Thanks. I don't need a doctor."

"Is there anybody else you'd like to see? Someone to keep you company here?"

He shook his head. "You're all the company I need, Chad."

The director sighed and gave it up. But two days later, shortly after noon, Brent heard a car drive up and stop at the front door. He made no effort to get up from his chair on the deck; he was already on his third long drink of the day and he had no inclination to move. Hope Andrews came into the house, saw him and walked through to the deck.

"Hi, there!" The lusty young greeting startled him; he hadn't even bothered to turn around. She was wearing a sleeveless short yellow dress over her tanned, voluptuous body and a bandana around her blonde hair. She leaned over and kissed him warmly on the cheek.

"Ain't you the lucky guy—you've got the beach all to yourself."

He forced a smile. "What brings you out here, Hope?"

"I'm not hoping for anything." She giggled at her little attempt at repartee. "I just came to see you."

"Chad give you the day off?"

"Chad? He had nothing to do with it." She lied transparently. "I mean you and I are friends. Well, aren't we?"

"Of course we are."

"Then aren't you going to invite me to sit down?" She didn't wait for answer but drew up a chair opposite him and flopped down, throwing out her arms to the sky. "That sun! What a glorious day!"

"Can I get you a drink, Hope?"

"It's a little early for me, thanks."

"You don't mind if I mix myself another?" She watched him do it.

"You writing another script?" she said then. "I hear great things about *Women, Money and Weather*. I'm sure you'll get a nomination."

"I appreciate the thought."

They sat in silence. In her candid way she seemed to be studying him, the artless smile encouraging him to speak what was in his mind, get it out of him. "We had fun that day, didn't we?" she said abruptly, as if she'd made the assumption that he was remembering their lunch together and what happened afterward.

"Yes," he said, and noticed that she'd drawn her knees apart and was naked under her dress.

"I owe you, David."

"No, I'm in debt to you."

She shifted in her chair almost clumsily, like a child, and widened her knees still further to make sure he could see what she was offering. "Any time, dear David," she said softly, "you know that."

He stood up and felt himself sway slightly; the drinks were getting to him earlier than usual. "You're very generous and very sweet," he said to her, "and I'm going to ask you to go now because I have some things to think about. Tell Chad I'm glad you came."

She was smiling and she flushed a little under her tan. "It wasn't Chad. Well, yes it was. He did suggest it, but I really wanted to come, you do believe that?"

They walked to the door together. It felt strange to him to have his arm around another woman's waist. "Yes, of course I believe it."

In the doorway she said, "Let me see you smile. You have such a good smile, David, and I haven't seen it today.

Your face is so different when you don't smile. You look
like you're feeling sorry for yourself. Vivian wouldn't want
that. You know she wouldn't."

She kissed him quickly and almost ran to the car,
waving a cheerful hand as she revved up and drove off. He
raised his arm in goodbye, and turning away from the
door he touched his cheek where she had kissed him.

# 57

It was only after Hope Andrews' visit that Brent began to see himself in a new light: the image of a man feeling sadness for himself and inflicting that feeling on his closest friend. Neither man mentioned Hope in the days that followed, but Brent was sure that Chad shared her opinion. Yet at no time since Vivian's death had Chad reproached him for his attitude except in the gentlest terms; even Vivian's name no longer left his lips. Now Brent realized it was unfair to burden Chad or anyone else with the weight of his despair, and one afternoon, through the mist of alcohol, the decision finally emerged: he would move out. Not to the house in Palisades, never that again; nor would he bring his private woes to Cathy's happy household in San Francisco. There would be a hotel somewhere up the coast, a motel or whatever, where he could retreat and nurse his gnawing sorrow.

He was ready to tell him when Chad arrived that evening, but Chad's first words postponed the plan. "Gotta whip back to New York, son," he announced breezily as he came in. "Early flight tomorrow—dunno for how long, four or five days anyhoo. Hold the fort for me, right?"

It could wait till he returned.

Chad was on the phone the rest of the evening and by the time he finished Brent was ready to call it another day.

"Do me a favor, old buddy." Chad stood in the bedroom doorway. "Ease up on the sauce while I'm away."

"I'll try."

But switching off the light and collapsing on the bed he knew he didn't mean it. For the first time since he lost Vivian he would be really alone. He hadn't realized till now how much he'd come to depend emotionally on Chad—just his voice in the house, his physical presence,

the certain knowledge he'd return at evening. Daytime
didn't count: there was sunshine and the sounds of life;
it was the dark that brought emptiness and dread, the long
night of sleeplessness or tortured dreams of a little boy
running across rain-slicked pavement, the waxen face of a
dead woman opening her eyes, distorted words echoing in
a hospital corridor. Only that bottle close at hand could
help him through the nights, but even whiskey was beginning to lose its effects, though the hangovers were as brutal
as before.

It wasn't going to be easy to leave this house.

He woke to find Chad gone. The beach lay under an
overcast sky; the surf was gray and sullen, and an unaccustomed wind blew off the water, scuffing up little bursts
of sand. On impulse he picked up the phone and called
Dr. Edelman. The nurse said he was with a patient and
would call back.

Nathan Edelman did better than that: he didn't call
back; two hours later he came. Still better, he listened.
And for the first time, without urging, without prompt-
ing, Brent unburdened his heart.

The silence when he finished was broken only by the
dull thudding of the surf. A chill breeze penetrated the
room where the two men sat and Brent got up to shut the
glass doors to the deck. Edelman's gaze followed his movements with careful attention. He spoke when Brent sat
down again.

"Your motor reactions are better, David. You were
drunk when I arrived. Did you feel you needed a drink
while you were talking to me?"

Brent looked at him. "No."

"Does that tell you anything?"

"I hadn't thought about it."

"Do you want a drink now?"

"Not necessarily, no."

"But you will later on, especially when it gets dark."

"I guess so, yes."

"You know, David, you haven't told me yet why you
called my office today."

"The liquor wasn't working any more. I wanted some
pills . . . strong pills. I figured I'd have to have your
prescription."

A pause. Edelman's steady gaze held him. "You don't

need my prescription. One or two aspirin might help your headaches, but what you were looking for was a powerful drug that would only make matters worse. Do you want to become a user? Because this is the way it begins, with no end but tragedy. Ruin. Ruin of character. Ruin of career. Believe me, I know what it does. I see the effects all around me, here in the colony, in Hollywood, in Beverly. I deal with it every day, and I don't want to add David Brent to my list."

He stopped, as if waiting. Brent said, "But . . ." His voice trailed off.

"But it's not as simple as it sounds—that's what you were going to say, right? Wrong, David. It *is* as simple as it sounds. The fact is that you can come out of this emotional pit all by yourself. You don't need doctors, or prescriptions. You need only an effort of will. You are organically sound. You are not an alcoholic. Remember that only a few months ago you told me a great deal about yourself, and I know you well enough to say these things with confidence. You're a sensitive man who has had a very rough time. In the space of less than a year, two terrible disappointments have shaken your life. You may not know this—I don't know whether Vivian ever told you—but I knew about her. I saw her ruining herself with troubles that began just as yours did, with a disastrous marriage. I know, from what Chad told me, that you saved her."

Brent spoke quietly. "We saved each other."

"Yes, and bitterest of all, you saved her only to lose her. And you won't accept it."

"Why should I?"

A long silence. Then Edelman spoke with finality. "You called me for a prescription. All right, here it is. It's something I want you to do tonight, David. Not for me. For yourself. Eat a simple supper and drink a glass of wine with it, nothing else. After I leave, and for the next three days, don't go anywhere near hard liquor and hold your wine consumption to that one glass with your meals. If you can't sleep when you go to bed, take a couple of aspirin, once. If you still can't sleep, turn on the light and read, or make notes for your book."

"My book?"

"The book you're going to start working on when I leave here. The story of your life."

Brent stared at him incredulously. "What makes you think a publisher would be interested in that?"

"You're not writing it for a publisher. You're writing it for yourself. Of course if, later, a publisher wants it, or some part of it, you can go ahead and give it to him if you want to." He smiled.

"And you expect me just to sit down and work, feeling like this?"

"You mean to say you can't outline your personal history to the best of your recollection? That's all I'm asking. Anybody can do that much. For the next three days, make it your only activity and lay off everything else. Then we'll see."

He glanced at his watch and stood up. "I have to go now. If any more questions arise, feel free to call the office. However, I anticipate no difficulties. Not with David Brent."

Slowly Brent shook his head. When he spoke his voice sounded weak and faltering to him. "I'm deeply grateful for your help, Nat. But I'm afraid I'm not up to doing what you advise. It's no use telling you I'll try when I know I can't do it."

The response was curt and unsmiling. "If the operative word there is *afraid,* then you're a coward. This is not advice, this is a challenge. Turn away from it now, tonight, and you admit defeat—you may never again be the man you were and should be."

He was gone with a crisp wave of the hand, so quickly that Brent reached the door only to see him already at the wheel of his car and moving away. For a long time he stood there staring unseeing up the drive, then returned to the chair where he'd listened to Edelman's last stinging words. How long he sat there, utterly motionless, he couldn't know; he seemed to have lost consciousness of time. Across the room the bar with its row of bottles stood as in silent mockery, as if waiting, and he remembered Edelman's warning: the crisis was now, on which everything in the future would depend.

Still he hadn't moved. The afternoon drew toward dusk; the air was cooler; the first shadows fell across the house. Suddenly, as if impelled by an inner compulsion, he got up and went to his bedroom, found the steel box he hadn't opened since New York and unlocked it, looking down at the mass of old letters and pictures he had resisted the impulse to destroy long ago. He spread out several of the snapshots under the lamplight, one of them of a blonde handsome girl hardly in her twenties. Photographed in summer sunshine on the tiles of a patio, she squatted nude on the heels of her pumps, her knees apart, turning a fresh and artless smile to the camera. A shirt and a pair of brief shorts lay discarded on the canvas chair beside her. He looked at the picture a long time while emotion rolled over him in waves, as near and new as the original moment long ago.

Next to it another picture, this one taken indoors of a dark-haired slender young woman stretched out on a sofa, the dainty face calm in submission, lips parted, long lashes half closed. She was naked under her dress, which was drawn up almost to her breasts, one slim, curving leg thrown indolently over the back of the sofa, a high-heeled shoe still on the narrow foot, her loins wide open to the camera's eye.

Staring down at the photograph he felt his breath come more quickly and his mouth went dry. In astonishment at himself, he gripped his erection until he winced in pain. He turned away abruptly, went to the windows that opened on to the deck and stood there looking out across the beach while his excitement subsided.

But there was to be no relief. A new fascination drew him back to the box. At random he picked up a page from a yellowed letter protruding from the heap and read the faded, graceful script:

> our wonderful last night still haunting me. I smell Fiesole, you, the lilacs, hear that phrase from *Gianni Schicchi*, you, taste the Orvieto, and you, see the little red car and the green tiny roads, the pines and the clouds, you, on and on until it's unbearable. If only

He shook his head and dropped the page from reluctant fingers, then locked the box again before returning to the living room. This was the hour of the day when all at once you didn't know who you are or why you're here or where you're going. When you crave the false assurance of a drug, a friend for solace in your empty room, anything to ward off the shroud of loneliness gathering around you. The French called it *l'heure bleue*. And all at once he saw Paris again, city of his happy youth, the Seine at evening, the Pont des Arts . . . the image unleashing a flood of memory, forgotten faces and their voices, cherished pictures and places crowding his mind. It was as though sluice gates were opening on the past, back, back over Europe and the years before Europe, the earliest years, to young and eager Nicky a thrilling long-ago night in Central Park; to Julia and the college rites of manhood; to Eileen and Maggie, those lusty evenings on Patchin Place; the all-night bus to the South with a nameless soft-spoken passenger at his side; and Jean, the last Village summer . . . Then Paris of the *Trib*, of Hap and Helen Osgood, Josette in the mirror room of Le Sphinx, Helen and the night of the lesbians, Tanya in Fontainebleau forest, the Impasse des Deux Anges and the bittersweet memory of Claudine. The images passed before his eyes in the changing pattern of a kaleidoscope: the Riviera like a dream come true, the incredible film star encounter at the Réserve de Beaulieu, Jamie, the dream that ended too soon. And London: Audrey's tainted welcome, Mildred and little sister Becky in the streets, but most of all Daphne. Later there was London again, but not before Pupi's Rome, and Clare, and hail and farewell to the work of art that was Elena . . . One by one the faces, the bodies reappeared and faded: had the exquisite interlude with Cathy really happened to him, so long ago it seemed, so many joys before and after? Washington and the Senator's wife, and Lee, an hour with little Sarah Lou. Once more the call to wartime England, Judy, the wild unreality of Liberation Day, Odile and Paris in his arms, Loren in combat, Anne-Marie. And finally New York, Alison's New York, his own New York, with Sandy . . .

So many, and so much had been given him. *You were born to love many women and overcome many obstacles and do a variety of things well*—Chad had said that. And where were they all in this moment of time, what were their lives today? Had he really known them, those distant worlds that are other people? He'd watched them pass him like ships at sea, come nearer, recede and disappear, but not before they were part of him, ineradicable, as he was part of them; and what had they taught and learned of each other? So swiftly had it all gone by, so intense and different each individual experience, so busy his other life, he'd looked back only in hasty glances; not yet had he spared himself time to seek a pattern. Or was it because he feared to find it all meaningless, with tragedy at its end?

He stirred in his chair, suddenly aware that he was sitting in darkness, that night had fallen. Patterns . . . designs . . . the voices struggling to be heard. He had thought that living only for the present was the wisest way. And yet something was eluding him, some sense of himself, of what he'd been and was and would become. *Your book,* Nat Edelman had said, *the story of yourself.* The way to understanding. The way to peace.

*The man in the house at Malibu got up and walked out on the deck, into the world of murmuring surf and mist-filtered moonlight. The beach was empty and he was alone. At first he stood listening to the voices only he could hear, still staring into the mirror of the past, still haunted by the death of love. But gradually, as his eyes grew accustomed to the gloom, a vision took shape in the dimness at the water's edge, a drifting cloud resolved into human form: the nude figure of a woman. She was moving now, gliding, swaying, her arms outflung in silent rapture—an invitation to life, the renewal of hope and desire. She seemed to beckon to him . . .*

All Futura Books are available at your bookshop or newsagent, or can be ordered from the following address:
Futura Books, Cash Sales Department,
P.O. Box 11, Falmouth, Cornwall.

Please send cheque or postal order (no currency), and allow 55p for postage and packing for the first book plus 22p for the second book and 14p for each additional book ordered up to a maximum charge of £1.75 in U.K.

Customers in Eire and B.F.P.O. please allow 55p for the first book, 22p for the second book plus 14p per copy for the next 7 books, thereafter 8p per book.

Overseas customers please allow £1 for postage and packing for the first book and 25p per copy for each additional book.